Invitation to Ruin

Invitation to Ruin

BRONWEN EVANS

BRAVA

KENSINGTON PUBLISHING CORP.
www.kensingtonbooks.com

BRAVA BOOKS are published by

Kensington Publishing Corp.
119 West 40th Street
New York, NY 10018

All Kensington titles, imprints, and distributed lines are available at special quantity discounts for bulk purchases for sales promotion, premiums, fund-raising, educational, or institutional use.

Special book excerpts or customized printings can also be created to fit specific needs. For details, write or phone the office of the Kensington Special Sales Manager: Kensington Publishing Corp., 119 West 40th Street, New York, NY 10018. Attn. Special Sales Department. Phone: 1-800-221-2647.

ISBN-13: 978-0-7582-5919-6
ISBN-10: 0-7582-5919-0

First Kensington Trade Paperback Printing: March 2011

10   9   8   7   6   5   4   3   2   1

Printed in the United States of America

To my darling Jock

Thank you for showing me that life is to be lived and that should I chase my dreams. I know you are often with me and that when I open the cover of this book you will be right there reading over my shoulder and enjoying every word. Thanks for the encouragement, your belief that I could do it, and for letting me share some of your way-too-short life.

I miss you.

ACKNOWLEDGMENTS

Thank you to the BI50Ders for putting up with me, and for your unending, unselfish support.

Plus, what would I have done without my critique partners? Gracie, your endless patience, knowledge and encouragement when I first made the decision to write amazes me to this day. Without you I would not be writing this acknowledgment. Rhea, my historical writing friend, I look forward to reading your first acknowledgment.

Thanks to my lovely agent, Melissa Jeglinski, for coming to New Zealand and giving me the opportunity to meet you.

I have fallen on my feet by landing the wonderful Megan Records as my editor. You have made this amazing journey to publication so easy.

Finally, I'd like to thank the Romance Writers of New Zealand—a fabulous organization that showed me I wasn't alone, and that there are loads of us consumed with the stories and characters floating in our heads.

Chapter 1

The rogue Society had dubbed "The Lord of Wicked" lurked in the dimly lit recesses of Lady Sudbury's ballroom. To most people the room was the epitome of warmth, with its blaze of candles and displayed finery, but for Anthony James Craven, the fifth Earl of Wickham, it held absolutely no appeal.

He was here to partake in his favorite pastime—sin and vice. Appetites that a notorious rake craved drew him like a malefactor summoned to hell. Thanks to his father, he was full of sin. Sin he could never atone for. Instead, he chose to lose himself in pleasure. Pleasure, at least temporarily, helped him block the memories he would give his very soul to forget.

He kept to the shadows, hiding from the sycophantic throng, while he searched for the one woman who'd enticed him into breaking all his own rules and attending the event of the Season.

His lips curved in anticipation of the night's forthcoming liaison. He raised a glass of burgundy to his mouth in mock salute, letting the alcohol take the sting out of the unenviable position of having to hide from mothers of young unmarried daughters.

In the concealing darkness he felt the primitive stirrings of the hunter. His eyes had begun seeking their prey as soon as he'd arrived, over an hour ago. He sank deeper into the shadows, searching for the flesh-and-blood goddess he intended to seduce.

Lady Cassandra Sudbury, a curvaceous young widow with a taste for the erotic, would be his by the end of the night. Anthony stirred from his position propped against the ballroom wall and observed his quarry's bold approach.

With each dainty step she took toward him, his amusement grew. She worked her way through the masses with an air of innocence reborn; yet if tales were to be believed, Cassandra could corrupt a nunnery.

The blazing draft-buffeted wall candles cast flickers over her burnt-orange silk dress, which indecently hugged her every curve. The gleaming Sudbury diamonds, attracting as much attention as her cleavage, emphasized her pale slender neck. Like an opium pipe to an addict, the exposed skin called out for him to lick, suck, and taste.

Moist pink lips parted in an inviting smile. Cassandra moved behind him, using one delicate hand to cup his left buttock while the other slid under his evening jacket and up his back.

Her soft form molded itself against him, her person hidden from the crowds in the ballroom by his height and size.

"Lord Wickham, is there a reason you're lurking in the shadows?"

Her husky voice caressed him more than the insistent fingers stroking his backside through his tight, and ever-tightening, black breeches. Both tactics achieved their desired outcome. His member instantly stood to attention, and Anthony smiled to himself. Lady Cassie, as he preferred to call her, was recently out of mourning, and she was playing with fire.

Anthony let his silence hang expectantly before murmuring, "I knew if I ignored the most beautiful woman in the room she'd come to me."

Light laughter mocked his senses as she moved to stand directly in front of him. "You know me so well." She trailed her hand over his hip to rub the most intimate part of him, her body shielding her actions from the pomp and ceremony in front of them. "Something's hard. . . ." Her hand moved more purposely. "Speaking of coming . . ."

Anthony soaked in the beauty of the woman bold enough to service him in full view of her guests. Very soon she would be his mistress—this very night, in fact. He'd waited long enough.

He did not move, or give any sign of the sparks searing through his body at the practiced fingers stroking him. "If you do not still your hand, I won't be responsible for my actions."

She gave a throaty laugh. "In view of the guests? I don't think so."

Gritting his teeth, he flashed Lady Cassie a taut smile. "Take a peek over my shoulder, sweetheart." His jaw tightened as he struggled to control his body. "Where do you think that door leads? If you don't behave, I'll pull you into the billiard room, lock the door, and ravish you on the table until you can no longer walk." He lifted her free hand and kissed the air above her glove. "Guests or no guests."

At his promise she moaned softly, and he felt her fingers tremble with desire. Cassie stood on tiptoes to whisper in his ear, "Come to my bed tonight, and we shall see who wears out whom."

If she thought he'd not accept the challenge, she was sorely mistaken. Cassandra thrived on games of flirtation. Anthony thrived on challenge.

He inwardly smiled as she peeped up at him from beneath incredibly long lashes and rubbed her hand longingly one more time, caressing his erection to the point of pain before she set him free. "Tonight?" she whispered.

Anthony's pulse ratcheted up a notch as Lady Cassie moved close, pressing her plump white breasts against his waistcoat.

"Do not keep me waiting," she almost pleaded, tapping his chest with her fan before drifting off to converse with her other guests.

He watched her swaying hips. She wouldn't have to wait.

Lady Cassie's beauty had driven Anthony to the point of

madness over the past week. He felt like a Thoroughbred racehorse that hadn't been run in over a month. Now he'd been given his head, he wanted Lady Cassie—rumored to be the most beautiful woman in all England—with a need verging on desperation.

She had jet-black tresses, almost a midnight blue in the candlelight, framing creamy milk skin that made you want to lick from toe to breast and back again. He almost lost himself in her exotically framed feline eyes, their color such a vibrant green they appeared to be made of emeralds. Lady Cassandra Sudbury came packaged in a body so curvaceous, so soft, it would drive a saint to sin.

And Lord knew Anthony was no saint.

Finally Cassandra had let him know she was ripe for plucking, and here he stood, a starving man, his eagerness to appease his appetite almost making him grovel.

He shook his head. Anthony James Craven did not grovel. He did not prostrate himself at women's feet, quite the opposite in fact. Women were usually fighting over him, the Earl of Wickham. Referred to as the Lord of Wicked by ladies who counted themselves among the ranks of those he'd seduced, and there were many. His "Wicked Club," as the ladies penned it, was most likely the largest female-members-only club in all of England, if not the continent.

Women were his biggest vice. Not his worst vice, but pretty close. He loved women. All women, but in particular women whose beauty could start a war, or those he would have to fight tooth and nail for. His childhood had been starved of beauty, and as an adult he could not help but gravitate toward it.

"What have we here? The mighty Earl of Wickham hiding behind a potted palm?"

Anthony's shoulders automatically tightened, and he turned to scowl at his twin brother. "A man of my standing—a wealthy, titled bachelor—has an excuse to hide." He paused and raised an eyebrow, "Who are *you* hiding from?"

Richard John Craven, younger by only thirty minutes, had

the grace to blush. "Mother, of course." Richard shrugged. "If you would hurry up and do what the head of the family is required to do, marry and produce an heir, Mother would not be bothering me."

Anthony cursed. "What a difference half an hour makes."

Richard slapped him on the shoulder. "Duty, Anthony. With the title comes responsibilities. It is time you did yours and saved me from Mother's constant attentions. There should be no pressure for the second son to bear fruit. I should be free to enjoy all the world has to offer. Seeing Lady Cassandra across the room, I am reminded that there is a lot to enjoy."

Anthony growled low in his throat. "Can't you find a woman of your own for a change?"

"Tut tut, can't handle the competition, eh? She is obviously immune to your charms. I have already given you three nights' head start, only because you spotted her first. You have not bedded her, or made her your mistress, so I feel free to step in and claim what you have been unable to procure."

Anthony looked at his twin with a cynical smirk. Richard was correct about one thing—Cassie had made him work harder than any other woman.

Richard looked at him with all the innocence of a man who had just strangled his wife and issued a challenge. "Care to make a game of it, brother?"

Anthony feigned boredom as his gaze swept the dancing guests. "Game?" His blood raced with the challenge. "What do I get if I win, besides Lady Cassie's delights, of course?" He flicked a spot of lint from the arm of his jacket.

Richard thought on it for a few moments. "I shall agree to allow you the first choice of any woman we meet over the course of the next year, and I promise not to seduce them first."

Anthony laughed. "That's not even worth considering. The female sex prefers the bad boy—and you, dear brother, are too angelic looking by far."

"Isn't that what we are about to put to the test? What are you scared of? Losing?"

"You'll lose. I have it on good authority that Lady Cassie will invite me to her bedchamber tonight." Anthony leaned back on the ballroom wall. "In fact, you just missed her issuing me a personal invitation."

Richard's handsome features, so different from his own, crinkled into a grin. "Well, that still leaves me a few hours. I don't need a bed. If I win, if I tup her before you bed her, I get Dark Knight."

Dark Knight was Anthony's prized stallion, and he would hate to lose him. He shook his head. Lose? Richard might be his twin brother, but they were nothing alike. Anthony always won their wagers because, when it came down to it, Richard simply was not ruthless enough.

Richard was the family cherub, full of goodness and light. Fair haired and blue eyed, he took after their mother in terms of facial features. He stood a few inches shorter than Anthony with a much leaner build, but well muscled. Anthony was the complete opposite, large, dark haired, with dark eyes and looked like his late father—brutish.

He was the dark-brooding twin, the wicked devil.

Anthony tipped his glass to his mouth and drank with relish; he had earned his reputation.

For the past ten years, the Craven twins had been inseparable. At thirty-three, their lives were spent fighting over women, brawling together, drinking themselves into stupors, and they were rumored to have seduced more women than all the rest of the nobility combined. Alarmed mothers of Society warned their daughters of the dangers of the notorious Craven twins.

A cunning plan formed in Anthony's head. He smiled at Richard. "If I win, you will marry within a month and sire a son. The son who will become the next Earl of Wickham."

Richard gasped.

Anthony stared at his brother without blinking, before raising an eyebrow, "What? Is the wager too rich for your blood, brother dear?"

"You are really determined to thwart Father. Not that I

blame you," Richard added hurriedly. "But you are the right and proper heir, and as such it should be your son who inherits, not mine."

"A half hour is all that separates us. It was chance I was born first. Society thinks I am lucky for it, but we both know differently. You know damn well I will never father a legitimate child, nor will I ever marry. I'll ensure Father's plans for me come to nothing. I won't ever let Father win."

Richard thumped the wall. "The only man who will lose is you. Think of your life. If you insist on this plan of self-exile, Father wins. And for what? Father is dead. Let it go. Get on with your life."

Anthony raised his hand and traced the scar that ran down his left cheek. "That man, long may he rot in hell, should never have been born . . .""

"I know he was tough on you . . . but you cannot let our sire continue to dictate your life from the grave."

Anthony turned away from Richard's prying eyes. Tough? His father had regularly beaten him until he was almost unconscious. His father had starved him into submission—all in the name of creating a strong heir-apparent, someone ruthless enough to carry on the Wickham empire. He would never let his father's legacy live on through him.

"I'm sorry. I didn't mean that, Anthony. I know my childhood was a bed of roses compared to yours. I just don't want to see you isolate yourself from all life has to offer."

Anthony gave a harsh laugh. "I would hardly call pursuing my next mistress as isolating myself. My father wanted me cold, devoid of human feelings, and totally focused on nothing but making money." He gave a wicked grin. "Tonight, money is furthest from my mind."

Richard took another sip of wine. "You're nothing like Father. So give up this pretense that you are. You've done more to improve the lot of your tenants than Father ever did in his lifetime."

Anthony looked at his brother, suppressing the shudder that racked his body. He was exactly like his father. Richard had no idea the lengths his twin went to in order to ensure his dark inner demons never surfaced. Anthony couldn't let down his guard for one moment. The memory of his father's evil and the part he had played in it had almost destroyed him.

His past was tarnished with evil. They were too much alike, father and son. Dark, deadly, and dangerous.

When Anthony was young, it had taken weeks to submerge the malevolence back into his soul. It still screamed to get out. Another slip and he might never recover; the wickedness buried deep within would rise up and take him over.

"If I did not know you better, Richard, I would think you were trying to distract me from our wager." Anthony turned to scan the crowded ballroom for Lady Cassie. There she was, just to his right, at the edge of the dance floor. He started to take a step forward, but his eyes narrowed; that wasn't her—not unless she'd changed dresses.

Richard pointed. "I see you've spotted Miss Melissa Goodly, Lady Cassandra's cousin. Almost a doppelganger for her, is she not? The two women look more alike than you and I."

Miss Goodly had black hair, too, but not as glowing. Her eyes were a pretty shade of hazel, maybe green in a certain light, but not as dazzling. Her skin was alabaster, but not as alluring, and she curved in all the right places, just not as temptingly.

She was definitely not mistress material. She was too much like wife material—absolutely not what he was looking for.

"Although," Richard added, "if I were you, I would stay away from Miss Goodly. Lady Cassandra does not like the comparison. I've heard the two women cannot abide each other."

As Miss Goodly placed an empty glass of champagne on a tray proffered by a servant, and helped herself to another full one, Anthony could see why. The younger woman was still an arresting sight, and those men not fortunate enough to have gained Lady Cassandra's attentions stood with gazes riveted on Miss Goodly.

She wore a gown of sea green, trimmed in gold, worn off

her shoulders in the current style. Her hair was artfully twisted, held in place by a pearl-encrusted comb. A pair of small pearls dressed her lobes, and a single pearl on a gold pendant rested above the swell of her pert bosom.

Miss Goodly was rather pretty but lacked the depth of beauty radiating from Lady Cassie. The young cousin reminded him of a copy of a Rembrandt, not quite as aesthetically pleasing as the original but still a magnificent work of art. The fact she was young and unmarried likely clouded his judgment.

Then Miss Goodly smiled, and the air rushed from his lungs. Her smile was breathtaking, and she suddenly appeared to be illuminated.

No. Miss Goodly was forbidden territory. Why risk the parson's noose when Lady Cassie was equally, if not more beautiful—and experienced?

He raised an eyebrow in his brother's direction. "Perhaps there is a way we would both be satisfied. As the eldest I get Lady Cassandra, but I won't stop you from taking the cousin."

Richard choked on his wine. "Miss Goodly? Do you think me stupid? She is one and twenty, an unmarried sister of a Baron. If I dally with her I'd be married before I could yell 'save me,' and that would be too convenient for you." Richard shook his head. "No, my original wager stands. If you do not bed Lady Cassandra before me, I get Dark Knight. I have plenty of time." He grinned at Anthony. "I'll wager you don't even know where Lady Cassandra's bedchamber is? You wouldn't want to stumble into the wrong room. Think of the scandal."

Anthony's jaw tightened. Damn. He'd forgotten to ask Cassandra for directions. The house was huge, and it could take all night to find her room. He would prefer to spend all night on the pleasure, not on the seeking.

His brother quietly chuckled. "I will give you a fighting chance. Her room is in the west wing, the fourth door along the corridor on the right."

"And how would you know that?" Anthony asked suspiciously.

Richard held out his arm and studied his immaculately groomed fingernails. "Where do you think I planned to stay tonight? If I have my way I still will. After all, it's a woman's prerogative to change her mind."

"You will accept my terms, then? You will marry and have a child if I bed Lady Cassandra before you?"

"Of course. You have my word as a gentleman."

Anthony scoffed and permitted himself a cold smile.

Richard put a hand to his heart. "I am mortally wounded at your lowly opinion of my honor." He grinned. "I won't lose, and I want Dark Knight."

Anthony couldn't still the prickle of distrust making its way up his spine. Richard was agreeing to his terms too readily. Had Richard already planned to meet her earlier in the library? He would have to keep his eye on his prize until the ball was over.

Feigning indifference, Anthony pulled out his pocket watch and looked at the time. "I accept the wager. The longer I keep you here the easier it will be for me. In fact, I feel so sure of winning I'm going to stir the pot. I shall ask Miss Goodly to dance. That should have Cassie burning to distract me from her cousin."

With that final gloat, Anthony tugged on his gloves and moved deliberately toward Miss Melissa Goodly, who, he noted, had just finished her glass of champagne. His body surged with adrenaline. The chase was on. If it took his last breath he would never let his brother win. Tonight he would bed his new mistress and move one step closer to ensuring his twin provided the much-required heir.

"May I have the pleasure of this dance, Miss Goodly? That is, if your dance card is not already full."

His deep, rich voice—rough with a bite yet thoroughly intoxicating—made her giddier than the cheap champagne she was drinking. She swung toward the tower of masculinity encapsulating her in his shadow, sending the bubbles splashing over the side of her glass.

The Lord of Wicked wished to dance with her. With her!

It was hard to remain composed with champagne dripping from her gloved fingers. "I don't believe we have been formally introduced, my lord." She tried to shake the drops off her gloves before she had to give him her hand.

Anthony's wolfish smile made her grip the glass harder. "My brother, mother, and I are Lady Sudbury's houseguests, as you well know. You were here when we arrived this afternoon. She's kindly taken us in while my house is uninhabitable." He raised a dark eyebrow. "You have heard about the fire?"

All she could do was nod. Her tongue felt like dried bread.

"I saw you peering down over the banister when we arrived. No one but ourselves will know we have not been properly introduced." His wicked smile widened. "It shall be our little secret."

Melissa's face heated as she stared at the large hand he held out to her. She gripped the champagne glass, looking around for somewhere to put her drink. She wouldn't miss this dance for the world.

"Shall I take that for you?" Without waiting for a reply he pried the glass from her hand and beckoned a servant. Glass dispensed with, he turned his full attention on her. "Shall we?" and he offered his arm.

The crowd of guests turned to vapor. All Melissa could see, feel, hear, and sense was him.

She was blind to the glittering candles and immune to the music filling the ballroom. She simply let him guide her, his arms holding her gently in the waltz. His scent filled her being—sandalwood, whiskey, and masculinity. Masculinity. He oozed it from every pore.

They twirled around the floor, unrespectable in their closeness. Melissa didn't care. His lean hardness thrilled her. The cut of his evening coat accentuated his broad shoulders. His breeches fitted like a second skin, leaving nothing to the imagination.

Melissa had a wonderful imagination.

His hulking frame and dark, brooding looks, together with his rakish reputation, made most of the young ladies terrified of him . . . But up close, his arresting features held her spellbound.

His black hair fell in thick waves almost to his shoulders, his fringe hanging low on his forehead like a silk curtain shielding his eyes. In the candlelight, his eyes flickered from silver-gray to dark charcoal, so appropriate for such a renowned devil.

She couldn't pull her gaze away. His eyes were disconcertingly direct and totally hypnotizing. The decidedly aristocratic nose, firm mouth, and chin declared that here was a man used to dominating his world, while the scar that marred the left side of his face contributed to the air of danger surrounding him.

The effect was like a mild stomachache, enough to make her tummy churn but not enough to make her faint.

She racked her brain for something intelligent to say, but his nearness made her brain turn to mush. "Was your house badly damaged?"

"Um . . . what was that?"

His attention seemed to be on another couple dancing across the floor. Melissa turned her head. Cassandra. Cassandra and Lord Spencer. Disappointment flooded her being. That's why he'd asked her to dance. So he could keep an eye on Cassandra.

Everyone knew Lord Wickham was pursuing Cassandra to be his next mistress.

Irritation sharpened her words. "The fire, my lord. Was there a lot of damage?"

His eyes flashed with amusement at her tone. "Luckily only smoke damage. We should be able to move back to Craven House in a few days' time, once the house has been properly aired."

This time he kept his dark gaze on her, the attention making her heart pound. His eyes roamed her features and slid down over her breasts, where they lingered indecently. She felt the flush heating her cheeks. His lips curled in a rakish smile of recognition.

"Will you and your brother be staying with Lady Sudbury long? She is your cousin, is she not?"

She tried to concentrate on his words, but he'd pulled her tight into his embrace in order to avoid another couple. She felt warm and delicate against him, her head barely reaching his chest. *Answer him, you fool.* "I am unsure of how long we will be here. Cassandra is sponsoring me for the Season."

"You wish to marry?"

She bit her bottom lip and lowered her gaze from his, too scared in case he saw the truth. "If I found the right man, then of course I want to marry. A home and children, isn't that something everyone wants?"

He stiffened at her words and remained silent. She raised her eyes to his. They appeared even more shielded.

"I assume your brother has someone picked out for you?"

It was her turn to stiffen in his arms. "I do my own choosing, my lord."

He smiled wryly. "Is that so?"

"I'm sure you'd not let anyone else make the most important decision of your life, why should I?"

He inclined his head, somewhat amused at her words. "I don't envy your brother."

How did she tell a peer of the realm, a man who'd likely marry for land, titles, or money that she would not marry except for love?

All her life she'd been treated as an afterthought. She was a very late child, eight years younger than Christopher. Her parents, both dead, never really wanted her. They had their son and heir, and that was all that mattered. Of course, their opinion changed when they needed looking after. Until their deaths, she'd dutifully seen to their every need. That was why, at her ripe age of one and twenty, this was her first Season and her first visit to London.

Upon her parents' deaths, she'd vowed she would never

again let herself be someone's obligation, a burden to bear, a person of no interest. She would never marry, not unless the man needed her, wanted her, and loved her.

With the dance finished, Anthony escorted her back to the place he'd found her, ensuring another glass of champagne found its way back into her hand, and with a bow excused himself. His eyes were already riveted back on Cassandra.

Melissa took a long sip from her glass.

If she were alone, she would close her eyes and twirl, pretend he still held her in his arm. She'd dreamed of him asking her to dance again, and more—a nightly fantasy she dare not fool herself into believing would come true.

Lord Wickham was not called the Lord of Wicked for nothing. As much as she mooned over him, she could never let herself fall in love with such a man, a rake of the first order. When she gave her heart, it would be to a man who wanted her beyond measure, a man who loved with all his heart and soul. A man who would cherish her forever.

Melissa stood on the edge of the ballroom, drinking more champagne. The alcohol kept her senses heightened and gave her courage. Was she brave enough to engage him in further conversation?

Melissa watched him from across the room. He did look a little frightening. Yet his crisp white shirt and immaculately tied cravat lessened the severity of his attire—to the point that Melissa decided he was, quite simply, the most beautiful man she had ever seen.

Her body still trembled as if she'd just returned from an afternoon fox hunt. Her heart raced with excitement, and her legs wobbled like custard. Lord Wickham was a heady mixture, especially coupled with the multiple glasses of champagne she'd drunk . . .

A movement to her left captured her attention. Christopher. She turned, stumbled a bit, but managed to catch her balance. How many glasses of champagne had she drunk? Four—five? Focusing on every step, she aimed for the library—away from her fast-approaching brother.

Lord Christopher Goodly, Baron Norrington, reached her seconds before her hand clasped the latch. *More like "barren." You've spent and lost everything we own*, she murmured under her breath.

"You will not run from me." His brandy fumes assaulted her nose.

Perfect. He was drunk as usual. A small giggle escaped. For once, she, too, was a little worse for drink. However, she needed the alcohol for courage, not to escape the mess she'd made of her life, as was her brother's crime.

"I was not running. I need some air."

"In the library?" His hand clamped down on her shoulder and swung her to face him. "I don't think so. Lord Wickham danced with you—danced the waltz with you. You are the only unmarried woman at the ball tonight to receive such an honor."

She kept quiet. It would do her no good to explain that the only reason the Earl danced with her was so he could keep an eye on Cassandra. A stab of envy hit her squarely below her left breast.

She removed her brother's hand from her shoulder before his sweaty palms stained her dress. They didn't have enough money to buy another. "That does not signify anything, Christopher. Go back to your drinking and leave me be."

He leaned in close and tried to smile. His face distorted, and he looked like an old man pained from gout instead of a man just under thirty. He poked her shoulder with his finger. "We are nearing the end of the Season. You will marry, and marry soon. Either you will accept Lord Carthors, or you will ensure Lord Wickham maintains his interest."

She drew a steadying breath and gripped the dresser beside her. Damn the champagne. "Lord Carthors is close to seventy and would likely die in my arms upon the wedding bed."

"Precisely. Then we'd be rich."

"No. I'd be rich."

Her brother growled. "Don't play with me."

She tried to push past him, to escape the conversation. But

his arm rose to cage her in. She was trapped by the door at her back, Christopher's arm and the large dresser on her right. "I will not marry a decrepit old man to save your skin."

He laughed in her face and sneered. "Not just my skin. Yours, too. If not for Cassandra's generosity, we would be in the poorhouse. Let's see how long your principles last when the men running such establishments start pawing you."

She kept her face blank, refusing to show how his threat affected her, but her stomach churned at the thought of what lay ahead of them if either she or Christopher did not marry well.

"Miss Trentworth is here tonight. If you are so worried about our position in Society, line your pockets by marrying her. Her father is rich. The Textile King they call him. Mr. Trentworth is after a title for his daughter."

He stood up straight. "I'm not going to marry any girl with a face like a horse's arse. It is my duty to see my young sister married first. At one and twenty you'll be left on the shelf if you are not careful." He hesitated, and his demeanor altered. "Come now. If Carthors is not to your liking, surely Lord Wickham is. He is handsome, rich, and in his prime."

She stamped her foot. "Don't be ridiculous. Even if I did— admire his lordship—the Earl is legendary in his abhorrence for the state of matrimony. He wants Cassandra as his mistress, and I'm sure she's willing to oblige. Why would he be interested in me?"

"You look exactly like Cassandra. He could take her as his mistress and you as his wife. His mother is determined he marry this Season. They need an heir. Wickham's father has been dead ten years. Wickham is in his midthirties. It's time."

Melissa's hands fisted in the sides of her dress to stop herself slapping her brother's face. How could he be so indifferent to his own flesh and blood? He wouldn't marry a woman not to his liking, yet he was quite willing to barter her off, giving her away to be used as a brood mare, so long as his debts were paid. Well, she had other ideas.

Seeing the determined look in her brother's bloodshot

eyes, she tried another tack. "What would Cassandra say if I tried to woo the Earl? Perhaps she wishes to marry him. If she becomes annoyed, we will be flung into the streets. I can't see the Earl or any other man wanting to marry me then."

His face paled at her words. Distracted by his thoughts, Melissa reached behind her and turned the latch. It released with a loud snap. Before she could escape, her brother grabbed her arm. "Then it will be Carthors. By the end of the Season you will become engaged, either to a man of your own choosing or Carthors. Am I clear?"

Melissa fought the tears filling her eyes at his painful hold. "Let me go." She tugged her arm free; the sound of the material ripping startled them both. "Perfect. Now look what you have done," she snapped. Anger propelled her to defy him. "I won't marry Lord Carthors. You'll have to drag me kicking and screaming in front of the vicar to ever get me to marry that old leech."

He simply smiled. "Not if I give you a few drops of laudanum. That would subdue you. You'd be pliant all the way to the altar." Christopher crowded her against the door frame. "Don't underestimate me, Melissa. Come the end of the Season you will be married. To whom is your choice. If you don't want Carthors, then pick someone else—as long as they are rich."

Melissa stepped into the library and slammed the door in her brother's face.

Christopher swayed his way back across the ballroom, failing to notice the man stepping out of the shadows from the other side of the large oak dresser.

Richard had heard every word of the siblings' conversation, and it was as he thought. The plan he'd set in motion would be welcomed by all concerned—except his brother. He could live with that. Eventually, he felt sure, Anthony would come to thank him for his deception.

Chapter 2

Damn her brother. Melissa stumbled her way up the stairs. At the top of the landing, she steadied herself. Bracing a hand against the wall, she headed for her room, alcohol and seething anger blinding her way. Once again, Christopher had ruined her night. She couldn't go back downstairs to Cassandra's ball, not with a torn dress.

She'd not be able to converse with the Earl again this night. He'd be all Cassandra's now.

Even so, Melissa was grateful to her cousin. The ball was being held to relaunch Cassandra back into Society, her mourning period at an end. But it also helped Melissa since it gave her a chance to see and be seen. From the beginning of the Season, Melissa's hope was to find a man who would love her, for her. Simply the way she was—with no dowry and no obvious benefits.

Cassandra introduced her to Society and grudgingly gave Christopher and her refuge in her home. Due to Christopher's debts—they had lost the Goodly family estate and the only home Melissa had ever known.

Melissa hesitated at the door to her room. She vowed she'd not let the disgrace of her brother's gambling distract her from the joy of her night. She had waltzed with him—the Lord of Wicked.

She twirled about her bedchamber with arms outstretched, only to have the room spin so much she fell back onto the bed laughing. Her heart soared, and she giggled with pure happiness.

He had danced with her, this time for real, not just a fantasy.

In her dreams she belonged to him. Lord Wickham had owned her dreams since the start of the Season when she had caught a glimpse of him at Lord Moning's ball.

She'd heard all the gossip about how handsome he was and also about his black soul. Lord Wickham's late father had been persona *non* grata within the *ton*—something to do with his business practices. Dark and dangerous the Earl may be, but she had to admire his strong business acumen. He'd turned the family's situation around.

Of course, he'd hardly noticed her. This evening he seemed consumed with pursuing her cousin. That didn't stop Melissa from wishing, just once, he would turn his devastating charm her way.

And he had. Never in her life had she been so thankful for champagne. She'd never have remained so composed without the added inducement of alcohol.

Melissa hugged herself tightly and waited while Cassandra's maid helped her undress. She didn't want to relive the night until she was alone.

In fact, over the past few weeks, she'd spent a great deal of time fantasizing about the wicked Earl. Tonight she had consumed more champagne than was respectable, not deliberately, but it enabled her to relax and have discourse with the one man who set her heart a-flutter, yet who must never know she had feelings for him. No one could know.

Melissa and her brother needed to be in Cassie's good graces to survive. If Cassie knew her thoughts, knew she desired Lord Wickham, they would be out on their ears. No, until she or her brother made a marriage contract that would inflate the family's coffers, she must do nothing to upset her cousin. Stealing Cassie's man would most likely destroy her begrudging kindness to them.

Melissa scoffed at her thoughts. Stealing Cassie's man?

What man would ever prefer her over Cassie's legendary beauty? Next to her cousin, she was the ugly duckling.

But Cassandra couldn't touch her dreams. In Melissa's dreams, the handsome Earl was besotted with her. She belonged to the Lord of Wicked.

To her disappointment, the anticipated dreams never arrived, and she quickly fell asleep. So Melissa was quite pleased when a while later she slipped into that space somewhere between waking and sleeping.

Her sensual dreams flooded her being. Lord Wickham's hands were not just holding her, as was her normal dream. They were roaming quite freely and fervently over her breasts, stomach, and scandalously between her thighs. The sensations his hands evoked were so satisfying she could not hold back her enjoyment. The sounds from her lips seemed to encourage him to explore further.

If too much champagne could do this, she would sneak a glass or two each night before bed. She didn't want to open her eyes, didn't want this dream to end . . . ever. Pleasure. Her body hummed with it, hungered for something more—a satisfaction she did not know how to reach.

Her body ached. She pictured Lord Wickham's strong arms holding her while her pleasure built, an agony she didn't want to escape, but her body felt like it would explode if she did not.

Lying on her side with one knee bent in front of her, the heat continued to escalate. Her nightgown rode up around her chest. She felt something hard and unyielding between her thighs, and she could not seem to roll onto her back, a wall of strength kept her on her side.

The kisses along her shoulder and neck continued to bedazzle her, allowing her no time to analyze where the dream was taking her.

She drowned in new sensations. Her skin pricked with awareness. Her dreams had never gone this far. She reached for—something, a gift; it thrilled her like a present she had yet to unwrap.

And then she felt the searing pain. Her eyes flashed open . . .
Intoxicated she might have been, but she wasn't drunk
enough to miss the hard wall of flesh at her back or the throb
between her thighs. This was real. There was a man in her
bed. A man!

Her throat closed, choking back her screams. Her body
shook with more than fear. He wasn't just in the bed, he was
in her.

Her mouth opened, but her voice scattered soundlessly in
her terror. She was paralyzed by a mixture of pain and fear,
until she heard his grunt of surprise. "Christ, bloody hell . . ."
and a few other choice expletives that followed.

She knew who the rich, gravelly voice belonged to. She'd
recognize Lord Wickham's articulation anywhere. The velvet
tones haunted her very dreams. Her mind reeled with the implications of his mistake. She gulped back a mortified cry.

She tasted bile in her throat at the horror of the situation.
Her dream was now a nightmare. A nightmare of gigantic
proportions. A nightmare that would continue on. Come
morning there would be repercussions.

Her life would never be the same.

Melissa's face flamed with shame and embarrassment. She
had been enjoying his caresses, encouraging his attentions.
What would he think? She'd behaved so wantonly.

For an instant she thought about the benefits this grievous
blunder could bring for her and her brother. It would be the
answer to Christopher's prayers. She quickly suppressed
those emotions. It would not be advantageous to her. Not
with this man, a man who was reputedly incapable of love.

With that thought, panic ignited her action. "Get away
from me." She tried to move, but his steely grip had not loosened. "Let me go. What do you think you are doing?" she
cried in distress.

The Lord of Wicked rose up to lean over her shoulder, but
she could barely see him in the dark room, which had only a
banked fire giving off heat but very little light.

"What sort of trick is this?" His voice was low and deadly in her ear.

She tried to turn to face him, wiggling in this strong grip.

"Christ, do not . . . move . . . do not . . . wiggle . . . oh, my God."

Melissa felt him surge inside her. Once, twice, his grip on her arms vice-like. She knew her skin would be bruised in the morning. He all but roared in her ear, his breath coming in ragged pants. He was trying desperately to withdraw from her, but in her frantic panic they seemed to tangle further.

Finally, he eased his hold and he was gone from between her thighs. He rolled away from her and onto his back, rubbing his hand over his eyes and muttering under his breath. She thought she heard more cursing.

Stunned, she curled into a ball and lay completely still. She was the one who had just been violated, yet he rolled away from her as if he'd been burned by a flame. He made sure he was no longer touching her, as though she were diseased.

Her temper flared at his dismissal of her. She rolled onto her side, facing him, trying to ignore the dull ache between her thighs, noticeable, along with the wetness. She wasn't innocent about the world of men. Cassie had been quite forthcoming with details of the marriage bed.

"Your reputation as a renowned lover is somewhat overstated." The sarcasm all but ripped from her mouth. "It would seem only one of us is quite satisfied."

"I have not had a woman in over three months. I'm sorry, but your enthusiastic response got the better of me. Give me a few minutes and I will redeem myself." He added sardonically, "Since the damage has already been done."

"Damage?" Melissa spat. "I'm still a person. A person you have abused."

He let vent another expletive.

"Your vocabulary is much lacking. Is cussing all you can do?"

"It won't work, you know." The velvet in his voice replaced with tones as cold and rough as tombstones. "I will not be captured into matrimony by this obvious trap."

"What trap would that be? How to be deflowered by a stranger in the night? How to be ruined for any other man? How to be shamed through no fault of my own?"

He snorted. "The trap of swapping beds with Lady Cassandra, so I would take your innocence and be made to marry you."

The darkness hid her anguish. She would never stoop so low as to try and trap a man into marriage. No matter how she played this, she would be the one to pay for his grievous error. Well, she had her pride, and she would not beg him to believe the mistake was all his own.

She swallowed her anger. There was no way she'd let him know the devastation enveloping her. "This is—and always has been—my room. Ever since we came to stay. Cassie's room is one door further along. It would appear, in your haste you miscounted."

More silence.

"Cassie's door is the fifth door along the corridor. Mine is the fourth."

"You should have locked your door." His tone was scathing, letting her know exactly whose fault he thought this situation was.

"A mistake I will not make again. However, do you always enter without an invitation?" she threw back.

"I had an invitation, if you must know."

"You certainly did not."

He frowned. "Did I say it was from you?"

"Well, you should have counted the doors more carefully. Your math is appalling."

"I can count. My information was incorrect." He finally uttered in a tone verging on resignation, "I will kill my brother . . ."

Melissa gasped in horror, his mistake suddenly obvious. "Once I have your apology, you'll have to line up to get to your brother. Now get out!"

He ignored her command, seemingly lost in thought. His voice softened. "Why on earth did you not stop me?" The words were almost a plea.

"I thought I was dreaming."

He finally turned his head to look at her. "But you were a virgin. Virgins do not dream of men . . ."

"Of men what?"

He growled, "Of men ravishing them."

"And how would you know what virgins dream about? Have you asked them?"

"Not bloody likely. I try to keep as far away from them as possible."

"Well then, there is no need for you to keep away from me, since I am no longer an innocent."

Another expletive. "Do not remind me."

He lay silent, staring intensely at her, his features shadowed in the half light. She could make out his high forehead and strong nose. His face bore a resemblance to the Greek statue of Aries in the London museum, classically planed and chiseled. The God of War. She tried to stop her body's shiver. She really wasn't afraid of him . . . or was she? She did not want to fight with this man. She instinctively knew she would not win.

"You're taking this rather well," he finally uttered.

"This situation is not of my making. I am not to blame. Besides, I am not hurt." She winced as she moved. "Well, maybe a bit sore, but I shall live."

He sighed. "You'll be blamed. You can hardly tell everyone you did not stop me because you thought it was a dream."

She smiled, thankful for once of her sensible nature. Creating a fuss would help neither of them. "Who says I am going to tell anyone. I am hoping you can be as quiet leaving as you were arriving. I'm sure you don't want your mistake known. Not only will you be the laughing stock of the clubs, you would be forced to marry me, and I know you don't want that."

"If I was not so relieved, I would be offended. If this is my mistake, you do not put much store in my honor. Most women would demand I marry them, and I should be honor-bound to do so."

She turned from him then. "I will not marry a man who is being forced to marry me. I have seen the pain that brings, and I would not wish it on my worst enemy."

"Like all women, you're a romantic."

"I know marriages are arranged for mutual benefit, dowry, land, money. But I want love." She added truthfully, "And if I can find a man who loves me, why shouldn't I?"

"Do you have someone in mind? Was it your true love you were dreaming of?"

Melissa stiffened beside him. Had he guessed? "A woman does not kiss and tell, not even on her dream lover."

"I have never met a young woman like you. Most ladies would be in hysterics by now, demanding marriage." He studied her face for a moment. "I thank you."

She held his grateful gaze. "I know what it is like to have no say in your future. I could not, in good conscience, put you in the position I so long to escape."

She's not demanding marriage. Thank the Lord. *You're such a bastard*, his conscience screamed.

Guilt and remorse hit him like a fierce drumbeat pounding in his head. Reminding him he had taken her virginity, roughly, quickly, with absolutely no finesse. She was ruined.

You can't leave her to Society's wrath. He ran his hand through his hair. Could he? He didn't want to see her hurt or disgraced. Perhaps he could turn this disaster into the answer to both their prayers.

He'd heard of her brother's dire financial situation and that she had no dowry. If he took a wife, his mother would stop her insistent hounding. Just because he married did not mean he had to father a child. There were ways to prevent conception, the obvious one being never to share his wife's bed. There were plenty of willing females to take care of his carnal needs.

His life wouldn't have to change at all.

His mother had to oversee his many staff, in all four of his households. It took a lot of work. Miss Goodly would be kept busy enough for her to lead her own life, separate from his. She would have everything a woman could dream of— title, position, security, and wealth.

But not children. Anthony frowned. His mother and all of Society would never know the reason he did not produce an heir was simply because he never had conjugal relations with his wife. They would assume she was barren.

He inwardly grimaced. Was this fair on Melissa? He sighed. The point was moot. If he was honest with himself, he had to marry her. He had no choice, and she definitely didn't have a choice.

He would not tell her it would be a marriage in name only. There was no point in upsetting the situation further.

But the chance of making his wife pregnant was not one he would ever take—again.

He turned and looked at the now not-so-innocent woman lying composed beside him. Her eyes locked with his and held him spellbound, his breath hitching in his throat. Their color was a beautiful tawny-brown, with shards of jade, glowing in the dim light. They appeared luminous globes welling with unshed tears, the chocolate specks adding to their troubled depths.

Even now his body began to stir, his mind remembering the feel of her soft curves and satin skin beneath his hands. His eyes were drawn to her rose-red lips, plump and luscious. He wanted to taste her, to devour her with his need, to set her passion soaring, and teach her that their joining could be so much more.

At the thought of making love to her again, his blood thundered loud through his veins. He wanted to reach out and tear her offending nightgown from her body. It was a sin to cover such a vision of beauty.

His heart stilled at the implications of his body's response to her. Perhaps this plan was not very clever after all. He definitely shouldn't want with such consuming desire, a woman who would become his wife. He shook his head. *No. It's simply that you haven't had a woman in so long—*

The bedchamber door crashed open, and two men were silhouetted in the doorway.

Melissa's elder brother stepped into the room. "You will obtain a special license first thing in the morning, or I will have my satisfaction on the dueling field."

Melissa shrank down into the covers. "Christopher, desist. It was an honest mistake. Anthony thought he was in Cassie's room."

Anthony rolled onto his side, blocking the sight of Melissa from those in the doorway, his eyes never leaving her brother's. "Be quiet, Melissa. I don't need a woman to beg for me."

She stiffened beside him.

Her brother's sarcastic words were biting. "Anthony is it?" The Baron strode farther into the room. "A mistake is when he apologizes for entering the wrong room and turns and leaves. There is no mistake when he stays to defile the mistake anyway, to simply sate his lust between a willing pair of thighs."

Melissa gasped.

Anthony exhaled. "You best watch what you say about the lady beside me before I decide to teach you some manners."

"I think we've both learned she is no lady."

Despite his nakedness Anthony leaped out of bed, his fingers wrapping around Christopher's throat, a dark rage engulfing him.

A familiar voice said, "As you seem to have such strong protective feelings for the lady, it would seem it's to be the special license."

His brother's calm voice broke through his haze of anger. Anthony shoved Goodly aside and stalked toward Richard.

"So you were behind all of this." In a deadly voice he said, "Do you know what you have done?"

"I have saved you from years of torment," Richard smugly replied. "I've stopped Father from destroying the rest of your life."

Anthony stood looking at his brother as if he were a total stranger. "No. You have simply ensured Miss Goodly will endure a life of misery."

He retrieved his dressing gown from the floor. Donning it, he walked to the door and turned to address Melissa. "I am truly sorry for what has befallen you tonight. I did not mean to hurt you."

Anger at his brother's deception flooded his being as he watched Melissa's eyes flood with tears.

"I do not want either of you to fight a duel over me. We will find another way. I won't force Anthony to marry me."

"You misunderstand, my sweet. I will get a special license. I am merely apologizing in advance for the lifetime of disappointments you will endure as my wife."

Chapter 3

Anthony stormed into his bedchamber, slamming the door behind him. The fire in the grate cast his shadow over the room, making him appear like a monster out of a child's worst nightmare. He hung his head. He was a monster.

Standing in the middle of the room, naked except for his robe, he fought to bring his temper under control. His hands fisted at his sides and tremors wracked his body. He needed a drink. He moved to the table in the middle of the room and grabbed the bottle of whiskey as if it were a lifeline. He poured himself a large measure and drank. The smooth alcohol soothed the coldness seeping into his bones.

Damn, damn, damn. God damn his brother to hell.

Black spots danced before his eyes. His brother's betrayal made the contents of his stomach begin to crawl up into his throat. Richard was one of only a few he'd allowed close since his father died. He'd opened up and let Richard in, and now his brother, his friend—his own flesh and blood—had betrayed him.

The door opened behind him. Anthony didn't need to look over his shoulder to know who dared to enter. He spun to face his betrayer and snarled, "You are either suicidal or stupid to enter my room after what you have engineered."

Richard held up both hands defensively, but his tone remained belligerent. "It was for your own good."

"More like protecting your own position." Anthony gritted his teeth. "How could you do this to me after everything I've endured? If you weren't my brother, I'd beat you within an inch of your life." He refilled his glass and swallowed the fiery liquid in one gulp. "But that would be a typical Earl of Wickham response. Too much like Father."

"You are nothing like our father. I mean to make you finally see the truth of it."

Anthony took a threatening step toward him.

His brother's eyes flared with a sliver of alarm before masking the fear behind calm indifference. "A woman like Melissa Goodly is perfect for you. She is not a simpering young nincompoop. She is sensible, kind, generous to a fault, and above all else, a woman who is so filled with goodness, it would eventually rub off on you. For Christ's sake, her name is Goodly. What more can I say?"

Anthony turned away in disgust. What could he say? His brother had no idea the things his father had done to him or the things he'd made Anthony do, all in the pursuit of making the perfect ruthless, coldhearted tyrant.

His father had almost succeeded. Anthony knew he wasn't nearly as evil as his late father, only because he'd trained his dark soul to stay hidden. Yet, deep inside, he knew he was the product of his upbringing.

He was a man not good enough for Melissa Goodly. He did not have the capacity to really care for anyone. Melissa deserved a man who would cherish her and hopefully love her. That is what she'd said she wanted. He doubted he could love at all.

Anthony sank down into the chair by the fire and rubbed his temples. What a mess. He raised his eyes to his brother's concerned face and hardened his voice, going in for the kill. "I will never forgive you for what you have done to me this night. We are no longer brothers. I hope acquiring Dark Knight was worth it. Now get out."

"I did not do this to acquire Dark Knight, and you know it." Richard could not hold his steely gaze. He turned and moved to the door. He hesitated with his hand on the door latch. "One day you will thank me."

Anthony took a swig of whiskey directly from the bottle.

"I see as usual, your answer is to drink yourself into oblivion." Before Anthony could reply, Richard left the room, quietly shutting the door behind him.

Anthony's whole body shook with suppressed rage. Thank him! He never wanted to see his brother again. If he did, he wasn't sure he would not pound Richard into pulp.

Everyone thought the brothers were close because they were twins. Anthony leaned his head against the high back of the chair and sighed. They were only close because Richard looked nothing like him or his father.

Anthony, being the first born, had been named after his father. Tony, as he disparagingly thought of his father, was the reason Anthony never let anyone shorten his name.

Swapping the near empty bottle for his glass, he gulped back the rest of his drink and poured himself another.

His late father, Tony, was a contemptible bully. He was a tyrant who leaned toward misogyny. To all intents and purposes, Tony had the *ton* completely fooled. No one outside the immediate family and servants knew the true nature of his father's business, or the cruelty he had heaped on Anthony, his oldest son and heir.

Richard. Anthony knew he shouldn't, but he blamed Richard for his father's ability to fool Society for so long. His father's other son, Anthony's twin, was the perfect picture of a happy child.

The *ton*'s opinion changed very quickly once Anthony came of age and made it known what "business" his father was in—the slave trade. While still perfectly legal, Society viewed the trade as distasteful.

Anthony's earliest childhood memories were now only flashes filled with violent images. His nurse cowering as his father whipped her for giving him a cuddle, his father's black groomsman beaten for condoning one of Anthony's childish pranks. Being young, Anthony had tried to stop his father, only to be backhanded across the yard and whipped with him.

With glass still in hand, but once more half empty, he let his fingers creep toward his face, hesitating before tracing his scar. The thick welt was a constant reminder of his torturous upbringing by a man not fit to own animals, yet alone sire children.

Anthony dropped his fingers from his face and took a long swig of whiskey. Even with his eyes wide open he couldn't stop the vivid memories of being beaten, starved, and worse by his own demented father. It had taken him to near adulthood to perfect the art of masking his feelings. He closed his eyes and swallowed down the bile at the remembrance of his fourteenth birthday. By his early teens Anthony thought his wall of practiced indifference was impenetrable.

When he was fourteen, his father had proved Anthony very wrong.

Tony showed Anthony that he had not conquered the soft side of himself. Anthony still cared too much. Tony had made Anthony hurt someone, lest Tony would hurt them more. The young girl's face haunted him even now. What he had done to her, and the disgusting knowledge that he had physically enjoyed it, still made his stomach clench and bile ride up in his throat.

From that moment on, Anthony realized he was evil. Capable of hurting someone, and worse, he was able to enjoy it. Now he could never relax his guard. One slip, one moment of weakness, and he would unleash the monster within. He would become like his father.

His father's "gift" had chased away any warmth in Anthony's soul, and he learned that if he felt nothing for anyone or anything, then his father would not be able to hurt him. His father would not be able to use anyone's pain against him—ever again.

He drained his drink hoping to wash the acrid taste from his mouth. He'd learned no amount of alcohol could ever dim his disgust at his own behavior.

As he'd grown older, Tony became incensed that he could no longer affect Anthony with his masochistic tendencies, so he turned to threatening the people Anthony cared about.

Eventually, unable to take the degradation anymore, he surrendered. Anthony told his father he'd won. Told him to do his worst to those he loved because Anthony no longer cared what happened to them.

His father had given him a smile so filled with evil it had chilled Anthony's soul, and said, "Finally, you are truly my son."

He had put Anthony through all this pain and agony, all in the name of producing a son capable of carrying on the family business—trading in human flesh.

Slavery—his stomach heaved. The whiskey threatened to come up the way it had gone down, burning his throat. Images of the things he had done while under the influence of his father simply reinforced his desire to ensure an evil like that never walked the earth again. He felt a shudder of disgust ripple through his soul. He alone could not be held responsible for procreating; he might produce another Tony Craven.

He poured himself another drink and tried to analyze the best possible outcome of the dilemma he faced. He must now think of Melissa. She was the one who was in for a life of misery. She would become a wife in name only, for he would never give her a child. He would never bed her again. He remembered her body eagerly enjoying his foreplay. Melissa did not know it, but for a woman who had been clearly enjoying his attentions, that was going to be a prison sentence.

A sentence because he would not permit her to take lovers. He of course would continue to take his pleasures when and where he wanted; he was a man after all. He wanted a Wickham heir—just not his own. Richard's son would inherit the title. Richard took after their mother and didn't have an evil bone in his body.

Melissa could not be allowed to bear another man's child and jeopardize the true Wickham succession.

He would hurt her, of this he was certain. But there was no other way. She was ruined. He had to offer her the protection of his name. He would give her a comfortable life, nice homes, and a position in Society.

His body unfurled, his muscles flexing, the tension draining from him. For the first time since making this dreadful mistake he knew what he had to do. He would strive to make Melissa's life as full as possible. Just not full of passion or love. He hoped the material things he could provide for her would be enough. Remembering the way her body sang at his touch he somehow doubted it.

The next morning Melissa was amazed her brother waited until nearly lunchtime to arrive in her bedchamber. She'd been sure he'd come to her room at sunrise, to check if last night had not been a drunken dream. From the look on his face, he was obviously pleased at the developing situation. You'd think he'd had a windfall at the gaming tables rather than having seen his sister compromised, but then he'd never really cared for her.

"I could kiss you, little sister," he said as he took the only chair in her bedchamber, not worried that she'd have to stand. "For once you've proved yourself useful."

"I have always tried to be useful. I looked after our elderly parents for instance."

"I meant useful to me."

She clasped her hands loosely in front of her. "And of course I have lived my life to be useful to you."

He scoffed. "Useful." He completely missed the fact she was being facetious. "This is the first useful thing you've ever done. You've finally taken my advice. Trapping Lord Wickham into marriage was genius."

She gritted her teeth. "I did not trap him."

"I don't care how it happened. All I care about is that you've saved this family."

"Family? Since when have we ever been a family? Don't you mean saved you? You paid me no attention until I came of age. Until it was time to parade me around the marriage pool, waiting for a shark to bite."

His gaze hardened. "It is my duty as your brother to make an appropriate match for you."

Society knew the precarious state of her brother's finances. She was not without her own appeal, regardless of her lack of a sizable dowry. Her brother hoped to attract a man desperate enough to pay for the privilege of wedding her—or rather bedding her.

"You've thwarted all my previous attempts at finding you a suitable husband. You won't defy me now."

She held in the flash of anger coursing through her body, and her spine stiffened. "That is because your view of 'suitable' and mine differ greatly. I would like a husband who is likely to live out the first year of our marriage."

He gave her a cold smile and stretched his legs out in front of him. "Then for once we should be in accord. The Earl of Wickham is a man in his prime, robust and healthy. He should meet your long list of requirements. I challenge you to state otherwise."

Melissa paced across her room to the window. The view of the damp back garden did nothing to improve her mood. For once her brother was right. She couldn't deny that the Earl would make any woman a fine husband, just not her.

She did not wish to wed Lord Wickham. Not like this. If she thought for one minute that he could conceivably come to care for her, she might at least think something could be salvaged from this dreadful situation.

But the Earl had not wanted her; he'd wanted her cousin, Cassandra.

She sighed. Christopher fully expected Lord Wickham to ensure the family's survival. In truth, a forced marriage to the Earl would be nothing but beneficial to him.

However, not to her. When had anyone ever considered what was best for her?

Melissa frowned. She was not at all sure her brother's plan would work anyway. Why would a man of Wickham's ilk, a man who did not wish to marry, a man who did exactly as he pleased, whenever he pleased, with whomever he pleased, settle Christopher's debts? If anything Lord Wickham would want to see her brother rot for forcing him to wed.

"I don't wish to marry Lord Wickham." She had kept her voice calm, but as she turned to face her brother, her shoulders tensed in preparation of the backlash.

He did not disappoint.

A sound like a starter's gun echoed around the room as he surged to his feet, the chair tipping backward and crashing to the floor. "You will not defy me again. I will not have our good family's name thrown in the gutter because of your disgraceful behavior." He moved toward her, but she refused to back away. Her brother had threatened her before, but she'd learned if she stayed composed, his snarl was worse than a fox's bite. He gripped her chin, and his eyes narrowed to angry slits. "My patience is at an end. You will marry him, even if I have to force you."

Her face heated with shame. Everyone would think she had done this on purpose, trapped Lord Wickham into marriage. Yet she was in fact the innocent party—well, not so innocent anymore.

Her skin felt clammy, and a chill swept through her. Her worst nightmare was coming to pass. A man was being forced to marry her. A man for whom she brought nothing to this union, nothing he valued and nothing he truly desired.

Yet last night, Melissa conceded, she acknowledged a profound truth. She was excited at the thought of marrying the Earl. He aroused strong feelings in her. Her stomach did little flips, and her heart raced whenever he was near. After seeing his naked body and having felt the masculine strength of him, having to share a bed with the Lord of Wicked would not be a hardship. In fact, she looked forward to it. Did that make her as wicked as him? Perhaps they *were* well suited.

But would that be enough? Would passion fill the empty void in her chest?

She shook off her brother's hand and rubbed her temples.

Christopher was intent on marrying her off. The Earl was the first contender to ever set her heart to wishing for more.

Even if she wed another, there was no certainty that would be a love match, either. Perhaps desire, passion, ardor were all she could hope for. Lord Wickham stirred her in a way no other man ever had.

She tried to imagine what her life would be like as the Countess of Wickham. She would want for nothing. He would likely take care of every one of her needs. A quiver skittered down her back. When he was close, there was only one need she wanted fulfilled.

Her body warmed at the thought of children. She wanted a big family. They'd make beautiful children together. She wanted at least six, four boys and two girls, yet she hoped for many more. Their children would never be lonely. It would not be like her childhood.

"He does not wish to marry me, Christopher. You won't be able to force a man like Lord Wickham. A duel would mean nothing to him. He's rumored to have wounded men in several fights. Be careful he does not call your bluff." She laughed. "You were never one to be the hero."

Her brother, Christopher, was all but a stranger. Even now he saw her as nothing but a means to his ends. He couldn't wait to get her married off—as long as he profited.

He moved to right the fallen chair. He set it on the ground and rested his hands on its back. "That is where you are wrong. We have already come to an understanding. The Earl will apply for the special license, and the marriage is to take place in a matter of days."

"So soon? No wonder you are extra chirpy this morning," she drawled sarcastically. She turned her back on her brother. She closed her eyes and tried to get a grip on her irrational fears. She swallowed. Her biggest fear was that she would fall in love with the Earl, only to never have her feelings returned. What could be worse?

She knew what could be worse. She might be viewed as a duty or obligation. She could not bear it if he came to despise her or worse yet, if he grew tired of her and spent all his days with his mistresses.

Yet, what alternative did she have? Once news of last night's escapades leaked out, no decent man would ever offer for her hand. She looked up at her brother. His smile said it all. She had only two choices, Lord Carthors or Lord Wickham.

It really was no choice.

She smiled at her brother, hiding the anger churning in the pit of her stomach. "It seems you will finally be rid of me. Are you going to wish me joy in my new life?"

Her brother turned and walked to the door. "I'm pleased you're finally being sensible about this. You should be grateful for such a good match." He opened the door before adding, "Once you become the Countess of Wickham, I trust you will remember your brother and all he has done for you today."

She would remember. She would never forget—or forgive.

As he closed the door, a triumphant smirk marring his features, she vowed to make the most of her situation. She wanted a husband who loved her, and she was determined to get one. She would devise a plan of her own. A plan that might never come to fruition, but a plan she would have a lifetime to nurture. If she was forced to marry, she would win the heart of the notorious Lord of Wicked.

The gong sounded for lunch. Melissa made her way downstairs to the dining room. Head held high, she entered and spied her cousin, Cassandra, wrapped around the neck of Melissa's betrothed, her body pushed scandalously against his. To Melissa's horror, Lord Wickham was not pushing her away.

Pain knifed through her. Already his callous treatment of her began. How was she to compete with her cousin?

The tears swimming in Cassandra's forest-green eyes made them sparkle like the finest emeralds. Her lush tresses were tied loosely with a purple ribbon and hung down her back almost to her bottom. Anthony was running his hand down the length of it as if stroking a cat.

His cheek was touching hers. The paleness of her skin against his tan made her look so ethereal. She looked like a fairy waif in her white muslin day dress with lavender twirls. He stood towering over her. He was her dark knight, her protector.

They made a striking couple.

Melissa felt sick to her stomach.

She cleared her throat. She had done no wrong. She would not be the one to run away and hide in shame.

"You viper. I could scratch your eyes out . . ." Cassandra flew at her, but before she could swipe Melissa with her claws, Anthony caught her around the waist, holding her back.

Melissa looked down her nose. "I do not see how I am the villain here, when you were stupid enough to give your paramour incorrect directions to your bedchamber."

Cassandra hissed. "Knowing the Craven twins and their mother are guests in my house, you should have locked your bedchamber door."

The Cravens were Cassandra's guests due to the fire at Craven House, two days previously. They were staying until the smoke damage dissipated. The fact that Cassandra was infatuated with Anthony was the driving force behind Cassandra's kind offer. Everybody knew it.

"I have already had that pointed out to me, and it is not a mistake I will make twice." She gave Anthony a scathing look.

Cassandra couldn't hide her bitterness. "You won't need to make it twice. Once has seen you catch the prize. Very well planned out."

"I did not invite the Earl or his brother to stay. You did. If anyone had ulterior motives, it was you! Don't get upset just because your plan has gone astray."

"Why you ungrateful wench . . ."

Lord Wickham appeared amused. "Now, ladies, tempers please."

Cassandra pushed his arms away and moved toward her, shaking a finger. "I knew I shouldn't have taken you and your brother in. You traitor—"

"I . . ." Melissa bit back her words as nerves tightened her throat.

"That's quite enough, Cassandra. No one betrayed you. My brother, however, betrayed me. The mistake was mine, and now I must pay for it."

His words seemed to pacify Cassandra while they heaped pain upon Melissa's festering pride. Melissa lost her appetite. She turned to leave the room.

Lord Wickham called after her. "Are you not hungry?"

She leveled a cool look over her shoulder. "No."

"Then I would like a few words with you. Cassandra, my dear, may we use your late husband's study?"

Not waiting for a reply, he gripped Melissa's elbow and shepherded her out the door. "This way . . ." He indicated up the stairs to the first landing. "It's the door on your left."

"Unlike you, my lord, I know every room in this house . . ."

He chose to ignore her remark, and once they'd entered the study Lord Wickham walked to the large windows that overlooked Cassandra's back garden. His shoulders were tense, and he seemed to lose himself in thought.

Melissa cleared her throat.

Still he did not respond. The silence was nerve-wracking.

"I'm sorry the situation has got so complicated. I would've hoped that I might have been able to talk my brother around this morning, but he was not inclined to change his mind."

Anthony nodded, still looking out the window.

"I'm pleased you did not take up his challenge for a duel. Getting yourself killed wouldn't have helped anyone." She gave a shudder. "I couldn't bear to think I'd been the cause of anyone's death, whether it was actually my fault or not."

He gave her a piercing stare over his left shoulder. "No, killing your brother would not have been the solution."

Melissa licked her lips. "Speaking of which, my lord—"

"Please, we are well beyond formality, call me Anthony."

"Yes, well, Anthony—" She counted to ten. "Can't you turn around? It's difficult talking to someone's back. It's rude and very off-putting."

His big shoulders rippled beneath his navy coat as he sighed and turned to face her.

Her breath hitched; he was so handsome. His gray eyes pinned her beneath a probing gaze. She moved, hoping to distract herself from the effect he was having on her. She crossed the room to one of the large leather armchairs and sat demurely. "I may have a solution to our situation. You do not wish to marry me—"

He raised a perfect dark eyebrow and gave her a smile that literally took her breath away. "We are getting married. I will brook no argument. I will not have the Wickham name disgraced. There has been enough scandal in my family."

If she didn't already have a *tendre* for him, or if she knew she could never come to love him, the marriage might have worked. But she wouldn't dare love him while he simply saw her as a woman to bear his children, run his home, and plan his entertainments. A woman who never questioned his liaisons. In time she'd be left languishing in the country, missing him terribly, while he cavorted in London with his latest paramours. She just knew it.

Her friend Lady Sarah Campbell endured her husband's disinterest. She bore the humiliation of his affairs and was often the subject of gossip and pity.

Melissa would rather not love at all than love a man who would never love her. So it was imperative to nip this indiscretion in the bud, before she fell under his spell any further.

Melissa felt her cheeks heat. "I don't want to marry you."

His gray eyes darkened to the color of coal. "Am I that terrifying?"

She shook her head.

"I realize my deflowering of you could have been better, but I won't hurt you again, I promise."

Melissa's bottom lip quivered as she tried to forget the feel of his body holding her, or his enormous member inside her . . . "I have no doubt you would make a marvelous lover, but you would likely be a wretched husband." She shrugged her shoulders. "To me anyway."

He ran his hand through his hair. "You are right of course. I would make a terrible husband. But you forget one thing."

"That is . . ."

He strolled over to her chair and looked down at her. "You have forgotten the most important thing of all. You might be with child." The word "child" seemed to stick in his throat, and his eyes widened as if he was in shock. He shook himself, drew in a deep breath, and added, "I am not heartless enough to leave you to face Society's wrath pregnant with my child."

Melissa felt the blood drain from her face. She hadn't thought of that. "We could wait and see if I am with child before rushing into anything."

Anthony's face clouded in anger, his eyes narrowed and darkened like the sky before a thunderstorm. Melissa watched the tick in his taut jaw with fascination. She'd just given him a way out, yet he seemed very displeased.

"You must think I have no honor at all."

She pleaded with him. "No, it's not that. I think, so far, you've proved to be very honorable; I applaud you for it. But there is no need to sacrifice yourself for me."

He crouched down before her chair and swallowed her hand in his. "I want to protect you from a Society that would hurt you. Why are you fighting me on this?" His eyes never left hers as he raised her hand to his lips.

A hurricane of emotions swirling around her, Melissa could hardly think. What was he up to? For a man so vehemently opposed to marriage, he seemed desperate to find reasons for the marriage to go ahead. She eyed him wearily.

That was a mistake. Her body stirred at his closeness. No man ever aroused her the way Anthony could. Merely looking at him now rekindled the delicious sparks between them.

She swallowed, aware of her humming nerves, the hollow flip-flopping sensation in her stomach, and the tingling warmth between her thighs.

Before she could help herself she uttered, "I just want to be happy."

"Your pulse is racing, I can feel it." His lips brushed the sensitive skin of her wrist like a feather. "At the moment what would make me extremely happy would be to lock the door and make love to you in a manner more fitting than last night's performance. To hear your small cries of passion, to make you wet with desire, and to sink between your soft thighs and let you touch heaven."

Now she was afraid. Something was wrong. He was trying to beguile her into this marriage—why? Melissa couldn't hold his seductive gaze. Warmth seared her skin at his touch.

Before she could even think to pull away, he leaned forward and kissed her . . . giving her a long, lingering, completely devastating reminder of the sensual power he held over her.

When he straightened, leaving her dazed and longing, his face was serious. "We will be married as soon as I obtain the special license. That is the only course open to us. I know it's not what you would have chosen, but I could make you happy. I can't promise to ever love you, but I can make your life comfortable. You'll want for nothing."

Except love, Melissa thought glumly. "I want to be happy, that's true. I'm just not sure you're the type of man that could make me happy." Melissa knew with certainty he would never be faithful. The ache in the vicinity of her heart sent pain lancing down her arms until she had to clench her fists.

Lord Wickham's eyes noted the movement.

He was reputedly a man of insatiable tastes where the opposite sex was concerned. She did not expect him to change his ways overnight—or ever—not for her.

He was staring at her intently. "Can you say that any other man would make you happy? Are you in love with someone else?"

She sucked in a short breath. "No. I am not in love with anyone."

"Then there is nothing more to discuss. You will become my wife. Society will feed you to the wolves with any other outcome."

Society. With sinking heart Melissa's hopes of avoiding becoming the Countess of Wickham died. She would never win against the might of the *ton*. Her charity work, her fight for people's freedom, was all she had. She would surely lose her ability to secure funds, to lobby for changes to the law. As the Countess of Wickham she would be afforded entry into the highest echelons of Society. She could do a world of good, perhaps speed the passage of change. But she was going to have to give up her freedom to achieve her goal—the abolition of slavery in all forms—first Negroes and then she would help women. Women who, often, were no better than slaves. Owned by men. Men who could treat them as they saw fit. The *ton* was full of examples of men's cruelty.

She would fight for freedom by giving up her own. The irony was not lost on her.

Melissa looked into Anthony's silver-gray eyes and shivered. What was it about this man? She should be petrified of the brooding rake. She licked her lips, not quite believing she was so readily capitulating. "Before I accept your proposal—"

"You don't have a choice."

"Before I accept,"—she leveled a serious gaze at him—"I have one favor to ask of you. Call it an engagement gift of sorts." She watched his eyes narrow into cautious slits. "Anthony, I have no wish to be the laughing stock of the *ton*, nor do I assume would you."

Melissa was pleased to see Anthony's confident smile dim slightly. "I will grant you any favor in my power to give."

She tried to keep a blush from scalding her cheeks. "I would like your promise that you won't take my cousin as your mistress. Put bluntly, I do have some pride. I don't want my husband sleeping with a woman I am related to."

Chapter 4

Anthony's face remained a mask; not a flicker of emotion crossed his handsome features. "You do know I am likely to take a mistress once we marry? I won't have you interfering in the way I conduct myself."

Her face heated further, and pain lanced through her chest. She fixed her gaze firmly on his face, willing her hurt not to show. "I am not naive of the ways of gentlemen. Just promise me that it is not Cassandra."

He stood looking at her for what seemed like several minutes, the silence deafening. Finally, he nodded and gave a small bow. "That is not too much to ask given the circumstances. My engagement gift shall be my promise not to pursue Cassandra." He hesitated before adding, "Know this, Melissa. I will never intentionally hurt or humiliate you, if I can help it."

She inwardly sighed in relief, and his warm smile lessened some of her pain. "Thank you."

"However, there will be some talk."

Melissa's lips lost their smile. "Obviously. Your views on the horrid state of matrimony are well known."

"I will do all I can to contain the gossip."

Melissa nodded. "I shall leave the story of pacifying the *ton*'s curiosity to you. Everyone will know why I have accepted—it's a great honor."

Anthony clapped his large hands together. "Good, then it's

settled. I shall go and give Mother the wonderful news. We'll marry as soon as I have obtained the special license. Shall we say Friday morning?"

Melissa clutched her hands tightly. In just under a week, she would be the Countess of Wickham. That hardly scared her. What turned her insides to ice was the thought of being married to the notorious Lord of Wicked. If she wasn't careful, he'd undoubtedly break her heart.

Anthony patted her hands, taking her silence for acquiescence. "Leave everything to me. I'll get the special license organized and the vicar. If you require a new dress or bonnet, speak to my mother. She'll organize any bills to be sent to me."

He opened the door and walked out.

Slumped back on the settee in his mother's temporary sitting room, off her bedchamber in Cassandra's house, Anthony could not hide the hard edge to his features or the blatant coldness about him as he stared at the woman seated across from him. A woman the world called his mother but who was in fact a complete stranger to him.

He sprawled in his seat with forced elegant ease, analyzing the Dowager Countess of Wickham—the woman who'd borne him but who was never a maternal figure in his life. An ease that did nothing to disguise the air of contained hostility emanating from his bulky frame.

His mother sat stiffly in her chair, to all intents and purposes looking as if she were poised for flight. Her hair, although graying in parts, still shone golden in the sun just like Richard's. Her eyes, still a vivid blue, reminded him so much of his brother it hurt looking at them. He envied Richard his mother's small nose. Anthony's nose dominated his face, as had his father's. She was still a remarkably beautiful woman, if it wasn't for the coldness radiating from her. He tried to make allowances for her. Being married to his father could not have been easy.

He looked at his mother. Not once had he experienced the

comfort of his mother's arms, or been given any feelings of maternal love. She'd lavished the little love she had on his brother. Richard had been hers while he'd been left to their father.

"You have finally got your wish. It appears I am to marry." Anthony tried to feign some measure of joy in the news he had just imparted to his mother.

He shifted uneasily in his chair. He hoped he was doing the right thing—for both himself and Melissa.

"Appears? Either you are betrothed or you are not. Which is it?" Her mouth set in a grim line. "Let me guess, you have succumbed to Lady Sudbury's delights. I have watched her leading you around like a bull with a ring through its nose this past week. If she won't bed you without marriage, she's risen in my estimations."

"Mother, really," he started in an offended tone. The fact she was quite correct in her deduction annoyed him somewhat. He was becoming too predictable. At least this announcement was anything but predictable.

He took great joy in correcting her. "It is not Lady Sudbury." He hesitated, wondering if she'd be pleased at his choice, not that he gave a damn. His mother's wishes were never a consideration in anything he did in his life. "It's Miss Melissa Goodly, Cassandra's cousin."

A hint of a smile curled on the Dowager's sullen mouth. "Caught in the wrong bed were you?"

Richard. He'd already told her. His blood began to pound through his veins. Had they planned this together? Had Richard been working for his mother? Anthony recoiled at the thought. Richard professed he'd engineered this situation for Anthony's own good, but perhaps pleasing Mother had been forefront in his mind. He briefly closed his eyes. God, could he trust no one?

His features remained impassive. "News travels quickly in this household."

His mother sniffed. "Miss Goodly is not the woman I would have picked. Her temperament does not suit you."

Anthony frowned. "What has that got to do with anything?"

"Like any mother, I do not wish you to be unhappy."

"I beg your pardon?" Anthony could not believe what he was hearing. "Since when have you ever been concerned with my happiness? You have left it a bit late haven't you?"

She hung her head. "I realize you have not forgiven me for deserting you when you were young, but your father was a hard man. If I created any fuss at his treatment of you, he threatened to take Richard, too."

Anthony tried to hide the emotions her words provoked, but he could not help the note of pain in his voice. "And we could not have precious Richard hurt, could we?"

A flash of anger entered her eyes. "Richard was not strong like you. You take after your father. Richard was softer. Your father would have broken him."

Anthony leaned forward and through clenched teeth said, "What do you think he did to me?"

The anger left her eyes. "He did not break you. You're your own man. You survived. That's why selecting the most appropriate wife is so important. The right woman, a woman you could come to love, will be the making of you."

Anthony blanched. Love?

"There has not been enough love in the Wickham dynasty. I was hoping you'd be strong enough to change that."

Anthony looked at his mother as if she'd gone mad. He rose from his chair, a sudden chill unsettling him. Love was something he'd never contemplate. Love and hate, the two sides of the same coin, both led to heartache. It was far safer not to feel at all. If you succumbed to real emotions, either love or hate, you could be manipulated or hurt. Care for nothing and you had nothing to lose.

His father had taught him well.

Anthony came to a halt in front of his mother's chair. "I wouldn't know love if it dropped down from heaven on angels' wings. I think you have overestimated me, Mother."

She stared at him for a moment, and then she shrugged her

delicate shoulders. "It hardly matters now. You have made your choice. She is very beautiful of course. If it wasn't for a lack of dowry, I'm sure she would have had several proposals of marriage by now. As it is, Lord Dashell has been very attentive. He has no need of money. He must like the girl."

Anthony's frown deepened. Beautiful? He sat down with a bump. He didn't want to acknowledge Melissa's looks. Her beauty was a gaping flaw in his plan. When not being compared with Cassandra, Melissa was indeed pleasing to the eye. This marriage would only work if he treated Melissa's looks dispassionately. He could not come to desire his wife.

His temper piqued. He did not like the prick of jealousy burrowing into his side. Dashell? He balked at the thought she preferred another. She'd told him she'd been dreaming when he came to her bed. Was it Dashell she dreamed of? Had he destroyed her hopes of a match with the man she loved? No. Melissa had told him she loved no one. Had she lied?

Anthony's hands fisted on his thighs. God help him. No, God help her. She was his. For some unknown reason, he did not want her dreaming of another man. Why was beyond him. He wasn't territorial about his women, and he did not care enough for any of them to care about fidelity. Why was the thought of Melissa with another man choking him with anger?

He did not like the feelings pouring through him. The sooner they were wed and he could send her away from him the better. He'd simply find a new mistress, and then Melissa would be forgotten.

His fists slowly relaxed.

"I have always wanted a daughter, a young lady to dress and introduce to Society." Turning to him, her face animated, his mother added, "She only has her brother, doesn't she? Her parents are dead. I shall have to take her in hand immediately. She will need a whole new wardrobe. Her clothes are not fashionable enough for a countess. Her brother has not taken very good care of her."

His mother was going to enjoy this. "I will be happy to pay for anything you deem appropriate for my bride to be."

His mother rose and surprised him by placing a kiss on his cheek. He stiffened at the unexpected contact.

"For your father's son, you are a very generous man."

Anthony's good mood vanished with her words. He rose to leave.

"I shall leave Melissa's fate in your hands. I have seen to the other particulars. You will know the invitations to accept once news of the wedding becomes public."

"You will be expected to escort her to many of the balls. It would look peculiar if you did not."

Anthony gave his mother what he hoped was a dazzling smile. "I am looking forward to the prospect of squiring my wife through the vivacious *ton* immensely."

If his mother believed that she was sillier than he thought.

Lady Wickham watched her son leave her room with mixed emotions roiling in the pit of her stomach. She gave a satisfied smile. Anthony must never know she thought Miss Melissa Goodly was precisely the woman he needed.

She'd been watching and assessing Miss Goodly since the beginning of the Season, and she liked what she saw. The young lady knew her own mind. Miss Goodly did not simper, flirt, or preen to attract a man, even though her brother faced financial ruin. Melissa remained composed while Lord Norrington paraded her before elderly widowers, hoping her obvious earthy charms would entice an offer of marriage.

The Countess of Wickham shuddered at the realities of life. Miss Goodly's own brother would sell her innocence to a decrepit reprobate simply to save his own skin. She smiled to herself. She was pleased to have been able to set Richard down the right path. Although she'd never have foreseen how quickly or how expertly Richard managed to accomplish what she never thought she'd ever see in her lifetime.

Anthony married.

She stood and let out a nervous breath. Her plan could

have gone terribly wrong. She'd suggested to Richard that Miss Goodly was the type of woman who would be the making of his brother. Bless Richard; his quick thinking had done the rest.

She moved to her writing desk and drew out a piece of paper. She would write to Selby and ensure Wickham Manor was ready for her return immediately following the wedding. She didn't want there to be any distractions in Craven House; they deserved time alone.

She paused in her writing. Miss Goodly was not only intelligent, refined, and selfless, but also beautiful. What convinced her that this match would be Anthony's salvation, however, was Melissa's charming disposition.

Melissa had a very kind heart. Her goodness was evident in the friendships she kept and the work she did for the Ladies Freedom Charity, a charity that raised money to buy slaves their freedom and then found them paid employment.

The Countess knew that would strike a chord with Anthony. Once married, once alone at Craven House, how could Anthony not succumb to Melissa's many charms—both physical and spiritual? At least Anthony would have someone by his side. Someone who might come to love him—if he let her.

If Melissa's quiet strength and beauty couldn't rattle her son, then no woman could and her husband would have won.

The Countess's smiled faded. She'd die before she let that happen. Her son had been hurt enough. She was going to do everything in her power to make this marriage a success.

Cassandra wanted to slap the triumphant smile off Christopher's face as he lay panting beside her. As usual, he had not satisfied her.

Probably because she was still angry with herself.

Her plan had not worked. Why, oh why, had she tried to play a game with Lord Wickham? If she'd simply let him seduce her straight into her bed, the first night they'd met, she would not be in this situation.

As if reading her mind, her lover said, "Do not look so upset, Cassandra. You'll still be able to take Wickham as your lover. A man like him will never be satisfied by one woman, let alone his wife." Christopher laughed. "But thank god I caught them. He is the answers to my prayers. If I'd known how easy Melissa'd be, I might have set her up in a compromising situation earlier."

Anthony was supposed to have been Cassandra's salvation. No one but her man of business and her lawyer truly knew the state of her finances. Christopher's debts paled into insignificance next to hers.

That two-faced milk-sop Melissa had ruined everything. Cassandra would have to look for another potential, yet rich, husband.

She sighed. With her beauty it should not be difficult. It's simply she wanted more than a rich husband. She wanted a real man, a man who made her body wet and needy with one seductive look. A man whose erection was so huge she'd feel as if he'd impaled her on it—a man like Anthony James Craven, the Earl of Wickham.

His sexual prowess was legendary. Her feminine folds became wet merely thinking about the pleasure his instrument of passion could give her.

How she'd longed to join his Wicked Club. She was not jealous of the women before her. She planned to be the only member of the club that succeeded in becoming his wife. That's why she'd tried to play her silly game. She'd built his desire for her until she could see it flaming in his eyes every time he looked at her.

Her fait accompli was when he'd agreed to move in while his town house was undergoing repairs. The fact that she'd paid a man to set the fire had luckily escaped notice.

She tried to keep her tone even. "Tell me, how exactly did you happen to catch them?"

Christopher frowned. "His brother, Richard, came and got me. I thought that strange. I always thought they liked each other. Most thought they were very close."

It made perfect sense to Cassie. Richard had been pursuing her, too. She was accustomed to men fighting over her, yet to force your own brother into marriage seemed extreme. Plus it wouldn't stop her bedding Anthony anyway. She bit her lip. No, something else was going on here.

Christopher turned to face her. "I may need help with Melissa. She has not taken her situation well at all. I wouldn't put it past her to do something stupid, like run away. This morning she was in tears begging me not to force her into this marriage. The girl's insane. She is completely ruined, a wealthy earl has proposed marriage, and yet for some reason she seems afraid to marry Lord Wickham."

Cassie gritted her teeth. How did she tell Melissa's brother that the likely size of Wickham's member probably hurt his sister to the point that she's terrified of sharing Anthony's bed. "Losing one's virginity can often be a most painful experience. She is probably simply fearful of further hurt. I will reassure her."

Christopher smiled in relief. "You are most kind. I had forgotten the talk about Wickham's size."

Cassandra had most definitely not, and she could not wait to feel the full hard length of him as he drove into her. She would marry him, for nothing was going to stop her.

But what to do about Melissa? A delicious shiver of evil slid down her spine. She knew a man who might help. This could be quite profitable for her in more ways than one.

She licked her lips and fingered her wet folds. Then, the Earl of Wickham would be all hers to enjoy and savor.

She rolled on top of Christopher and began stroking him. "Tell me, how soon are they to wed?"

Christopher's voice hitched. "Friday," he panted.

Cassandra kissed and sucked his nipples before she rose to her knees and moved up to grip the headboard, perfectly positioned above Christopher's face.

"Then I suggest we help them plan this happy event." She looked down expectantly at her lover. "Now that you are connected to an earl, it should not take me long to find you a suitable bride. A suitable, wealthy bride. Why don't you show me how grateful you can be?"

His tongue stroked her; her eyes glazed over and her head fell back. Soon she was riding his face, his mouth sucking and licking until she exploded in ecstasy above him, dreaming of letting the Earl of Wickham do this to her until she fainted from the pleasure.

Chapter 5

The next morning, Anthony, having let his mother extract a promise to escort Melissa riding in the park later that afternoon, badly needed some good news to lift his foul temper. He arrived at Craven House to inspect the fire damage. He couldn't take another night under Cassandra's roof, knowing she was only a few doors away yet due to his promise to Melissa—untouchable.

He took a deep breath. Quincy, his man of business, was quite correct. The smell of smoke had dissipated.

"You were very fortunate, my lord. The fire damage was not very extensive. The house will be ready for you to occupy in a few days' time."

The two men made their way back upstairs to Anthony's study. The actual fire damage was contained to the back of the property, near the kitchens. The rest of his house had simply been affected by smoke.

Thank goodness, for Anthony loved this house. Craven House was a substantial dwelling. He'd bought it five years ago, so it held no degrading memories of his childhood. It was a free-standing Mayfair mansion surrounded by extensive gardens and a high stone wall. There were enough rooms in the grand residence that Anthony rarely had occasion to see his mother.

Not that she stayed in Town often. She preferred to stay at Wickham Manor in Selby near Bath. His father had bought the Bath property to be near Bristol, which up until last year was the largest slave-trading port in England.

At this moment, Anthony had never been more thankful for the house's size. He'd need the space to avoid his wife. Wife! His chest felt as if it had been caught in a blacksmith's vice.

Anthony cleared his throat. "That is good news, because I will be holding an intimate wedding breakfast here on Friday."

Quincy's moon face puffed with surprise, his thick, brown brows furrowing. "Who's getting married, my lord?"

He could not help but give a bleak smile. "Me. Last night I proposed to Miss Melissa Goodly, and to my joy she has accepted."

Quincy jerked in his seat, nearly falling off his chair. "Er . . . ah . . . congratulations, my lord. May you be very happy."

Very happy might be pushing it, but he hoped for at least happy. Melissa seemed a sensible girl, not so full of unrealistic notions that a companionable relationship could not develop. Besides, she was very aware of her precarious financial state and the privilege that would come with her marriage to an earl.

Turning to more important matters, Anthony asked, "Have they managed to ascertain how the fire started?"

"No, my lord. One of the grooms found a cheroot near a box of old papers the maids keep for lighting the fires. The theory is a box of paper caught alight when a cheroot was carelessly thrown over the wall."

"Then I suggest we move anything flammable away from the area."

"It's been done."

"Good." He took his seat at his desk. "Shall we get on? What needs my attention today?"

Quincy handed Anthony a sheaf of papers. "The shipping reports, my lord. Both your ships should arrive this week as expected."

Anthony looked forward to their return. He expected

Captain Hawker to provide an update on the effects of the Anti-Slave Trading Act. The House of Lords passed the bill in March last year. Slavery had not been abolished, but they'd made it illegal for any British ship to carry slaves.

There was a knock at the study door. Stevens, Anthony's long-serving butler, entered and presented Anthony with a calling card. "Viscount Strathmore to see you, my lord."

Anthony raised his head, surprised. He'd not expected his friend until Thursday when they were due to meet at White's before enjoying a night of entertainments.

"Send him in, Thompson." He wondered what his good friend, Rufus Knight, wanted.

Anthony rarely saw his old school chum. Rufus had been his best friend since Anthony's first day at Eton. Richard had attended Eton from a young age, while Anthony's father tutored—if that's what you could call it—him at home. When Anthony turned sixteen, his father relented, and Anthony accompanied his twin brother back to school.

Most of the boys thought Anthony extremely odd and paid him very little attention. Except for Rufus.

Anthony to this day did not know what Rufus saw in him. Rufus had pestered him until Anthony finally accepted the slight shadow, as he called Rufus. He followed Anthony everywhere. At sixteen, Rufus was small next to Anthony's hulking frame. Perhaps it was the protection Anthony provided Rufus with that made him so loyal. For whatever reason Rufus had picked him to be his friend, Anthony was grateful.

Rufus strode into the room, an irritated scowl hanging from his auburn brows. A troubled look darkened his golden-brown eyes, startling within a face conveying a dark tan, which indicated his life of outdoor pursuits, and setting him apart from the rest of the nobility.

Anthony rose to shake hands with Rufus, who before his time at Eton had finished matched him in height and build.

"Rufus, this is a pleasant distraction." Rufus kept much to himself. As did Anthony—one of the things they had in common. "My ships have not arrived in port yet. Or could you not wait for Thursday night's entertainments?"

Rufus gave a bark of laughter. "I am most eager, as you put it, to visit Madame Sabine's. I hear she has two new demimondes just for us, but I'm afraid I'm here on business."

Anthony sank back down on his chair. "I don't like the sound of that." Rufus worked for the Foreign Secretary, in what capacity Anthony was unsure and he knew better than to pry into government business. "Quincy, leave us please."

Quincy bolted out of his seat. "Quincy, a moment." Anthony looked at the clock on the mantel. "Inform Monty I need the grays harnessed and ready by quarter to four. Thank you." Deliberately, he added, "I am taking Miss Goodly for a turn in the park."

Rufus's jaw dropped.

Anthony laughed. "I have some news of my own, and believe me, you will need a drink."

"I go away for a few weeks, only to return and find you escorting women in the park." He raised an eyebrow. "Perhaps I should go away more often."

Rufus often disappeared for weeks at a time on government business. The last time Anthony had met with Rufus, the man informed him that some English merchants were risking life and limb to slip through the Royal Navy blockade. The new Anti-Slave Trading Act made the gamble highly profitable for those who succeeded in breaking the law. "I've a feeling that your business here will require a drink anyway. Brandy or whiskey?"

"Whiskey," Rufus said, his sun-bronzed hand tugging the last riding glove off. "You? Taking a woman riding in the park?"

He tossed his friend a grin and moved to pour them both a drink, waiting for Quincy to close the door behind him.

"Don't tell me." Rufus claimed a seat on the other side of a large mahogany desk. "Your mother's match-making again."

"Worse than that I am afraid." He handed Rufus the glass of whiskey, then gulped his own shot straight down. Hissing the heat out of his throat, he turned to pour himself another. "You owe me congratulations. As of this morning, Miss Goodly is my fiancée."

"Miss who?" Rufus scowled at him and shoved his unruly auburn hair out of his square face. "I've never heard of her. What is going on here? Why are you marrying?"

"Why, indeed?"

Rufus took a sip of his drink, and his mouth curved up in amusement. "I find I am quite pleased you are and that you have given up this nonsense about not spawning future Tony Cravens."

Anthony rolled his eyes. "Don't you start. You're as bad as Richard." Taking the whiskey decanter with him, Anthony sat behind his desk. "My so-called brother, a brother I have now disowned, has achieved that which no woman ever has. He's managed to get me leg shackled."

Rufus threw back his head and roared with laughter.

"It's not funny," Anthony snapped.

"Not to you," Rufus said, sobering. "I shall have to find Richard and congratulate him. How on earth did he manage that mammoth task?"

With more than a little embarrassment, he told his sorry tale and ended it with: "The moral of the story is, do not go without bedding a wench for more than three months. It addles the brain and makes you susceptible to all manner of treachery."

Rufus stuck out his glass for a refill. "I know you too well, friend. You do not seem as miffed as you make out. If she looks like Lady Sudbury, she must be a rare beauty. So, are you pleased or disappointed in your betrothal?"

Anthony put down his drink. A flitter of nervousness somersaulted in his stomach remembering Melissa's horror at the knowledge she would have to wed him. He could not for the life of him work out why. She wasn't afraid of him. Her calm refusal was not made in fear. He'd almost lost his nerve to carry out his plan when he gazed upon her serene features. She was so composed.

He'd been lost in the ethereal beauty of her, her narrow nose, the dark sweep of her raven brows, and the lush curve of her rose-kissed lips. She was a most lovely creature, and the urge to crush her in his arms had stolen over him so suddenly, he'd almost made love to her again before remembering his plan.

A wry smile twisted his lips. "She is very pleasing to the eye."

"Ah . . ." Rufus leaned back in his chair and shook his head. "Desire is a good way to begin a marriage. I still cannot believe Lord Wickham has accepted being hog-tied into matrimony so easily. Hell, if I'd known you'd have crumpled so effortlessly, I would have tried to compromise you a long time ago." He raised his glass. "Here's to Richard."

Anthony checked the alignment of his cravat with his fingers. "I have my reasons for wanting this marriage. If you are so enamored of the state of matrimony, why are you not wife hunting?"

Rufus stilled. "You know why. Once I have uncovered the truth about my father and restored my family's honor, I shall marry. Not before then."

They exchanged knowing looks. That's why they were friends. Rufus's father was reputed to be as despicable as his own. A traitor who'd sold secrets to the French. The only difference was Rufus thought his father was innocent. Anthony knew his father wasn't.

Rufus's eyes narrowed. "You mentioned you have a reason to marry. What reason would this be? I thought Richard was supposed to provide the Wickham heir?" Rufus's smile faded. "I doubt it could be love. You haven't been pursuing any woman except Cassandra as far as I am aware."

"Don't you have something of more importance to discuss with me?" Anthony desperately wanted to change the subject. "Or are my impending nuptials of more interest?"

His expression bland, Rufus slid a cool, unaffected gaze at him. "I do have more pressing business, but I shan't forget to further this conversation at a later time. I'm looking forward to meeting Miss Goodly." Rufus stood and moved to the window, his shoulders immediately tensed. "It's about the Royal Navy slave blockade."

Anthony stiffened. "You know my ships are available to help if needed."

Rufus swung around to face him. "It also involves your old friend, Baron Rothsay."

A cold chill shot down Anthony's back, and he pushed up out of his chair. "Let me guess, Rothsay is still carrying human cargo."

"Nothing that we can prove—yet. That is why I'd be interested to hear what Captain Hawker thinks on his return. I have some information I would like him to verify—if he can."

Anthony sat on the edge of his desk, his voice strained. "The last time we met, Rothsay laughed in my face. Telling me the Anti-Slave Trade Act would make his fortune and that he'd always wanted to be a pirate. I knew he had no intention of stopping. The problem is, even when the Royal Navy intercepts these pirates trading in human cargo, none of the ships can be traced directly back to him."

"Are you sure they belong to him?"

Anthony sniggered. "I'm certain. My father and Rothsay and his father were the biggest in the business. Rothsay was taught well. He revels in the trade. The power over another human being thrills him. He's cruel. I've told Captain Hawker to ignore his ships on the open ocean because if they tried to catch him, he'd simply throw the evidence overboard, killing all on board. No human cargo, no evidence, no ship confiscation."

Rufus frowned. "So if we want to catch him we have to do so before they leave port."

"Even then, Rothsay's not stupid enough to have a ship traceable to his name." He gave Rufus a solemn look. "I probably won't be much help. Rothsay would like nothing better than to see me dead after I stopped his last slave shipment. He's never forgiven me for the money I cost him, or for the fact I have turned traitor and joined the Abolitionists."

"We need your help again." Rufus cleared his throat. "The Foreign Secretary, Lord Ashford, has received intelligence that Rothsay's behind an increase in shipments."

"I already told you he was." Stopping Rothsay's three slave ships last November had been such sweet victory. Anthony knew nothing could make up for the atrocities he and his father had committed, but he could look at himself in the mirror with less revulsion. "He's trying to make as much money before the world forces men like him into retirement."

Rufus held up his hand. "Yes, I know. But Ashford needed confirmation. He now has it."

"From whom?"

Rufus grimaced. "I cannot say. Not because I do not trust you, but because I do not know. Ashford is a need-to-know man, and I didn't need to know."

"I am not sure if there's any more I can do, Rufus. My ships relay any and all information they collect, but Rothsay's clever." He returned to his chair. "I've already told the navy which ports in Africa Rothsay works out of. If I hear anything else, I'll let you know immediately."

"I'm sorry, Anthony." Rufus spoke in almost a whisper. "Rothsay's no longer only working out of Africa—"

"Don't be ridiculous, he wouldn't bring slaves to England. It's too dangerous."

An ominous silence filled the study.

Rufus hung his head. "He's not taking African slaves to America. It seems he's opened up a new market."

Anthony gasped. No. Rothsay wouldn't. Bile tasting of whiskey rose in his throat. He swallowed it back down.

Rufus stood and moved to the window. "He is rumored to be operating out of British ports, selling women throughout Arabia, the Barbary Coast, and the Ottoman Empire."

Anthony gagged. "White women?"

Rufus nodded. "God knows how long he's been doing

this. The Royal Navy is not even looking at ships leaving English ports for destinations other than the Americas."

"Christ, I should have killed him when I had the chance." He rubbed his temples. "What can I do to help?"

"Information." Rufus had the grace to look embarrassed. "Ashford thought, given your background, you might know how he would set up such an operation and who he'd likely trade with. Any help you can give us would be appreciated."

"I have no idea. This is a new low for Rothsay. Even my father balked at selling white women."

Rufus looked crestfallen.

"But I could find out. With my contacts, it shouldn't take me long to uncover something. Rothsay has made many enemies; someone's bound to talk."

"Do it quickly. The sooner we stop him the better." Rufus glanced at the clock sitting on his desk. "I best leave or you shall be late for your drive in the park. Perhaps I could join you? I'm interested in meeting your bride—"

"I don't require nor wish for a chaperone."

A faint smile touched Rufus's golden-brown eyes. Eyes that had women drowning in their depths to the point they very rarely said no. "If Miss Goodly is as beautiful as Lady Sudbury, you may well need my services. As I recall, you were never very happy about sharing. You are very territorial about your possessions." He casually picked up his gloves and walked to the door.

Anthony's smile did not reach his eyes. "That won't be necessary. I shall be the perfect gentleman."

A knowing gaze slashed in his direction. "And then . . ."

"Once we are married, once she belongs to me, I shall carry on as I always have."

Rufus hesitated at the door, the warmth fading from his eyes. "Let me guess. You will be more like a lord and master than a husband? Be careful, my friend. Sometimes slavery takes many forms."

Rufus closed the door before Anthony recovered from the shock and hurt Rufus's words created.

Marriage was nothing like slavery. Melissa would have all her heart desired . . . except her freedom.

Anthony called on Melissa exactly at four. But it was Cassandra waiting for him in the entrance hall to Sudbury House.

"Your mother has informed me you are to escort Melissa and I to Lady Cavendish's ball tonight." She slid her hand up Anthony's arm. "We should be able to find a moment alone. I know where Lord Cavendish keeps the key to his study."

Anthony had no doubt. Cassandra had been sleeping with Lord Cavendish, on and off, since the day she'd married.

Before he could reply, Melissa made her way down the stairs. He saw her start at the sight of Cassandra's hand on his person. He moved forward, brushing aside Cassandra's hold on his arm and bowed low. "You look lovely, Miss Goodly."

She deigned to nod her head, refusing to return his smile. She swept past them, frowning at Cassandra before descending the front steps toward his barouche.

Anthony turned to address Cassandra. "We have much to discuss, Cassandra." He bowed and took his leave. "Until tonight . . ." He would explain to her that there could be nothing between them. No matter how much he desired her, he had given Melissa his word. He would not break it.

Melissa stood waiting beside his barouche, still refusing to look at him.

He bowed over her hand, allowing his lips to linger a moment longer than etiquette allowed, while taking in the heavily lashed hazel eyes and raven-black hair. His body hummed; she was stunningly beautiful.

"I hope you have remembered your promise to me, my lord?"

"Of course."

He helped Melissa into the carriage.

At the feel of her, his body tightened. Damn, she truly was

a very desirable woman. He dropped her hand as a jolt of pure pleasure rocketed through him.

He was annoyed at his reaction to her. His blood wasn't raging, but the heat was there, a constant simmer each time she was near. *Please do not let me desire my own wife.* It would be just his luck to want the one woman he could not have.

God, he needed a woman beneath him and soon. A woman he could ride until he was exhausted, until he was thoroughly sated. A woman who was not Melissa.

He took his seat on the other side of her. She sat stiffly beside him, looking straight ahead.

Their drive in the park was not off to a good start.

"Chin up, Melissa. We are supposed to be a couple in love. You look like you're about to be led to the guillotine."

She turned to him and gave a remnant of a smile. Her wide eyes appeared almost catlike. He had the sudden urge to stroke her. Would she purr? He shook his head; what was he thinking?

But she looked quite lovely in her pastel-blue day dress with a deep navy pelisse trimmed in fox fur. Her clothes were not the height of fashion, but any man would not even see the clothes once they gazed upon the beauty of her face.

He was surprised to inwardly acknowledge that he was proud to have her seated beside him. He reached over and took her small gloved hand in his. "Has Mother talked with you?"

Anthony felt her stiffen at his contact. Good; the less responsive she was the better.

"Yes, we had a pleasant chat this afternoon just before I got ready for our excursion in the park," Melissa stammered.

Anthony took his eye off the street traffic for a second. "I hope my mother said nothing to upset you. You must come to me if she does. Once we are married you will be in charge of my households, not my mother."

Melissa flushed. "Your mother was most kind. I shall look

forward to her help when we marry. I am not used to such a large number of households to manage."

He squeezed her hand. "I am sure you're up for the task."

At the gates of the park they slowed to await their place in the line of carriages. The park was very busy on such a pleasant summer afternoon, and their arrival caused quite a stir, as he expected.

Melissa hadn't spoken since they'd left the house. Something was troubling her; she'd never been short of words before. "Is there something on your mind, Melissa? If you wish to know something, all you need do is ask. I am not, contrary to belief, an ogre."

The word "ogre" made her wince slightly. "Thank you, Anthony. It's just that I should very much like to know . . ." she said quietly.

"Know what?"

She glanced up, assessing him. "Well . . . I should like to know how you see our marriage working."

"Working?"

She sobered more, if that were possible. "Yes. For instance, where would we live?"

That should not have caught him by surprise, but he did not think the answer that sprang to mind would be the one she wanted to hear. She would stay anywhere he wasn't.

He cleared his throat. "I have three estates: Glenforay, in Alyth, near Dundee in Scotland; Wickham Manor in Selby near Bath; and Bressington House in Cambridge. Plus Craven House in Mayfair, as you know. I travel between them on business and to oversee the estates. You must decide where you would feel most comfortable."

A soft frown creased her brow. "The houses must take a lot of organization."

He smiled charmingly at her. "I'm sure Mother is looking forward to handing over the reins."

She nodded and squared her shoulders, unconsciously he thought, before meeting his gaze again. "I believe our marriage should be built on respect and honesty. We both know it does not involve love—"

"Of course," Anthony interjected, hating himself. He could not even give her that. He was starting the marriage with a lie by not informing her of his plans for a white marriage—a marriage of no intimacy between husband and wife.

Coloring slightly, she gave him a tremulous smile. "Trust, as with respect, is earned," she continued, deflating him a little, "but I hardly think one earns respect and trust until one has had appropriate time to get to know one another. We won't have that luxury."

He shrugged his shoulders, not quite sure where this conversation was going.

She drew a deep breath. "What will we be to each other? How will we live our lives together? What do you want this marriage to become?"

Christ, his hands tightened on the reins. Melissa was still having doubts. Perhaps a tad more seduction was required.

"I would like us to become friends," he blurted out.

Nodding thoughtfully, she leaned back in the curricle.

He felt the need to clarify. "Is that not to your liking? As you said, we do not have a love match. I have always valued friendship over love; it tends to be less fleeting."

"I quite understand that, my lord," she said hastily. "But I want to be a good wife to you. I want to know in advance what you will expect of me, and I think you should know what I will expect of you." Her face had flushed a lovely shade of pink.

Expect of him! What the hell did that mean? He was not expecting his wife to lay down any rules. "I beg your pardon?"

"Well, for instance, I would expect you to keep your affairs discreet and not make me the ridicule of the *ton*. I also hope you will allow me to continue with my charitable work, perhaps support and become involved in my charities financially on occasion. My philanthropic work is very important to me," she added nervously. "I realize I am lucky to be given your good name and title, but as we are both aware, you shall carry on your life as if nothing has changed. I would like something in return, for agreeing to become your wife."

The horses jerked under his tight reins, the animals feeling the tension instantly invading his hands and arms. He tried to relax. Involved in her charities, in her life? That just wasn't plausible. He did not want his life to change in any way. Already he could feel the pull of physical attraction. If he had to be around her constantly, how was he to resist her? His wife, a woman he could have at anytime, anywhere, anyway he pleased. No—he could not become involved in her life—she was too much of a temptation.

"I shall try very hard to be discreet. I despise being fodder for gossips, and I would not stand in the way of your charity work. However, it is highly likely I will be too busy with my estates and other business to be involved in most aspects of your life."

She nodded thoughtfully. "That seems a fair response." She fiddled with the edge of her glove. "But you wouldn't deny me my freedom, would you? You wouldn't lock me away and keep me from doing the things I love to do?"

He felt a burning sensation in the pit of his stomach. Freedom? What kind of freedom was she thinking of? Did she wish to take lovers? Was she already planning to carry on with the man she'd been dreaming of?

"You may live however you please, madam, as long as you do not disgrace the Wickham name, and that includes taking any lovers once you become my wife."

She gasped. "That is not what I meant, Anthony. I would never dishonor you or myself with such behavior."

He briefly closed his eyes at her words. She may think that an easy promise, assuming as she did that she would be sharing his bed. Yet as the long, cold, lonely years passed by, how strong would she be then? God, he was a cruel man.

He gave her a cool glance. "I thought that might be what you wanted your freedom for. I will not tolerate infidelity from my wife. I require to know that any children we have are actually my own."

He did not give a damn what she did with her life, but she would not share her body with another. He wanted Richard's children to inherit the title, not some by-blow.

"You like children then?"

He did not like where this conversation was heading. Her question tore at his soul. He did not want to lie to her. He worded his reply carefully. "I like children, yes."

Her face broke into a radiant smile, and her other hand drifted to her stomach. "I have always wanted children. It is one reason why I have agreed so readily to this union."

He cringed; he could not bear the thought that he may have got her with child. That was his worst nightmare. He would have to banish her to Glenforay if a child was born. He wouldn't risk subjecting a child to a man with his dark soul. He believed, deep down, he was his father's son. That was the reason he'd been so careful in his liaisons with women. He always withdrew, ensuring his seed never took root.

Over the years, he'd fought so hard not to succumb to the evil of his upbringing, but what if a child was his tipping point? Perhaps it had been his birth that had set his father down the path to darkness. Hadn't their mother said he'd changed once his sons had been born.

This was so unfair. Melissa had done nothing wrong except be in the wrong place at the most inconvenient time.

His gloomy thoughts were interrupted by the approach of a man on a fine black stallion, Lord Dashell. *Perfect. Just what this afternoon's ride needed. The first person to approach would have to be the man of her dreams, the man she would likely turn to for comfort.*

Anthony hardened his features.

What did he care? She was to be his wife in name only. She could pine her life away for all he cared. As long as she remained faithful to him, she would not suffer.

Anthony's grip on the reins tightened further; the horses

neighed in protest. He could not name the emotion suddenly gripping his innards at the sight of the intimate smile Lord Dashell gave Melissa, and worse, he felt the beast in him rising, fast and furious, as she returned it.

"Miss Goodly, how lovely to see you this afternoon."

He should have heeded Rufus's words. Dangerous at any time, he recognized he was becoming more so. He wanted no other man near her, especially the man who she dreamed of taking to her bed. The emotion and sexual hunger rising together were unforeseen, a fireball streaking through his gut, burning his blood, sharpening his appetites.

He could not believe it—he was jealous. He went absolutely cold, frightened out of his wits.

Then he let vent to his fury, how could he be jealous of a woman he'd not wanted or desired? A woman, who if he got her pregnant, threatened his very sanity.

Because she's yours, a voice in his head whispered.

He was so consumed with anger he'd missed her initial greeting to Lord Dashell. She was attempting introductions. "Lord Dashell, may I present Lord Wickham"—she hesitated for a few seconds—"my betrothed."

Lord Dashell did not even try to hide his surprise.

Anthony's fingers curled into tight fists until his knuckles turned white, watching the look of horror and then anger flit over Dashell's face. Dashell it seemed did have his eye on Melissa.

With barely concealed contempt, Lord Dashell's eyes raised to his and he said, "Lord Wickham and I are well acquainted. Congratulations, Wickham. What act has brought this unexpected turn of events to pass?"

Anthony gave a lazy smile, hiding his inner turmoil. "When I see something I want, I go after it."

Melissa gave a start beside him, the movement so small hopefully only he'd noticed it.

Anthony knew Dashell disliked him intensely, ever since he'd lost his favorite mistress to Anthony almost two years ago. Anthony couldn't even remember her name, but it obviously still irked Dashell.

Dashell's cold blue eyes moved arrogantly over Anthony's face before they swept indecently over Melissa's, imprinting each delicate feature before coming to rest on her lush mouth.

The beast inside wanted to lash out at his opponent.

"You had us all fooled, Wickham. We thought it was Lady Sudbury you'd set your cap at. It would seem you're changing hats, one wonders why? Perhaps you're simply being very greedy."

The implication that he'd already had Cassandra and was moving on to greener pastures was not lost on Anthony. Nor was it lost on Melissa. Her face had stained a brilliant red. The urge to jump from the carriage and pound Dashell into the ground set a fiery rage blazing inside him. He made to leap from the carriage, but Melissa's hand stilled him.

He attacked from the front. "I did not know you were intending to call on Miss Goodly. History seems to be repeating itself."

He felt rather than saw Melissa shrink back in her seat.

Dashell's face flushed with color. "We have no understanding." He addressed Melissa. "I see the rumors are true. Your brother will be pleased. Lord Wickham has a very fat wallet."

Melissa gasped.

Anthony's voice lowered and his tone was ice cold. "I always knew underneath that façade of nobility you had no manners. I'd move on before my patience runs out. If you'd like to discuss the topic further, meet me at my club later."

Dashell grinned at Anthony's obvious anger. "That won't be necessary. I cannot see anything here I'm interested in," he said, and turned his horse around and cantered off.

Anthony's rage still blazed. "I apologize, Melissa. There was no need for you to hear that. Lord Dashell has a grudge against me for a matter that occurred a while back. His words had nothing to do with hurting you, but more to do with annoying me."

" 'Tis of no concern. I was silly to have thought him a gentleman." Her soft words, filled with hurt, did nothing to alleviate his anger.

The rest of their ride was uneventful, yet they'd accomplished what they'd set out to do. Dowager Countess Millington had stopped their carriage and hadn't wasted any time finding out the significance of the ride in the park. It would be all over London by this evening—Lord Wickham was to marry.

As they turned for home, Melissa still noticed the anger ruminating from the man sitting like stone beside her. Gone was her charming companion. In his place was the brooding, dark devil.

He still couldn't be angry over Lord Dashell's appalling behavior. She'd all but forgotten it. She had no idea if she'd said or done anything to upset him, but she could see he was barely holding on to his temper.

Tentatively she placed her hand on his arm. She felt him tense at her touch. "Is there something troubling you?"

"I won't have you flaunting yourself to attract other men. I'll not be made a cuckold." It was not a polite request; it was a barked order.

"You have me confused with my cousin. I do not flirt to attract men. I find the less I have to do with men, the better."

He turned hard, coal-black eyes, flaming with suppressed fury, on her. "Make sure it stays that way."

Refusing to be intimidated, Melissa returned his hard gaze. "It would seem the less I have to do with you would be very desirable."

"Don't provoke me. You'll not like the outcome."

Melissa shivered. What had started as a pleasant ride to get to know one another had disintegrated into bandied insults. She decided to be the bigger person. "I'm sorry. I am not usually so defensive, but your behavior does make it hard to like you."

He studied her for a moment. "I don't require you to like me, just to honor your vows."

She raised an eyebrow. "All of my vows?" He did not answer. "Because the vows require me to love, honor, and obey. I am assuming you only require two of the three?" she added sweetly.

His mouth thinned. "Love is a fallacy." Melissa blanched. "Don't mention the word love again," he said flatly.

She swallowed back a retort. What on earth was the matter with the man? Their ride had been progressing amiably until the encounter with Lord Dashell. Yet, Lord Dashell had insulted her, not him. Why, anyone would think Anthony was . . . jealous. Her mouth dropped open in amazement as she took in the rigidity of his shoulders and the way he tightly gripped the reins.

Was he jealous?

Warmth bloomed in her chest like a bud blossoming in the spring sunshine.

A tiny sliver of hope filled her. Perhaps she could make something of this disaster. Could she make a man like Lord Wickham fall in love with her?

Melissa felt slightly sick. She'd resigned herself to a life not of her making, a life where she was a piece of property changing ownership, and now dangling in front of her was an opportunity for more. Here was a chance to attain her dream, to find love.

She glanced sideways and looked at the man beside her. His expression was hard and sensual and more than a little fierce. Yet, he did not scare her. She wasn't fooling herself. A man like Anthony would not succumb to love easily. He would see it as a weakness, something to be avoided at all costs.

She gave a small smile. But she had two things on her side: time and proximity.

Shortly she would become his wife, locked to him for a lifetime. If she had to go to hell and back to do it, she'd find a way to make her husband fall in love with her.

But where should she start? How did you make a man, not just any man, a rake, a renowned lover, fall in love with you? She needed to learn as much as she could about the private and reclusive man beside her.

Perhaps his brother could be of help. Richard seemed very keen for this wedding to take place. She'd start with him. What secret was Richard hiding? Why did he want his brother wed so desperately he'd compromise her to force the issue?

Like everything she tackled, she wasn't about to rush in. If Anthony sensed what she was up to, he'd freeze her out of his life before she had any chance of claiming his heart.

No, she needed to do her research. She needed to find out as much as she could about the man who in a few days was to become her husband.

She risked a gaze at her betrothed. His anger had begun to dissipate; his jaw was less taut.

"I believe we are to attend Lady Cavendish's ball tonight."

Anthony turned to look at her. "Yes, I'll escort you and your cousin."

"Will your brother be attending?"

Anthony eyed her suspiciously. "I do not know. My brother and I are no longer on speaking terms."

Melissa bit her bottom lip. This wasn't going to work. Anthony was still too angry at his brother to be of any help in learning Richard's whereabouts.

But his mother would know. She'd start with Lady Wickham. She'd know where her other son was hiding.

Chapter 6

That evening, the entourage walked into the Cavendish ballroom and joined the queue waiting to greet their host and hostess. As they descended the stairs, the whispers behind twitching fans started. Melissa could well imagine what the other guests were saying. She had her arm through Lord Wickham's, and on his right, so did Cassandra.

She knew the men were praising Lord Wickham's skill in keeping the ravishing beauty on his right as his mistress, while marrying the plainer, quiet, demure cousin on his left. A raving beauty to bed for pleasure and a wife to bed to provide the much-needed heirs.

Melissa lifted her head high and kept her eyes looking directly ahead, hoping her cheeks had not colored. Never had she wished so fervently for the floor to open up and swallow her. Cassandra played up her part and was spitefully pleased with the *ton*'s interpretation of events. To reenforce the perception, Lady Sudbury stroked her hand down the arm of Anthony's jacket until he bent his head and let her whisper something in his ear.

At his gruff laugh there was a surge of activity; the array of fans were fluttering wildly.

This evening was going to be torture.

The line of guests shuffled forward until, with the pleasantries completed, they could move fully into the ballroom. Letting go of Anthony's arm, Melissa began scouring the room trying to see if Anthony's mother or brother were present.

"Are you looking for anyone in particular?" he asked, his voice radiating about as much warmth as a snowflake.

Melissa turned to look at him. Her traitorous breath caught in her throat. How did he do it? She tore her gaze away from the intoxicating sight of him, trying to quell the fluttery sensation developing in her stomach. He was so handsome this evening. The white on black ensemble set his physique off to perfection. The material was tight enough to be considered indecent. Yet Melissa would wager every woman in the room longed to run their hands over the ebony velvet. She longed to feel the hidden strength beneath the soft fabric, the urge as overwhelming as the man himself.

This evening, in his finery, he screamed Lord of Wicked. His silver-gray eyes seemed to deliberately issue an open invitation, a temptation sent to make her sin. Every married woman in the room envied Cassandra, while the young debutantes were miffed they'd not been as brave as Melissa and caught him in matrimony. Her legs felt as if she'd just ridden at full gallop all day. She didn't dare return his avid gaze. She wasn't brave or courageous or fearless enough to accept—yet. She let a satisfied smile curve her lips. But she was his.

He leaned nearer, the tantalizing scent of expensive cologne mixed with raw maleness made her dizzy, and as he placed his large hand at her back, guiding her toward a chaise upon which Lady Millington sat, she wondered if tonight would be the night she'd finally swoon.

"Remember my warning. I trust you will conduct yourself appropriately. You are to be my wife."

The sudden bolt of awareness flashing down her side—the side he'd touched—had nothing to do with the anger his harsh warning provoked. She could sense him, hard, strong, and very male, a potent living force beside her.

His nearness was pure pleasure. She glanced at his face, but he'd already turned to see to Cassandra.

He must have felt her gaze though, because his eyes swung

back to her. He saw her studying him intently, and his gaze grew direct; his eyes searched hers.

Her lungs seized.

The introduction for the first waltz cut through the hypnotic moment. She heard Cassandra stir. *Please do not disgrace me by dancing the first dance with Cassandra.*

His eyes still held hers, and perhaps he read the desperation there. His fingers closed about her hand, and he lifted it fleetingly to his lips. He then elegantly bowed, his eyes never leaving hers. "My dance, I believe?"

She let out a huge breath, gratitude beaming from within her smile. At that precise moment he truly was the most wonderful man in the world, her knight in shining armor. She inclined her head and let him draw her to the floor.

Her body responded as soon as he gathered her close and steered her into the swirling throng. Her chest felt tight, and her skin came alive. She became a young giddy schoolgirl, taut with anticipation, expectations. This man would soon be her husband. She remembered his naked body lying next to her, and her gaze dropped to his groin.

Even in his nonaroused state he was large; she could see the bulge quite clearly. A sweet tremble filled her being. What would it be like to have him make love to her properly, to feel those large hands caress her naked skin?

She swallowed. This man wasn't going to stay her imaginary lover. He would become her husband. Since their last dance together, everything had changed. The planes of his face seemed harder, more chiseled, more austere. His body seemed more powerful, and there was something in his eyes as they rested on hers—something . . . was it regret? Whatever it was, her instincts recognized enough to make her shiver—either in fear or anticipation, she wasn't sure which.

Without thinking she uttered, "How did you get your scar?"

His countenance changed immediately. She could feel his muscles tighten beneath her hands, and he almost led them straight into the path of another couple.

"Is that why you did not wish to marry me? You find my face repulsive?" His words were uttered harshly, and her face heated in mortification. She had offended him.

She made sure she looked him straight in the eye. "I find the scar interesting. It gives your face character." She paused, not sure if she should utter what she really thought, but given his reaction she decided she owed it to him. "Besides, you would be too extraordinarily handsome without some slight imperfection. It makes you look more human and less godly."

Typical man. He was trying to stop the smile hinting at the edges of his lips. "I'm no saint, and my behavior is far from that of the Lord Almighty."

She blushed. "No. I meant like a Greek or Roman god."

She saw he was pleased with her compliment.

"And which god do you believe I take after?" Now he was teasing her.

"When you are trying to be dark and mysterious, then I believe Aries, God of War. When you smile I think of you as Apollo, the God of Healing."

His brow creased and his smile vanished. "Healing? Ironic really, for if anyone needs healing it is me."

"How so?"

He straightened and pulled her closer. He seemed to realize he'd said too much. "Never mind." He changed the topic. "I have made the wedding arrangements. Mother is organizing the event. We will hold the ceremony and wedding breakfast at Craven House. I hope that will be suitable?"

She wondered if he had deliberately changed the topic so as to avoid answering her question. She decided not to push the subject in full view of the gossiping *ton*. But later when they were alone she would press for her answer. How had he got the scar, and why did he need healing?

A god, she thought he looked like a god. His male ego could not help but be puffed up. His betrothed was unique, he would give her that. She did not simper and praise him with false flattery; she told him straight, in a frank and totally forthright manner.

He pulled her closer than was respectable in this company because he had a sudden craving to feel her softness. He wanted to lose himself in her scent and beauty, so as to block out the degrading memories her question invoked.

He should have been prepared for her query about his scar, but no one had ever dared ask him before. Of course his wife would likely want to know. He would think of some suitable reply, perhaps a fall from a horse. There was no way he was telling her the truth. He did not want her pity. He did not want her to glimpse the man he kept hidden from the world.

He became so engrossed in thought, he did not notice how crowded the floor had become. He had to suddenly guide her expertly through a knot of dancers, which proved a tight squeeze. For a brief moment they came together so that he felt her ample bosom and erect nipples against his chest. His body tightened with want. A shiver of raw sensation ripped through his groin.

He heard her soft gasp, and he drew back to survey her face. Was it a gasp of shock or pleasure? He shook his head. Why should he care? He did not want her in his bed.

So quietly he almost did not hear it she whispered, "Thank you for dancing with me first."

He flashed a charming smile. "I do not plan to feed the flames of the gossips. I will not dance with your cousin at all tonight. I see my friend Lord Strathmore across the way. I shall accompany him into the gaming room until you wish to leave."

Melissa glanced over her shoulder, and he watched her give Rufus a thorough inspection before turning back to give him a grateful smile. His stomach twisted. She no doubt found his friend handsome; most women did. Rufus never had trouble finding a bedmate. Anthony tried to dampen down the jealousy that arose with his thoughts. Worse, he did not seem to care that Rufus was staring down Cassandra's bodice or that Rufus was signaling his interest with his eyes. Anthony realized he didn't care if Rufus took Cassandra to his bed. All he could think about was that Rufus was not focused on his fiancée.

All his instincts shouted that this marriage was a mistake. Anthony felt a muscle flex in his jaw. He had never been jealous of a woman in his life. Melissa was bewitching him.

When he looked into her eyes, he could not tear his gaze away. Her eyes seemed to be able to look into his very soul and see the man he truly was. Which was probably why she did not wish to marry him and why he should flee while he still could.

She was smiling in happiness at him now, or was it a show for their audience? When she smiled her lips became so inviting he had to battle the urge to crush his mouth to hers.

Anthony felt a twinge of disappointment as the music came to an end. He would miss the sultry feel of her in his arms.

She said, "I see my friend Lady Albany has arrived. I shall join her after you have introduced me to your friend."

He became instantly on guard. "Why do you wish to meet my friend?"

Her nose turned up as she frowned, a look of puzzlement on her face. Her hand rose, and she opened her palm in a helpless gesture. "Because he is your friend. As your wife I should be aware of your acquaintances. Or are you ashamed of me?"

"Of course not. What man would be ashamed of a beautiful woman on his arm?" He held himself stiffly as he gave her his arm. "I thought it might be because he was a handsome man. You wouldn't be the first lady desirous of an introduction."

She sighed. "He is only handsome in a pretty sort of way. I like my men dark and mysterious, preferably with a scar." Although amusement tinged her voice, it was said with a modicum of truth, and his heart thrilled at her words.

For a moment he dropped his guard. He let his happiness

at her words show in his smile. Anyone watching would believe the two were madly in love. "Come then. Let me introduce you to the most renowned rake in all of London."

"You mean other than you."

He laughed and steered her toward Rufus at the far side of the room, where he was blatantly seducing her cousin. As they drew near, Anthony cleared his throat and Rufus swung around to greet them. His friend's smile died on his lips, and he saw Rufus's eyes widen and then fill with obvious appreciation of the woman on his arm.

"A man should not be so spoilt as to meet two such beauties in one night," he gushed as he took Melissa's hand and kissed her glove.

Anthony's hands began to itch. If Rufus did not drop her hand soon, he might just ensure Rufus's face was not quite so pretty.

Rufus broke into an amused smile, recognition of Anthony's thoughts clearly visible in his eyes.

"Lord Strathmore, I have the pleasure of introducing my fiancée, Miss Melissa Goodly."

Still holding her hand, Rufus said, "You are indeed a lucky man, Anthony. She is very beautiful."

Melissa blushed under his words while Lady Cassandra humphed. "Thank you, my lord," and she curtsied.

"Call me Rufus. May I have the pleasure of a dance later?"

She saw Anthony's frown. So she gave Lord Strathmore a devastating smile and uttered, "It would be my pleasure."

Lord Strathmore once again placed a kiss on her fingers.

Anthony cleared his throat. "I thought we'd leave the ladies to it and take a turn in the gaming room. I have some news about the matter we discussed recently."

Rufus's carefree disposition changed at his words. Turning to the ladies, he bowed and said, "Until our dances, ladies."

Anthony said to Melissa, "I shall look for you later in the evening when it's time to leave. If you wish to leave earlier, simply come and find me."

As the two men walked away, Rufus said, "You're a lucky man. She's beautiful and already a little in love with you."

Anthony laughed. "How on earth can you tell that from such a brief meeting?"

Rufus smiled. "Her fingers did not tremble when I kissed them. My charm did not work on her. She had eyes only for you."

"How did you get so vain?" But Anthony was secretly pleased at his words. Rufus was right. Most women couldn't resist his friend. For instance if she could, Lady Cassandra Sudbury would bed both of them. The fact Melissa wanted only him warmed his heart.

A cold chill quickly followed his thoughts—heart. He scoffed to himself, not likely, he didn't have one.

As soon as the men left, Melissa turned to scan the crowd. Where was Richard Craven? She couldn't see him anywhere, and she was just about to give up her search—he was probably in the gaming room with the other sought-after bachelors—when she spied him standing over by the open doors to the terrace.

He was conversing, in a very intimate manner, with Lady Spencer. Melissa began to move toward the couple, but it was a slow process with so many people stopping to wish her congratulations on her upcoming nuptials.

By the time she made it across the crowded floor, she saw him disappear out the door to the terrace, Lady Spencer in tow.

Blast, this might be the only chance she got to speak with him alone before the wedding. Looking quickly around her, she noted that for once she had nobody's attention. She quietly slipped out the door after them.

The rush of fragrant evening air was exhilarating. Melissa made her way down the short flight of stairs from the terrace onto the gravel path.

She'd spotted Richard leading Lady Spencer toward the garden, and she hesitated to follow. Descending into the garden could mean only one thing. Yet if she did not speak to him tonight, she mightn't get another chance before the wedding.

She picked up her pace and rounded the bend in the path, hearing a woman's soft voice and careening sighs. Goodness, Melissa's face heated. She had a fair idea of what Richard was up to with the young widow. She moved forward, hoping she'd interrupt before they became too amorous.

She drew near, just in time to see Richard expertly free Lady Spencer's breasts and lower his head to take her nipple in his mouth.

She shrugged off a shiver of annoyance at being put in this situation. Melissa coughed loudly. A man with his mouth on a woman's breast was not about to deter her from getting the answers she required.

But Lady Spencer's moans drowned out her approach. She moved closer and in a firm, strong voice called, "Excuse me, I would like a word with you, Mr. Craven."

Melissa heard Lady Spencer's shocked gasp as her hands flew to her bodice to try to cover herself. Richard did not even stand up. He merely lifted his mouth from her breast and, turning his head, gave a cool glance and said, "Very bad timing, Miss Goodly."

"Just returning the favor, Mr. Craven."

He stood up, his mouth relaxing into a wicked smile. "Touché." He gave a small bow.

"I have been trying to have a word with you all evening."

He helped lace Lady Spencer back into her dress. "I have rather had my hands full."

"So I can see. I am sure Lady Spencer will excuse us. I'd like to discuss a private family matter with you."

He bent and whispered something in Lady Spencer's ear, which resulted in a lot of giggling but which thankfully saw Lady Spencer, after throwing a sullen look at Melissa, trot back along the path toward the ballroom.

"I am ready for my ribbing, Miss Goodly. Have you come to box my ears?"

"If I wanted to box something, it would not be your ears," she growled at him. "No, what has occurred cannot be changed no matter how much I wish it. Hurting you would still find me betrothed to your brother."

He crossed his arms over his chest and frowned. "Then what is it you want from me, Miss Goodly?"

"May I?" She pointed to the bench he'd previously been using for his liaison.

He stood aside, sweeping his arm toward the bench. "Of course, forgive me. I am not used to a dalliance being so rudely interrupted, especially by a young lady. My wits seem to be in a muddle."

Ignoring his teasing, she settled on the bench while he regarded her suspiciously. It was difficult to remember Richard was Anthony's twin because they looked nothing alike. Richard was not as tall, not as solid. He had a leaner frame but was still well muscled. His hair was fair, with the shape of his face more rounded than Anthony's chiseled features. She could not quite see the color of his eyes, but they seemed to be sparkling in the moonlight. He was rumored to be as much of a rake as her betrothed. Seeing him fondling Lady Spencer only confirmed the rumor.

It would seem, even though they were nothing alike, the twins were alike in their pursuit of the opposite sex.

"I do not wish to appear rude, but is there something urgent you'd like to discuss? I do have plans for this evening." He was tapping his foot.

Melissa raised her head and gave him a scathing look. "Oh, I am sorry. Have I disrupted your life of pleasure? Do please forgive me, but I'd say having to wait half an hour for your liaison with Lady Spencer is nothing compared to destroying my life, which you appeared to be able to do with casual ease the other night."

Richard stood up straighter and pulled at his cuffs. A look of seriousness steeled over his features. "I will admit that in my endeavours to help my brother I did not properly factor in the consequences to you. I assumed given your family's money situation, and the fact your brother was trying to arrange a suitable match for you, having to marry my brother would not be disagreeable to you."

She hoped her eyes stabbed him with her anger. "You thought wrong. I do not want this marriage."

Richard shrugged. "It's a little late for that now."

She hung her head and sighed. "I am well aware of my predicament."

"If you don't want to tear a strip off me, then what is it you want?"

"I want to know about your brother."

His eyes narrowed, and he shoved his hands in the pockets of his trousers. "What exactly do you wish to know?"

Melissa paused for a moment. How did she ask Richard to reveal his brother's secrets? Especially as Richard did not know or likely trust her.

"It's no secret that I do not want this marriage. In fact, I have made more of a fuss about having to get married than your brother. Don't you find that surprising?"

Richard's head cocked to one side.

She continued. "Anthony's views on marriage are well known. He is vehemently against the institution."

Richard allowed a wry smile to curve his lips. "Come, Miss Goodly, most men of my age feel the same. I for one, am in no hurry to marry."

"Exactly."

He moved to sit next to her on the bench. "I don't quite follow."

"Your brother has not complained once. He has not ranted and raved against the injustice of the trap you set for him. He hasn't tried to buy his way out of this mess. He does not even appear to be angry."

"Perhaps he's fallen for your charms."

Melissa scoffed. "Don't be ridiculous—"

"Are you fishing for compliments, Miss Goodly? You know very well you are beautiful."

She flushed at his words. "He does not know me, and he

certainly did not wish to share my bed. He craves my cousin Lady Cassandra and you know it." Her hands, resting in her lap, balled into fists. "If I am to have any way of making this marriage bearable, I deserve to know what I am up against. Your brother is up to something and as his fiancée I demand you tell me what it is."

Richard stilled beside her.

"You know I am right. Why has he so readily embraced this union? What does he gain with our marriage?"

He was ignoring her, lost deep in thought. Even in the dark she could see the lines of worry crease his forehead.

"I am not sure what he hopes to achieve, but I am hoping he gains back his soul."

Melissa gasped. "His soul?"

Richard stared deep into her eyes. "Can I trust you, Miss Goodly? My brother has been hurt too much for me to hand you the weapon to destroy him."

Melissa felt her heart clench in her chest. "Does the scar have anything to do with it? Tonight I asked him where he got it and he refused to even discuss it."

He rose and began pacing up and down in front of her. She knew he was debating what was best for his brother. He obviously cared for Anthony a great deal, so why had he forced his twin into marriage? "If it helps I would never knowingly hurt your brother. I have admired him for many months."

Richard stopped and swung to face her. "Then why have you been so opposed to the match."

She instinctively knew she was going to have to trust him before he would trust her. She whispered softly, "I am scared of marrying a man I could easily come to love and of never having that emotion returned. If I did not care for your brother this match would be far easier."

Melissa sat very still. Would he help her?

He smiled at her warmly, dropping down on his knee before her and taking her hands in his. "Those are the sweetest words I have ever heard. All I want is for my brother to find love and to be happy."

She raised an eyebrow. "And he could not do that on his own?"

He rose and retook his seat beside her. "Not could not—more like would not."

"I don't understand."

"Do you know anything about our family history—about my father's business?"

She pursed her lips. "I know there was something distasteful with your late father's affairs, but my parents wouldn't speak of it in front of me. I was very young at the time."

Richard drew in a deep breath. "I am not sure I should be telling a young lady our seedy past, but as you are marrying into the family, marrying Anthony, it's best you know."

Melissa felt her shoulders tense.

He could not look Melissa in the eye. "My father inherited nothing but debts from his father, the third Earl of Wickham. He was on the brink of losing everything. So he married my mother, a very wealthy heiress in her own right."

"Did that save the estate?"

Richard shook his head. "However, a good friend of my father's, Baron Rothsay, offered him a business solution." He hung his head and seemed to take a big swallow. "My father became a slave trader. One of the largest in all of England."

Melissa felt sick—a slaver—the most distasteful practice she could ever imagine. To deprive a person of their free will, their dignity, and their hope. The perpetuators of such trade were evil. They had little or no humanity. She tried not to let her horror show.

"Mother says the trade changed him. In order to survive the despicable vocation, he became cold, cruel, and unapproachable."

"But what has this got to do with Anthony?"

Richard sighed. "When we were born the coffers were still not at the level needed for the family to survive. Father was determined to groom Anthony, to prepare him for what he'd need to do in order to ensure the Wickham legacy survived."

Melissa began to tremble. "Anthony's a slave trader?"

Richard quickly uttered, "No. No. Anthony closed the family business down when he was four and twenty, the year my father died. His trading business is cargo—nonhuman cargo." Shaking his head, Richard continued, "I don't know how to tell you this, how to make you understand."

She put her hand on his arm and gently said, "Just tell me. I am not a simpering miss; I won't swoon on you."

He gave her a grateful smile. "My father's version of grooming was very severe. Anthony won't even tell me the terrible things Father did to him, but he received the scar on his face from the man who sired us."

Melissa felt her eyes brim with tears. She'd thought her parents cruel with their disinterest, but her heart clenched with sorrow at the thought of a father beating his child, any child.

"I was raised by my mother, while Anthony was given to my father. I have to live with the guilt of knowing, but for an accident of birth, it could have been me." His face contorted in pain. "My brother's wounds are deep. He guards himself, his feelings, his desires, ensuring he doesn't give in to any imagined weaknesses. He denies himself love. He is under the mistaken impression that he is evil. Evil like the father he so closely resembles. He believes he does not deserve love."

Richard lowered his head and said softly, "I love my brother. But I don't know how he feels about me. I've never heard him speak one word of love to anyone. I think Father beat every feeling out of him except hate and bitterness."

With a heavy heart she stood, her legs trembling from the story he'd told her. "I still do not understand. How does my marrying your brother change this?"

"Once again I have taken the cowardly route. I can't seem to get through to him. He has sworn to never marry, and I hoped the love of a good woman would break through the cold shield he's put around his heart. That with time, and with children, and a loving family, he'd learn to love and live again. I owe him to try because I did nothing to help him while we were growing up."

Richard stood and moved toward her. He took her two hands in his. "Are you a good woman, Miss Goodly? I was hoping with a surname like yours you'd be the perfect foil for his dark, brooding temper. Will you fight for my brother? Will you love him so well he'll not stand a chance of not loving you in return?"

She looked into his eyes; they gleamed with a combination of hope and sorrow. She cleared her throat. "You ask a lot, Mr. Craven."

His hands tightened their grip. "I don't ask it for myself. I ask it for my brother who has suffered more than any human being should. Can't you try?"

She shook her head. "You misunderstand. I am already partly in love with your brother, but what could I possibly offer a man like him? To a man who has legions of women succumbing to his every whim at the wiggle of his little finger?"

Richard raised his hand and stroked one finger down her cheek. "Your love. Just love him, not his title or wealth, but the man."

She swallowed and gave a small smile. "I can do that."

"Thank God." And he raised her hands and placed a kiss on her knuckles.

"How touching. My brother and my bride-to-be, sharing a rather intimate moment in the garden. How sweet, how conniving, how distasteful."

Chapter 7

Richard dropped her hands as if they were hot coals. "This is not what it looks like."

"You wed her." Anthony stalked toward them like a beast sniffing for blood. "If I've got her with child, you can raise it to inherit the title."

Melissa clenched her fists at her side, tipping her chin up to hide the pain slicing through her body. Who did he think he was?

Richard shook his head. "Anthony don't . . ."

"We've been known to share women, often at the same time." His voice dripped with sarcasm and anger. "I've only had her once, and it was over in a minute, literally. I'm sure she prefers a man who can whisper sugary nothings in her ear while he drives into her. You always were much better than me with the sweet talk."

Blushing hotly, Melissa swallowed the lump in her throat. He was trying to rid himself of her, his burden.

"Miss Goodly has done nothing wrong." Richard's voice was a harbor of calm in a rising tide of anger. "She is the innocent party in all of this."

"Not so innocent anymore," Anthony snapped back. "I have been taken in by a pretty face. You were obviously in on my brother's plan to trap me in marriage from the beginning. Well, you both look pretty cozy to me. You'll be pleased. She's enthusiastic in bed."

Melissa gasped and stumbled backward, as if Anthony had kicked her in the belly. She turned around and retched into the rose bushes.

Anthony heaped on the pain. "What's the matter, my sweet? Does the thought of missing out on becoming a countess upset you?"

"Enough!" Richard roared.

Tears of humiliation and anger welled in her eyes.

Richard continued, "You and I have never raised a fist to one another. But by God, if you continue with this slander . . ."

Anthony laughed an ugly sound. "Lord Dashell was right. She's not worth the trouble." He gave her a mocking bow. "As you seem to prefer the company of my brother, I shall leave you with him. Try to convince my brother to take my place, will you?"

Anthony looked at his brother with dead, cold eyes. "If you aren't prepared to make an honest woman of her, kindly unhand her. I don't share my property—not with anyone. I warn you, if I find you've cuckold me, not only will I never forgive you, but I shall demand satisfaction on the dueling field."

With that, he pivoted and marched away.

Melissa sunk onto a sitting position on the bench, her knees shaking. What kind of man was he? How could he be so vicious and cruel? He wanted his brother to take her. He was handing her off like a piece of garbage.

"I'm sorry," Richard said softly. "He'll calm down shortly and feel like a cad. He knows I'd never dishonor him or myself by seducing you. It's just his dark temper gets the better of him. He fights first and thinks later. With the life he's led, he instantly assumes the worst."

"How can you excuse him?"

"I know the pain he's had to endure. If you knew what my father did to him, you'd be amazed at how he's managed to stay sane all these years."

Sniffing, Melissa wiped her tears away with her gloved hands.

"Miss Goodly, what my brother just did was inexcusable, but believe me when I say that he was not striking out to hurt you. He was protecting himself. Please do not turn away from him. He needs you, he needs love."

"I can't . . ." She shuddered. "You ask the impossible. He seems incapable of love."

"A man who can be that fired up with jealousy is a man who can also love." Richard's face lit with a slow smile. "He's just demonstrated he's not as immune to feelings as I suspected. Hmm . . . Anthony jealous." Chuckle. "I never thought I'd see this day. Miss Goodly, you are an angel!"

Melissa shook her head. "Jealous? Because of me? I don't think so."

"You've won half the battle, and you don't even know it. He doesn't like the idea of any other man being with you. Use that. Jealousy is a powerful emotion."

She looked dumbfounded up at him. "Are you mad?"

"Jealousy is part of desire," Richard insisted. "If you make him desire you, want you, it's a beginning."

Could she make a man like Lord Wickham, the Lord of Wicked, desire her? Did she want to? She had no choice now. If she didn't, she'd have to live her life with a man who could barely stand the sight of her.

"I wouldn't know where to begin." What would it be like to bring a man like Anthony to his knees with longing? "I'd make a fool of myself."

"That, Miss Goodly, is impossible." Richard smiled. "Your allure of innocence will tempt Anthony to distraction."

Moments later, back in the ballroom, Melissa escaped to the ladies' retiring room in order to gather her thoughts. Upon entering, her stomach plummeted at the sight of Cassandra sitting before the mirror. Tonight had been horrible enough without suffering Cassandra's resentment and insults.

Their eyes met in the mirror. Cassandra's smile could freeze hell. "I have underestimated you, little cousin. From the balcony, I saw you with Richard Craven. It was very clever of you to join forces with him."

Frowning, Melissa strode deeper into the room. "I don't know what you're talking about."

"Who would have thought a country bumpkin like you would outsmart me and land the Lord of Wicked? And in your very first Season, too."

"You know why I've not had a Season, and it has nothing to do with being a country bumpkin." Melissa halted next to Cassandra, in front of the wide mirror. "Some of us put duty and responsibilities before our own needs."

"Hogwash. You all but steamed with resentment at playing the dutiful daughter while you cared for your sick, invalid parents—"

"But I still did it. What have you ever done for anyone but yourself?"

"You ingrate," Cassandra sneered, her face reddening. "I was foolish enough to take you and your brother in—"

"I hear my brother is repaying your kindness with favors of his own."

Cassandra's eyes narrowed, her beautiful face hardening. "You don't want to make an enemy of me, Melissa."

Shivering at the threat, Melissa lowered her eyes. "If I could find a way out of this mess I would, but Christopher is set on the match." Unable to help herself, she turned and took her cousin's hand. "Please talk to Christopher on my behalf. Make him see this is not what I want. Please—"

"Your brother is no fool; you are." Cassandra shook her hand away. "You have landed a prized catch, and his debts will be paid."

"If you pay Christopher's debts, he'd listen to you."

"Why on earth would I want to do that?"

Melissa's face flushed with heat. "Because then you'd have Anthony."

"I am not sure he's worth that much blunt, not when I can have him for free." Cassandra shook her head. "No, whether you like it or not you will be married to the Earl. Not that you will know what to do with him." She half turned on the stool and ran her eyes up and down Melissa's person. "He's too much man for you. Hell, he's too much man for most women."

Laughing, Cassandra circled her delicately gloved wrist with her fingers and moved them up and down. "His shaft is rumored to be as thick as my wrist. His cock can drive a woman to orgasm simply by entering her. A timid virgin like you won't be able to handle him. It won't be long before he comes crawling to me for satisfaction."

Melissa grimaced at her crude words. A flash of apprehension snaked through her. He was huge. Yet his reputation as a renowned lover meant there must be more to it. Melissa knew the first time was always painful. Perhaps Cassandra was simply trying to scare her.

Then Cassandra's words seeped into her consciousness—his shaft is rumored . . . Cassie did not know. Anthony hadn't slept with her cousin. Relief swamped her, and she could not help goading her beautiful rival. "I have experienced exactly how big Anthony is firsthand." Leaning down she whispered in her cousin's ear, "And you never will. My betrothal gift is his promise never to bed you."

Before Cassandra could utter a response the door opened, and Melissa smiled at her friend Lady Sarah Albany.

Clad in a muted gold gown that brought out the highlights in her chestnut-colored hair, Sarah strode deeper into the room, returning her smile. "I thought I'd find you here. I saw you slip away a few minutes ago. The *ton* is abuzz with the news of your betrothal—"

"How appropriate," Cassandra cut in, sweeping to her feet. "I shall leave you to discuss your plight with a woman who understands what it means to marry a man who does not love or desire her." Cassandra halted at the door. "Pass on my regards to your husband, Lady Sarah. I have not had the pleasure of Lord Albany for a few weeks. I look forward to our reunion." Her laughter echoed down the hall through the closing door.

"I hate that woman," Sarah muttered, her pretty face flaming.

Melissa gave her tall, slender friend an apologetic look. "One good thing to come of this betrothal is I can escape from her household."

The two women sat on the stools before the mirrors. Melissa's heart warmed when she looked at her friend.

Sarah's pale blue eyes met hers in the mirror. "So it's true? You're engaged to Lord Wickham? I would not have credited him with such fine taste. And how lucky you are to have won the heart of the man you have been mooning over for weeks."

Melissa dropped her eyes from Sarah's joyful gaze, trying to find the words to tell her friend the truth.

But before she could form any kind of answer, Sarah gave a choked sob and grabbed her hand. "You are so lucky! Never marry for your family, especially if the man is a monster in disguise."

Sarah collapsed on the dresser, her body racked with sobs.

Melissa laid her head on Sarah's shoulders and put her arms around her, trying to comfort her friend. "Ignore Cassandra's words. They are probably not true. She is too busy bedding my brother to be bothered with your husband."

Sarah's sobs weakened to tiny sniffles. She raised her head and gave a tiny smile. "I don't care who Charles beds as long as it isn't me." She shook her head. "It's Theresa . . ." She let out another wail.

"Calm down, you'll give yourself the vapors." Theresa was an elderly black slave who had been in Sarah's family since Sarah was a girl. The woman was now Sarah's Abigail and came with her to the Marquis' household as marriage property. "What has happened?"

Sarah took several deep breaths and flushed a pretty pink. "I refused Charles my bed the other night. He came home drunk and tried to claim his husbandry rights. I'd told him that I would not have him come to me in that state. Theresa managed to thwart his plan by hitting him over the head with the chamber pot."

"Good for Theresa," Melissa said with a giggle. But the situation was not funny. Sarah had tried to get her father to free Theresa on many occasions, but he had always refused, and now Sarah's cruel husband owned Theresa. "I would have loved to have seen that."

Sarah flung her arms up. "Yes, it was rather funny at the time, but it is not me that has to pay the price. He is going to sell Theresa. He's such a coward. He knows that would hurt me the most, and he's always been scared of her."

The unfairness of Lord Albany's actions made Melissa's stomach churn. She stood and paced the room. "We can't let him do this."

"How can I stop him, Mel? He owns her, not I. I own nothing, not even the clothes I stand up in."

"When is he selling her?"

Sarah gently shook her head. "He has not told me. He is happy to let me stew in his threat."

"You must find out where and when the auction is to take place, and I shall ensure I'm there to bid for her." Where would she get the money? "Once I own her, I shall give Theresa her freedom."

"She will need a job. There is no way Charles will allow her on his staff."

"I shall take her as my lady's maid when I marry." Would Anthony let her? "I will need my own maid when I become the Countess of Wickham. I'm currently sharing Cassandra's."

"This all sounds too easy. Where will you get the money? Can the Ladies Freedom Charity provide it? I have twenty pounds saved up from the meager allowance Charles gives me, but Theresa will cost a lot more. One hundred and fifty pounds, at least."

Melissa walked over and hugged her friend. "You leave it to me." She wiped Sarah's tear-stained face dry. "Come. Let us rejoin the ball and show the throng that we are ecstatically happy in our lives."

"At least you are happy. You are, aren't you? Your engagement is what you want?"

"Of course, who wouldn't be happy at becoming the next Countess of Wickham?" She smiled, not wanting her friend to worry about her, too. "I am marrying the man of my dreams. What more could a girl wish for?"

Later that night, Melissa slipped quietly from her room. The candle she held scented the corridor with the sweetness of beeswax and cast eerie shadows over the walls. The carpeted floor creaked beneath her slippers. She winced. The only other person who would walk the corridor this night would be her brother, who would most likely head for Cassandra's bed. The Cravens, Anthony and his family, had moved back into Craven House this morning.

Hand shaking, she slowly opened the door to Cassandra's private sitting room and closed it behind her. Relief whooshed through her; Cassandra's bedroom door was shut.

She glanced around, unsure of where to look. She knew what the book looked like. It was small. The brown leather cover was worn and the green leather binding cracked, undoubtedly from constant handling.

Her skin heated remembering what little she'd glimpsed of the book. She had interrupted one of Cassandra's afternoon sessions with her married acquaintances. They'd been discussing the book and twittering over the images. Both abruptly halted once they discovered her presence in the room. But they were not quick enough to hide a page showing a man and a woman in the most convoluted of poses.

Where would someone hide a book of that nature? *On the bookshelves? No, they were too out in the open.*

Melissa tiptoed toward the writing desk and slid open the drawer. After a quick ruffle through, she realized it contained only papers.

She slowly turned to scan the room, her nightgown wrapping around her legs. She kicked out at the garment. *Think. Where would you hide it?*

There didn't appear to be anywhere else it could be. The room contained only two settees, two French mahogany chairs, and a small tea table. Her eyebrows rose as she spied the round wooden footstool; its tapestry cover depicted a scene from ancient Rome. She had one in her room just like it. With growing excitement, she crossed to the stool. Dropping to her knees, she put the candleholder on the floor and used both hands to play with the stool until the lid popped open. Raising the candle for more light, she peered inside. She lifted two novels up, and there at the bottom was the book. Her hand shook as she reached for it and flipped the page.

The book was written in French by Madame du Barry, and was titled *The Secrets of a French Courtesan*. It said du Barry had been the last chief mistress to King Louis XV of France.

Melissa snapped the book closed and drew a breath so deep she thought her lungs would burst. Her fingers clasped her prize reverently. She glanced around the darkened room like a burglar looking for a way out. She couldn't very well read it here.

Quickly and quietly, she skittered out of the room, down the hall, and into her bedroom. She hopped under the covers and grinned. "Lord of Wicked, I shall challenge your wickedness."

Melissa opened the book, *The Secrets of a French Courtesan*. Her hands were shaking, and she felt so naughty merely reading it. The book began with a letter from Madame du Barry.

COURTESAN. *Without a doubt, the word conjures images of rare beauty, impeccable grooming and poise, a woman who is not worldly enough to be hard, but who is charming, has a high level of intelligence, and is able to captivate a man with a glance. She must be selective with her patrons and is always very expensive. The idea of sexual expertise is usually implied. Some self-described courtesans emphasize the romantic, lover-like quality they bring to each encounter. Others emphasize their wild sexual abandon. Yet all know what it takes to please a man.*

Most women are born to be obedient. Raised with no expectations or ambitions other than to marry and serve their husbands in all things. To put their wishes aside in the pursuit of safety, respectability, and duty. A life where they are protected, cared for, and—unfortunately, mostly—bored beyond reason.

Why, I ask myself?

I find it hard to fathom that a woman would condone her short life to only duty. To be used to bear children and run a household, while their husbands engage in all the delights life has to offer, with no penalties except those imposed by the Almighty at the gates of heaven. The tedium alone would kill me, let alone the soulless existence of being denied the rush that comes with desire.

I believe women choose this monstrosity of an existence because they are afraid. They are afraid to embrace one of life's greatest gifts—passion. Or, too often, women confuse passion and desire with love, and feeling content dim their passions believing they have ensnared their man's heart.

Too late they learn desire must never dim or the love flies the coop to a more welcoming perch.

Men never get confused. For them there is no love without desire.

What most women do not understand is desire is our most formidable weapon. Brandished effectively, desire brings many rewards, both monetary and in the form of delicious pleasure. More importantly,

*wielded with skill, it binds a man to you more firmly
than any marriage vow.*

*I write this book in the hope that women open
their eyes to the joys only a few of us know. That
they can embrace the knowledge that there is no
greater skill than that of learning how to pleasure a
man. To set the fires of desire burning deep in his
soul, until it all but consumes him, and he wants you
with an ardour that stirs your senses and makes you
believe in love . . . More importantly makes him
worship and adore you. Makes him want to lay
down his life for you, give you everything your heart
desires, and, finally, fervently believe he cannot live
without you.*

After all, is that not the true definition of love?

Melissa chewed her bottom lip—was that the definition of
love? For a rake like Anthony, it most likely was. She could
not imagine Anthony worshipping any woman he did not desire. A slight shiver skittered over her frame. But was Anthony capable of love?

More than anything she wanted Anthony to want her. To
be important in his life. If desire achieved that—if it made
him "fervently believe he cannot live without her"—then
she'd embrace it gladly.

With trembling fingers, Melissa turned the page to the first
chapter of Madame's book—"Setting the Scene for Seduction." The chapter was focused on gaining a man's attention
to the point of forming some kind of attachment from where
a woman could use her skills to flame his desire. She skipped
those pages. She was already betrothed to Anthony. She already had a relationship of sorts. She jumped directly to the
next chapter, "Tantalising and Teasing."

*In the previous chapter I showed how to gain a man's
interest by stroking his ego. Now you have gained his*

attention you must move to the more physical aspects of ego stroking. A feat easy to achieve because, for most men, their egos tend to hang between their thighs.

His member, or as I like to tell him, his potent love stick, is responsive to sight, sound, and touch. You have many mediums in which to cause his passions to flare. Luckily for us you can immediately see any effect you are having and change your tactics if need be.

Let us start with sight. A glimpse of skin, a tease of bare flesh, stirs a man's senses. He cannot help but imagine what you would look like completely naked. That is the nature of the beast.

You must learn to be comfortable with your body. Stand in front of a mirror and learn the art of display. How to move, lean, bend, and pose in order to display glimpses of tantalizing skin. When seated in a chair, bend to pick up your handkerchief which you have artfully dropped on the floor. Watch his eyes latch onto the fall of your breasts, when you lean forward, making your cleavage available for his eyes to drink in. Of course having the correctly cut bodice is an imperative.

Melissa lay the book face down on her stomach and chewed her bottom lip. She had never considered that her body could be used as an enticement. She'd never preened and flirted with gentlemen, preferring to try and attract a man who preferred a woman with a brain. But she had ended up trapped in marriage to Anthony, one of the most seasoned rakes in all of England. He, most likely, would be brought to his knees by the temptation of her body, rather than her brain. Did she have a body that could tempt him? The night he had mistakenly come to her bed, he very obviously enjoyed her body. In fact, he couldn't hold back his enjoyment, spilling his seed.

Melissa read on, skipping over the art of showing a little leg and other various tricks of slowly revealing yourself. She wanted to know how to entice Anthony to her bed . . .

> Remember my earlier advice. You must own the bedroom, while letting him believe he is in charge. One of my favourite places for seduction is a bath. He is naked and vulnerable in the water. It also seems to calm them down, perhaps it reminds them of their youth when they were bathed. To set the scene I suggest you change into an appropriate negligee. A garment that teases—transparent enough for him to realise you are naked underneath but not enough to be able to clearly see your body's treasures.
>
> Have a warm hot bath drawn (preferably in front of the fire). Invite him to bathe. Dismiss his valet and undress him yourself, using the process of disrobing to stroke and fondle, kiss and lick, every bare inch of him until he sees nothing in the room he wants, except you.

Melissa's heart began to dance in her chest as she imagined touching Anthony in this intimate way. Her face flushed and her body burned with longing even though her room had grown cold as the night approached dawn. Could she do it? Was she bold enough to forget her upbringing, forget that she was a lady and act the courtesan for him? Would she be experienced enough to hold his attention? Would he desire her as he had their very first night? Her body knew the answer before she did—yes. She wanted him and she wanted him to want her. She would be brave enough because all her dreams hinged on her success.

Sleep beckoned. Yet, Melissa kept reading. She would become the most well-trained courtesan in all of England if it meant winning the heart of the Lord of Wicked.

Chapter 8

Anthony tapped his riding crop against his gleaming hessians. Thompson, his valet, had done him proud this morning considering the condition he'd arrived home in as daylight was breaking.

How Thompson had the time to clean his boots, so clean Anthony could see his reflection in the leather, was beyond him.

Last night, he'd been at his favorite gaming haunt, Faeroe's, until the sun rose at six o'clock. Gambling was his second vice. But he couldn't concentrate on cards with his mind whirling about his fiancée and his brother's betrayal.

Fortunately, he didn't go there to gamble. He'd managed to gather information about Rothsay and the white slavery ring. Lord Langtry, one of William Wilberforce's colleagues, confirmed that Rothsay had closed down his dock and holding pens in Bristol. Anthony knew Rothsay wouldn't be stupid enough to continue to operate out of what had, until recently, been the largest slave-trading port in all of England.

Unfortunately, no one seemed to know where Rothsay was currently based. They all agreed he still owned a huge fleet of ships and was engaging in trade. The funny thing was—no one quite knew what he traded. Some said wool and grain, others said coal. The fact Rothsay's cargo was unclear only confirmed Anthony's suspicions. Rothsay would carry anything that made him a vast profit—including white women.

Langtry had mentioned Great Yarmouth. He said he'd heard Rothsay had recently purchased a house there. That could mean only one thing, he was using the port, but for what?

Blast this wedding. Anthony tried to still his growing resentment. If not for his wedding he could head directly to Great Yarmouth. Instead, he'd have to send Quincy.

Not being able to attend to the matter of bringing down his nemesis wasn't the only thing his temper was flaring over. He tried to still his rising irritation at being summoned to Lady Sudbury's well before lunch. Melissa needed to see him urgently, and it could mean nothing but trouble.

He paced the drawing room, swearing beneath his breath. The woman was punishing him. She'd kept him waiting longer than twenty minutes now.

He'd not seen her since the terrible scene in the Cavendish garden two nights ago. He rubbed his temples. He'd acted like an arse. He let his emotions get the better of him. Something he never usually did, mainly because he very rarely had any emotions worth mentioning. He hated feeling so vulnerable. He had let her see his weakness—possessiveness.

His blood still boiled thinking about the sight of his brother holding and kissing Melissa's hand. The interlude looked so intimate. He should have demanded Richard take his place and marry her instead of him.

She was in league with Richard. Worse, she played him for a fool, pretended it hadn't been a trap. Dreaming! What virgin dreams of a man ravishing her? He'd been completely taken in by her story.

He hated the dark disturbing feelings she invoked in him—anger, fury, and God damn it, the most terrible of all, jealousy.

He slapped the crop against his thigh. Like a lion trapped in a gilded cage, he prowled from the bright windows, along the burgundy-upholstered sofa, and back to the windows. The urge to roar was eating him up inside.

For the first time in his life, a woman was keeping him waiting like some lap dog. The hiss of his crop was the only sound in the empty room. Did she think he had nothing better to do? He checked his watch. Damn it, he should be pursuing leads regarding Lord Rothsay . . .

The handle of the drawing room door turned, and the rustle of fabric caught his ears. He shoved his watch back in his pocket and stood with his hands behind his back, legs spread wide, in the middle of the room. His mood, which was already dark, deepened to pitch black.

He watched Melissa, with her usual contained manner, enter the room. She held her head high, and her eyes did not waver from his. They issued a silent challenge. His appalling behavior at the Cavendish ball had not made her cower.

As if hit by big surf in the ocean, Anthony felt waves of embarrassment wash over him. How did this young woman do it? His tongue felt thick. For once, he was at a loss for words, and he lowered his eyes.

Regrettably, they came to rest on her ample bosom, prettily displayed by the style and cut of her pastel-pink gown. His pulse gave a little kick. She folded her hands demurely in front of her, and he wondered what they'd feel like running all over his body. He struggled to control the crescendo beat of lust that surged through his veins.

His irritation grew.

"Good morning, Anthony," she coolly said, walking to where he was standing and giving a deep curtsy. "Thank you for sparing me a moment out of your busy schedule." He took a moment to respond, dazzled by the display of soft white flesh and the tantalizing view of her cleavage. The cut of her bodice was low.

He raised an eyebrow. Today he was Anthony, rather than Lord Wickham. She must want something.

His eyes quickly rose to meet hers. She flushed a pretty rose color that matched her dress. She turned away, gracefully strode to the settee, and sat.

Her thick black hair, arranged in a pleasing style, showed off her delicate neck to perfection. Her jugular jumped, telling him she was not as composed as she pretended.

Good. He wanted her unnerved.

"I am a busy man, Melissa," he said, striding toward her. "Why have you summoned me here at this ungodly hour of the morning?"

Melissa clasped her hands against her lap to hide her shaking. Anthony stood before her clad in a burgundy riding jacket, striped waistcoat that matched his beige shirt and cravat, and a pair of fawn breeches. His dark stare held no warmth, only irritation.

So much for Richard's theory that with time, Anthony would calm down. She doubted if he'd apologize for his behavior any time soon.

She cleared her throat. "I have a favor to ask of you."

He spun, and for a moment, she thought he'd march out of the room. Instead, he strode to the mantelpiece, leaned against it, and looked down his aristocratic nose at her. Silence. The man was deliberately making her squirm.

Straightening her spine, she gave a nervous smile. "I suppose you're waiting for an explanation—"

"After your behavior at the Cavendishes I rather think I'm not in the mood to grant favors."

Damn the man. Even in his bad mood she couldn't ignore how handsome he was.

Keeping her voice steady, she began her farce. "As the future Countess of Wickham I assume you would not want your wife's debts left unpaid."

His eyes narrowed, and he crossed his arms over his chest. "So your little charade, pretending ignorance of my brother's scheme to trap me into marriage, was all about money. Is it not enough I have seen to your brother's debts?"

Melissa blushed. She wanted to tell Anthony about Theresa, but he'd taken over his father's slave-trading business. Although he'd closed down the business after his father's death, he had worked for his father. Anthony would likely think buying a slave's freedom a waste of money, and she couldn't risk him saying no. Not when Theresa's life hung in the balance.

"I have a small debt that I raked up at Lady Humphrey's last evening, and I am without funds." Lady Humphrey, a renowned gambler, often held card evenings for the ladies of the *ton* since women could not openly visit gaming houses. "Her ladyship will expect the debt paid, and I am sure you would not like the embarrassment of me having to plead insolvency."

"How much is the debt?"

"Two hundred pounds." Her words spilled forth without hesitation.

Jaw tight, he stalked toward her and halted in front of her. He jammed his hands on his hips and towered over her like Goliath, his face carved with fury. "Am I to expect this behavior will occur on a regular basis? I suppose like brother like sister."

His eyes swept over her, his contempt making her feel ten inches small. "Everything is slowly becoming clearer. You agreed to Richard's proposition to trap me in marriage, not just for your brother but for yourself as well."

"No—"

"Do not add more lies to the ones you've already spouted," he growled. "You played me well. Let me see if I remember your words." He tried to mimic her voice. "I won't make you marry me. I want to marry for love." He gave a hollow laugh. "You should be on the stage."

She dropped her head. Waves of nausea rose up into her throat. It was pointless to argue, he'd never believe her.

"Since I am left in no position but to grant you this favor I shall call it your engagement gift."

Her head jerked up. She whispered, "No. As you have already given me an engagement present, I would like to call this a loan against my allowance."

"I think not." A bitter smile twisted his lips. "This shall replace my previous present, which due to your underhandedness, I shall take back."

Melissa slowly rose to her feet, shaking her head. "Don't do this."

"The choice is yours—the money or a promise not to bed your cousin." He gave an ugly smile. "What makes it so interesting is I shall see what means more to you. Money or a faithful husband?"

The room spun. She reached out and grasped the back of the settee. He meant it. Bastard. She sucked in deep breaths. She had no choice. Her pride was nothing compared to Theresa's life. "I shall take the money."

His nostrils flared and his eyes hardened. "At last you are finally being honest. Now we both know where we stand." He spun and marched toward the exit, saying, "I shall send the money to Lady Humphrey's on your behalf—"

"No." Without thinking, she flew after him. She grabbed for his arm, but at the feel of his sinewy muscles, a jolt of awareness made her drop her hands to her side. "I would prefer to deliver the money myself. I would not like it known that I run to my husband to pay my debts."

He halted and stood staring at her for what seemed like an eternity; then with a slight bow he said, "I shall have the money delivered here by lunchtime."

She let out the breath she'd not known she was holding. "Thank you," she whispered, but he had already left the room, and he was now free to bed Cassandra . . .

She sunk onto the settee before her legs collapsed. Her hand moved to hold her stomach to stop herself from being sick. She'd really done it now. Anthony could not stand the sight of her, and in two days' time she would have to stand before God and swear to love, honor, and obey him.

Anthony swept his hat and gloves off the entrance table, and without waiting for the butler to open the door, he marched out of the house, impatient for the groom to bring

Dark Knight. Since neither brother had actually bedded Cassandra, he had kept his stallion.

To think he'd intended to apologize to Melissa for his behavior the other night. As he swung into the saddle, he was thankful Melissa's gambling problem came to light. He'd order Quincy to set up a tiny allowance for her, one that should curtail her excesses at the card tables.

Thankfully, he was finally free of the creeping soft feelings he'd begun to harbor for his fiancée. After they married he'd have no qualms about sending her to Bressington or even Glenforay if it meant keeping his finances and sanity safe.

He entered the gate of Hyde Park, Dark Knight prancing with excitement at the promise of a gallop. As he battled control of his excited stallion and with his mind still analyzing how big a fool he'd been, he did not immediately hear the voice hailing him. He looked up to see Lady Samantha Dorrington. She was the wife of his good friend and business acquaintance, Lord Freddie Dorrington, the Marquis of Skye. If anyone could cheer him up, it was Samantha. He'd played a key role in bringing the couple together. He'd never seen his friend so happy.

"Anthony," she said as she brought her steed alongside Dark Knight. "A bit early for you, isn't it? Or have I caught you slinking home?"

"No, I . . ."

"Good." Her hazel eyes twinkled. "I would hate to think you have been up to mischief behind your fiancée's back."

He could not help smiling in return. "Speaking of slinking, does your husband know his pregnant wife is galloping in the park? Unescorted."

"Men." She pressed one gloved hand to her small belly. "You all stick together. I'm near term yet still hardly showing. Freddie keeps threatening to send me to the country, but I want to wait until after your wedding. Besides, my son loves the ride. Feel for yourself."

Before he could protest, Samantha grabbed his hand and placed it on her slight bulge. "He is kicking again, demanding I resume my ride."

Anthony was surprised by the awe he felt at the feel of tiny feet kicking against his hand. He saw Samantha's face soften as she took in his expression. "I told Freddie you were all hot air. Who wouldn't want a son? Now that you're marrying Miss Goodly, I expect your views on children will greatly change."

His smile faded. Blast Freddie. Did the man have to share everything with his beautiful wife? He felt his face flush.

Samantha continued, "I never thought I'd see the day you'd take a wife." She laughed. "Having met Miss Goodly, I believe your mistake was a blessing."

Hah! She didn't know everything. Underneath Melissa's beauty lurked a conniving liar and gambler. "I didn't know you'd made her acquaintance."

"We had a lovely talk at Lady Carmichael's ball last night."

He could not keep the hint of puzzlement out of his voice. "Lady Carmichael's ball? I thought the ladies were playing cards at Lady Humphrey's?"

"What nonsense. Lady Humphrey left town last week. Her daughter-in-law gave birth to twin boys a month early, and she raced down to the country to oversee the household."

A prickle of unease spread through his body. "So you played cards at Lady Carmichael's?"

Samantha hit him gently with her riding crop. "What is with you and gambling? No, there were no cards—"

"My mistake." Was there no end to Melissa's treachery? If she didn't need the money to pay off a gambling debt, then what did she need the money for? "I must have my nights confused. May I see you home? I need a word with your husband. He should not allow his very pregnant wife to prance about the park unescorted."

"Gosh, you sound so much like a husband already. Women are not helpless creatures, Anthony. I'm sure Melissa will soon teach you that we are capable of much more than you gentlemen credit us with." He didn't have the heart to tell her she was right. His betrothed was something of a conundrum. "Thank you for your kind offer, but I have Jefferson with me." She turned in her saddle. "He can't keep up with Twinkle Toes here."

"What a ridiculous name for a horse."

"At least it is more original than Dark Knight. How are you, boy?" She rubbed the stallion's nose and slipped him a sugar lump.

"Don't spoil him."

Samantha leaned close and gently cupped Anthony's cheek. "I think both of you could do with a little spoiling. I shall instruct Melissa to take extra special care of you."

Her words cut him to the bone. No one had ever spoiled him. No one had cared enough to bother, and he didn't have the heart to tell Samantha his new wife wouldn't care, either.

More gruffly than he intended, he said, "It was a pleasure to see you, Samantha. If you will excuse me, I have some urgent business I must attend."

"Of course. We shall both see you at Craven House for the wedding. Tell Melissa to call on me if she requires any help." With that, she turned her mount and took off at a gentle canter.

He shook his head thinking of Samantha pregnant with Freddie's child. A stab of envy surprised him. He'd never considered remaining childless as a hardship. The thought of being responsible for a child's emotional welfare terrified him beyond reason.

What if he couldn't love his own child? What did he know of raising a child? He'd learned what he knew from his father. What if he became his father? He would not subject a child to what he'd had to endure. Years of coldness, years of feeling unwanted, years of knowing he was unloved.

He spurred Dark Knight, and the stallion lurched forward and took off at a gallop across the park. No matter how fast they ran, he couldn't escape the question chanting in his head: What if he'd already gotten Melissa pregnant?

At lunchtime, Anthony organized for the money to be sent to Melissa as promised. However, he instructed one of his men to keep watch. Why did she need the money so badly she would lie to him?

He was finishing a late lunch when Stevens, his butler, entered and bowed. "Excuse the intrusion, my lord, but Jacob has some urgent news."

Anthony wiped his mouth with his napkin and nodded his head.

Jacob, the man he'd assigned to watch Melissa, came forward. "I did as you instructed, my lord. She left the house and went . . . and went—"

"Out with it man," Anthony said, rising to his feet. "Where did she go?"

Jacob wrung his hands and glanced at Stevens, who gave an encouraging nod. "She went to Smithfield markets, my lord." He paused, and looking distressed, added, "I didn't really wish to leave her there, but I knew I had to get back to tell you as soon as possible."

"What on earth is she doing at Smithfield's?"

Jacob's hand-wringing took on new proportions. "She is at—that is, she is watching—a slave auction . . ."

"What!" The mention of the slave market brought him up short. He could hardly manage to hide his incredulity. Anthony shot Jacob a bristling scowl. "Stevens, summon Monty. Have Dark Knight saddled." To Jacob, he said, "Who is with Miss Goodly?"

"Her groom."

"And you left her there with only a groom in attendance? Could you not have sent me a messenger?"

Smithfield market was the meat district. The market was

often used to sell meat of the living kind—slave auctions. Most slavers thought of their wares as nothing more than pieces of meat. It was no place for a lady.

"I-I'm so-sor-sorry, sir. I th-thought it best to ensure the message was delivered quickly and-and with all discretion."

Anthony stormed out of the room, grabbed his riding crop and gloves from Stevens, and walked around to the stable. His temper flared as he waited for Dark Knight to be saddled.

He cursed as he swung into the saddle. No fiancée of his was going to buy slaves. He'd put that side of his life well behind him. He gritted his teeth. God help her if she had bought a slave.

Chapter 9

Melissa pulled her cape tightly around her body. The hood hid her face in its shadows. She did not wish to be recognized. The thought that someone might think she supported trading in human flesh disturbed her greatly. She was a founding member and current president of the Ladies Freedom Charity. The charity raised money to purchase freedom for slaves. Thus far, they'd freed over one hundred slaves, something she was rather proud of.

The men surrounding her were rough and frightening. Already several of the men began watching her more than the slave auction, something the auctioneer was not pleased about. His frown was getting deeper the longer she stood next to Cassandra's carriage. At first glance, she'd recognized Mr. Rawlings, the man conducting the slave auction. She prayed he did not recognize her; he would likely have her escorted away. She and some of the charity members had disrupted one of his auctions last month.

She gave small thanks that it was Mr. Rawlings. He at least was known to treat his merchandise well. Theresa would not have been abused in any way.

Still, there was no sign of Theresa. Melissa did not know how much longer she would have to wait. Apparently, the men were being auctioned first. The majority of the slaves sold in England were men. Men were needed to work the land, to replace all the Englishmen killed or those still off fighting the war with France.

Finally, Mr. Rawlings led the first female slave onto the auction block. A murmur swept through the men with a few calling out crude comments. The young Negro woman, or girl in this case, was barely dressed. All she wore was a thin dress over her chemise, indecently covering hardly any of her body.

Melissa's face flushed as she heard several men beside her discuss what a versatile slave she'd make—a worker during the day and a bed warmer at night. Her heart broke thinking of the life the young woman, who stood so proud and defiant onstage, would lead. If she had more money, she would have tried to buy her freedom, too.

The bidding flowed thick and fast and quickly rose beyond her two-hundred-pound budget. She chewed her bottom lip. Would she have enough money to secure Theresa's release?

A hand suddenly gripped her arm, and Melissa nearly shrieked with surprise. She tried to jerk away from the tightening grip, and her hood fell back. "You will come away from here this instant. Move," a deep, silken voice growled in her ear.

Anthony. What was he doing here? Did he come to buy a slave? She jerked her arm away, but his gloved hand tightened its grip until she grimaced with pain. His face was a mask of barely concealed fury. The afternoon sunlight gleaming on his jet-black hair tousled from his ride, added to the vehemence pouring out of his tightly controlled body.

She spun to face him and scowled at him for all she was worth. "Let go of me. You are not my husband yet. You don't own me."

"Listen to me, carefully," he sneered in a voice that she imagined the devil used. "If you don't leave this place with me right now, our marriage is off. You can rot in your own disgrace, your brother will end up in debtors' prison, and you'll be ostracized from Society. I won't have my future wife partaking in this despicable trade."

Melissa stared at him, speechless. She should have trusted him. It was obvious he was as vehemently opposed to slave trading as she was—at least they shared that in common. She smiled. "I can't leave. I promised to secure Theresa's freedom. That is what I needed the money for."

His hand loosened its grip on her arm. "Who is Theresa?"

She eyed the young black girl before her. "I will explain in a moment, but can you please help her?" She pointed to the stage. "Look at her. Listen to the men bidding. She can't be more than sixteen years old. You know what will happen to her once she is sold. We have to save her, but I only have enough money for Theresa."

She watched Anthony raise his head and take in the actions going on around him. He ran a hand through his hair. She could sense his hesitation.

"Save her," she urged. "Please, Anthony, free her."

"I can't save them all." She heard the note of despair in his voice.

"I realize that, but look at her. You know what will happen to a young girl of her beauty. Her life will be a living hell."

"Yes," he whispered, his face paling. "I know exactly what will be done to her."

"Please—"

"Two hundred and seventy pounds," he called out.

Melissa clapped her hands together and silently thanked God.

She saw a softening in the hard intensity of Anthony's eyes. She was suddenly aware of a new tension that charged the air. He dropped his gaze to hers. It felt unbearably intimate, while his hand on her arm turned gentle and reassuring.

She drew in a sharp breath and stared at his sensual, inviting mouth. As if he could feel the sudden flare of awareness in her eyes, he released her arm abruptly and turned toward the auction block to concentrate on his bidding.

Anthony had to bid up to four hundred pounds before he

won the auction. He quickly made his way through the crowd to fetch the young girl and bring her to Melissa's carriage. The young slave was shaking with fear but held her head high. Once settled in the carriage with blankets, Melissa explained that Anthony had bought her freedom. She burst into tears and fell to the floor of the carriage at Anthony's feet. "Thank you, thank you."

Melissa's heart clenched as he gently lifted her to sit back on the seat and softly asked, "What is your name?"

She swallowed back her tears and wiped her face. "I'm called Alice."

"I am Miss Melissa Goodly. You may call me Melissa."

Anthony said, "Well, Alice, you'll need employment and a place to live." He turned and gifted Melissa a genuine smile. "My fiancée will no doubt need a laundry maid once we are married. The position comes with room and board and pays ten pounds per year. The job is yours . . . if you want it."

Melissa blinked back tears.

Alice smiled at Anthony. "Thank you, sir. I would be honored to work in your household for your beautiful wife." Alice turned and beamed at Melissa.

Returning the girl's smile, Melissa warmly covered Alice's trembling hand with her own. "Wait here in the carriage. We have one more slave to free."

Anthony alighted and helped Melissa down. He held her close, longer than necessary. The air fairly hummed with tension, a tension neither of them seemed to deny. In unison, they faced the auction block and grimly waited for Theresa to appear.

"I wish we could save them all," she murmured.

Anthony's shadowy gray eyes regarded her speculatively, and then he grimly nodded his head. "One day we will. One day the House of Lords will see reason and support Mr. Wilberforce's bill. I and several others intend to ensure that happens." He smiled down at her. "I wanted to throttle you when I learned you were here."

"You don't know, do you?"

"Know what?"

"I'm the president of the Ladies Freedom Charity. We raise funds and try to educate slave owners and influence Society to see how wrong it is to own another's life. It's difficult to get men to take us seriously. Most think women are dim witted, too delicate to understand the economics of it all." She sucked in a breath. "We understand. Money. Sometimes I think God's word is right. It is the root of all evil. We just don't have enough funds to buy them all their freedom. I can't understand how anyone can condone the ownership of a human life."

He took her hand and wrapped it possessively through his arm. Warmth streaked to the pit of her stomach, and for a brief moment, the horrors of the slave market faded. She felt stronger, more capable, now Anthony was by her side. Her fear that she may not be able to save Theresa gone.

"Greed. There are men like . . . like my late father, who'll do almost anything for money." He frowned. "When I learned you'd not been playing cards at Lady Humphrey's, I thought you might have wanted the money to run away."

"Once you know me better, you'll learn I never run away from my problems," she said, smiling a little. "I face them and try to work out a logical solution."

"Logical? You made me think you'd sold yourself to me, to cover your brother's debts and your own." He shook his head. "Your logic is twisted. But I suppose you did it for Theresa. How do you know her?"

"Theresa was Lady Sarah Albany's maid. Her father bought Theresa, many years ago, when she was a young girl, and when Lady Albany married, Theresa came with her into her husband's household and became Lord Albany's property."

Anthony frowned. "I still do not see how Theresa ended up here."

"Lord Albany was displeased with Sarah, and as punishment he took the one person Sarah called a true friend. Theresa was the one woman who protected her and who would never leave her."

Anthony shook his head. "I still don't understand. Lord Albany is quite capable of protecting his wife . . ."

At Melissa's raised eyebrow his words petered out, and he made a small hissing sound. His eyes flashed with anger. "It is her husband she needs protection from."

"Sarah is my friend, and when she asked for my help I couldn't let her down." She paused. "Now you know why I would prefer to marry for love. I wouldn't want to be left in Sarah's situation, with a man who despises her and cares nothing for her needs. It's nothing short of slavery. Women are at the complete mercy of their husbands."

Anthony stared at her for several minutes. "Are you afraid of me? Do you think I'll act like Lord Albany?"

"No, Anthony," she said with feeling. "Everything I have learned about you points to you always doing the right thing. Besides, you would never hurt someone weaker than you."

Melissa felt the heat from his eyes leave a hot trail of fire as they studied her. "You are a remarkable woman." His voice took on a husky sound. "I am sorry for the harsh words I spoke in Lady Sudbury's drawing room and in the Cavendish garden." He raised her hand to his lips.

Melissa blushed. "I was only asking Richard questions about you. I should have been braver and asked you directly, and then you would not have misunderstood. And this morning I should have trusted you enough to ask for your help."

"Why didn't you?"

She looked to the ground and shuffled her feet. "Richard told me about your father and that you'd at some stage worked for him. I couldn't risk your displeasure at my objective. What if you had said no?" She reached for his hand. "From now on, if our marriage is to be comfortable, I realize there should be no secrets between us."

Gritting his teeth, he damned his father for forcing him into this dark world of deprivation. His father's business had always nauseated him.

Then equally, he damned himself for wanting the woman standing beside him too much.

No secrets. Hell, his whole life was a secret. No one truly knew what he'd had to do to survive his father. A woman like Melissa would never understand, or likely forgive the horrifying things he'd done. He couldn't even forgive himself . . .

"It's Theresa."

Anthony's head snapped around to look at the stage. Theresa was neither a young woman nor a beauty, and as such, there was not much interest in the bidding. It was all over relatively quickly, and very soon, Melissa was hugging Theresa and helping her into the carriage.

Anthony swore under his breath. With her cheeks flushed with delight, Melissa looked stunningly beautiful. Damn, even in this disgusting place, she aroused him. She was going to be trouble. He knew it. Gruffly he stated, "I shall tie Dark Knight behind us and we can take the women directly to Craven House in your carriage."

Melissa was about to thank him when a shadow fell over them. A man stood a little to his right, the stranger's face hidden by the glare of the sun.

"Wickham," a familiar voice said in a menacing tone. A voice that haunted Anthony's nightmares. "Two slaves purchased. Doesn't that go against your holier-than-thou sensibilities?"

Anthony practically shoved Melissa into the carriage to get her away from the bastard's foul presence, and he slammed the door shut.

The carriage door closed before she could get a good look at the stranger talking with Anthony. More startled than hurt from Anthony's shove, Melissa wobbled onto the color-upholstered seat and peeked out the window. The brown-haired man stood with his back to her. The noise from Theresa's and Alice's excited chatter drowned out the conversation between the two men. But Anthony's thunderous face told her the man was not a friend.

When Anthony finally entered the carriage, his horrid mood silenced Alice and Theresa. They set off for home in ominous silence.

"Who was it you were talking with?" Melissa calmly asked.

Anthony met her eyes, and she could read the anger still blazing in them. "No one of importance and no one you would know."

Melissa opened her mouth, but one look at Anthony's face had her questions dying on her lips. He didn't wish to speak of it, and he needed time to gather his temper, so she snapped her lips shut.

She let her eyes drink him in, and his gaze pinned hers. A sharp flare of heat clutched at her as a hungry, almost predatory expression hardened his features.

In the confines of the crowded carriage, she experienced her first pang of sexual frustration. After everything he'd done for her today, she wanted a few moments of privacy to thank him properly—personally. She licked her lips. Perhaps even kiss him. And . . . well, there were all sorts of things possible since they were to be married.

She wondered if the light in his eyes meant his thoughts were along the same lines . . . She hoped so.

Surely they would have a few minutes to themselves at Craven House. Her pulse raced at the thought. *Couldn't the horses go any faster?*

Lord Philip Drake, Baron Rothsay, watched the carriage drive away. He tapped his cane on the cobblestones. Who was the delectable creature with Wickham?

She was obviously someone Anthony cared a great deal about, for Anthony had sworn never to set foot in a slave market ever again.

She was a woman capable of getting the one man who never wavered from his path to do the one thing he'd sworn never to do—buy a slave.

This meeting was quite fortuitous. Philip thought of himself as a patient man, and he had waited and watched Lord Wickham for a long time. His revenge would be all the sweeter for knowing his enemy intimately. Finally he had stumbled across an opportunity.

He turned swiftly and walked back to Rawlings. "Do you know who the woman with Lord Wickham is?"

"Miss Melissa Goodly. One of them Ladies Freedom Charity women. She's been here before but never to buy, only to disrupt."

"Did she arrive with Wickham?"

Rawlings shook his head. "No. She was here for quite some time before he arrived. I remember because I was going to have the boys turn her away. I didn't want no trouble. Some of the punters were more interested in her than the market."

From what little Drake saw, she was a beauty, almost familiar, yet he hadn't gotten a good enough look. He couldn't think of where they might have previously met. Her name was not familiar.

Snapping at Rawlings he uttered, "Find out all you can about her and what she is doing with Wickham."

This day had just become very interesting.

Chapter 10

Anthony needed a drink. A very large drink. His emotions were in turmoil. He didn't want to feel anything for his fiancée, but God damn he admired her. He admired her selflessness in trying to help someone less fortunate than herself. She was prepared to shoulder his scorn and contempt to save a slave. He was proud of the way she put someone else's needs before her own happiness. He'd never known another human being to be less self-serving.

He took a deep breath. But most of all he felt desire. A total, all-consuming need to lose himself in her softness. To feel her body wrapped around him, letting her goodness wash him clean. He didn't deserve her.

But he wanted her. All of her.

Instead, he had to sit politely sipping tea while his mother monopolized the conversation. Lady Wickham was enticing Melissa into providing thorough details of what they had been up to this afternoon.

The butler had taken Theresa and Alice to show them the servants' quarters and to explain what was expected of them in the future. Since their new mistress would not be taking up residence until the day after tomorrow, there was no need to rush.

Anthony heard his mother say, "Of course I'd heard of your work with the Ladies Freedom Charity."

He frowned. If she'd heard of Melissa, she'd never mentioned it to him. But, then, they seldom had two civil words to say to each other.

He wished his mother would stop asking questions. He wanted them finished and Melissa gone. He could feel his defenses crumbling under the onslaught of the goodness radiating from her.

Like a hawk watching a fat, juicy field mouse, he observed her. She had noted the obvious heat in his eyes, and she returned his gaze boldly. The way she kept flicking her tongue over her lips had his body tightening. She was nervous, yet her skin had a hint of flushed awareness. He longed to feel those sweet lips all over his body.

God, he needed a woman, and soon.

On the carriage ride home, he'd given up all pretense that he could ignore his soon-to-be Countess. He couldn't. Her self-sacrifice was compelling. Compelling him to believe there was still good in the world, and he craved a taste.

Driving him on was the thought that there were ways to pleasure a woman without impregnating her. Not foolproof, of course, but he'd made love to numerous women and as yet had not fathered a child.

He watched her while images of what he'd do to her body—the pleasure they would share—crashed through his head, making breathing difficult.

He remembered her naked and in his arms, moaning as his hands stroked her at the juncture of her long slender legs. He could almost feel how tight and hot she'd been.

He tried to get the naked image of her to leave his mind. He fixed his gaze on the fully clothed Melissa. The sunlight from the window behind her was lighting her dark tresses as if she wore a halo. He crossed his legs to hide his arousal. Halo. Yes. She was his fallen angel. He'd ensured her fall.

Watching his angel's pink tongue once again flick over wet, ruby lips was once too much. He rose and crossed to stand directly in front of her. Knowing his actions verged on madness, he held out his hand. "Mother, I wish to show Melissa the gardens. Please do excuse us. If the weather was up to it, we could hold the ceremony outside. I would like my bride's valued opinion."

"I must say it took you long enough. I was wondering how much longer I would have to keep up this prattle." He watched Melissa's mouth drop open in surprise at his mother's words. "Go—be off with you. Due to circumstances there is little need for a chaperone."

Melissa, with a perfectly respectable hint of hesitation, gave him her hand. At the feel of her fingers, so tiny in his, he almost shuddered.

It took a moment before she looked up at him, her face closed, masking her emotions. "I would be delighted to see all that Craven House has to offer."

Once they stepped outside, the warmth from the sun was not nearly as hot as the feel of her arm through his.

"Is there something in particular you'd like to show me?"

He glanced at her suspiciously, trying to understand the siren-like murmur of her voice.

"The rose garden."

Her smile deepened. "Is it private?" It was one of those smiles that every instinct he possessed distrusted, especially as she let her hip brush his. Who was seducing whom here?

His eyes locked on hers. He replied in a way that would ensure she would not suspect his motives. "At this hour the gardeners will be working in the orchard down the back of the garden. We should be quite alone."

"How lovely. I shall have you all to myself. I haven't thanked you properly for helping Theresa and Alice this afternoon."

His rake's instincts were functioning normally; his member was hardening at her clear invitation to seduction. Hunger for a dalliance raged through him. He'd not had a woman since their mistaken tumbling and none three months prior to that. Their brief bedding had hardly been satisfactory.

Walking through the hedgerow arch, between the lawn and the rose garden, she halted, facing him. Her eyes searched his, then she smiled—one of those smiles that left a man in no doubt as to her current appetite.

She stepped closer. "The garden is beautiful. A perfect place for me to offer my thanks. Don't you agree?"

Her hand rose to his chest. She was close, almost in his arms. The rutting beast within came out of hibernation. He battled the primitive urges to simply pull her down on the manicured lawn and lift her skirts.

His inner rake wanted to very much come out and play. "It would be interesting to see what a lady of limited experience would likely offer in way of thanks."

She laughed and settled against his chest, her face tilting up to his.

He teased. "Perhaps she would like a few lessons first?"

"I may surprise you." She ran her hand down his chest and over the ridge of his erection. "I'm a very quick learner."

He sucked in his breath at her touch. He growled against the silken skin of her neck. "As long as I'm the only one to teach you, I don't mind a quick study."

Her voice vibrated with laughter. "I think it would be pointless to wait until our wedding night. You've already taken my virginity. Who would care or even know if we indulged now?"

"I would know."

He went rigid, worried about his ability to resist. About his potential lack of control, of the primitive need feeling her voluptuous curves evoked in him. That need even now was driving him to claim what she so readily offered. That need wanted her beneath him, above him, any which way he could have a woman. He wanted her surrender—wanted her.

It was a need unlike any he'd ever known—infinitely more powerful, more compelling than his normal longing to couple. It was a need that drove him as no desire ever had.

He tried to come to grips with what this driving need indicated, what it would mean to him. He looked into her eyes, trying to formulate a reason she'd accept for the Lord of Wicked to decline her gracious offer.

Finally he shook his head at her offer. "I want our first night together to be memorable." How weak was that? The Lord of Wicked suggesting they wait for the proprieties to be completed.

Melissa listened to the words; even more she listened to his tone. Hesitant, worried, uncertain. Her Lord of Wicked was afraid. He'd said the words of denial. His lips had moved, but his body sang a different tune. She caressed him intimately. He was as hard as rock under her fingers.

If not for the evidence, she could well believe he did not desire her. Why was he declining her offer? Apparently his customary mode of dealing with such an offer would have had her on her back, skirt hiked up with no further conversation.

She eyed him warily. "It will be memorable because I've become your wife. It does not stop us indulging here, now."

His voice as hard as his member under her fingers, said, "I would prefer to wait. For once in my life I am trying to do the right thing."

She continued to smile invitingly at him. "The Lord of Wicked trying to do the right thing." She couldn't imagine it. After reading her book, and seeing the tightness in his shoulders and thighs, she was confident matters between them could progress precisely as she'd planned this afternoon, precisely as she'd pictured on the carriage ride back to Craven House.

Still, she was truly wicked if she destroyed his one attempt at behaving as a true gent. Which suggested she should treat his current vacillation with some degree of magnanimity?

With reluctance, she dropped her hand from the most intimate part of him, and letting her lips curve more definitely, she reached up and wound her arms about his neck. "Very well. If you wish."

The suspicion that flashed into his dark eyes made her smile even more. She drew his head down, lifting her lips to his. "Perhaps just a small taste of the pleasure to come."

*   *   *

Their lips met. He relaxed. He was an accomplished rake, and setting the pace of any seduction was all but second nature to him. Why was he scared of allowing a few stolen kisses?

She broke the kiss, and giggling like a schoolgirl, she took his hand and dragged him deeper into the garden until they came across a stone bench next to the bird fountain. She pulled him down to sit next to her.

Sincerity clouded her kaleidoscope eyes, a true array of green and brown flecks. "I do thank you for your help today. It was most kind considering how I deceived you." She smiled beguilingly. "How exactly would you like me to show you my thanks?"

Sliding into habit, he pulled her into his lap, into his arms, and felt her soft form through her gown. It was a mistake. The rake hiding deep down burst forth.

"I'm sure I can think of something," he all but growled.

She eagerly reached for his face to bring it to hers. He found the hooks of her day dress, and without thought, as if he was simply following a script, he undid them. She wriggled closer and sank against him, her hands on his chest, her lips teasing and taunting—flagrantly tempting.

He answered her challenge, confident of staying in control. His words of restraint almost forgotten under his burgeoning desire. His hands roved her soft body, roved her curves, the experience all the more potent since he'd never actually had the pleasure of seeing her naked body before. He pitied blind men. To feel a woman's curves but not be able to see them would drive a man mad.

She kissed him with unfeigned delight, openly encouraging. His mind refocused.

All too soon the kisses grew headier, more evocative; she grew softer, he commensurately harder. He'd made a logical rational decision that indulging her with kisses and caresses was only fair, since it would be dangerous to indulge once she was his wife. Besides, she was already suspicious of his magnanimous gesture to wait for their marriage bed.

At no point did he entertain the notion that the Lord of Wicked could not, no matter how hard she tried, overcome his determination not to take her.

God help him, she didn't.

It wasn't Melissa who tumbled them onto the warm, fragrant grass. It wasn't Melissa who trapped herself beneath him. Nor was it Melissa who swept aside her bodice, revealing her bountiful breasts, encouraging him to admire, caress, and taste that which he commanded himself to resist.

He'd touched her breasts before, but he hadn't viewed them, hadn't feasted on the soft flesh and dusty pink nipples. She arched wildly beneath him; her willingness to oblige him caught him unawares. Caught him with his defenses down, and before he realized her strategy, he'd almost lost the battle. His fortress of denial breached.

His lips were on hers, hard and demanding, his hand on one pert breast. His body roared for satisfaction, pressing her down, his intention brutally clear.

And she fed the flames. She smashed his battlements to dust, showing no fear. He kissed her more ravenously, more explicitly than he ever had before—with any woman.

She took, savored, and urged him on.

Her hands roamed freely over his shoulders and stroked his back, frantically clenching his hair. Then his waistcoat and shirt were undone, and her palms spread like liquid heat across his chest, fingers flexing, sinking in as she tweaked one pebbled nipple. She made small encouraging gasping sounds, her body arching under his experienced hands.

The sounds of her passion sent a primitive and unrestrained need slamming into him, filling him, shaking his resolve.

Through his raging desire, he glimpsed one instant of clarity. She was his—his to take whenever he wished, here, and now—if that was what he wanted.

The devil take him. He wanted to have her with a need so acute, every fiber in his being hurt. He hadn't expected his own instincts to betray him, delivering up to him that which was his deepest fear—he must prevent his seed from taking root. Not easy to remember when his body craved her to distraction.

He could ease his pain. He could have her now, here: Even as his lips returned to draw one peaked nipple deep into his mouth and his body moved over hers, one thought flashed through his mind: don't get her with child. The thought was almost enough to cause an extremely hard part of him to become morosely flaccid.

With a shaky breath, he acknowledged that indulging in his favorite pastime with Melissa could lead to his condemnation . . . to a child, a child whom he would never love.

He'd been captive of the flames often enough to know he had the willpower to wrestle back control. Now that he remembered the danger, his will kicked in and he began his withdrawal. She might have won the battle, but he'd win the war.

However, Melissa's tortured breathing, her greediness for every touch, told him how close to release she hung. He couldn't leave her disappointed for a second time. The night he'd taken her virginity had been rough, fast, with no finesse. His pride wouldn't let him leave her on the edge once more— he wasn't that cruel.

Melissa was floating in a sea of sensation. She knew she was close to experiencing her first orgasm. The book could never have prepared her for the spine-tingling, exquisite torment. Beneath the staggering heat, urgency gripped her— drove her on. Her senses could barely cope, yet seemed to have expanded, heightened. Her skin was over-sensitized, yet greedy for all he could give her.

Her body melted, all resistance gone; his in contrast had only grown harder. Nevertheless, his strength wasn't his source of power over her. His power stemmed from his expertise, the way he made her body surrender. Her arms clung to his shoulders as if her life depended on it.

She felt the hard, hot evidence of his erection pressing into her stomach; all the while his lips ravaged hers. His hand kneaded her naked breast, his palm shooting sharp desire to the very core of her. She longed to feel him inside her. She heard herself moan deep in her throat. The hard rigidness of him held a promise of all she hoped would come.

She did nothing but encourage him when his hand left her breast, slid over her hip, and started to gather and lift her skirt. She didn't care that it was daylight, or that anyone could stumble across them. She'd stopped breathing entirely—caught in a vise of anticipation, excitement, and sheer hungry desire.

Melissa was caught up in the masculine scent and feel of this man. A man who would on Friday become her husband. Never before had she wanted a man the way she desired Anthony. It was as if her body knew, before her head, that this was meant to be. Her heart clenched deep in her chest. Anthony was sweeping her past infatuation, heading directly down the path to love. She should be terrified. Terrified that a man like Anthony, a seasoned rake, who was only marrying her to protect them both from scandal, could ravage her heart.

She let out a gasp at the touch of his heated palm sliding up her leg. He shifted over her, pushing her skirts and chemise to her waist, leaving them bunched there, his hand sliding immediately to tangle in her curls. Then he thrust his tongue deep into her mouth as he cupped her—the tantalizing dance in her mouth distracting her before he opened her body and slid one finger into her softness.

Like a well-trained courtesan, she reacted, hips lifting against him. Being a quick learner, she picked up the rhythm of his tongue and finger, her movements triggered by instincts as old as time.

For one long minute she felt a flutter of panic. Her body was no longer hers. The heat within her built and built, until she struggled against his attentions, wanting to break free and breathe. His charcoal eyes, their flint-edged heat, captured her gaze as he lifted back, his fingers continuing to work their magic between her legs. He watched, his eyes darkening, soaking in her gasps, and pants—while the weight of his body held her down, held her at the mercy of his incredibly amazing fingers.

"Open your eyes. Look at me." His voice was raspy and his breathing heavy.

She felt him come up on his elbow and shift back. Her lids felt heavy, but she didn't want him to stop, so she obeyed his command. She opened her eyelids and looked down his body, watching him watching her, where his hand rhythmically flexed between her naked thighs. His knee held them spread and she could feel the grass tickling her naked skin.

Slowly, at odds to the fingers working her steadily to the point of fracture, she watched his gaze roam back up over her hips, over her bare stomach, up over her midriff, over her rucked skirts to her exposed breasts, heaving, with their tight peaks pointed and begging for his mouth.

He captured her gaze. His expression was hard, etched as if in pain; yet something in the line of his lips suggested a softness, an intangible emotion she longed to see forever in his face. Between her thighs, his hand shifted; slowly, deliberately, he probed deeper. Then his thumb caressed, circling, increasing her pleasure. Tensing, she rose off the ground, her breathing ragged. "Please—make it . . ."

"Give yourself to me." His lips twisted in a half smile. "Let yourself fly free." His mouth bent and claimed her pebbled nipple. His tongue flicked. Then his lips suckled, hot and greedy on her breast. The sharp sensation of his mouth at her breast, coupled with the wicked intimate caress of his marauding fingertips, set her skin afire. Her lungs seized. Then his finger withdrew, and he pressed—breathless, she gasped his name as his clever thumb began its stroke against the nub of her womanhood.

She surrendered; she let him take her to the dizzy heights, to the moon and the stars.

She gave herself up to his expertise and floated on the tide of a sensual delight. Nothing she had read could have prepared her for a man's touch, let alone Anthony's clever ministrations.

Briefly she wondered what it would be like when he truly took her, when it was more than his fingers deep inside her.

She lay boneless, watching him feast on the sight of her naked body. His gaze was hot and erotic. His eyes glinted like burning coals, and she could still feel his thick erection pressing against her leg.

She reached for him to see to his needs. She knew what she could do to satisfy his aching hunger, but he said, "Not now," and pulled her into his arms, kissing her deeply.

Anthony took a dark pleasure in ravaging her mouth, taking from her that which he could not take from her more explicitly.

Ever.

He stifled a groan, his body's protest at denying his own needs. He gripped her hips and held her to him, stealing a moment to glory in her suppleness, in the evidence of how well she would fit him. He took in the womanly warmth that ultimately he would never be able to claim.

This was his punishment, his torment. To be madly in lust over a woman he could never have. A woman who didn't want him to stop—she'd be quite happy if he drew her back down, kissed her swollen ruby lips, and sunk deep between her thighs.

It took serious willpower to release her luscious mouth and deny himself. God give him strength.

Her lashes fluttered down, and she sighed. "Would you like me to pleasure you?"

His gaze fixed once more on one tightly budded nipple; it was an effort to draw enough breath to answer. "Thank you for the kind offer, but I fear we have run out of time."

He gathered his wits and rose, pulling her upright and letting her skirts fall to cover her long slender limbs. He tweaked her chemise back up and, with a resigned sigh of unfulfilled longing, helped her set her bodice to rights. But when he reached for her waist and gripped, intending to turn her toward the house, she stayed him, sliding one hand past his jaw, curling her fingers into his hair.

She looked up into his eyes, studied them, her gaze direct, and then she smiled like the cat who'd drunk the cream. "Suddenly I am looking forward to our marriage."

She pulled his head down to meet her passion-raked lips. She kissed him long, lingering, and sweetly. She lifted her head and whispered against his lips, "Until our wedding night . . . I'm looking forward to all the Lord of Wicked can teach me."

Anthony had refused to take his own pleasure. It seemed strange that the Lord of Wicked declined an opportunity to indulge in his favorite pastime. She couldn't have been more obvious in her desires than if she'd written him a formal invitation.

His control had been admirable. But she didn't want him controlled. She wanted him wild, desperate for her. Only then could she perhaps hope to tame and capture his heart.

Conceivably he was being gentlemanly, not wanting to overwhelm her all at once. Yes that was it, Melissa concluded. Gentlemen of the *ton* believed their wives did not covet sexual intimacy. She would have to reassure him on that point. Perhaps even show him her book. She'd like his advice on some of the positions. She'd been puzzled by the physicality of some. Even with pictures, she couldn't work out how the man and the woman fitted together without breaking something.

Melissa reassessed her fiancé's character. He was obviously more of a gentleman than most of Society thought. His control this afternoon was admirable. Perhaps the Lord of Wicked was not as wicked as she'd thought.

That might be a problem. How could she win his heart if he kept such a tight rein on his passion? She would have to ensure that once she became his Countess, he would not be able to resist her. Cassandra often told her men took mistresses because they had funny notions about carnal relations with their wives. They didn't feel comfortable asking their wives to act the whore in the bedroom, even if the wife was happy to oblige.

Melissa's body shivered in impatient contemplation at the prospect of being in his bed when he unleashed all that pent-up control. She patted her flat stomach. What's more, the idea of children thrilled her. She couldn't wait to hold their child in her arms.

The one person who would always offer her unconditional love.

Richard had been right. Anthony's response to her proved the way to his heart lay in pleasing his sexual appetites.

Armed with the courtesan knowledge gained from Cassandra's borrowed book, Melissa was confident she was up for the challenge.

Chapter 11

The following morning, it startled Melissa when Anthony arrived early at the house and joined her in the breakfast room. Her teaspoon clattered against the side of her teacup as she drunk in the sight of him. Her eyes feasted on his sensual lips, and her face heated, remembering the way he'd made her respond with his kisses and magical fingers.

She smiled on the inside, realizing she'd soon have the pleasure of his company every morning. He would be sitting across from her having breakfast. The vision of him would certainly aid her appetite—but not for food. This morning, his dark beauty was enough to make her forget she was supposed to be a lady.

Her heart rate sped up another notch noting the newfound companionship between them, evident in his amiable greeting. While she watched enraptured by the ripple of muscle beneath his tight-fitting breeches, Anthony filled a plate from the sideboard, accepted coffee from one of Cassandra's footmen, and then took the chair beside her. The deep blue of his jacket made his gray eyes look almost violet. She felt her body stir with want.

"Good morning, my sweet," he uttered with a grin.

She wished she'd taken more care getting dressed. She knew she was not looking her best. She'd tossed and turned all night, reliving the magic of his touch in the garden of Craven House yesterday.

What was he doing here this early? Had he stayed the night? If so he had not come to her bed. She froze. Cassandra. She shook her head. No, he wouldn't. He'd promised. Her hands fisted on the knife she was holding. *He could have lied; you hardly know this man.*

Forcing those foolish thoughts away, Melissa made herself take a mouthful of egg and swallow before addressing him. "Good morning—Anthony. This is a pleasant surprise. You are up early."

The servants returned to refill the platters on the large mahogany sideboard, for when Christopher and Cassandra joined them. Silence reigned until the servants completed their tasks and left.

Anthony was attacking his breakfast with gusto. It wasn't until his plate was clean that he answered her.

"I often ride early in the morning. Dark Knight likes a good gallop, and any later in the day the park is too full to really let him have his head. Besides, I wanted to try and catch you before you were engaged for the day."

Her pulse picked up its pace. "Oh. I do have rather a full schedule, with the wedding tomorrow. The final fitting for my dress, organizing my move to Craven House . . ."

"Quite." She felt his light gaze examining her face. "Are you nervous?"

She shrugged her shoulders. "As much as most brides I would suspect."

"It's to be expected considering we barely know one another. In that vein, I was wondering if I might have the honor of escorting you to the theater tonight. Do you enjoy Shakespeare?"

Melissa swallowed her excitement. It wouldn't do to turn into one of his fawning admirers so quickly. He was reputed to thrive on a challenge.

"I love his work and would enjoy accompanying you." He did not need to know that she'd planned an evening of pampering so as to arrive for her wedding fresh, utterly appealing, and ready for a long night of pleasure with the Lord of

Wicked. Yet, she'd readily give that up to spend more time in his company.

This was the first occasion he'd ever sought her out, and she was conscious of a rush of warmth swamping her. He wanted to spend time with her.

"Good. It will help quiet the scandal for us to be seen together and pretend to enjoy each other's company before we wed."

Pretend? At his words, her rush of happiness began to fade. "Yes . . . I suppose that would help."

He rose then and took her hand. He raised it to his lips. "Until this evening."

Melissa shivered, feeling the tingle of his mouth all the way down her arms to her loins.

She stared after Anthony long after he was gone. Finally she felt her breath return to normal. He hadn't really wanted to see her. He was merely obliging the niceties of the *ton*. She yearned for a time when for once, someone would visit or call on her with the sole purpose of wanting—no—needing her company. She wondered what that would feel like.

She prayed one day Anthony would ask to be with her purely for pleasure. Solely because he wanted to, not because he felt obligated to.

Melissa shook her head, desperately fighting the emotions he unleashed in her. Anthony woke in her a hungry longing. A longing to matter. A longing to be wanted. She feared the power he held over her.

She threw her napkin on the table and rose. She had a lot to do today, since tonight would be busy. She'd have to call on Sarah earlier than expected. Sarah needed her advice regarding their plan to disrupt a slave auction next month.

She hoped Anthony would not oppose her attendance. Given his distaste for slave trading, she prayed he would be considerate of her need to help bring down slavery in her own way. As women they lacked the power to openly change policies, but they found creating nuisances drew the attention of those that could—fathers, husbands, brothers, lovers . . .

The Ladies Freedom Charity meant the world to her. When she'd had no one, when she'd felt lost and alone, her work for the charity helped her realize there were souls worse off than her. There were far worse things in this world than being the unwanted sister of a destitute baron.

It felt good to know somebody, somewhere, needed her. She had purpose. She was important to the world in her small way. She felt sadness at the fact that many of the slaves she helped, those she was most important to, would never meet her.

Those around her, those closest to her, found little use for her at all.

As they entered the Wickham box at the Globe Theatre, all eyes turned to view Lord Wickham and his future Countess. She straightened her back and stood up tall, smiling to hide how nervous she truly was.

Her excitement at attending the theater was heightened by the man at her side. Her heart pounded against her ribcage. He should be on the stage. His performance as a man besotted with his fiancée had the audience riveted, with eyes straining on their box.

The effect on her was like the hot summer winds, profoundly appealing and unquestionably dangerous, filling her lungs with hot, smothering air. She couldn't lose her heart to him just yet. Not until she'd had a chance to ensnare his affections. A lovesick, clingy wife was certain to ensure he did not come near her.

Melissa did her best to battle the whirlwind of emotions and maintain a cool demeanor. From the stares pointed their way, she knew they made an appealing couple. She'd taken extra care in her appearance tonight. She wore her hair piled high on her head with tiny ringlets softening her face, while her gold slip with its overskirt of rich copper was daringly cut, displaying her wares to their best advantage. She could tell by the sudden darkening of Anthony's silver-gray eyes that he greatly admired the effect. She was smugly pleased.

Anthony's performance for the *ton* rivaled those of the actors onstage. From the moment he was settled beside her, he played his role to the hilt, taking her hand and bringing her fingers to his lips, all the while gazing deeply into her eyes. The delighted audience was totally convinced the pair was in love. Even though there was no real sentiment behind the gesture, the sheer intimacy of the act made her body pitch and roll as if sailing the high seas. She found it difficult to keep her seat.

Her heart was going to be extremely difficult to protect if he continued to wield the power of his sensuality. She would be wise to speed up her own strategy of seduction.

They were barely seated when visitors started arriving at their box, no doubt wanting to gaze upon the woman who'd managed to trap his lordship into matrimony.

If she hadn't already been infatuated with Anthony, she was completely under his spell now. His pretend display of the lovelorn rake had her beginning to believe in a love match. Even before the play commenced, the audience seemed to be there for one performance only—Anthony's.

His continued closeness had Melissa's blood racing. She could feel his body heat, and she watched mesmerized as his smile dazzled all and sundry in the theater while his gaze raked her from head to toe, staking his claim. Like everyone else, she entered make-believe land, and for once became the cherished and desired fairy princess of her youthful dreams.

Once the play began, she still couldn't relax. Even with her body strung tight as a bow, Melissa found the onstage performance riveting. As the curtain fell for the first intermission, she gave a sigh of delight.

She clasped one of Anthony's hands between hers. "Thank you for bringing me here, Anthony," she said sincerely. "I know it's really for the benefit of the gossips, but I have never enjoyed myself so much."

He bowed gallantly. "I take it you have not been to the theater much?"

She felt her face flush. "I have never been. This is my first

Season in London, and Christopher would not waste money on the theater—or on me."

"Another first for me." Anthony teased softly. "The pleasure of introducing you to your first play." He continued to hold her hand. "As my wife you can visit the theater whenever you wish."

Before she could stop herself, she asked, "With you?"

The smile faded from his face. "I've seen almost all the plays there are to be seen. But do not let me spoil your enjoyment of attending with friends." Like the curtain onstage, his fringe swung forward and veiled his eyes. Melissa could have bitten off her tongue. She'd sounded far too eager.

She was relieved when a visitor appeared in their box. Lord Strathmore, Anthony's friend, joined them with, of all people, Cassandra, and her brother, Christopher.

The Viscount and her cousin made a dashing couple, while her brother was worse for drink as usual. Anthony excused himself to go procure drinks for their party.

Melissa felt nervous being in the presence of Anthony's close friend. What if he found her lacking? Lord Strathmore sat staring at her with a teasing smile on his face. She refused to let him ascertain how unsettled he made her. "Lord Strathmore, have you been enjoying the play?"

"One rarely comes to the theater to enjoy the play. One comes to be seen." He took her hand and placed a kiss on her glove. "Please, call me Rufus. Tomorrow you will become the wife of my closest friend. I hope you will come to think of me in the same vein."

"Have you known Anthony long?"

He gave a slight pause. "Since my last year of Eton."

"So you were not friends from when you first entered Eton?"

"Anthony didn't attend Eton until my last year."

Melissa frowned; that was odd. She opened her mouth to inquire why, but Rufus changed the topic—rather quickly she thought.

"Rumor has it you visited Smithfield's market recently. Do you make it a habit of buying slaves, only to set them free?"

Was he mocking her? She responded, unable to hide her haughty tone. "I make no apologies for helping those trapped in slavery. Ownership of another human being is morally wrong."

Rufus raised one dark eyebrow. "How liberal of you."

His condescending manner infuriated her. "It does not surprise me that a man like you, a man of wealth and privilege, does not comprehend the plight of slaves." She looked him up and down. "I suspect you've never been forced to do anything you don't want to do in all your life. For some of us freedom of choice is a luxury."

"You surely do not count yourself the same as a slave?"

The knowledge that he was as big a rake as her husband ensured she couldn't hold her tongue. "Slavery takes many forms, my lord. Women, in the eyes of the law, are little more than slaves. Subject to their husbands', fathers'—brothers' tempers, whims, and desires."

Rufus nodded, his smile somewhat diminished. "However, the majority of men want what is best for their loved ones."

"Not always." She flashed a look at her brother. "Some are more focused on their own self-interest, giving their female relatives little choice."

He studied her silently a moment before venturing to ask, "Given a choice, are you saying you would not freely marry Anthony?"

"Why would I freely choose to marry a man I've known less than a week? I am literally handing my keeping to a man I hardly know. I have simply been foisted onto Anthony to be looked after." She shivered. "I loathe being someone's obligation. Would you like it?"

Rufus threw back his head and roared with laughter. "Anthony, I'm sure, shall enjoy his obligation."

"Until he tires of me. I see little difference in my position than that of a kept mistress. Except a mistress has more freedom."

Rufus sat up straight. "You will be the Countess of Wickham. There is a big difference. You will have the protection of Anthony's name and his wealth."

"Money. Yes I will not want for material things." She turned away in disgust. "You would not understand. You think nothing of using a woman and discarding her. Most women do not sell their bodies because they wish to. Without an education or the ability to work, other than on our backs, most women have little choice. Men see to that."

Rufus still appeared horrified. "I would hope any woman I have a relationship with gets far more than simply money. Pleasure is most definitely mutual."

She turned to him. "Pleasure does not provide the financial freedom to make your own choices. Men, by ensuring we have no education, no skills, make certain we are reliant on them."

Rufus sat back in his chair and scoffed. "Reliant but well protected. We are the stronger sex. How would you protect yourself against an enemy?"

"By not making one in the first instance."

"Come, Melissa, you are not that naive. There are men out there who commit such atrocities you would be ill if I listed them. How would you protect yourself against such men?"

"Do not bore Lord Strathmore with your preaching." Cassandra leaned forward to rest her arms on the back of Rufus's chair and interrupted their conversation. "Ignore her ranting, Rufus. She resents her life. She fumes about having never had choices, of never having freedom. Yet she'd give it all up for love. Melissa does not understand the realities of life." Cassandra slid her arm over his shoulder and down his chest. "She has never understood the true power a woman holds."

Rufus halted Cassandra's wandering hand and lifted it off his chest. "That is to her advantage, I think."

Cassandra sat back in her chair, her lips pursed in anger.

Rufus under his breath whispered, "I must warn Anthony, you'll likely be an expensive wife. He won't have to worry about you gambling or wasting his money on finery, but you might bankrupt him with your passion for saving the underprivileged and the shackled." In a louder voice he added, "The Ladies Freedom Charity is obviously important to you. If you ever require funds or assistance in any way, please call on me."

Melissa's mouth dropped open in astonishment. "Thank you, my lord."

Rufus cocked his head on one side. "You will be good for Anthony. He needs people with passion in his life, those who think of others before themselves." He gave her a beguiling smile. "He'll try to push you away, but don't you dare let him. Underneath his gruff exterior is a man who is fiercely loyal and fiercely in need of love. He deserves to be happy."

"For a renowned rake you seemed indecently pleased your friend is to marry. If the prospect of marriage is such a sought-after union, why are you not married?"

Rufus shifted uneasily in his seat. "I have a matter of honor to address before I wed."

Melissa sat waiting for more, but it became very clear he would not tell her. "We all have something to atone for, my lord," she added softly.

That made him smile. "I cannot believe you have done anything for which you must be forgiven."

Melissa rolled her eyes. "I am atoning for the fact I was stupid enough not to lock my bedchamber door on the night Cassandra had guests."

Rufus broke into a loud laugh. His gaze roamed her person, not entirely appropriately. The rake was back at play. "Anthony has chosen well."

"I do not believe there was any choice involved, my lord. We had little option but to wed."

His eyes twinkled. "Did you? Do you think a man like Anthony, the Lord of Wicked, would be forced into a marriage he did not want?" Rufus studied her face intently. "He recognized something in you that night. He just needs encouragement to understand what it is. He shields his heart." His smile faded and he leaned forward to whisper in her ear. "You, my dear, must learn how to pierce his armor. Not putting up with his irritability and barked dictates would be an excellent place to start. He needs a woman who can manage his brooding temper, and I believe you are such a woman."

"You wouldn't be trying to seduce my fiancée, Rufus?" a voice from the door uttered dryly.

Rufus gave no apology; he only laughed. "Do you blame me? She is quite the most gorgeous creature here. I'll wager you're glad I value our friendship."

"Quite," Anthony said, giving Melissa a glance so warm she felt herself blush, as he handed her a glass of champagne.

"I have been busy persuading her that you do have some good points. For instance did you know, Miss Goodly, that it was Anthony who provided detailed personal testimony on the treatment of slaves to the House of Lords. It is largely due to his support of Wilberforce's bill that the Anti-Slave Trading Act got through the House."

"Stop it, Rufus," Anthony growled.

"The House of Lords were not interested in abolishing slavery. However, if the Earl of Wickham, whose father ran the largest slave-trading operation in all of England, closed shop and became an Abolitionist, his peers were intrigued enough to take notice."

Melissa nodded her head. "True. Few noblemen would bother to care for lowly slaves." She turned to Anthony. "I admire your stance even more, considering your upbringing. It's worthy to note that you could rise above your father's business and see slavery for what it truly is." She hesitated. "Did something happen to make you see the moral bankruptcy of the trade?"

Shocked silence descended on the box as if she had uttered an extremely unladylike word. Her curiosity grew when she saw Rufus and Anthony share a look.

Just then the lights lowered, ready for the second act. Anthony turned to gaze at her in the darkness. "If you want the truth—" She nodded. "I was looking for redemption."

"Why? You are not responsible for the sins of your father."

"Oh, but I am." He let that sink in before adding lightly, "I have sins of my own that to this day haunt me. I can't share them with anyone but myself. Who would want to shoulder the burden of the horrors I have seen and inflicted? It makes for lonely and objectionable company. Most of us are too wrapped up in our own sins to take on the burden of others."

Anthony's self-condemnation echoed in her ear, but it was the pain in his voice that unsettled Melissa. She had the urge to pull him close and stroke away his fears.

His tone was quieter, more reflective when he continued. "I offered my testimony not for any noble reason, but purely to unburden myself and cleanse my soul. Now I choose to block out the memories with pleasure. Only when I am with a woman do the nightmares dim." He sighed into the darkness. "But the euphoria never lasts. My cloak of guilt still sits heavy upon my shoulders," he said softly. "It will take more than my lifetime to throw off."

Perhaps his play-acting was affecting him as much as it affected her. Melissa was taken aback to hear him sharing such confidences with her. Her fists clenched at her sides in anger, picturing the childhood Anthony must have endured to make him feel this despondent.

"So, now you know the type of man you are marrying. Now you understand how I earned my name, the Lord of Wicked. It is well deserved."

"You are not wicked or evil or the devil, Anthony." She would not hear him talk of himself in that way.

Anthony hesitated as if searching for the right words. "Perhaps by marrying you, some of my sins will be offset by your goodness. Just promise me you won't let me corrupt you, too."

She digested his admission in silence. Is that why he was so determined to marry her? It wasn't concern for scandal, an obligation to the *ton*. He believed she could help him.

"I didn't realize," she said quietly, "that anyone could have had a worse childhood than me." The remembrance made her feel rather . . . small. How self-involved she had become, when in fact her upbringing, while lacking in any true emotional warmth, was nothing compared to what Anthony had suffered.

Melissa reached out and took his hand. "I am more than willing to listen. You have my shoulder to lean on. Slight though I may be, I can carry quite a load. I will share your burden."

She felt rather than saw him go still. Then Anthony shook his head abruptly, as if recollecting who she was. "They aren't tales for a lady's ears." His tone had turned suddenly grim, but she could sense his despair.

Ugly or not, Melissa wanted to hear them. The man sitting beside her was a stranger. A stranger she longed to understand. To unravel the psyche of such a complex man, she would gladly share his sins.

She barely remembered the second act. Her mind was too busy contemplating his unexpected attempt at openness. By the time the carriage drew up before Sudbury House, she had made her decision.

To help Anthony—and to help her—she would be brave and embrace his need for love. She knew he might never come to love her, but she would risk it. Risk everything. Now she knew her purpose in life. It was to heal a man who'd endured a life void of any tender feelings. Void of love.

She smiled and hugged herself . . . A man who needed her, yet didn't know it.

Philip, Baron Rothsay, was now in serious discomfort, rock-hard and desperate for release. He'd not had a good whipping for days.

There was enough light from the large number of candles illuminating the room to appear as if it was broad daylight instead of nearer to early dawn. He preferred to see every inch of the woman he amused himself with. He had to see their pleasure, and he thrived on seeing the pain he inflicted.

To him, pain was the world's most succinct aphrodisiac. He relished the giving and receiving of pain.

He'd used the woman standing before him numerous times. If he wasn't in such a heightened state of arousal he'd recommend they move to his town house. The room at club Spare the Rod was looking decidedly shabby. It had lost most of its grandeur since the last time he'd visited. He had not been in London for almost a year. He would be here for a week. He'd save inviting her to the dungeon he'd installed at his house for her next session.

Many would say he needed saving; however, years ago he'd sold his soul to the devil, and he had no complaints. His smile belied his true evil nature. As the devil's follower, he had no rules to pursue. He could do what he liked, when he liked, to anyone he liked. He felt a familiar adrenaline rush at the freedom having no conscience brought him.

His partner in pain for the early hours of the morning stood in thigh-high leather boots, completely naked except for her mask. He didn't need to remove her mask to know who she was. She'd asked for this liaison. He knew her well. He'd ridden her many times and still he never tired of her. That was unusual for a man like him. He'd learned years ago that everyone was disposable.

Perhaps it was her ferocious appetite for the perverted, the fact that it nearly overwhelmed his own. They shared equal desires for the giving and receiving of pain and pleasure. His groin throbbed thinking of her specialty, using his lighted cheroot to burn him as she rode magnificently above him. If he came before her, she'd whip him almost senseless. He'd often obliged.

Her whip hung around her neck like a beckoning diamond necklace. Not as valuable as diamonds, but the whip brought far greater pleasure . . . for both of them.

She spoke, her voice a gravelly entreaty that set the hairs

on his arms to prickling. "I am flattered you have come, Lord of Pain. I was not sure you'd desire me after so long."

He kept his smile even, neither confirming his pleasure at seeing her nor denying it. He simply began to remove his jacket, waistcoat, cravat, and shirt. Her masked face never left his as he undressed. "I would prefer less talk. I can think of more pleasurable things you could do with your mouth than talk." He unbuttoned his trousers and let his erection spring free. "Come here."

The leather of her boots crackled as she moved in sultry steps toward him. Her lush breasts swayed in time to her hips; her nipples had peaked into hard points at his words and the sight of his manhood. She moved to stand directly in front of him. Then she licked her lips. He grabbed the ends of the whip around her neck and roughly pulled her down, forcing her onto her knees before him.

"Take me, suck me, bite me." Rothsay yanked her hair hard, forcing her face to his groin. "I want to feel it all."

At the first lick of her tongue, his member surged against her face. Her mouth opened and slid down the full length of him. He squeezed his eyes shut and drove deeply into her throat. He could hear her gagging. He savored the sounds of her sucking him, but it was her first painful bite, her teeth sinking into his soft-hard flesh, that finally made him groan and shudder.

This is why he permitted himself to have her again and again. She was the only woman who knew how to give him the right amount of pain while sucking him dry—without turning him into a eunuch.

He gripped her hair harder and drove firmly into her mouth, his groin grinding her face. He loved the sound of her mixed cries of passion and her gagging. It drove his desire higher.

She knew what he would have planned for the evening. His arsenal of drugs would have him hard again within minutes. As her lips and tongue worked their magic, he pictured her above him. He couldn't wait for her to ride him with a cheroot between her lips, burning him when he least expected it. At the pictures forming before his eyes, he grabbed her head with two hands and drove deep down her throat. His seed spilled forth as she gagged and struggled to breathe.

He almost didn't let her up. If she wasn't so good at giving him pleasure, if she wasn't a lady of the *ton*, he might very well have simply suffocated her with his cock. He'd done that before. It simply added to his pleasure. But tonight he wanted more—she was lucky. Tomorrow morning, by the time he'd finished with her, she wouldn't feel so lucky. But she would have enjoyed herself. She was as twisted as he was—that is why she came back for more.

Rothsay let her go, and she fell backward in a heap on the floor gasping for breath.

His chest heaved with his ragged pants. "A most enjoyable performance, my dear. A good beginning to our evening." He moved to sit in a chair to begin removing his boots and the rest of his clothing.

The woman sat up slowly and gave him a devastating smile. She crawled across the floor, the leather boots whooshing in the thick carpet. He watched her heavy breasts swing as she moved toward him on all fours. He couldn't wait to get them in his mouth.

She helped him tug off his boots. "It is my pleasure to give you pleasure." She hesitated before adding with a roguish smile, "One good turn deserves another, don't you agree?"

He kept his face impassive, but inwardly he admired her chess-quality move. She was informing him she would let him use her body in whatever way he wished. His mind immediately filled with images perhaps even she would never comprehend. She expected something in return. Plus she had let him use her first. Giving him a taste of what she could do before playing her hand.

A strategy worthy of any man.

"You may be quite right, my dear." He sat back in the chair and studied her as she came up to her knees and slid her fingers up his thighs to grip his breeches and begin pulling them toward his ankles. "What is it you require of me?"

At his words, he felt her tremor of relief in the small fingers sliding on his legs. She must require help desperately to come to a man like him. Something illegal no doubt.

"I think you will find helping me would also bring you something your heart desires."

"I have many desires, but I can satisfy them whenever I want. No one can stop me."

"I know of one desire even you have been unable to fulfill."

He raised a cool eyebrow. "You have me even more intrigued. Go on."

"I need your expert help in removing an annoying obstacle."

He stirred in the chair. His hand reached out to stroke her breasts. "That does not seem so onerous; there must be more."

She shoved her breasts fully into his hands. "I need a woman disposed of. A lady of the *ton*."

He tweaked her hardened nipple. "A nobody is easy to dispose of. A woman of the *ton* is something else. Questions will be asked. A thorough investigation will be undertaken. Why would I be interested in risking the gallows? Even your skills are not worth that."

She smiled, the evil within escaping as her lips parted. "Because she is about to marry the Earl of Wickham."

He squeezed her nipple hard until she cried out in pain. Rothsay's breath caught in his throat. His stomach churned and his bile rose at the mention of Wickham's name. Wickham had sworn to him he'd never marry and father children. Like everything about the Earl, it was a falsehood. Wickham—he choked on the name. The one man who Philip had called friend. The one man who had turned his back on him. The one man he wanted to destroy—to bring to his knees. To inflict so much pain Wickham would never recover.

Now the woman on her knees before him handed him a weapon, but he'd not let her think she'd given him anything of interest. He did not like the fact she knew him even this well.

He sat up and pushed her out of his way. Rising to his feet, he kicked the trousers away that pooled at his ankles and stood staring down at her.

"Don't play with me, Cassandra." It was a measure of how unsettled he'd become. They never used real names.

On her knees, she walked to him and stroked his bare thighs. "I'm not playing. He was found in a compromising position with my cousin, Melissa Goodly, thinking he was in my bed. He has to marry her, but he does not want her. He told me he'd never bed her. It's obvious why. A frightened virgin would not interest a man with Wickham's appetite."

Rothsay knew exactly why Wickham would never bed a woman he was married to. He was terrified of siring the next Earl. God the man was pathetic.

Melissa Goodly, the woman with Wickham at the slave auction. The way Wickham had pushed her into the carriage before he could get a good look at her told Rothsay all he needed to know. The Earl felt something for her.

So Wickham still did not plan to have children. Philip's adrenaline surged. Here was his Achilles' heel. He almost burst with . . . could it be happiness? He'd never experienced that emotion before, and it was hard to recognize the senses reeling around his body.

He looked down on Cassandra, pretending contempt. He let it enter his stare. "Why would you be concerned at that? What is it you want?"

"I want Anthony for myself." Her skilled hand moved to fondle and squeeze his balls, making him groan in delicious pain. "I want him as my husband."

"Mmm . . . you mean you want his money."

She gasped.

He unwound the whip from around her neck and trailed it down over her breasts. "When will you learn, Cassandra dear? I know everything."

She tried to hide her flash of annoyance, but he caught it. This pleased him. She was more vicious when she was angry.

"I also want a real man in my bed, not some elderly fat lump that cannot pleasure me."

"Yes, you like to play rough. You'd likely kill an older gent. I wonder exactly how your husband died." He used the ends of the lash to tickle her taut nipples. "I think I can safely say I am thrilled at the information you have brought me."

"So, you will help me?"

"Leave everything to me." His shaft began to harden at the thought of taking his revenge on his longtime enemy. Not only that, he would also thwart Cassandra's plans. That gave him immense pleasure. His erection grew, lengthened, and hardened. He had no intention of stopping the wedding. His revenge would be all the sweeter once they were married.

He pulled Cassandra to her feet and bent her forward, placing her hands on the table in front of them. He brought the lash down firmly on her bare buttocks before forcing the whip handle between her legs and spreading them wide.

With no ceremony, he took her from behind, driving deep into her hot, wet sheath. "God you're so tight." She let out a moan of pleasure. He murmured, "Let me show you how grateful I am at the news you have brought me tonight." As she pressed her bottom more firmly against his groin, he brought the whip down hard on her back—the tassels made to sting, not mark, her flesh. She arched back up and gave a cry of ecstasy. He kept whipping her as he withdrew and slammed back into her.

He was suddenly glad he'd taken such a high dose of his wonder drug. He wanted to make this night last forever . . . imagining the slut he was whipping belonged to his dear old friend Anthony.

Chapter 12

The wedding took place early on Friday morning in Lord Wickham's rose garden with the local bishop residing. Images of what they'd done in this very garden made Melissa's heart thud in anticipation.

She couldn't wait to do it again.

There was an odd assortment of guests in attendance. The special license Anthony had obtained eliminated the necessity of reading the bands, yet most of London knew of the wedding and had jostled for invitations.

The ceremony was a solemn, swift affair, certainly not even remotely like the cherished ideal of her dreams. The groom in particular did not radiate happiness. He looked pale, as if he were about to be sick. The entire event seemed unreal to Melissa. She felt like an observer rather than the glowing bride.

She smoothed down the skirts of her high-waisted wedding gown. The soft ivory satin with a tulle overskirt shot with silver threads complemented the groom's superbly tailored blue coat, the silver matching the color of his eyes.

She could scarcely believe this was happening to her. After bearing the brunt of Christopher's rages at her refusal to marry a suitor of his choosing, a man who would ease his debts, here she was, repeating vows to love, honor, and obey the Lord of Wicked. A man she was completely infatuated with and already a little in love with.

She glanced covertly up at Anthony standing beside her. The sun glinted off his jet-black locks, but the warmth didn't reach his eyes. His face was hard and unsmiling. That he did not wish to marry her was humiliatingly obvious to everyone present. Melissa was thankful they'd come to some understanding. Although he did not love her, he did not hate her, either.

So far, the main point in Anthony's favor was his obvious desire for her. Without that, it would have been almost impossible for her to demonstrate her feelings and to shower him with love. There had to be something to base the relationship on. Knowing he wanted her in his bed, coupled with the fact he stirred all her senses, had been the deciding factor.

When it came time to declare her vows, she did so with unfettered passion. With all her heart she hoped love would blossom. Without love she'd once again be nothing more than a woman owned by a man, a wife to take care of and nothing more. Not really wanted and never loved.

Only she would know how much Anthony really needed her.

If she could ignite his passions, ignite them until he couldn't get enough of her, then she might stand a chance to make this a real marriage, a love marriage, a marriage to be proud of.

She wanted a family. A family of her own. A family where she truly felt she belonged.

With an unsteady breath, Melissa studied the immaculately groomed fingers of the large hand clasping her own. She knew the visceral images swirling in her mind were wicked when they were declaring themselves before God, but she couldn't wait to feel his fingers on her bare skin.

The only dart of unease piercing her outward calm was thinking this marriage was still not to his liking—not one tiny bit.

After all the guests had departed, Anthony walked into the drawing room, steeling himself against the rush of desire when he saw—his wife. He almost made a direct beeline to her side but checked himself. It wouldn't be wise to spend too much time with her.

He hesitated on the threshold wondering where to sit. Cassandra was still vying to become his mistress even though her cousin was now his wife. He'd promised Melissa not to indulge, and he meant to keep that promise. He owed her that at least.

The large room became deathly quiet at his entry. It had been a long day, and everyone looked a little weary.

His mother, seated next to Melissa, paused in her conversation. A shiver of dread raced from his neck, along his arms, and down to his fingers. God knows what stories his mother was filling Melissa's head with. If Melissa was not pleased with her situation, she'd be even more distraught after his mother informed her of all the family's darkest secrets.

Halting close to the threshold, Anthony surveyed the cast in this marriage travesty. Baron Norrington, Melissa's brother, looked extremely smug. So he should; he'd fleeced Anthony out of twenty thousand pounds. Christopher was in for a shock if he thought Anthony would hand over any more. If the Baron gambled away Anthony's generous marriage settlement, he could rot in one of London's workhouses for all Anthony cared.

Anthony had very deep pockets. The increase in world commerce meant the Wickham fortune had not diminished when Anthony put a halt to his father's slave-trading venture, switching to wool and coal. In fact, he'd managed to quadruple the family money not merely by increasing his trading business but by making sound investments. He had no intention of throwing his money away on Christopher Goodly.

He saw Richard was in residence. Anthony was still as mad as hell at what his brother had done. But he realized Richard had no understanding of his inner torments and thought he had been helping. Richard sat in the chair by the fire, staring into the flames, no doubt racked with guilt over his treachery. Good. It wouldn't hurt for Richard to experience a little suffering for a change.

Cassandra was seated next to Christopher, a frown marring her beautiful face. Upon seeing him enter, her frown eased into an uncertain smile.

Dismissing her, he spied the powerful grande dame seated beside his mother and swore beneath his breath. His mother had called in reinforcements.

Lady Horsham wielded more power, political and social, than any other lady of the *ton*. Whatever she decreed, Society would support. Anthony respected her. His father had taught him the meek did not inherit the earth. Seeing Lady Horsham's rise to power, he well believed it.

He walked to the chaise, inclined his head to Melissa, his mother, and Lady Elizabeth Horsham.

His mother's intensely blue eyes—true indigo—fixed on his face. "I was just discussing with Lady Horsham the events you and Melissa should attend."

He stiffened to stop his shoulders from flinching. Then bowing to his mother's acquaintance, he took the bony-gloved hand the silver-haired woman offered, careful not to overdo the observance. She had never been fond of his father, nor of him. "Lady Horsham, a pleasure as always."

"Congratulations on your nuptials." Lady Horsham's droopy brown eyes studied him for a moment. "About time you were married."

He inclined his head and declined to rise to her lure.

She gave a cluck. "Whatever the circumstances, you have made yourself a fine match. Your bride has a good head on her shoulders. She complements you."

Anthony arched an eyebrow.

"Don't give me that dark scowl. You're all fiery temper. She's calm, moderate, and thinks before she acts." Lady Horsham turned her gaze on Melissa. "Fine children you'll make together."

Swallowing his horror at those words, he moved and took a chair across from Melissa, leaving his mother to pick up the conversation.

"Lady Horsham is fully supportive of your marriage. She has agreed to pacify the gossips."

Richard coughed. Anthony silently agreed with his brother's assessment; no one would believe any story Lady Horsham told, but they would never dare to openly show their incredulity. Not when Lady Horsham was endorsing the version.

"Thank you, Lady Horsham. I personally don't care what the *ton* thinks, but my wife isn't keen to be the subject of gossip."

"I told you she is too levelheaded by far to let a little scandal destroy her." The Baroness sniffed. "By the time I'm finished with her, Melissa will be the *ton*'s latest darling." She turned to Christopher. "If you'd spent less at the gaming table and more on ensuring your sister was appropriately attired, she would have been married long ago."

Christopher's face reddened.

Melissa quickly jumped in. "Lady Horsham, it would not have made any difference. I was waiting for the right man."

Lady Horsham chuckled. "How the young think. Don't be foolish, gal. There is no such thing as the right man—only a man who can be molded into the right man." She flashed a grin at Anthony. "Lady Wickham, I do believe you have caught yourself one. Now it is up to you to ensure he becomes all that he can."

Melissa's face paled.

Lady Horsham reached over and patted the bride's hand. "I have every faith in you."

Melissa's eyes locked with Anthony's. He felt something stir deep inside him as her lips curved into a smile blatantly challenging. "You may be right, Lady Horsham. Perhaps I can make something of him."

He couldn't pull his gaze away. His senses, ensorcelled simply by her look, refused to ignore her. Noting the silence in the room and all the pairs of eyes on them, Anthony felt his throat constrict. The tension was thrumming through the room when Stevens announced a late luncheon was served. *Thank God.* Anthony leaped to his feet. However, he was not to be spared. His mother's look clearly indicated he was expected to escort his wife.

Reluctantly he moved to his wife's side. At the touch of her hand on his arm, he reacted like a stallion sensing a mare in heat. He did not understand it. She wasn't doing anything to attract his attention, and her dress was modest, with very little cleavage showing.

It was the smile. It was her knowing smile. A smile that said *"I have power over you. Should I choose to use it, you will be at my mercy."* With an effort, he hauled his mind back from dwelling on the loveliness inside her demure gown, from the image of her curled naked against him, and surrendered to duty and strolled with her toward the dining room. The lingering elusive, wantonly feminine scent of her was making his task extremely difficult, and it was with thanks he took his seat at the head of the table to hide the growing evidence of the effect his wife had on a certain part of his anatomy.

The late luncheon proved to be a torturous affair. His groin ached, his head hurt from trying to ignore Melissa's presence, and every pair of eyes around the table watched him with growing amusement.

His gaze tracked to Richard, seated at the other end of the table next to Melissa. Whatever he was saying to her, Richard was keeping her amused. She was relaxed, smiling up at her new brother-in-law. An emotion akin to envy snaked through him. Melissa had never gifted him that type of smile. This was an open, friendly, unguarded smile, and happiness illuminated her beautiful face.

He gripped the stem of his wineglass until he thought it might break. What was Richard playing at? Did he have designs on Melissa? He frowned. It was true, as brothers they'd often shared women, but surely Richard did not believe his generosity applied equally to his wife.

Why did he care? He never cared. One woman was much the same as another. An all-consuming possessiveness attacked his system without warning. Melissa was his wife. She was his.

Emotions swirled around him. When Melissa reached and put her hand on Richard's arm, obviously trying to stop his teasing, a fist clamped about Anthony's heart. The effort not to react—not to snarl and show his teeth—stole his breath. His heart thundered in his chest.

As if his glare scorched Richard, his twin blinked at him. Then Richard smiled and shook his head as if to say, "*Don't be stupid.*" Their gazes locked and held an instant longer.

Anthony's heart began to calm its frantic beating, clearly seeing the denial in his brother's eyes. Even after what Richard did to him, Anthony instinctively knew his twin would never betray him when it came to Melissa.

He returned to his lobster curry and made conversation with his mother, who was seated to his right.

Finally, once they had eaten far too much, his mother led the ladies back to the drawing room, leaving the three men to enjoy a smoke.

With his wife not in the room, Anthony could relax. He walked to the sideboard, filled his glass with a shot of whiskey, and gulped it back. With a refill, he turned and flopped back in his seat. Christopher had taken his mother's chair, and Richard took the seat on his left. Both men opted for whiskey, too. The three sat in silence, savoring the smoky liquor.

After a minute Richard's brows rose. "Something bothering you, brother?"

"No."

"I could have sworn earlier during the meal, you were about to leap from your chair and stab me with your knife." He smiled knowingly. "I have never seen my brother jealous before."

"It was not jealousy igniting my temper."

"Was it not? Then pray tell, what has you so riled up?"

Anthony took a sip of his drink before answering, his voice all but a rough growl. "It's simply that since my betrothal, I have not had enough physical exercise of a personal nature."

"Sex? Abstinence, they say, is good for the soul."

"As if you'd know." Anthony scoffed at his brother. "Abstinence annoys the soul and is hell on the temper."

"Ah, well—it will only be an hour more," Richard added with a knowing smile.

Anthony gritted his teeth. That was what was worrying him. The sexual abrasion of her nearness was a constant reminder that being near her, without touching her, or wanting her, was like living in his own personal hell.

The silence lengthened.

"You do desire her?" Richard stammered. "I—I mean, she's a beautiful woman. I'd hate to think I'd selected a woman who did not—let's say—have you rising to the occasion."

If only his brother knew. Richard had picked well—too well. "I don't think you have any worries on that score."

Richard sat back in his chair and sighed. "Thank goodness. So, it shouldn't be long before the heir of the Wickham dynasty arrives."

Anthony remained silent. What could he say to that? *I won't be sleeping with my wife!* Richard would never understand. Besides, who he chose to sleep with—or in this case not sleep with—was no one's business but his own.

Anthony remembered his childhood; the memories ate at him every day. For years he'd thought he was a wicked child, that that must be why his father didn't love him, and why he was punished so severely for any minor misdemeanor.

Every time he tried to get close, his father pushed him away, or worse, physically beat him away. Soft and loving emotions were not to be tolerated.

Looking back, he cringed at the pathetic attempts he'd made to gain his father's approval and love. He'd soon learned that his father didn't have a heart.

On one particular occasion, at the age of eight, Anthony had been thrilled when his father had consented to allow him one of the orphaned pet lambs to keep as his own. He'd named the lamb Little John. He'd play for hours in the hay barn with Little John; his role was always Robin Hood. Together they'd fight the wicked Sheriff of Nottingham. In his mind's eye, the sheriff had always resembled his father.

After one afternoon of thrashing the sheriff, Anthony was summoned before his father and told that tomorrow they would be slaughtering his lamb. The Earl's hunting hounds needed food.

He begged and pleaded with his father not to take his friend. As his tears fell in streams down his face, Tony coldly told him to be a man. But sobbing Anthony begged for Little John's life.

"All right," his father said. "I won't let Carter kill the lamb."

Anthony's heart burst with joy. At his happy face, his father sneered, "Carter won't kill the lamb; you will."

The next morning Anthony had been forced to slit Little John's throat. If he didn't do the deed, his father was going to whip Richard, in front of him, until Anthony gave in and did as he was told.

It wasn't until Anthony was much older that he'd realized his father had given him the lamb with the intention of making him kill it. He let him befriend Little John, grow to love it, and then forced him to kill it, simply to teach him a lesson. Don't let emotion enter your life. If you do, you're at its mercy. He'd never given his heart to another living thing since that day.

Even now, he kept his heart all to himself. If he loved his brother once, he couldn't remember the emotion. He . . . liked his brother, only because Richard was his exact opposite.

If he had a child, he would like it, too. But he knew how it felt to have a cold man for a father. He wouldn't want that for his own child. He knew he was incapable of giving the child what it would need. He wouldn't know how. And he didn't want to know, didn't want to feel any type of weak emotion.

If he felt, all those innocent lives he'd hurt would haunt him even more than they did already. Christ! He wouldn't be able to survive the guilt and horror.

What's more, he couldn't live with the knowledge that his children would grow to despise him. He hated his father with more passion than it took to love. Hate was an easy emotion. It took nothing from him. In fact, it simply gave him strength to endure, to survive, to win.

Love was castrating. It grabbed you by the balls and made you a prisoner. It made you petrified of loss. It made you weak and exposed your fears. Love destroyed; hate helped you to survive.

Christopher interrupted his morose memories. "Richard, I would be happy to escort you to Madame Sabine's tonight. I hear she has some new talent in from Paris. Perhaps later, after Anthony has performed his husbandry duties, he'd like to join us."

Anthony's hand fisted on his thigh. He'd just married the man's sister, and yet Christopher didn't seem to care what became of Melissa. "Melissa may have different views on how I conduct myself within marriage."

"Don't be ridiculous. She's a woman. She will expect you to keep a mistress. Cassandra has already informed Melissa she is willing to take on the role to save her indelicacies."

"Did my dear bride agree?" Anthony's temper hummed, vibrated in his chest. "What else do you think Cassandra will have taught her? How to cuckold a husband?"

"I'm sure Cassandra has explained to Melissa what is expected of her in the marriage bed," Christopher babbled, not realizing the danger he was walking into. "Apparently she was unnerved by her—by your—that is the night you were caught in her bed. Cassandra promised me she'd soothe Melissa's mind about . . . ah . . . er . . . your size."

Richard jumped in with a short laugh. "Soothe her mind? What on earth are you talking about? The deed's been done. Anthony has already taken her virginity. It should be plain sailing—"

"Enough! It's my wife we are discussing."

Christopher stumbled on. "I wouldn't worry. You'll only have to bed her until she's with child. There will be plenty of women willing to warm your bed the rest of the time."

Anthony's temper hum headed toward a full symphony.

Muttering to himself he said, "And whose bed will Melissa be warming?"

"Pardon?" Christopher cocked his head. "I didn't quite catch that."

"Just ensure Cassandra doesn't teach my bride any games played outside of the marriage bed." At Christopher's shocked expression, Anthony narrowed his lids and growled. "I wouldn't want to hurt your sister, but I will if she cuckolds me . . ."

Richard chuckled as if he heard a joke. "Relax, Anthony. I'm sure Melissa wouldn't dishonor you or herself with a tacky illicit affair."

"I agree," Christopher said. "She's infatuated with you if you haven't noticed. That's why I've had a devil of a time trying to interest her in any other match. Since the start of the Season, she's only had eyes for you."

"Don't be ridiculous. I only met her a few nights ago."

With closed eyes and head back on the chair rest, Richard lazily drawled, "You're wrong, brother. You met her at Lord Moning's ball. Why do you think I instigated my plan? I caught her worshipping you from afar. I would never have set her up to be compromised if I didn't think she'd have welcomed the match."

Bloody hell! This changed everything. He couldn't let himself enjoy any physical pleasure with Melissa. It would leave her wanting more, wanting him, wanting everything. He was incapable of tender emotions, but he wasn't heartless or stupid. He didn't want to deliberately hurt her, and he didn't want to encourage her fairy-tale dream. He lusted after her, but he didn't want a wife who was infatuated with him. When emotions were involved, sex became complicated. He must simplify everything . . . tonight.

Melissa knew something was wrong the minute the men rejoined the ladies in the drawing room. Anthony's intense gaze locked on to hers. His held no warmth and his lips were thinned, hard and angry.

Cassandra decided to take an interest now the men had returned. She moved away from where she had been staring into the fire to sit on the settee across from Melissa. Lady Horsham and the Dowager Countess of Wickham sat on another settee, leaving room for Anthony to sit next to her on the day couch. She inwardly cringed at the obvious move.

Melissa resisted the urge to twist her hands in her lap.

"We saved you a seat beside Melissa," Lady Horsham told Anthony.

Melissa watched Anthony hesitate, saw the moment of indecision. He did not want to sit next to her. She could see the truth of it in the tenseness of his body. Unable to politely refuse, he took the space beside her, careful not to let any part of him touch her.

Melissa's mouth felt dry, and words stuck in her throat. She didn't know what to say to a man who radiated so much anger. She glanced at her brother, who, taking the seat next to Cassandra, was whispering low and urgently in Cassandra's ear. Melissa prayed her brother had not upset Anthony.

With what she hoped was a delightful smile on her face, rather than a scared grimace, she said, "We are to attend a luncheon put on by the Duke of Richmond tomorrow. I hope the fine weather holds."

He nodded. "I am to meet with my mother tomorrow morning to apprise myself of our public calendar," he said smoothly as he flicked a piece of lint off his trousers, not bothering to hide his boredom.

She swallowed the instant bolt of anger. It was hardly fair of him to take his displeasure at this marriage out on her. It was not she who had hopped into the wrong bed.

She bit her tongue to stop herself issuing an angry retort. Not in front of family and Lady Horsham. She would wait until she got him alone.

He moved, and his thigh briefly brushed her leg through the silk material of her skirts. Heat flared and her belly clenched. She struggled to remain composed as her mind brought forth the image of his naked torso propped against her headboard.

Soon, he would expect to become intimate with her. She'd been studying her book diligently. To have a remote chance at claiming his heart, she had to become a sensual siren.

Lord help her.

Still, she couldn't wait to practice her learnings on Anthony. If Madame du Barry could capture a king, she hoped her untutored knowledge could at least ensnare her husband's interest long enough for her to practice. After all, practice makes perfect.

Her eyes wandered over his form. She would enjoy the practice. Melissa remembered the twin ropes of muscle that cut his lower stomach and had disappeared under the sheet, beckoning her eyes to follow. He had the most perfect male body. Wide shoulders, a steel velvet chest with rippling stomach.

A wave of lust made her dizzy, and she breathed deeply to slow her pounding heart. She remembered every single detail about their one night together. His hard body holding hers, his hands roaming every inch of her, and the feel of his rough, naked skin.

Her face flushed with color now as his obsidian eyes met hers. As if he could read her thoughts, and didn't like what he discovered, his full lips thinned and his face grew dark and foreboding.

He stiffened beside her and then rose. "Ladies, if you'll excuse me, I have a previous engagement to attend."

Anthony's mother pierced him with a cold, brittle look. "But this is your wedding day."

"This wedding was unexpected, and I am committed." His voice seemed to suck the warmth from the room. "I have business that urgently needs attending."

Christopher choked on a laugh. "Oh, yes, I'll say. The gentleman's business we discussed earlier, no doubt. I shall join you."

Dowager Wickham would not let it rest. "And what business is so urgent that it must be discussed tonight?"

Anthony stood and bowed to the ladies; then he swung back to stare at his mother. Melissa felt herself shrink back against the settee, but his mother seemed to brazen out his mocking smile. "Do you really want me to spell it out, Mother, in front of company? I will if that is what you wish. I am doing what I do most nights; my marriage does not alter a thing."

Lady Horsham gasped.

Richard jerked in his chair. "There is no need for this, Anthony."

The dowager's lips pursed into a thin line of disapproval. "Well, really."

It took Melissa a few seconds to gather her wits before she understood the implications of his statement. He was going to a pleasure club or to his mistress. No, not a mistress. He'd been chasing Cassandra to fill that role.

Hurt knifed through her until every inch of skin exuded pain. Her stomach heaved and she fought down the bile. *"My marriage alters nothing . . ."* He had deliberately embarrassed her in front of everyone. She threw a glance at him. His eyes glittered in the light from the candles, hard like diamonds, his face a mask of indifference. She would never forgive him.

Melissa lowered her eyes and smoothed her skirts, but she refused to rise to his obvious bait. He'd been in a fowl temper the minute he'd stepped into the room. She would not let him see how much his words hurt her.

She rose to her feet. "It has been a long day." Flicking him a look of utter contempt she added, "Due to a rude and unwanted intrusion, I haven't slept much the last few nights. If you excuse me, I shall retire for the evening."

As she turned to leave, she felt a small measure of satisfaction at the look of astonishment on his face and the delicate laugh from Lady Horsham.

Lady Horsham's words floated softly behind her as she left the room, "Oh, yes, you might just have met your match, my boy. I can't wait to see how this marriage progresses."

Chapter 13

Anthony grudgingly admired Melissa's response to his abysmal behavior. Her back straight, her head high, she swept from the room like a princess.

It wasn't quite the reaction he expected, but he'd caught the flash of hurt in her eyes. Good. He must destroy her infatuation with him. Then she'd never love him. He didn't need an irritating love-struck wife demanding his time.

Richard shook his head at him. Anthony shrugged and stared him down, before the men followed Melissa from the room.

As he walked out into the night, he didn't know what he was more annoyed about. His brother's sanctimonious proffering as he accompanied him or his niggle of conscience about the petty wound he'd inflicted on Melissa.

Hours later, Melissa lay curled up in her bed, watching the fire sputter and spark in the white marble fireplace, her mind racing, imagining what Anthony was doing . . . with other women.

She would not cry—she would not cry—she would not . . .

If she said it often enough, the tears might not flow.

Unlike her, the women he was now with knew how to pleasure him. Knew what a man of his appetites would want, would need. She'd never keep a man like Anthony interested. He would undoubtedly always seek his pleasures elsewhere.

That was the message he had sent her tonight. She was not to expect fidelity in their marriage.

Did he think she was a halfwit? She knew a man dubbed the Lord of Wicked would not take the vows of marriage seriously. But this was her wedding night.

Torn between hurt and anger, tears finally spilled down her face. She smeared them away with the back of her hand. Crying and feeling sorry for herself wouldn't solve anything. She'd married a man who wanted nothing from his wife . . . save perhaps an heir.

Well, she was no broodmare. She wanted a man to love and cherish her. A man who would never intentionally hurt her.

A tear slipped from her eye. She snuggled deeper into the down covers, cold with fear. She gulped back a sob. Could a man filled with passion, angst, and sensuality come to love? He needed the right encouragement, a reason to open his heart. She knew there was goodness in him; he could have left her to her ruin. He could have turned his back on Alice and Theresa, but he hadn't.

Did he have a heart? Was she brave enough to risk finding out? She chewed on her bottom lip. If she set out to entice him into love, she would be the one risking everything. He'd been deliberately cruel tonight, warning her not to get too close.

What was he afraid of? And he was afraid. Analyzing his actions after dinner, Melissa clearly saw the fear that had filled his eyes. That's why he tried to push her away. That's what the scene in the drawing room had been all about.

She would most certainly have to be fearless for both of them. Well, she told herself, she needed her sleep so her wits would be sharp tomorrow. Tomorrow she had a husband to woo.

Somehow she'd have to work out how to make the Lord of Wicked desire her. *You must make him desire you, want you . . .* Richard's words were her final, slightly wistful, and utterly ridiculous thought before she drifted off.

*   *   *

Anthony paused in the doorway of Madame Sabine's sin club, forcibly repressing his sense of right and wrong, surprised at the layers of guilt cloaking him. He was, after all, a man. He was entitled to indulge.

The elegant drawing room glittered under the crystal chandeliers and pulsed with the gaiety of satisfied guests. It was still early, so the club had yet to fill with the smell of smoke and stale body odor. Instead, women's perfume scented the air, tickling his senses. Coupled with the female flesh blatantly displayed, his body stirred with a restless hunger.

"I'd forgotten how wonderful this place was," remarked Christopher as he grabbed a passing young blonde whose charms could be seen through a transparent silk negligee. "I shall see you gentlemen later." Anthony waved a careless hand and turned away, determined to enjoy himself. But Melissa's face popped in his head, and the memory of her pain-filled eyes made him grit his teeth.

Blast the woman. He'd enjoyed this club more than any other London hell—

"Brings back happy memories, does it not?" his brother quietly said in his ear. "Are you of a mind to indulge tonight of womanly charms or gaming—or perhaps both?"

He didn't like the sound of the challenge in his brother's voice. Setting his jaw, Anthony strolled into the room. Almost immediately, he spied the evening's prime entertainment. He halted, and Richard almost stumbled into him. Their gazes were drawn to the dais at the far end of the room, where two nude beauties were onstage lustily cavorting with each other. One had her head buried between the other's thighs, lapping her with a long, talented tongue to tempt the avidly watching gentlemen in the audience.

Anthony's annoyance grew. In his wilder days, he would have joined the beauties onstage. But his mind swirled with images and thoughts of Melissa. He pictured her as she'd been when he'd mistakenly slipped into her bed. Had he not been so lustful, he should have noticed how innocent she acted. But he was caught by her eagerness and delightful inhibition. Compared to her freshness, scenes like this one lost their appeal and roused little more than a feeling of disgust in him. Melissa had given him a taste of something other than mindless sexual gratification. She'd given him a taste of innocence.

If he were to indulge in a fantasy such as this one being enacted onstage, he would replace the beauties with one specific woman.

The image of Melissa, naked and on her back, her thick black tresses spread out across his pillows, was arousing enough to make Anthony instantly hard.

Damn her. She was like a shot of opium in his blood.

"The gaming is more to my taste tonight," he growled, and headed to a table in the far room.

Anthony would not have been pleased to see the triumphant, knowing smile curve upon Richard's face as he watched him move toward the card table. Richard said below his breath, "That's a first." He followed, then, careful to keep his victory concealed from his eyes, took the seat next to his twin, saying, "There is hope for you yet, brother."

Anthony played through the night and into the early hours of the morning with a fervor nobody missed. He played frantically, betting wildly, mainly to distract himself from his fantasy about Melissa.

It unnerved him that in a house filled with enticing, sensual, and beautiful women, he couldn't prevent his erotic musings—the pictures of him ravishing Melissa—from invading his mind.

It unnerved him that she had feelings for him. He was flummoxed; he was used to grasping and shallow beauties, who pursued him for his title and fortune. God knew, her brother needed his fortune, but she'd still refused to trap him into matrimony. She would have let him dishonor her and walk away. He couldn't in all honesty say he hadn't thought about snatching her offer with all that he had—hands, feet, teeth . . . Melissa Goodly was unlike any woman he'd ever known.

That's what scared him. He didn't know how to deal with her.

He couldn't recall any woman who was less afraid of him. Nor could he remember one who actually dealt with him as an equal, without trying to impress him or control him.

She *was* beautiful. But that didn't explain why he wanted her so badly. Why he lusted after her almost to the point of obsession. There were plenty of beautiful and available women—he looked around him—here for instance. Women who'd do almost anything he asked without ties or commitment or risk of producing the next Earl of Wickham.

More likely it was the forbidden fruit aspect that was attracting him so strongly to Melissa.

He would resist her delights, and tomorrow, search for a new mistress. A woman who'd sate his desires and leave him immune to his wife's temptations.

He looked around. He could start the hunt now. What better place than a sin club? As he gazed with heated blood at the naked rouged flesh on display, Melissa's face flooded his mind. He pulled at his cuffs.

"Something bothering you?" his brother asked. "You've lost quite a lot of money tonight. That isn't like you. Perhaps we should move to the settee to enjoy other entertainments."

Anthony eyed the curvaceous redhead lying completely naked, prone, upon the divan against the far wall. At his stare, her lips parted in a beckoning smile, and her tongue slipped out from between moist pink lips. She swung her legs down to the floor and parted them, running her hand provocatively down between her thighs.

He hardened immediately at her blatant sexual invitation.

"She is a beauty, is she not, my lord?" Sabine's husky feminine voice whispered in his ear as he sat, eyes firmly entranced by the woman pleasuring herself directly across from him. He had not seen or heard the Madam's approach. "I trust your marriage won't diminish your attendance here. I'd hate to lose my best customer—so would Karla. As you can see she's a true redhead."

Anthony grinned. "My compliments, love, on your exquisite taste in women. As a matter of fact I might be in the market for a new mistress."

Richard shoved back his chair. "Since when?"

"I am always open to offers for one of my girls." Sabine smiled, money her favorite topic. "I'm pleased your marriage has not diminished your appetite."

"I have no desire to be tamed, and I prefer my women wild and willing."

"Karla will be as wild as you require. She doesn't look as if she's far from orgasm. You'd disappoint my other patrons if you interrupted her now."

Both Anthony and his brother swiveled their heads to watch Karla, along with every other man in the room. Her breasts were heaving, her eyes were closed. Her hips were gyrating wildly, lifting off the couch as her fingers disappeared between her wet, glistening folds. She was emitting soft cries of passion, and for the first time in his life, Anthony was not aroused.

She came with one final scream and slumped back against the settee to a round of applause and catcalls.

He couldn't hide from the truth, he, the infamous Lord of Wicked, was not in the mood for a woman . . . other than his wife.

So he shook his head, feigning regret. "Richard advising caution is probably sound advice. For the moment, I should remain faithful. The gossips have been fed enough tantalizing details for now. After a few weeks, the matter will be another question entirely."

"Of course, my lord. Then I shall let you get back to your cards."

Once Sabine left, Richard leaned close. "A most provocative display. Did it not tempt you?"

"It's late. I'm tired. If you want her, take her."

"Tired. I see."

He resented the knowing look in his brother's eye. Richard knew damn well Anthony would normally have to be dying before he turned down an opportunity to be serviced by a woman of such obvious skills and beauty.

He pushed back his chair and stood. "I'm going home. Are you coming?"

Richard smiled and cocked his head at Karla. "I think I'll stay and play a while. At least one of us should be satisfied tonight."

Anthony left the club to Richard's laughter ringing in his ears.

Chapter 14

Anthony loathed balls of any kind, especially one where he and his hurried nuptials where the raging topic of conversation. He couldn't blame them.

His trip to Madame Sabine's, on his wedding night, had added fuel to the fire. *Idiot!*

He propped one shoulder against the fashionable matron's wall covered in the latest Parisian designs. He had no idea whose house he was in, nor did he care. Over the heads of the assembled throng, he studied Melissa across the room.

His wife needed none of the frippery or jewels that so many women seemed to prefer. Her plain, elegant, yet somehow seductive apricot-colored dress clung to her curves. Diamonds couldn't be more alluring.

Her curls shone midnight black in the candlelight, piled loosely upon her head, with artfully arranged pieces twinning over her shoulders to rest directly above her lily-white breasts.

She was a woman of elegance and simplicity, and Anthony admired her taste.

He shook his head. Admired?

His teeth still ground at the memory of her calm acceptance at his behavior last night. This morning, she'd acted as if there was nothing unusual about a husband not sharing his wife's bed on their wedding night.

For once, he was grateful the crowd packing the ballroom

gave him adequate cover. *Coward. You needed to converse with her.*

The wolves were circling.

He was in no mood to act the happy husband for the *ton*. He'd never cared one whit what anyone thought of him. Society had never cared for him; he certainly owed them nothing.

From the look of it, his Countess had forgotten him, her smiles charming every man in her vicinity. She did not understand they hovered for one reason only.

His more primitive self observed the men gathering about her through ever-narrowing eyes. When Lord Carthors swanned into contention, he inwardly swore. The rakes smelled blood—virginal blood. They knew he'd compromised Melissa and thought he didn't care about her. Plus, she was Cassandra's cousin. Men would likely think that Melissa was as enthusiastic for the sport as Cassandra.

Leaving her unattended was paramount to feeding her to the sharks. His mother's warning had been correct.

Anthony was just about to push away from the wall and head in her direction when he felt delicate feminine fingers lightly touch his arm.

"Do you love her?"

A storm brewed in his chest. How dare anyone ask him such an impertinent question? Love? Love was a fleeting emotion used to appease women who wanted an excuse to indulge in passion. Once the desire was gone, love died as quickly as the passion.

He turned to set the interloper in her place, but his harsh words died when he saw the look of hope on her sweet face. She took a step back when noting the scowl covering his.

She stammered, "I'm sorry. I have been observing you watching her. I am not usually so forward, but Melissa means the world to me and I would see her happy."

He stood silently assessing the young woman before him. She was tall, slender, with a full bosom. She was dressed in a rich blue dress that matched the color of her soulful eyes. She could be a very pretty distraction. Why had he not noticed her before? Her auburn hair glinted in the flickering candlelight. "Lady Albany, is it not?"

She nodded her head. "She loves you, you see, and I would not see her hurt."

Not only was the woman totally impertinent, she was rude with it. "For a lady I have never had the pleasure of knowing either in the biblical sense or otherwise, you seem to have no trouble attacking my character. Are you implying that I'd intentionally hurt her?"

Her face flushed with color. "Hurt is not always caused by the physical. Men do not always understand how easily they can wound, with a simple look or gesture."

"Come now. Melissa is made of sterner stuff than that."

"Forgive me. Obviously, I've made a grievous mistake in approaching you. I see that Melissa is simply another woman fooled by a handsome face and pretty lies. Like most gentlemen, you do not value that which you so easily gain." She moved close, her chin lifting. "Do not hurt her, or I will do everything in my power to make your life miserable."

He bit back the urge to laugh, her threat running off his back like bathwater. "I think you have been misinformed, my lady. She does not like me, let alone love me."

"Then you must have done something recently to earn her dislike."

"Nothing that any man has not done before me."

"And that makes it right?" Her distaste was obvious. "You should take the time to learn the character of the woman you have been so fortunate to compromise." She scornfully looked him up and down. "I pity you. You have won the most precious gift, yet you don't have the courage to embrace it."

He pushed off the wall and came to tower over her. "You go too far, Lady Albany. You may talk to your husband in that manner, but you will find I do not countenance insolence from anyone."

She glared right back. "I find I don't talk to my husband at all. It makes for a very tiresome marriage. I suggest that you don't make the same mistake. If you are man enough, get to know Melissa before discarding her, before trying to closet her at one of your country estates." With that she gave him her back and glided away.

Anthony stared at Lady Albany's straight spine as she walked away. Taking deep breaths, he clenched and un-clenched his fists at his side. How had she known his plan?

Stirring, he moved to the edge of the dance floor and grabbed a drink from a passing servant. *If he was man enough!* Who the hell did Lady Albany think she was?

She's in love with you . . . Lady Albany was the second person to make such a claim. He gazed across at Melissa and drunk her in. She looked perfectly content, fending off the bucks surrounding her. He remembered back to the night he had mistakenly ended up in her bed. She'd had plenty of men vying for her attention that night, too. She had calmly held court, very practiced at dealing with those who became overly familiar, Lord Dashell being one of them.

Anthony seriously doubted that Melissa understood just how appealing the rakes within the *ton* found her calm, con-tained, disposition. Her ability to remain unfretted, with a cool demeanor, was having her would-be suitors lining up to accept her challenge. To be the man to make her lose control. To claim the honor of her passionate surrender.

Her behavior had established her as a prize to be won, and with the added gossip of her fall into his bed, the vultures who circled her were perfectly cognizant of the intangible ca-chet attached to winning her favors.

Unlike the gentlemen hovering around her like bees to a honey pot, he knew the exquisite pleasure of seeing her cool façade fracture as she surrendered herself to passion.

His temper bubbled up to the surface again. Lady Albany was right about one thing, Melissa was a gift. A gift wrapped and ready to open, but a gift to be opened only by him.

He headed in her direction ready to do battle with any man who thought otherwise.

As he strolled down the ballroom toward Melissa, he thought it ironic that under normal circumstances he would be assessing the room and the house for places where he might later whisk a lady who'd caught his eye, so that he might indulge in his favorite pastime—pleasure. Tonight, the lady who currently commanded his attention—every bit of his anatomy stood to attention as his primal male possessiveness emerged—he was more concerned with avoiding precisely those same pleasures.

He gritted his teeth and willed his sex to quiet down. The last thing he needed was for his wife to think she held any sway over him—any part of him.

Melissa was holding her own against an annoying clutch of rakes when she glimpsed Anthony through the crowd. A whirl of emotions stole her breath, making her momentarily dizzy.

Trepidation, excitement, and a seductive thrill were a novel and unsettling mix. How could she be so angry with him, yet still be so delighted to see him?

She could tell from the scowl marring his features that he was not in an appealing mood. What on earth had she done wrong this time? She had stayed away from him, as directed the last time he'd deigned to talk to her, which had been early this afternoon.

Sternly ordering her stupid senses to buck up, she refocused on Lord Carthor's tale. He was presently holding forth on the lawlessness that was invading the lower class in London, having had his late father's pocket watch stolen by pickpockets last evening as he arrived at the theater.

The fact that most of the inhabitants flooding London's streets lived in abject poverty, and stole simply to survive, seemed to have escaped his lordship's notice.

Being the rogue that he was, however, just as he was expounding on the dangers of ladies traveling the streets unescorted, something she would not be stupid enough to do, he picked up her hand and placed a kiss upon it, declaring that it was not even safe for ladies to travel even if adequately escorted. Melissa prayed he would release her hand before she had to make a scene and vigorously pull it out of his grasp. As Lord Carthors was about to open his mouth, a deep, menacing voice interjected.

"If anyone is to escort my mother and my wife home this evening it will be me." A dark foreboding eyebrow lifted. "Unless of course you'd like to make my evening and argue over who has the right to that pleasure. It is too long since I have let my temper unleash and had the satisfaction of a good fight."

A snort sounded on Melissa's right—Lord Smithers, another rake of the first order, was smothering a laugh.

The younger gentleman knew when to retreat, and they made a space for Anthony beside her. That left her flanked by Anthony and Carthors.

Thinking to ease the tension, she smiled at Anthony and gave him the hand Carthors had dropped as if she had leprosy. Anthony bowed and placed a lingering kiss on her gloved hand, the pressure such that she could feel his lips all the way through the material. Her skin went all prickly as if she'd just dipped her bare toe into a cold fountain in midwinter. What was he doing?

"It seems rather stuffy in here." Carthors was not as stupid as he first appeared. "Please excuse me, Lady Wickham. I feel in need of some fresh air." He bowed. After a nod of her head, Lord Carthors disappeared faster than a rabbit down a rabbit hole.

With one glowering look from Anthony, the small gathering of men slinked off into the crowd leaving the two of them quite alone.

"Thank goodness he's gone."

Anthony stared at her. "It appears by neglecting my wife, every rake in town is setting their sights on bedding her."

"Every one of them, except my husband."

He gave a hollow laugh. "That does not give you leave to bait other men."

She gasped. He was accusing her of behaving like a jezebel. No wonder he'd looked like thunderclouds about to burst. She pulled her hand off his arm. "I assure you, my lord, I have no intention of bedding any other man. And you can believe that or not."

Anthony moved in close; his body's leanness and hardness had her skipping without moving. He trailed a finger down her arm. "That's the opening bars of a waltz. Dance with me."

It was a command, one her traitorous body instantly recognized. It wanted to seize the opportunity to feel his arms hold her and mold her to him.

Heart pounding in her chest, she tried to gauge what he was up to by his expression, but his features gave nothing away. *Calm yourself, don't let him see you're rattled.*

The music floated over the surrounding conversations. "How can I refuse such an—offer?"

One dark brow quirked. "It is customary for one to dance with one's wife on occasion." He studied her eyes. "As I recall you love to dance."

Inside, her nerves were all aflutter. She eyed him warily. "I do love to dance. From our conversation this afternoon, I just didn't think you were desirous of my company."

His black eyes swept her from head to foot, resting scandalously on her breasts and hips, scorching every inch until she thought she'd swoon from the heat. "There is much I find desirous about you, my sweet."

Drawing in a slow breath, past the constriction fast forming in her throat, she steeled her senses and let him guide her onto the dance floor.

He expertly twirled her around the floor; she prayed he wouldn't guess his touch was scrambling her wits and defrosting her anger at his previous behavior.

"You dance very well. Who taught you?"

Was it her imagination or had his arms closed more firmly around her? Her senses quaked—he had! The cheek of the man. He'd yet to apologize for his atrocious behavior on their wedding night. If she was to have any sway in this marriage, then he had to learn she was not a silly airhead whom he could abuse at will and then the next minute expect to fall willingly into his arms—or his bed.

She closed her eyes. Why had she thought the word "bed"? Heat pooled in her stomach and an ache blossomed and grew deep inside.

"I was taught to dance by the local vicar's son. In the wilds of Derbyshire there was no one else."

His gray eyes, warm in the candlelight, searched her face. "What of your brother? Did he not teach you?"

"He is eight years older than me and had left home by the time I wanted to learn how to dance. He showed no interest in me until he needed money." The reminder of her brother's debts had her face heating in shame.

Anthony pulled her deeper into the circle of his wonderful arms. She gave herself a moment to enjoy the sensation of floating around the floor, of strong thighs brushing her skirts as they whirled. His deep resonating voice whispered into her ear, his head so close she caught the masculine scent of cheroots and brandy. "Was it your brother's plan to plow you through the marriage mart and find a husband suitable . . . to fill Christopher's pockets?"

Her gaze locked on his enigmatic face and tried to think what the meaning behind his question might be. Did he still think she had played into Richard's game for his money? Was he hunting information in which to damn her and their marriage?

It was difficult to keep her thoughts in order. It wasn't simply the ease with which he moved her—she was slight enough that most gentlemen managed that—but the sense of power, of control, of leashed energy he brought to the simple joy of dancing.

She glanced swiftly at the couples surrounding them. Keeping her voice low she said, "Like most men, my brother underestimated my desires. I was not opposed to taking a

husband, but my husband would be of my choosing and selected for my own reasons—money not being one of them."

"I remember. You wished to marry for love. Before my
heavenly mistake, how was that theory advancing? How
would you know if a man loved you? Men use words of love
when it is convenient, and they soon forget that vocabulary
once they've grown tired of that they so falsely coveted."

She blinked back her surprise and calmly stated her ratio-
nale. "I would know. Why else would a man wish to marry
me? I have no dowry to speak of. I have a brother who is one
foot from the poorhouse. Any man who offered for me
would have to love me."

He gave a smirk. "Like Lord Dashell? Did you think he
was in love with you?"

He held her tighter. If she wasn't in the middle of the ballroom, she would have squirmed under his probing gaze. "I
hadn't made up my mind what to think of Lord Dashell."
Damned if she'd let him know how close to the mark he was.
She had thought Lord Dashell was pursuing her hand. She
had thought it must have been for love.

He gave a satisfied smile. "Lord Dashell was not in love
with you."

She eyed him wearily knowing her next words would
probably obliterate their night of truce. "We will never know.
You destroyed any chance of me finding out."

His eyes narrowed and darkened to the color of burned
ash. "Dashell gave you up without a fight. If I wanted you, I
would not let another man steal you away."

He looked down at her shocked face as he swirled her to a
halt—at those ruby lips slightly parted, at her normally calm
eyes now a storm of emotion. It was best she put all silly notions of love from her mind. "Wealthy men aren't always
drawn by large dowries." He pictured her naked. He let his
gaze trail slowly up from her slippered feet, up her long slender legs, halting briefly at the junction of her thighs, on up

over her flat stomach to rest longingly on her rapidly rising and falling breasts before meeting her wide eyes. Her breath was coming in soft pants. "They are also not drawn by love. They want a beautiful woman for a wife, so that the prospect of getting her with child, to produce necessary heirs, won't seem so onerous. You, my dear, are a beauty any man would want on his arm, as his wife, and in his bed."

He could see the storm brewing in her eyes, but she calmly stated, "Since I love children and want at least a dozen, it would seem I have the necessary prerequisite for my current role. I am so glad I do not disappoint."

The matter-of-fact statement annoyed Anthony. Why couldn't she react like most women and become a screaming shrew. Anthony immediately ran his finger around his cravat; Thompson seemed to have tied it extremely tight.

His words were meant to warn her and to make her understand gentlemen rarely took a wife for love. Their marriage was a marriage of convenience—his convenience. There would be no children.

Melissa watched his broad shoulders until he passed out of sight. Only then did she begin to breathe normally again and marshal her wits and try to understand what had just happened.

She bristled at his outright lack of apology for last night's behavior. Nevertheless, the tension that had been marking her body since this morning eased slightly due to his somewhat convoluted attempt at peace.

She tried to remember every word, analyzing their meanings. There appeared to be a lot of mumbling about love. Anthony seemed fixated on the topic.

He was clearly warning her that she must abuse herself of the notion theirs would be a love match. He must think her an idiot. She knew damn well he did not love her, or come to think of it, even like her.

She tapped the end of her fan against her chin. Nonetheless, his eyes declared he desired her. She wasn't vain, but she understood her features were pleasing to the eye. Men had always showered her with attention, that is, until they realized she was nothing like her cousin—rich and easy. She did not engage in flirtations. She was not interested in illicit assignations.

She thought back to Richard's words in the Cavendish garden. *"If you make him desire you, want you, it is a beginning."*

They did say gentlemen fell in love with their mistresses more often than their wives.

So, Anthony Craven, the Lord of Wicked, did not want her thinking of love. She knew he would not be an easy man to love, but as she'd set her heart on a love match she was even more determined to put him in his place. It was now patently clear to her that the way to Anthony's heart was through the appendage hanging between his legs.

With his notorious reputation for unending sexual prowess Melissa had her work cut out for her. It was either become more skilled in the arts of seduction than the highest paid courtesan, or simply become his broodmare, a woman he did not value above providing his much-needed heir.

The latter wasn't an option. He needed her love. And if she was to accomplish the former, she would have to study the book until she knew it cover to cover. Clearly without some help she was going to be unable to stir his interest in pleasuring her, let alone opening his heart to her.

Reading by candlelight hurt her eyes. Melissa welcomed the pain; it distracted her from the words and pictures she was reading. For one brief moment, she waved the book in front of her face to cool her ardor.

If Madame du Barry was as good at seduction as she was with words, she could have been a most popular authoress. *"This position is one of my favourites for it allows for mutual satisfaction. A man's tongue can make a woman faint, driving her to orgasm after orgasm. While a woman's lips and mouth can literally bring a man to his knees, sucking him dry. The power over him a potent aphrodisiac."*

Melissa turned the book sideways to better study the graphic picture. The man was lying on his back. The woman was on her hands and knees hanging over the top of him, but her head was facing his groin and her bottom was inches from his face.

The naked intimacy displayed within the picture had her face heating. She closed her eyes and gulped. Would she ever be brave enough to sit naked on Anthony's face so he could pleasure her with his tongue, while at the same time using her mouth to pleasure him?

She thought of Anthony's hard, lean body. She craved his touch. If her mouth could bring him to his knees and make him want her, she could do anything. The images and sensations Madame du Barry invoked tempted Melissa to barge into her husband's adjoining bedchamber and ravish him!

If Anthony was home, she would be ravishing him this very minute. Unfortunately, after the ball he saw her home, and before he left, he said, *"Don't wait up, sweetheart. I shall be at my club until very late."*

How stupid did he think she was? He was at a club all right, but it wasn't White's.

Anthony was like a slippery eel. The minute he sensed her presence, he slid away. Nothing she did convinced him to spend any degree of time in her company, especially if they were alone.

Well, he couldn't escape her forever. She would make sure of it.

Chapter 15

One lamp drew shadows inside the carriage. Sitting across from him, Cassandra hissed like a barnyard cat, all claws and ruffled fur. What fun. Rothsay longed to feel her claws dig deep in his flesh.

Her face reddened, brighter than the scarlet of her low-cut gown. "You gave me to believe you'd help me. How is Melissa being married to Lord Wickham helping me? Why did you not take your revenge before they married?"

"I made no such promise if I recall." He grinned, taking perverse pleasure in thwarting anyone's plans, especially Cassandra's. She tried to use him, and he would never allow that to happen. "You simply came to me with valuable information."

She hissed again. "You know very well what I expected you to do—what I still expect you to do. Why have you waited until they are married?"

"I thought you were clever, but now I realize you have no idea how satisfying the exact kind of revenge can be." Rothsay drew his leg up between hers and used his boot to lift the hem of her skirt to her hips, baring her silk stocking–clad limbs and creamy thighs. "What was the point in taking that which he had yet to own and did in fact not want?"

Women. They never understood that revenge was sweetest when your enemy had the most to lose. He had waited patiently to find the one thing that would cause Wickham the most pain. He could have sunk a few of his ships, but the Wickham coffers were full to overflowing, the loss of a small fortune hardly a dent. He'd thought about having Anthony's brother killed, but he was unsure what their relationship was. Anthony might not mind being rid of a sibling.

But a wife. A woman Anthony owned and who was under his protection. What could be sweeter?

Cassandra's lips curved into a self-satisfied smile. "You think hurting Melissa will hurt Anthony. You're a fool. He couldn't care if she lived or died."

"Is that so?"

He got down on his knees before Cassandra's raised skirts. His tongue licked up her leg, and then he buried his teeth deep into the soft flesh of her thigh. Her scream would have been heard above the din of the swift-moving carriage. Rothsay's staff would not bother with the sound of her distress. They'd learned to stay out of their master's business.

"Don't meddle in things you know nothing about, Cassandra. My plan is progressing perfectly. I would hate to think you would do anything to disrupt it." He raised his eyes to hers as he pinched the skin between her thighs hard. He hardened immediately at the sight of her tears.

"No—no—I would never cross you." Her voice, lanced with pain, made his breath quicken.

"You wouldn't like to see what pain I can inflict if you betray me. And you know how much I love pain." His lips found her womanly folds and licked tantalizingly.

She shuddered against the seat. He knew she enjoyed being pleasured by mouth. He didn't mind. She gave far more than she got. The image of her lips on his hard, aching shaft made him bury his head between her legs and lick, suck, and bite until she shattered on the squab above him.

He moved back to his side of the carriage. The lamp threw light on her glistening wet thighs. Now she was a purring cat, much easier to manipulate.

He began unbuttoning the front of his trousers. "I am not completely without gratitude. I have bought up all your debts. They are now mine." He gave her an evil smile. "I own you."

Her satiated expression turned to one of fear. He could smell it in the air. Thick, thrilling, and satisfying. His erection sprung free of his garments. He leaned forward and gripped her hair, pulled her up so she was forced to straddle his lap. He freed himself, and lifting her hips, slowly slid her down until he impaled her on his straining erection.

"If you please me"—he gasped as her tight sheath closed around him—"you will be at my personal beck and call. You will do anything and everything I tell you. If you behave"— he let out a moan as he plunged deeper into her heat—"then I shall never call in your debts."

He gave over to the ministrations of his new toy. He owned her body and soul. It was a long carriage ride; he did not wish his fun to end too soon.

To keep from succumbing to her tight ride, his mind wandered to the information he'd collected on the new Countess of Wickham. If you paid the most money or applied the best threat, information was easily obtained. He learned from a source in the Earl's household that Wickham did not sleep with his wife. What a fool . . .

Rothsay knew why. He'd been there the day the late Earl had forced his son to do what Anthony considered an evil act. He'd heard the words Anthony had flung at his father. He'd sworn Tony's legacy died with him. There would be no children. He would not carry on the Wickham name.

Wickham would not sleep with his wife. He did not wish to have a child with her. Once Rothsay had that knowledge, his revenge fell into place.

His orgasm built. His balls tightened, and he surged more forcefully into Cassandra's wet folds, thinking of Anthony's wife . . . of Anthony's helplessness.

Revenge . . . how absolutely delicious.

Chapter 16

Melissa busied herself preparing the tea in the drawing room of Craven House, her new home, swallowing the emotion welling inside at Sarah and Theresa's reunion.

"I hope you will be happy here," Lady Albany said to Theresa. Detangling her arms from around Theresa's neck, she wiped a tear from her cheek. "But I shall sorely miss you."

Once Melissa had filled three cups, she sat back on the settee, waiting for Sarah and Theresa to take the chairs opposite.

This was her favorite room in the house. She glanced at the small touches she'd added to the room, a vase of blood-red roses on the mantel, a small miniature of Sarah on her writing desk, some of her favorite gothic novels strewn on the side table. This had been Anthony's mother's receiving room, and Melissa drew comfort and strength from the soft red and gold furnishings. The fireplace, with its marble mantelpiece, dominated the room. Yet the petite French furniture ensured the room's femininity.

Sarah turned a grateful gaze her way. "I know you'll look after Lady Wickham. Is Lord Wickham at home? Before I leave, I'd very much like to thank him for aiding in securing Theresa's freedom."

"And Alice's," Theresa interjected. "Alice thinks he's her savior. A true saint."

Melissa gave them both an acutely uneasy look. "His lordship is not in at present, but I shall pass on your thanks when I see him." Sarah and Theresa looked at each other. Melissa shrugged. "He is busy. His business affairs take up a lot of his time. Do you take sugar, Sarah?" she asked, to distract them, and her, from the topic that plagued her every waking thought. Anthony's absence from her life—from her bed.

"His lordship has been absent far too much if you ask me." Theresa turned accusing eyes her way. "And it isn't purely business that is keeping him busy, now is it? He is never home, especially at night."

Melissa's cheeks flamed under her knowing gaze. As her maid, Theresa knew very well that Anthony had yet to share his wife's bed.

Sarah sat and took her cup of tea from Melissa's outstretched hand. "I don't understand. If I remember correctly you thought Lord Wickham was, and I quote, the 'most handsome man in all of England.' " Her mouth curved down. "Unlike me, you were looking forward to your husband's attentions. Lord Wickham is reputed to be the most amazing lover."

Melissa's blush deepened.

Theresa raised an eyebrow, waiting for her to confess.

Sarah continued on, oblivious to the silent communication between Theresa and Melissa. "I must admit I was surprised to receive your invitation to tea this morning. I would have thought a man of his appetites would not have let you out of bed for at least a week."

Unforgivably, Melissa slurped her tea at her words.

"Well," Theresa urged.

She put her cup down with a clink. "Since we married, he has not come to my bed. It would appear I am not to my husband's taste," she informed them defensively.

"Don't be ridiculous. Most men would sell their souls to get you into bed." Sarah paused. "There isn't anything wrong with the man? I mean, his reputation isn't a carefully developed cover is it, and he in fact prefers the company of men? I have heard of that sort of thing . . ."

Melissa laughed. "No, I'm quite sure; from my experience of the night he thought I was Cassandra, women are his definite preference. Just not this woman," she added unable to hide the hurt in her voice.

"Perhaps he's simply giving you time to get used to him. He's being considerate of your feelings. You are, after all, virtually strangers."

"Oh, Sarah, how sweet. But remember he compromised me. That's why I'm his wife. I'd say we know each other well enough in the bedroom department. Besides, he's the Lord of Wicked." She nodded vigorously. "No, it's me. He prefers other women to me. I am not who he wants. Up until a week ago, he only had eyes for Cassandra."

Sarah settled her cup on the table beside her. "So, what are you going to do about it?"

"Do?"

"I know you want a proper marriage, children, love! I allow Charles his mistresses because I'd rather not have him in my bed. If I wanted him, there would be no way I'd tolerate his other women." She leaned forward. "Have you told Lord Wickham how you feel? Have you shown him you desire him?"

Melissa scoffed. "He doesn't give me the opportunity."

Theresa sighed. "There's your problem, my girl. You sit back and let him dictate how you'll live your lives."

Lord Strathmore's words echoed in her head. "*Don't let him dictate* . . ." Could Theresa be right? "You're right. I know what I have to do. I've even been studying the topic. But I've been a coward. I'm scared of rejection." She lowered her head and softly said, "I'm not sure I could stand it if he turned away from me. I so want a child."

Sarah stood abruptly and pulled on her gloves. "Well, there is no time like the present." Turning to her former maid, she said, "Theresa, I suggest you make yourself scarce this afternoon. If his lordship returns, Melissa, I forbid you to let him leave this house before he's performed his husbandly duties."

"Duty! I was hoping he'd not think on it as a duty. I do have my pride."

"Silly girl. Seduce him, and he'll take care of the rest. With a reputation like his, the Lord of Wicked, I assure you, will find his pleasure. He won't ever think of bedding you simply as a duty!" Sarah was already at the door. "You have a chance to shape your marriage into something you want. Don't let fear stand in your way."

Melissa bit her lip. Sarah was right.

"I'll see Lady Albany out." Theresa stopped in the doorway and gave her a wink. "From what I've seen of his lordship, the way he follows your every move like a drunkard stumbling across a barrel full of fine French brandy, I don't think you'll have to try very hard to seduce him into your bed. I feel certain he'll be more than happy to oblige."

Melissa turned as red as the roses in the vase and smiled weakly. "I hope you're right. The rest of our lives together as strangers seems a very long time."

Melissa's inner tension rose to the screaming point as the afternoon dragged on. She shrugged, noting she'd read the same page three times but had not taken in a word. The afternoon silence of Craven House was driving her to distraction. At least here in the library, amid the books, she felt a little measure of comfort.

She knew Anthony had not returned until nearly dawn last night, because she'd laid awake listening and planning. She hugged her pillow tight. Where had he been and with whom? She let a single tear slide down her cheek. Why did he not come to her bed?

It was all very well for Sarah to issue directives, but it was a totally different matter putting them into practice. He didn't want her. Newlyweds, on their supposed honeymoon, did not avoid each other. She hung her head. But they were not a couple in love.

He liked her, of that she was certain. He smiled and conversed with her and politely asked after her and her day. He was attentive when they were together, except he never let the attentiveness go past a chaste kiss on her cheek or lips, and worst of all, he ensured he was not at home when darkness fell.

What happened to the man who gave her such pleasure in the garden before they wed? Where had he gone? What had she done to drive him away?

She closed her eyes and inwardly winced. She could no longer deny it. She had rationally thought through his behavior. It could mean only one thing. He did not find her desirable. Having tasted her passion, he preferred other women. He likely thought her not skilled enough. Yet, he'd given her no opportunity to use the teachings from her book. She prayed her new skills would be enough to enthrall the Lord of Wicked.

Last night, she'd been too miserable to sleep. She'd rubbed at the ache in her chest. He was a man whose notoriety for sins of the flesh was legendary. If he did not want her, who did he want? Who was he sleeping with? A man of his virility did not enjoy abstinence.

Which was why leaving her each evening made it so much harder to bear. She longed for him to hold her, to come to her bed and satisfy the longing rumbling inside her. If Anthony was intent on living his life as he wanted, then at the very least he could give her the one thing she desired—a child.

Last night after dinner, he kissed her good night, wished her sweet dreams, and disappeared into the night.

Instead of sleeping, she re-read Madame du Barry's book. It contained sound, descriptive advice. But if her husband never came near her room, near her bed, how could she seduce him?

She sniffed into her handkerchief. A persistent voice in her head kept whispering, *"Go to him. Didn't Madame du Barry stipulate that men enjoyed women who took the initiative?"*

But making love in the afternoon as Sarah suggested . . . ?

Yes, men were visual creatures. Even Melissa understood their passions rose when they saw even a flash of ankle.

She remembered the way Anthony's eyes had darkened and how his shaft had lengthened and thickened against her stomach, once he'd feasted on her naked breasts.

She jumped to her feet. *Fool! You have sat back like a ninny, letting him ignore you. Well, no more.*

She crossed the room to the bell pull and summoned Stevens, his lordship's butler. She walked up and down the Persian carpet chewing on her fingernail.

"You rang, my lady?"

She swung around to meet the impassive features of Anthony's butler. Stevens had been with the Cravens since a young boy. Stevens thought his lordship walked on water.

"Has Lord Wickham returned home?"

"Not yet, my lady."

"When do you expect him back?"

"He did not say, madam, but given the heavens have opened up and he is on Dark Knight, I would say soon. I have already informed Thompson to get a hot bath ready."

She nodded in agreement. "Good. I don't want him to catch a chill."

"Did you wish me to give his lordship a message, my lady?"

Melissa hesitated. What did she want? She needed to think this through. Ignoring Stevens' question she asked, "Is his lordship dining in this evening?"

Her face flamed as she saw the flash of pity in the butler's normally stoic eyes. "Indeed, I think not."

Her lips suppressed into a grim line. That meant she had limited time to enact her plan. She bid Stevens leave her and sat down before the fire, her hands absently stroking the material of her gown. Could she do it? Could she play the temptress?

She looked at her hands, took in her gown. Not dressed like this she wouldn't. Her drab and faded-blue day dress had seen better years. It was unlikely to tempt even a yokel farmer. However, she knew exactly what she would wear. She had the sheer silk, scarlet in color, negligee, so appropriate for the task. Sarah had bought it for her as a wedding gift. Her note accompanying the gift burned in Melissa's memory:

> *If you love your husband, it would seem to keep him faithful, it pays to be a whore in the bedchamber and a lady in the ballroom. A pity no one told me this on my wedding day.*
> *Your dear friend,*
> *Sarah*

How Sarah had found such a saucy piece of attire, Melissa hated to ask, but it was perfect. Perfect if she had the nerve to wear it. Even if she did, how did she get Anthony's attention? She could not very well flounce around the house dressed like one of London's best courtesans.

She drew in a deep breath, willing herself to calm down. *Think, damn it!* Her happiness might depend on this defining moment.

As peace descended over her, the answer became obvious. A devilish smile played upon her mouth.

Stevens greeted Anthony at the door, taking his sodden coat and passing it to a servant before he had time to flood the tiled entrance hall. His boots would need packing, they were soaking wet.

Ignoring the puddles Anthony was forming on the floor, Stevens ventured, "I have directed Thompson to draw you a bath."

Anthony's mood lifted. "As usual you are one step ahead of me." He turned to head up the stairs, but an umpf from the butler stalled his movement. Raising an eyebrow at Stevens, Anthony waited.

"Lady Wickham was inquiring as to your plans for this evening."

Stevens' face remained apathetic. Was that a hint of disapproval in his tone? Surely not. "You know my plans. I will be going to my club tonight."

"Perhaps you might personally let the Countess know your plans for the evening, my lord."

That was definite censor he heard. "Are you telling me how to converse with my wife, Stevens?"

He bowed. "I would never presume to do such a thing, my lord."

Anthony pulled at his sodden cuffs. "I should think not. You may inform my wife that I shall be dining at my club and won't be in until late." Not waiting to see the disappointment he knew would be reflected in Stevens' eyes, Anthony took the stairs two at a time. "Tell her not to wait up."

He rushed toward his bedchamber like a fox avoiding the hounds. Relief washed through him when he closed the door behind him and he was safe in his inner sanctuary.

Thompson was in his retiring room seeing to his bath. Anthony could see the steam rising. He waited for Thompson to help him undress all the while conscious of the guilt eating at his innards. Stevens was right. He had been ignoring his wife.

He inwardly cursed at the growing need to avoid her. Even now, he could feel the pull of attraction, the constant drumming of desire to take his pleasure of her. She was a woman of absolutely no sexual experience, yet she had his passions in such a stir. He awoke each morning hard as a steel blade, dreaming of going to her bed and taking that which by law was now his. The temptation she posed was perilous.

Melissa was too intelligent for her own good. She would work out, if she hadn't already, that he was deliberately avoiding her. With a twinge he recognized he admired that about her. She was independent and could think for herself. It only added to her allure. But it also added to the danger.

Of all the females he knew, she was unquestionably the most difficult to handle. She hid behind a wall of calm detachment. He never knew quite what she was thinking. She was never ruffled by his harsh comments or inexcusable behavior. Most wives would have, at the very least, sniped at him for his boorish behavior. But not Melissa. She still smiled politely at him across the breakfast table and did not censor him in any way for his lack of attention. He was not sure if that didn't anger him more. Did she not want his attentions? Most women he knew would go through the fires of hell to end up in his bed.

A flare of angry heat scorched his skin. Unless she was receiving plenty of attention elsewhere. Perhaps Lord Dashell was top of her mind.

With a weary sigh of surrender, he knew he would have to speak with her—tell her his position and set the ground rules for this marriage. But that would mean being in her company. It would mean smelling the flowery scent that sent his pulse galloping. He would be able to study her lush curves, picturing what lay underneath her clothes. He would be in torment, looking but not being able to touch. He wasn't at all sure what that would do to his sanity.

As he lowered himself into the tub, he vowed to have the conversation first thing tomorrow morning. It would be best if she was sent to Bressington. Out of sight, God willing, would help get her out of his head. He might finally be able to sleep. His libido couldn't take too many more nights under the same roof. Already the Lord of Wicked was screaming to take, plunder, and taste her. She must leave as soon as possible.

He relaxed deep into the tub; the lull of the heated water was invigorating to a man so bone-weary he could hardly lift his arms to wash them. He'd not slept the last four nights, his dreams of Melissa making him so hard he was in agony. He needed all his willpower not to slip into her bed and sate his lust.

He needed a woman, but the thought of any woman other than Melissa made him flaccid.

With eyes closed, he pictured the vision that was Melissa. His member hardened with thoughts of how her body had fit his. He'd had her in his arms, his member held tightly in her hot, wet sheath. The feel and scent of her had him imagining touching heaven.

His hand curled around his throbbing cock. Ever since she'd moved into his house he'd had to resort to self-pleasure in order to keep the beast at bay. He'd tried to find release at Madame Sabine's, but none of the ladies enticed him—only one—only Melissa.

He stroked himself, imagining Melissa riding him, hard, deep, and furiously. Her breasts bouncing above him. His hands gripping her hips, his eyes watching as his hard, thick shaft disappeared into her wet folds.

So caught up in his fantasy of ravishing Melissa—her luscious breasts in his mouth while his thick, throbbing shaft drove her wild with desire—he missed the soft footsteps approaching.

"Don't let me interrupt, although it would be my pleasure to aid you in your endeavors."

His eyes opened on a groan. Through his haze of passion, he took in the sight of her standing next to the tub, clad in red transparent silk. He froze and fractured. The luscious sight before him sent his hot seed erupting like an overactive volcano.

"Christ!"

He struggled for control, his chest heaving with each ragged breath. The scarlet—negligee—left nothing to the imagination. Her breasts were pushed up, exposing the soft swell of creamy skin, and her nipples stood rigid, poking through the scrap of lace supposedly covering them. He could see every curve . . . see the thatch of dark curls at the top of her long slender legs. The delicacy of prime womanhood displayed before him immediately had him hardening again.

Her voice was the sound of the sweetest symphony. "I'm sorry about the intrusion, but I thought it time we discussed our marriage. At least in the bath you cannot escape me by storming out of the house."

Chapter 17

Still mortified with shame, Melissa lifted her chin a degree higher. She did not miss the activity he'd been engaged in when she entered the room. Anthony would rather pleasure himself than make love to her.

Why?

Yet at the sight of his wet, muscled, naked body, sensations rippled through Melissa in a tangle of unthinking passion, overriding her hurt and anger.

She'd watched him in the act with heat and moisture growing between her thighs. He'd had his eyes closed, his head thrown back, and Melissa wondered who he dreamed of when he stroked himself to completion. She prayed it wasn't Cassandra. No doubt it was one of the demireps at his favorite sin club since it was obvious he did not want her.

He jerked upright in the bath; his passion-hazed gaze struck her. She felt its impact, felt the dark, heated intensity of his eyes locking on her. A searing heat sliced along her limbs at the rampant desire hidden in their depths. She quivered from head to toe.

He licked his lips. "What are you doing in here?" His voice was rough, like gravel crunching underfoot.

Melissa's anger returned with a rush. She swallowed it along with her pride. This was not the way she'd planned this seduction. He was not supposed to have given himself release. She was supposed to entice, tease, and he was supposed to be made so hot and needy, he'd take her regardless of his lack of enthusiasm.

Melissa stepped forward until she could see clearly into the tub. She bent forward, placing her hands on the rim, causing her breasts to fall free and the negligee to part to her waist, displaying her legs right up to her mound. She heard his sharp intake of breath.

She reached out and ran one finger from his firm lips, over his chin, down his throat and chest. "I want my husband," she whispered sultrily.

He stopped her hand before it dipped below the water, but she could see his member stirring into life at her touch. Interesting. She was having an effect on him.

"Why are you dressed in this manner?" He held her hand tighter. "You look like a whore."

His freezing tone made her cringe. Without raising her voice she calmly stated, "As you seem to be spending every night since our marriage with whores, I thought perhaps you preferred them."

Melissa was surprised by the flicker of remorse that briefly entered his eyes. But then his lips firmed, and he pushed her hand away from him.

"Who I prefer is my own business. You don't need to act the whore for me." His voice softened for the last sentence and contained a hint of apology in the tone.

She moved closer until her breasts were practically in his face. "But I do have your attention now, don't I?"

His eyes stayed fixed on her breasts. He rasped, "Yes. You have my attention. However, my valet will be returning shortly and I don't want him to see my wife displayed like some doxy."

She dipped her hand into the water, sliding her fingers over his rippling stomach and down toward his now straining erection. He did not stop her this time.

"I have told Thompson not to disturb us until you ring for him." His member jerked into her hand as her fingers grazed over the head of his cock.

His eyes briefly closed. His voice hoarse and choking. "Stop. Don't do this. I have to get dressed. I'm wanted at the club."

Her fingers wrapped firmly around him, and his body stiffened. He leaned back against the tub. She purred in his ear, her naked breasts hitting his rock-hard chest. A thrill surged through her blood at the contact of her hard nipples against the rasping black hair of his chest.

"There is no hurry. I checked with Stevens. You are not due at the club for another hour at least."

His eyes opened wide at her words. His tempting mouth only inches from hers.

Anthony didn't have time to think. The kiss was so unexpected that he was responding before he even realized. He couldn't help himself. He was instantly enveloped in her—in her scent, in the feel of her small hand wrapped firmly around the most intimate part of him. In the heat of her body, so close her nipples scorched his chest. In the taste of her as she parted his lips with an insistent urging.

The kiss deepened as her other hand roamed over his body. Something stirred inside him as she pushed against him, her breasts flattened against his chest.

A fire erupted deep within him. His body craved this, yearned for it, begged him for it.

He turned slightly and pulled her into the tub. Her mouth broke from his, and she gasped as she slipped into the warm water, her negligee molding to her skin.

Good God, he was kissing her. He *was kissing her*. He should stop. Stop before he lost himself in her charms and destroyed himself and her along with him.

He gripped her arms and held her away from him. She sat staring at him with eyes liquid pools of desire, water running over her hardened nipples, her thigh pressed against his erection.

He could not believe he'd allowed the kiss to happen, let alone that he'd pulled her into the tub. She'd planned her move well, he admitted admiringly. She had him at a distinct disadvantage.

He couldn't hide the evidence of his need. This was madness. A dark passion filled, riotous sort of madness, the type that could ruin all his plans for the future.

Anthony looked down at Melissa's wet, luscious body. It had taken every ounce of his strength to break the delicious kiss. His hands remained like shackles on her arms, simply because he didn't trust himself not to pull her up to straddle him and sink into her tight heat. She was as intoxicating and succulent as a fresh strawberry. The heady mixture of innocence and sensuality had his groin once again throbbing with need.

Despite his intentions otherwise, he was powerfully attracted to her, powerfully aroused, and powerfully fearful of what might happen next.

He was breathing hard, as was she. Desire swirled around them, rising to engulf them like the steam from the heated water.

Damn her.

Melissa was beautiful, unconsciously sensual, intelligent—too intelligent for his liking, and not about to be pushed aside without an explanation. His eyes roamed her flushed face. He could feel the tremble of her body beneath his fingertips, see the rapid rise and fall of her chest.

She was struggling to maintain her composure. Ordinarily he would be ecstatic. To have a beautiful, sensual woman in his arms, naked, willing to sate his every need. No wonder his body was reacting as if he'd never seen a naked woman before.

Anthony silently cursed. He steeled himself and lifted a hand to Melissa's chin, then raised her face from her study of his body to meet his gaze. She dropped her hands to his chest and challenged him with a look of pure carnal delight.

Through the heat of her stare and the warmth from the bathwater, he felt his body chill. He pushed her roughly toward the other end of the tub and rose from the water.

He stared down at her face, which was flashing anger, hurt, and most of all disbelief.

"I can see you want me," she said, nodding to his erection, which stood proudly against his stomach. "What on earth is wrong?"

He stepped from the tub and grabbed a towel to hide the evidence of his need. "This is not the time or place to discuss such matters . . ."

She dropped her head and her voice wobbled. "It's me. There is something wrong with me."

Bloody hell, he was a cad. She thought there was something wrong with her. He was such a coward, and now he'd upset her. All he'd really wanted to do was keep her away so he could resist the temptation of her abundant charms. How could she think it was her?

Anthony let out an oath. Melissa gave a heart-wrenching sob. He felt like a piece of turd stuck on his boot. "There is nothing wrong with you, Melissa. You are a beautiful woman. You can see I desire you."

She shook her head. "I should not have interrupted you. I just thought . . . didn't you enjoy the kiss?"

Her gaze flew to his. The pleading look in her eyes hurt more than his aching need for release. He could do it now. He could destroy her with a simple word and never have to worry about fending her off again.

He hesitated. The splash of water, dripping from her ebony hair into the tub, was the only sound in the room.

She gave another sob. "Never mind. I was wrong."

He couldn't do it. When he looked upon her heart-shaped face, full of innocent anxiousness, he couldn't do it. He couldn't bring himself to be so cruel.

"Yes I want you. I did. I do . . . however, I meant it when I said this was not the right time."

Relief flooded her features and she relaxed into the tub. Her mouth pouted. "When will be the right time?"

Before he could answer, there was a discreet knock on the retiring room door, and Stevens called, "I'm sorry to disturb you, my lord, but Lord Strathmore is below, and he says it's urgent."

Grasping at any excuse, Anthony turned to Melissa. "That is why it is not the right time. Rufus was due. We will discuss your behavior later. I must get dressed and meet with him."

He handed her a towel and tried to still the rush of desire that lanced through his already throbbing groin as she rose like a goddess from the tub.

The silk and lace negligee clung to her skin, her pert breasts exposed and nipples hard. At the visceral sight before him, he almost hopped right back in the tub. His body screamed to take her. It was pure torture for him to turn away. He suddenly didn't care about whether he might get her with child.

That drew him up short.

He was going to have to remove her and soon. Now he'd seen her naked, seen her desire for him, seen what pleasure she'd offer him, he wouldn't get another wink of sleep with her under the same roof. He did not have enough self-control.

Melissa was too big of a temptation.

He was weak, he knew it. If Stevens had not interrupted, he would have taken her—here and now and damn the consequences.

With the towel wrapped around her body, she moved, halting at the door, eyeing him warily. "We will continue this conversation later." Her eyebrows scrunched into an engaging frown. "In fact, as soon as you get in tonight, no matter how late. When next we talk I want some answers." With her threat she passed through his bedchamber to her own room, quietly shutting the door.

Anthony breathed a sigh of relief. *Coward. All you've done is put off the inevitable.* With a guilty start he thought, I'll not come home tonight. He rubbed himself briskly with the towel until his skin was almost raw. He'd sleep at the club. If Rufus had something to report, it would be a good excuse to avoid being home for a few days.

If he couldn't think of something to diminish her desire for him over the next few days, he'd have to confess to deceiving her—tell her about the white marriage. But that might not be enough. If she was this determined to have him in her bed, he would have to do something drastic to kill any feelings she had for him.

What chilled him to his marrow was the fact he cherished her feelings for him. When she looked at him with glowing warmth in her eyes, a tiny piece of his soul didn't feel so cold.

Rufus was pacing the study when Anthony entered—his face hard, his features sharp. He swung around and crossed the carpet swiftly, shaking Anthony's outstretched hand.

"I'm sorry to intrude like this, especially as you are recently married, but I needed to talk with you about Rothsay." He finally issued a smile. "Rude of me not to ask, I hope married life finds you well?"

Anthony raised an eyebrow. "As well as can be expected. Actually, I welcome your intrusion. You've just saved me from a particular tricky conversation with my wife."

"Really? From the look of you, it would appear I've called at an inappropriate time. I hope I didn't interrupt anything—pleasurable?"

Anthony ignored his friend's salacious inquiry. "Drink?" he nodded his head to the decanter of brandy on his desk.

"Thank you, yes. I can see you're not in the mood for teasing. Marriage has not improved your temper then?" Rufus sank into the chair on the other side of his desk. Not bothering to wait for an answer, Rufus uttered, "I think I've located Rothsay's base."

"Where is he?" Anthony demanded, pivoting to face his friend.

"He's operating out of Great Yarmouth."

"Yes—Yes. I know that. I'd heard he'd bought a property there. But have you proof of his shipments? Quincy could find nothing."

"Not exactly," Rufus answered.

"Then what is so urgent?"

"I came to warn you. Some of Rothsay's men have been watching your house and more importantly you. I'm not sure, but Rothsay has long held you accountable for his three shipments we intercepted last November. He might be out for revenge."

Rothsay did hold him responsible. But it went deeper than that. There was no love lost between the two men. "I can look after myself." Anthony cursed. Melissa. If Rothsay got his hands on her . . . He refused to think of the consequences. Would his enemy even know he'd gotten married? Of course he would. Rothsay was having the house watched. "I'll need a guard for Melissa. I want your best man."

"That's why I am here. If he got his hands on Melissa, he could ship her off and you'd never find her again."

Anthony took a sip of brandy to still the panic Rufus's words invoked. There had to be more to Rothsay's sudden interest in him. November was months ago; if he was annoyed why wait until now? "Are you sure he doesn't know about our latest investigation into his white slavery ring?"

Rufus shifted in his seat. "No. We can't discount that possibility, although only a handful of men know we have him under investigation. I'm hoping his sources are unaware of our recent foray into his activities. However, if he does know, he'll likely cause trouble."

"Sources? Damn it. I wondered how he got onto me so quickly last year. This time I've only made a few discreet enquiries. At least I know he's onto us. I shall be prepared. I'll have to be careful no one follows me."

"Follows you where? What do you mean to do?"

Anthony frowned. "I'm going to Great Yarmouth."

"Do you think that wise? The last thing we want is for Rothsay to know we have his ships under observation. If you leave Town now, they will follow. We can protect you—protect Melissa easier in London."

Anthony sat back in his chair and took a long drink. The fiery liquid took the edge off the tension strumming his body.

"If he means to hurt me or my family, it won't matter

where I am. Besides, if they believe I have taken my wife to Bressington. . . ." He leaned forward. "Think about it. What could be more natural than for the Earl of Wickham to take his new bride home to the family seat?"

Rufus began nodding his head. "I like it. You can leave Melissa guarded at Bressington while you slip away to scout out his lair."

"We could also leak out that it is to be the start of our honeymoon."

This would be perfect. He could escort Melissa to Bressington and then leave her and head to Great Yarmouth. Not only would he finally be close to destroying a man who should have been strangled at birth, he would escape the torment that was Melissa.

Once he'd brought Rothsay down, he could put off being with his wife until he got her completely out of his system. Until he no longer wanted her. Until his passion for her was as dried up as a harvested corn husk.

He would leave Melissa at Bressington, come back to London, find a new mistress, and carry on his life exactly as before.

"It will be harder to watch me at Bressington. I know the countryside so well. I can easily slip away, especially if in disguise."

Rufus drew a deep breath. "It won't fool them for long. As soon as they see your wife out and about without you, they'll be suspicious."

"She will have to have an escort with her at all times." He paused. "The man you assign to guard her . . . can you find someone similar to my height and coloring? We might be able to fool them for quite some time. By then I will be long gone and they won't know where."

"What will you tell Melissa?"

Anthony inwardly grimaced. Rufus knew him too well. He would know he'd not like to discuss Rothsay with Melissa. She would ask too many questions. Questions he would be ashamed to answer, questions that would make her feel nothing but repulsion for him . . .

But isn't that exactly what he wanted? Didn't he crave to push her away? He needed a way to destroy the infatuation she had for a man who didn't really exist.

"I'll tell her the truth. Tell her about the man I am."

Rufus frowned. "The boy you were. The man is nothing like his father."

"You sound like Richard."

Rufus leaned forward. "Richard is right. Your father died ten years ago. Stop holding on and let him go."

If he let go of his hate, who—what—would be left.

Chapter 18

The trip to Bressington was uneventful. Last night, Melissa had been so excited at the news of their journey, she'd left off interrogating him. They were to leave first thing in the morning for Bressington, and she quickly began to ready the household for the trip. He'd used having to tidy up his affairs as an excuse to remain out of her way for most of the night.

Now she sat next to him in his carriage, her head on his shoulder while she slept. Her abigail, Theresa, also slept. He'd suggested Theresa ride in their carriage to avoid any personal conversations. A few gentle snores from the maid was the only sound keeping him company, as he pondered the inevitable conversation to come.

He grew angry at his sudden feelings of contrition. Bleakly, he realized how angry Melissa would become when he told her the truth. Why had he thought this marriage such a good idea? What an idiot he was! He'd always been ruthless, his upbringing making him susceptible to hasty decisions, but it had never manifested itself with such a permanent consequence as this! He should never have married her. He should have left Melissa to her shame. Paid off her brother's debts and set her up in a house in the country. His life would have been so much simpler. But he had too much honor.

He glanced down at the woman beside him. Even in her sleep, her striking natural innocence stirred him.

He was a goddammed fool.

Her eyes slowly opened, and she smiled up at him. His heart bloomed and thudded against his ribs. Moments like these almost had him believing his life could be different.

Yes a fool.

He nodded his head toward the window. "You'll glimpse Bressington when we round the next bend."

She sat up and leaned toward the window.

The Elizabethan mansion held disturbing memories for Anthony, the ornate estate a perfect foil for the evildoings within.

Sure enough, as they rounded the curved driveway, stretched out before him in taunting splendor, he felt his stomach knot at the sight of his childhood home. The three-story seventeenth-century sandstone manor, with huge forward wings and steep rooftops dotted with chimneys, was as intimidating to him now as it was as a child.

As the carriage coasted around the long circular drive, Melissa turned a beguiling grin to him, her hazel eyes sparkling with enthusiasm. "It's beautiful. It looks like a palace with its graceful terraced steps leading up to the front door and the sunlight glistening against hundreds of panes of mullioned glass. You must have loved growing up here."

He nodded and tried to hide the absolute loathing he felt for the property.

This would be the perfect place to keep Melissa. He hated everything about Bressington. His memories of the house would ensure he was never eager to see his wife.

The butler stood waiting as they drew up. This was going to be embarrassing, Anthony thought as he helped Melissa from the carriage. Anthony couldn't remember his name. On his father's death, he'd replaced the butler, but he'd spent so little time here he'd forgotten the man's name.

"A pleasure to have you home, my lord," he intoned. At Anthony's pause he added, "It's Stubbs, sir."

"Thank you, Stubbs. Allow me to introduce my wife, the Countess of Wickham."

Stubbs bowed.

"It's a pleasure to meet you," she said, and smiled brightly.

Anthony noticed Stubbs immediately responded to the warmth in her greeting. Stubbs looked surprised—no doubt expecting him to have selected a woman as dour in nature as himself.

Stubbs's demeanor brightened considerably. "The pleasure is undoubtedly mine, my lady. I hope you shall find all at Bressington to your satisfaction."

"Oh! I am quite certain I shall. It's so very lovely, don't you think, Theresa?"

Theresa beamed her approval at Stubbs. "Yes sir'ee. The house is wondrous." She swept her arm toward the steps leading down onto a magnificent lawn, pointing on toward the pond. "The children will love playing in the pond over yonder."

Anthony watched Melissa's face turn to him and flood with pink. He had no earthly wish to answer that and simply smiled as he glanced over his shoulder at Stubbs.

It had been an age since he'd last visited Bressington. He would likely not know all the staff. "Lead on, Stubbs," he indicated with his arm.

He watched with growing unease as Stubbs swiftly led her to the row of servants who had filed out to meet them in the late afternoon sun. Melissa spoke with each and every one of the twenty-five staff gathered. Her quiet dignified yet friendly manner had them half in love with her by the time she reached the end of the queue.

Good. As they moved inside he hoped she would be, if not happy, then content at Bressington.

"Show Lady Wickham to her rooms, and perhaps a tour of the house would be in order. It's a house easy to get lost in." He should know. He'd found innumerable places to hide when a young boy. The fear of a whipping honed his skills to perfection.

He followed in his wife's footsteps. Once inside his mood darkened.

"If you will follow me?" Stubbs asked, and gestured toward a huge curving staircase spiraling upward beneath old portraits and coats of armor and one massive crystal chandelier.

Anthony followed them up the first lot of stairs. "I'll be in my study." He stopped and watched with chilled inevitability his wife being led to the rooms that would adjoin his.

His inner rake rejoiced. He was a fool.

Anthony sat staring at the papers before him on his desk. His study at Bressington should be a bastion of serenity, but with Melissa under the same roof, even here he couldn't hide from his all-consuming desire for her.

He knew tonight would be a night of reckoning. She'd held back her questions because he'd carefully planned for Theresa to ride in the carriage with them. Nothing would stop her from wanting to consummate their marriage tonight.

Her image blossomed in his mind—her gentle smile that was becoming increasingly strained as the nights passed and he did not come to her bedchamber. Yet every time that smile disappeared, he had to shackle an urge to kiss it back, to take her in his arms and . . .

Inwardly cursing, he jerked his mind off his wife. He would not risk Melissa getting with child. Unfortunately, ingrained habits were hard to break; Melissa simply being in his house, next to his bedchamber a couple of strides away, added to the already considerable strain of desisting. Resisting. But he would.

He knew his mood was darkening and that his craving for Melissa was the cause. Just how dark he'd only realized when he'd helped her down from the carriage. Denying his carnal needs amounted to self-flagellation with poison oak leaves. He could easily exploit her proximity to gain the ease his body longed for. Just how strong his desire for her had grown, he'd only then fully comprehended. He'd almost not care if any progeny resulted.

What was worse, she'd sensed his discomfort, sensed his growing need.

Eyes narrowing, he replayed yet again all she'd done as they'd ascended the stairs and entered the house.

She'd deliberately brushed against him, the swell of her bosom caressing his arm, one soft thigh bumping his, and she'd shot him a look so smoldering with desire he all but combusted on the step.

He trusted himself not one jot. He should leave immediately for Great Yarmouth.

A moment later, he grimaced and surreptitiously shifted in his chair. His body was trapped in the worst vise. If he were honest with himself, he was champing at the bit to have her, the woman who overnight had become a beaconing sensual siren. On the other hand, he was desperately reining back, fighting her allure. He still could not understand why he simply did not head directly to the nearest tavern and sate his lust between a pair of willing soft thighs that weren't his wife's.

How could he want Melissa so much when it could result in his worst nightmare—a child, his child?

A knock at the study door disturbed his musings, followed by Stubbs saying, "My lord?"

Relieved it wasn't Melissa, he blew a sigh. "Enter."

Stubbs did, bowed, and crossed the floor. "Lady Wickham requests your presence."

"She will have to wait until I have seen to the correspondence."

"I believe it is urgent. A small problem in relation to her maid." Stubbs looked uncomfortable.

"Problem?"

Stubbs flushed. "I think it best her ladyship explains. She's in her sitting room, my lord."

His blood turned to ice in his veins. The sitting room next to her bedchamber. "Thank you, Stubbs. You may go."

His inner instincts roared into life. He did not trust her. Melissa was all but virginal, yet if yesterday was anything to go by, she was not totally inexperienced in seduction. She only had to look at him with her large, hazel eyes and he wanted her. Who was he fooling? It was him he could not trust.

Her room.

Stifling a sigh and inwardly knowing he was being a fool, he rose. Whatever was behind her summons? It was still late afternoon. Sending Stubbs to find him bore no resemblance to an illicit invitation. His wife was a lady and far too innocent to think of sex in broad daylight. It was only the Lord of Wicked, with temptation in his grasp, who had visions of spending the remainder of the afternoon making love to his wife.

He mounted the stairs to her apartments with trepidation. He stood for a few seconds in front of her door before lightly tapping.

He heard her call. "Come in."

Steeling his impulses, he entered her sitting room. It was empty, but the door to her bedchamber stood ajar.

"Is that you, Anthony? I'm in here," she called in a sweet voice.

Like a man facing the gallows, he entered her room. Sunlight still streamed in through two sets of windows, both with their curtains wide.

His pulse quickened and his body—every inch—hardened at the stimulating vision gloriously displayed before him.

Melissa lay completely naked upon her large four-poster bed. The late afternoon sunlight illuminated her pale skin in a worshipful glow. She looked like an angel fallen into sin.

The diaphanous white curtains surrounding her bed were presently roped back, and the counterpane of sprigged ivory satin was rolled down and folded across the end of the bed, leaving silk sheets exposed. The purity of her lily-white skin was in complete contrast to the scarlet of the sheets she lay upon and emphasized her sensuous curves.

His mouth watered for a taste.

Her luscious midnight tresses, flowing like sable across the sheets, shone in the lingering sunlight. His fingers itched to thread through the fine strands, and then roam over her silken skin until he knew every inch intimately.

Knowing it was his house, his bed, his wife—seeing her so provocatively displayed, and knowing she had done this to tempt only him, Anthony's blood roared for possession.

"I'd close the door unless you want your servants to see me as God intended."

He pushed the door closed with his boot, his eyes never leaving hers. He watched her lips move as if in a trance, dying for a taste.

He stepped toward the bed.

Not a good idea.

The Lord of Wicked didn't listen to him.

Take, plunder, sate . . . his inner voice screamed. He briefly closed his eyes to still his rampaging desire.

Christ what was wrong with him?

This was his wife. *Think of all you could lose simply in pursuit of lust.*

He started—every muscle he possessed tightened as if he were being tortured on the rack.

Step back and escape, his brain begged him, but his body refused to obey. Give in, the devil on his shoulder said.

She lay flat on her back, smiling at him, and dropped her thighs open.

Lust slammed through him. His mouth dried. Her body drew his gaze like a river to a man dying of thirst. His senses, driven by instinct, had brutally focused. The sight of her open womanhood was enough to make his groin throb.

He could not drag his gaze from her. The delights of her body, embedded in his memory, were boldly and brazenly displayed.

For him.

He swallowed.

"I thought this the most likely way to capture and hold your interest—at least for this afternoon. Was I wrong?"

He felt the rein of his control quake; he managed to draw

enough breath to rasp, "No. You undoubtedly have my full consideration, madam."

Her lips curved gently—that sweet, understanding smile now openly challenging. "My husband," she whispered, the soft invitation making him hard and fit to burst.

Before he comprehended what he was doing, he was beside the bed. On his next breath, the heady scent of her, orange blossom mixed with arousal, filled him.

Sheer seduction . . . sheer torture.

She knew it—he saw the truth. She was fully aware of her power; her understanding was written clearly in her beautiful face, in the depth of her jade-brown eyes, in the inherently feminine set of her lips.

He felt his body surrender, a desire infinitely stronger than any that had come before, a passion immeasurably more compelling—she was his. She belonged to him and no other. Why shouldn't he take her?

Consequences—that's why.

He made one last attempt to cling to reason, to deny his driving need to possess her, to take her, to enjoy her obvious delights.

The Lucifer on his shoulder pricked until he was thinking with only one part of his anatomy, the part that was rock hard and eager to enter her. *Surely they could enjoy pleasure without conception.*

He felt her heated gaze focus on his lips. Her succulent berry-ripe lips begged to be kissed. He dragged in another breath and leaned over her until his face was inches from the mouth he wanted to plunder.

She stretched up, drew his head down, brought her lips close to his, and murmured, "At least I know you do find me desirable."

He could hardly deny it, for his erection was straining against his breeches.

Her other hand moved to fondle the bulge at his groin, and his last vestige of restraint evaporated at her innocent touch.

He covered her lips with his, kissing her voraciously, deliberately letting the chains he'd locked himself in break—rattling his very soul down to his bones. He couldn't do anything else. Hands splayed, sliding over the fine silk of her skin, he pulled her roughly, half off the bed and into his arms, molding her urgently against him.

Any chance he'd had of escaping died the instant he'd seen her nakedness and immediately pictured the pleasure he'd find between her thighs. Naked in his arms, she clung and returned his kisses greedily, avidly—flagrantly encouraging him to seize, take, and conquer.

Melissa's whole body trembled as she felt Anthony's arms lock tight, felt his lips bruising hers, hard and demanding, felt his surrender. He straightened, crushing her to him; without interrupting the kiss, he lifted her against him, sliding her down his body, his clothes rasping against her sensitized skin.

Her slide of pleasure stopped when her knees touched the bed. She knelt on the edge of the bed, her arms around his neck. His hands cupped her bottom, pressing her so she'd feel his need for her, while his tongue plundered her mouth, wreaking havoc with her senses. Within her, heat bloomed, burgeoned, grew—

Melissa was scared to break the kiss and destroy the moment, but she wanted him naked, his body displayed for her gaze, her touch. Hands on his granite chest, she pushed his jacket wide, trapping his arms. "Your clothes . . . I want to see you."

With a curse of impatience, he let her go and stepped back, wrenching the jacket off and flinging it aside.

The violence of his desire thrilled her. His eyes, dark and burning, narrowed on hers. He reached for her, palm curving about her jaw, tipped her face, and drew her close. He studied her; she poured everything into her gaze, all her desire, all her uncertainty, all her need.

He bent his head, murmured, "Yes, I want you, too."

That's all she needed. She acted on his words, grappling

with the buttons of his waistcoat and then shirt. Yanking the two halves apart until she found skin. Melissa touched, searched, and grasped the smooth marble. The sensation was just as she'd remembered it. She purred with satisfaction. The muscles beneath her palms flexed, hot satin, and alive. His chest was a wonder of rasping black hair and male hardness. She filled her hands with the hard contours of his chest and soaked her senses in his maleness.

She would win this battle. He yielded to her questing fingers, eager for her touch. She felt the evidence of his need pressed against her stomach.

He gasped, "You have driven me to the brink of madness these last few days."

His words fed her confidence, and she met his lips brazenly, hoping he'd let her glimpse, conquer, and tame the part of him she'd always known was there, lurking behind his false apathy.

She sensed the warmth hidden within him, felt the battle he fought to constantly force it back into his soul, as if he'd become a puddle of melted ice if he let it escape. She pressed her lips to his nipple and licked, hoping to send flames of desire ricocheting around his body. But the heat engulfed her, too. The fire spread, capturing her in its scorching blaze.

Yet her boldness had the desired effect. He hastily stripped off his shirt and waistcoat before he captured her mouth in a devouring kiss. Her arms wrapped around his back to hold him to her, for his escape was out of the question. She needn't have worried; his hands moved down to cup and provocatively knead the globes of her bottom. She felt the thick muscle framing his back flex like steel beneath her searching hands. She ran them down his back, marveling; then with more bravery than she ever thought she owned, she slid one finger over his ribcage and forward to caress the rippling bands decorating his abdomen. They quivered at her touch; he sucked in a breath as she sent her fingers questing lower. The breath exhaled as she lightly traced the line of his erection.

He did not stop her.

He stilled and broke the kiss, his eyes revealing his inner turmoil. She tentatively reached for the buttons at the waistband of his breeches. This time it was her holding her breath—would he submit?

The only sign of doubt was that he'd closed his eyes.

Like approaching a rose bush with prickly thorns, she slid one hand inside the open flap and, undoing the drawstring on his drawers, touched the silky length of him. Rigid, as she expected, yet so hot, and with skin so smooth . . .

She gripped him tightly, and his groan filled the bedchamber. His eyes flashed to her face, taking her lips in an urgent, unrelenting kiss, tongue plunging deep within her mouth. Her fingers continued to explore him. He was large; he more than filled her hand.

"God, you make me feel so big." His words came in short pants.

Closing her fingers as far around him as she could, she moved her hand slowly up and down the length of him, and felt him shudder.

She wasn't exactly sure what to do now. She experimented, hoping she could drive him over the edge, ignite his heated passion until he forgot that he did not want her, forgot that she was not the woman he truly desired, forgot everything except taking her.

To her growing frustration he ruthlessly held it back. Soon, please soon, let the dam break.

He was proving stronger than she expected, her continuing ministrations not having the desired effect, until without warning, he pushed her back on the bed. Within moments he had stripped off his boots and trousers and was lying naked beside her, his large hand guiding her back to his rampant member.

Anthony clenched his jaw and battled the wave of passion engulfing him, but his control grew more brittle by the second. She was such an innocent, yet her instincts were sound, her actions robust, and her hands on his pulsing member pure heaven.

The sunlight played to her advantage, the light letting him see her, all of her. What would she look like under him as he drove into her hot, slick folds, when he finally claimed her?

The image sent another surge of heat, of pure unadulterated desire lancing through him, hardening and lengthening his already throbbing shaft, the object of her focused concentration. She paused, seemingly fascinated by the bead of moisture seeping from his tip. He looked down as she sent her thumb stroking over his aching head, spreading the latent drop down the length of him.

The sight of her finger moist with his dew sent him spiraling out of control. He caught his breath, nudged her face up, and took her lips again, drawing her into a drugging kiss, then ruthlessly, deliberately, he let his walls fall. He seized and devoured, claiming her mouth, her lips. He wanted all of her.

He captured her wrist and drew her hand from him. He rolled on top of her, reveling in the sensation of her soft, satin skin caressing his chest, his arms, his erection, while he plundered her mouth and caught her up in his tide of desire. Anthony knew this was dangerous, but he could not think straight.

All he knew was he had to have her.

Melissa quaked with her victory. He was helpless against the passion she'd aroused. He was out of control. She did not fight his passion—she'd never stop him. This is what she wanted—for him to make her his. For him to make love to her. She sank into his arms, giving herself up to his commanding lips, his hands. She surrendered to his dictates, waiting with nerves strung tight with anticipation to be claimed, marked for all time by the one man who, in a flash of blinding light, she realized owned her heart.

Breaking the kiss, he bent his head and set his lips to her

breast. Set his hot mouth to one puckered nipple and sucked fiercely.

Her gasp echoed in the room, her head falling back, letting him feast like a king. She was a slave to his passion.

He laved her breasts, suckled, nipped, torturing the tightly pebbled peaks, his mouth sending arrows of heat downward to curl in her stomach, increasing the ache between her thighs. Her hands lifted to his head and held him to her, lost in the roaring sensations his mouth was creating.

His hands roamed her curves; he became the conqueror, and she almost wept.

Anthony stopped, still panting, and looked at his wife. He tried to control the savage need he felt to take her.

He'd made love to numerous women—some of the best courtesans in the world had pleasured him—but he'd never felt this hunger, this need to drive into a woman, before. She'd bewitched him. Likely his ardor for her was driven by the knowledge he couldn't have her. Not in the way he wanted, not in the way he craved her.

He wanted her so badly his body felt like it wasn't his own. He closed his eyes and dragged in a deep breath. He knew they could find pleasure without penetration, but his blood sang for more.

He rose up on his arms over her and drank her in. Melissa lay eager below him. Her thighs dropping open, her musky scent of arousal filling his nostrils. He thrilled at the thought he was the only man to see her like this—wet, hot, and aching with desire.

She looked into his eyes and, in a sultry whisper, said, "Take me. Make me yours."

Painful need twisted deep in his groin. Her words thrilled him—she *was* his.

Needing no further encouragement, he bent and quickly captured her left breast and suckled. He moved his head and laved her other breast with his tongue, torn with the need to take both breasts in his mouth at once.

He groaned as she reached for him and caressed his skin, running her hands up his back and down his arms as he devoured her breasts with reckless, fiery, suckling kisses.

He lifted his head and swept his gaze down her body, over her flat stomach, lingering over her brush of dark curls and down over her slender firm legs. She was beautiful. He shuddered with the need to feel her legs wrapped around his hips. But he wanted her wet and begging to be taken first.

He trailed kisses down her stomach, while his hand dipped between her legs. She was wet, and so hot he burned to taste her.

He moved between her thighs and, lifting her bottom off the bed, hitched her legs up over his shoulders so her mound was directly in front of his mouth.

"I want to taste you." Before she could protest, he placed his tongue on her wet folds and gloried in her shuddered response.

Her taste was intoxicating. He probed her sleek heat, and he soon had her bucking beneath his tongue's onslaught. He gripped her legs tighter so she couldn't pull away. He wanted to hear her come, to feel her juices exploding against his mouth.

He mercilessly drove his tongue deep within her over and over, and then he took her engorged nub in his mouth and sucked hard. He felt her body spasm, and her legs gripped his neck with incredible strength.

Her head thrashed on the scarlet sheets as he continued to drive her toward another completion. She still quaked when he began to lick her again, his tongue lapping every drop of her passion.

He kept up his ministrations, plunging his tongue deep within her, then suckling her with his mouth and then lapping at her folds until the room filled with her moans. He continued to work his tongue in time to her moans. Her hips moved toward him, her natural instincts driving her on.

He gripped her thighs more firmly, his tongue penetrating

her. He could feel her intimate muscles contract as her female musk surrounded him in a sensual cloud.

Her body quivered uncontrollably. She was so close to another climax. He gave one hard suck and she cried out his name, "Anthony!" Her voice cracked as she reached her shuddering peak. "Oh, Anthony!" she screamed before she fell back on the sheets, panting.

He placed her legs back down on the bed and moved between her thighs, his legs pushing them wide. He waited. Waited for her to focus on what he was going to do to her. He wanted her to watch as he claimed her. He wanted to see the passion burning within her eyes.

The delay was almost blowing the top of his head off.

For an endless space, she clung to the burning light and stars. She'd never felt anything like it. She opened her eyes and looked into his face. It was hard with his own need.

She looked down to where he was positioned between her legs, which were wide in invitation. He was poised above her, looking intensely into her face. He looked like a Greek statue carved in stone, yet the heat radiating from him was scorching.

Melissa reached between his legs. He jerked as her hand circled his hot, silken erection.

She spoke. "I want you inside me. I want to feel all of you as you move deep within me."

Anthony groaned.

She gripped him gently and began the rhythmic stroking Cassandra's book described to her.

"Harder," he groaned. "Grip me harder."

She tightened and applied more pressure until he closed his eyes and flung his head back. She could see the tautness in his jaw. He liked what she was doing.

"Christ." He surged in her hand, and his breathing grew more rapid. When she looked up, his eyes glared back at her, full of heat and fire. "No more, stop. I didn't perform particularly well the last time I was inside you. I want to make this joining last."

He slowly began to enter her, inch by incredible inch. He was big, and she felt his invasion. His eyes never left her face, and she knew he wanted her to feel every inch of him as he slid deep within her.

He leaned down and kissed her tenderly, catching her bottom lip between his teeth and swirling his tongue inside her mouth. Her body opened to him, and even without the knowledge gained from Cassandra's book, her legs lifted to encircle his hips, allowing him even greater access.

He filled her to the hilt. He paused above her, his arms straight, muscles taut, and then he lowered himself to her completely and buried his face in her neck as he slid deeper still. His hand stretched out to where hers clutched the bedcovers and covered it. With a soft groan, he lifted his hips and began a delicate and stimulating dance of penetration and withdrawal. It felt as if she were floating, almost above them, as he continued his even course of stroking her with his body, lengthening inside her. Melissa watched the sunlight dancing across the walls in time to his body's movement.

She shifted beneath him and felt the mound of her sex brush against the hair that covered his groin. A sharp bolt of pleasure seared her at the contact. She wanted more. She lifted her hips, meeting his thrusts. Carefully he withdrew, then stroked into her depths again until she was arching up off the bed. An unbearable, sweet pressure mounted, and she moaned and tried to find his mouth. He turned his head aside.

His hand tightened around her wrist. "Let me hear you. Your small whimpers drive me mad. I want to hear you scream when you come."

He increased his pace, the thrusts getting faster and harder, a torturous movement, pushing her toward an anticipation of ecstasy like she'd never experienced.

She began to squirm and buck beneath him, matching his

frantic pace. His strokes took on a new urgency, which she matched. The sound of their bodies meeting filled the room. He met her body with a fierceness that had her begging for more.

The grip on her hand loosened, and she eagerly sought the corded muscles in his shoulders and back, running her hands down to cup his flexing buttocks.

"God, you're heaven, so hot, so tight . . ." he whispered roughly as he slipped his hand between their joined bodies and began to stroke her. "I can't wait. Come for me—now."

As if her body understood his command, she was all at once soaring high above herself as overlapping waves of plea-sure spilled over her. His hand continued to torment her sex, and yet another erotic assault built to another mind-blowing climax. Gloriously, when she thought she could bear no more, her body released itself again and she screamed, "An-thony, oh, my God, Anthony."

At her scream Anthony's thrusts quickened, and he plunged into her over and over again, until with a roar, he flung his head back and withdrew from her, spilling his seed on the sheets between her thighs. He collapsed on top of her. She felt his heart beating rapidly against her breast.

She relished Anthony's heavy weight on her. That had been the most awe-inspiring experience. No book could have pre-pared her for what she'd just shared with Anthony. It was more than just the mere welding of two bodies; it was hearts and souls as well. It had to be. It was the intimate act of love, and she wanted to stay locked in his arms and revel in its glow. His embrace filled her emptiness with warmth and ten-derness and . . . love?

No.

He had withdrawn before . . . Why had he withdrawn from her? That was not supposed to happen unless . . . unless a man did not want his seed to take root in a woman. Madame du Barry detailed exactly how this practice could prevent women from getting with child.

Her world trembled, her heart fractured, and she came

back down from the heavens with a resounding crash. She pushed at his dead weight above her.

Anthony lifted his head. "Am I too heavy?"

She swallowed painfully and quietly asked, "Are you ashamed of me?"

Rising onto his elbows, his cool mask hardening his features, he replied, "Of course not."

Then why? A small tear slipped out of the corner of her eye. She shoved at his massive shoulders. "Get off me."

He rolled to her side and tried to pull her into his arms. She slapped his hands away and scurried off the bed, heedless of her nakedness.

"You do prefer whores; you just treated me like one. You didn't stay inside me. I picked the right outfit last night. That's what got your attention. Not me. Not your wife."

She watched Anthony go absolutely still, and his eyes narrowed. "Calm down, Melissa. You don't know what you are saying."

"Calm down. Calm down!" Her tears burned a trail on her cheeks. "Why? Why did you just . . . Why did you just ruin one of the most perfect moments for me? What is so wrong with me that you would deny me the one thing I crave in life—children?" She was sobbing and she didn't care. She hated him. Anthony had just taken her dreams and squashed them.

He had used her. She'd been convenient. He didn't really want her. Hadn't she learned by now that she was not special? No one truly cared for her. Especially her husband, who'd been forced to marry her when all he'd really wanted was Cassandra.

Had he been thinking of Cassandra the whole time he was making love to her?

She sucked in deep breaths, trying to gather her composure. "I know you did not wish to marry me, but you don't appear to want me—for anything. You don't even want me to have your children. I love children. I want loads of children. I could survive a loveless marriage if I had children.

Why did you work so hard to ensure I accepted this monstrosity of a marriage when you had no intention of including me in any aspect of your life?"

She angrily swiped her tears. She tilted her head, clutching her hand to her bosom. "Why did you bother bringing me to Bressington with you? I may as well have stayed in London." She felt the blood drain from her face, and she gripped the bedpost until her knuckles turned white. "Oh, God. You brought me here to leave me—Bressington is to be my prison. To discard me while you go back to London, back to your life. Didn't you?"

He said nothing, but she saw the flicker of truth flash in his eyes.

Her hands dropped to her sides. "Why Anthony? Why did you trap me in this . . . in this . . . I don't even know what to call it. What did I ever do to you?"

Chapter 19

Anthony stared at the woman whose life he'd just shattered, and guilt gnawed on his innards. Melissa deserved his honesty, deserved to know he was not ashamed of her—just deeply ashamed of his own actions. He should have told her before they married.

"I don't want children. I have nothing against you personally. I'm sure you'd make an excellent mother. I, however, would make a dreadful father."

Melissa's mouth gaped. Her hands curled into fists. "Then why marry me at all? You could have paid my brother's debts and provided me with an income to live quietly in the country. Why go through this charade?"

Anthony shrugged his shoulders. "I had several reasons if you must know. Protecting your reputation was one of them."

"I don't believe you. You're rumored to be coldhearted and incapable of love. I didn't want to believe it—but now . . ." She hissed, "I want the truth. All of it."

He swung his legs over the side of the bed and stood facing her. "I wanted my mother to stop shoving debutantes in my face. I wanted everyone to think I'd soon sire an heir, even when I have no intention of ever providing one. Now married, my mother and brother will leave me alone."

Melissa paled and gripped the bedpost for support. More tears slipped down her beautiful face. She tried to brush them away. In a voice he could barely hear, she whispered, "You selfish—loveless—bastard."

"I'd like to think of it as practical. As you so often advised, a logical solution. I saw a solution that would help us both."

"Help me . . ." Her head snapped up, anger shining through her tears. "Help me! You've taken everything from me—my ability to have a proper marriage, to find love, to have children, and now you're taking my freedom."

Trembles racked her small frame. His gut tightened. "I'm sor—."

She held up a palm. "Don't. Don't you dare say those words to me. Not after what you just did. You used me for sex. It wasn't me you wanted. It could have been any woman—any thighs to sate your lust between."

She stood there, her body gloriously displayed. Her pert breasts heaving in anger. She was wrong—he had wanted her, only her. He despised himself for it. He wanted her so much he'd almost given in and damned the consequences. It was true. Already he felt his body stirring at the thought of taking her again and again and again. . .

She was right. He should have told her about the white marriage before making love to her. He should have confessed all. But he'd been a coward. His self-loathing rose to throttle him. He needed to end this before his compassion for this beautiful woman overrode his common sense and he dropped to his knees and begged her for forgiveness. Begged her to be a real wife to him.

"I fucked you because you kept throwing yourself at me. I told you not to dress the whore for me."

She sunk down to her knees, arms folded on the edge of the bed, and gave a sob. "God, I'm such a fool. Richard told me you were nothing like your father, but he was wrong. You don't care what happens to me as long as I do my job. Stay caged at Bressington letting the world think—think what?" She gave a choked gasp. "That I'm barren?"

He turned away and reached for his trousers.

"Don't ignore me. Answer me like a man. Was it always

your plan to use my body when you saw fit—making sure I never conceived? Never created the one person who'd love me unconditionally?" Her hatred slashed him with each blink of her eyelashes. "You're just like your father. A cold-hearted bastard, incapable of one ounce of emotion. You've treated me like a lowly slave you'd buy at market. Well, that's the last time you ever touch me. Do you hear? I'm not here simply for your pleasure, at your whim."

"This is your fault. My plan was to find a willing mistress. But you asked me not to give the position to Cassandra. I have yet to find a replacement. I have waited too long to bed a woman, and your naive attempts at seduction overcame my good sense."

Like a queen she lifted her head off the bed. "Get out. Get out of my room. Now!"

"It's my room actually. Everything in this house is mine. You'd best remember that."

Melissa's face paled and she gagged. "You'll never own me. I'll not be a slave—not for anyone. You didn't stand up to your father, but I'm strong; I'll never submit to you—never."

Not stood up . . . she had no idea what he had endured under his father's dictates, how hard he had fought. He had the scars—both external and internal—to prove it.

Fury pushed him beyond reason. He leaped over the bed and pulled her roughly up and into his arms. His mouth took her lips in a punishing kiss. He lifted her, as she squirmed in his grasp, and threw her down on the bed. Her eyes widened with shock.

He came down on top of her before she could move, his weight pinning her beneath him. He grabbed her wrists and pinned them above her head. He could feel her lifted breasts squashing against his chest, still taste her on his lips. He nudged her legs wide and settled between her thighs.

"First and foremost you will submit whenever I damn well feel like it." Her body tensed under his, her eyes filling with fear. "Secondly," he growled, "this is my house and you are my wife; you belong to me." He took her lips once more, forcing his tongue into her mouth.

She twisted her head away from him and let out a gut-wrenching sob. "You told me once that you would never knowingly hurt me. If you take me now, against my will, you'll destroy me."

He stilled above her. Guilt knifed through him until his body was awash with pain. He felt ill. What was he doing? He rose up off the bed. He couldn't bring himself to look at Melissa, but he could hear her quiet sobs.

Anthony gathered his clothes off the floor. Rufus's words came back to haunt him—*slavery takes many forms*. He felt his world tip on its axis and send him spiraling down to hell. He *was* his father. He left the room without a backward glance.

In his bedchamber he poured himself a drink and dropped his head in his hands. What had he done? He loathed himself beyond measure. He could hear her soft cries through the open door. How could he almost have raped his wife, what was wrong with him?

The whole sickening scene reminded him of the time his father forced him to. . .

He gulped the whiskey down in one swallow.

Melissa's words had fed such a rage. A rage he thought he'd managed to conquer. He'd prided himself over the years of managing to contain his darkness. Yet, all it took was one taunt from her—his wife—and his inner demons surfaced with a vengeance.

What a pathetic fool he had become, a weak pathetic fool who had let a woman he did not even want to marry affect him!

Appalled, he knew he had to get away. Away from her. He had hurt her as he predicted. Ironically, he'd succeeded. He'd wanted to do something to make her hate him, to leave her repulsed by him.

He had achieved that and so much more.

He could safely say his wife would never want to lay eyes on him again.

Unfortunately, he hadn't expected to feel so desolated, and so alone, at the news.

He hadn't expected to fall in love with his wife.

The tavern was dank and stank of vermin, both the animal and human sort. The smell of alcohol didn't cover the stench, and Anthony had to stifle the urge to cover his nose with a handkerchief.

He'd ridden directly from Cambridge to Great Yarmouth, stopping to briefly rest over the arduous four-day journey. Yet every time he closed his eyes and tried to doze, he saw Melissa's tear-stained face, and self-loathing assaulted his body to the point where he felt too ill to sleep.

Now he'd been in this godforsaken town for three days, his disguise of a local farmer seeking refreshment after selling his wares at market seemed to be intact. In the days he had spent in and around the taverns near the docks, he'd had little luck in gathering any kind of information on Rothsay's whereabouts or if he had ships in port.

He was sitting in the Nags Head tavern waiting for Rufus's contact. One of Rufus's agents had uncovered a lead. He'd just lifted his tankard to his lips when a small boy appeared at his side and pressed a note into his hands. The boy took off before he could ask any questions.

As per the note's instruction, he left the tavern and entered the small alleyway at the side, ready for any treachery. He got almost halfway in where he heard a scrape and a match blaze to life as a man lit a cheroot.

"Lord Wickham, I presume."

Anthony tensed. "And you are?"

The man took a long draw on his smoke. "No names, if you please. If you'll follow me I'll take you to a man who may be of interest in your quest for Baron Rothsay. We are holding him in custody for a matter relating to treason, but he had the poor judgment to boast about knowledge of a white slavery ring." He moved into the lamplight, but his head was covered by a large hat. "He may have some information for you. Lord Strathmore says I am to provide you with every assistance."

"Lead on."

They reached the jail minutes before midnight. If he'd thought the tavern stank he was wrong. The prison smelled as if he'd stepped into hell. Nothing could cloak the smells of rotting flesh and excrement. This time he did use a handkerchief to cover his nose.

As they approached a cell, the jailer said gruffly, "You there. Get to your feet. You 'ave visitors."

A hulking brute of a man rose up from a pallet of straw and spat on the ground. He spied the man at Anthony's side. "Come back to try and beat more information out of me? You'll not get it. I'm dead anyway; do your worst."

The man beside Anthony quietly said, "Simon Clune, even though it goes against every principle I possess"—he sighed deeply—"in exchange for information on another matter, the Foreign Secretary has instructed me to offer you transportation to the colonies—for life."

An evil smile broke across the man's battered features. "I won't hang?"

"No," came the curt reply.

Anthony eyed the prisoner, trying to ascertain if he could believe a word that came out of the man's mouth. After all, he could tell them anything simply in order to avoid hanging.

As the silence drew out, Clune grew more triumphant. "You must want this info pretty bad. I'll not dob on my friends."

"We don't want details on your mangy pack. We'll have most of them rounded up by morning. It is a completely different matter."

Clune turned his gaze to Anthony. Unflinchingly, Anthony returned his stare. He kept his voice gentle. "I'm after information on a man named Rothsay."

Clune's eyes narrowed. "What sort of information?"

"You know him then? In that case, you'll have some idea of what intelligence I wish to gain."

Clune turned back to Anthony's contact. "Is this on the up? You'd spare my life for any information on a slavery ring?"

Anthony lost his patience. "Yes. A white slavery ring, Mr. Clune. Do you know of it?"

"Well, God is smiling on me. This is my lucky night. Aye, I know of it. Rothsay's been operating it since the end of last year, when the navy increased its patrols on the Atlantic route. I'll tell you all you want to know. The bastard almost killed my Alice after I lent her to him for the night. He's a pervert."

Anthony's breath hissed out between his teeth. That was when he'd provided the navy with information that led to the seizure of three of his ships. "Do you know which port he operates from?"

Clune nodded. "He doesn't use only one. He's clever. He uses smaller vessels to hold women on, schooners that the navy thinks are too small to be of any interest. Then sails them to wherever he has a merchant ship sailing out of a port and transfers them far out at sea. That's why he's never been caught. It could be any boat, docked anywhere."

Anthony's raised hopes were dashed. It would be nigh impossible to track smaller boats at every port. Rothsay was clever. But if they had to search every smaller vessel, at every port, just prior to sailing, he would see to it. Anthony stepped closer to the bars, the light revealing his face. "Is there a particular vessel he uses to ferry the women? Anything you could remember about these boats? Anything to narrow our search?"

Clune frowned. "I know you. You're Lord Wickham; you used to be in partnership with Rothsay. He pays good money for any information on your business. He's taken a real personal interest in you."

Anthony couldn't help the shiver that racked his body. "Stop wasting my time. Do you know anything else?"

The silence was deafening. Anthony was turning to leave when Clune uttered, "He sometimes uses his own pleasure craft. A thirty-foot schooner called *The Master*. It's often docked on the Thames near London. The streets of the city are easy pickings for a wealthy lord. Plenty of women to abduct and none the wiser. Who'd notice one missing from thousands?"

Contemplating the prisoner, Anthony was certain he'd get nothing more from him. "Thank you, Mr. Clune. Enjoy Australia."

Anthony followed his contact's lantern back out into the night. "Thank you. That has been most helpful."

"Thank Lord Strathmore. If I had my way, Clune would still hang. But I have given my word."

Anthony didn't return to his lodgings. He made directly for the stables and was soon on his way back to London.

Chapter 20

Melissa felt waves of nausea begin to rise. She was too ill to even lean over the edge of the bed to reach the bowl. Thank God for Theresa. Theresa held back her hair with one hand, the bowl with the other.

It wasn't just the guilt making her sick. Guilt from the afternoon when she had stood just where Theresa was standing now and told Anthony he was just like his father. She closed her eyes. What made her say such a thing? She knew nothing could be further from the truth; the mere remembrance of what she had said, what she had hurled at him, made her belly lurch again. But she was now certain it was not only her remorse making her ill.

"It's been over six weeks since his lordship left. Stop pining for him. You're making yourself ill."

Melissa gave a wan smile. Even though she was exhausted and emotionally spent, she knew Theresa was wrong.

Wearily she sank back on her pillows. The past few weeks imprisoned at Bressington had been an incredible, while horrifying, journey into Anthony's past. There were only a few servants remaining from when Anthony was a young boy, but the stories they told her still had her reeling.

Ted, the head gardener, had been a young lad when Anthony and Richard were born. His stories made her wish she could cut out her tongue for having lashed out at a man who had suffered more than she could have ever imagined.

What Anthony had endured as a child she could not begin to fathom, and she'd thought her upbringing had been devoid of love! She'd never been subjected to such abuse and cruelty . . . it was little wonder he was as guarded with his emotions as he was. She understood him better now and wished she'd known more before she irrevocably pushed him away. Her ache for him was sharply focused and wearing her down.

They both had something in common. They had both been denied the love of their parents. They both had no real notion of what real love was like—what it took to earn it and how hard it was to keep it.

She glanced at the ceiling, blinking back the glimmer of tears. Now, knowing about Anthony's childhood, she more than ever wanted to reach out and teach him about love. They could learn together.

She prayed with all her heart that she'd be able to show Anthony what it was to be cherished. That he'd forgive her enough to be in her company.

Anthony had wanted her, but not enough. Not enough to risk being hurt again. He did not love her. Now it was clear he would never let her close enough to try, not without a fight. And here she was lying here, as if beaten. She sat up. That would never do.

Richard, on his last visit, told her why Anthony was so scared of having a child. Anthony thought he was evil like his father, incapable of love. She briefly closed her eyes. She'd accused him of that very thing, here, in this bedchamber, the night he'd left.

That is why Anthony had lashed out.

But she didn't believe he was incapable of love. She knew there was good in him. He'd been so tender when they'd made love. It wasn't just about his pleasure; she'd felt his feelings for her.

"You're right, Theresa, I am wasting away. But I don't hate his lordship. I love him. I'm not sick because I'm pining for him. I think I'm with child."

Theresa's calm voice broke into her thoughts. "I thought you said he'd not—"

She raised her hand to her throat, willing her emotions to stop choking her. "The night he compromised me, the night he thought I was Cassandra, he did not withdraw." She tenderly cupped her stomach. That night, almost two months ago, the man who did not want her love had given her the most precious gift. How could she hate him? She was going to have his child.

"When are you going to tell him?"

Her hand stilled its stroking. "I don't know. I have to handle this carefully."

He'd made it very clear that he wanted to lead separate lives. More of a concern was his opposition to children. She had simply been a means to keep Society at bay. What would he do if he found out she was with child? Would he build even thicker walls around his heart? She had to think of a way to break through, even if it took months of chipping away the stone—block by block.

"He'll find out. You'll not be able to hide your protruding belly for long."

Melissa threw back the covers and sat up on the edge of the bed. The dizziness and nausea always left her by early afternoon. "I'll wear my riding habit today. I need some fresh air to clear my head. I need to think. I need to understand what Anthony is likely to do when he finds out." She stood and moved to the window. The splendor of Bressington lay before her. Though she never tired of its beauty, it was still her prison. A prison with no bars, but a prison all the same.

Melissa didn't know what to do. Perhaps a ride would reveal an answer.

"You want me to be what?" Anthony asked in stunned amazement.

Freddie Dorrington, the Marquis of Skye, stood before the fire, cradling his newborn son in his arms. The silliest smile plastered across his handsome face. "Samantha and I would like you to be Philip's godfather, and Melissa to be his god-mother."

At the mention of his wife, Anthony's stomach churned. He missed her. He still wanted her. He feared her and what she made him feel.

Then again, his greatest fear was currently sleeping in his best friend's arms. The thought of being this tiny infant's godfather gripped his innards. He broke out into a cold sweat. "No. Absolutely not."

Samantha, sitting across from him on the settee, gave a warm chuckle. "A grown man scared of such a tiny babe. You're being ridiculous."

The drawing room of Freddie's home became oppressive. Anthony ran his finger around his cravat. His gaze hardened on Freddie's face. "You don't know what you ask."

Like an assassin sent to kill him, Freddie approached, one foot before the other, bringing the danger ever nearer. Anthony was frozen, unable to move from his chair.

Freddie held out his precious bundle. "Hold him." Freddie smiled. "Go on, he won't bite. He might throw up on you, but I'm sure the mighty Earl of Wickham can survive a bit of vomit." He tenderly laid Philip in Anthony's arms.

Anthony became a statue. He was too scared to move. What if he dropped him? He looked down at the babe lying peacefully in his arms, and something tugged in his chest. Lord Philip Dorrington was so small. So vulnerable.

Protective feelings reared inside him. He'd never let anything hurt something so tiny, something so precious.

Samantha watched the play of emotions flicker over Anthony's face. She couldn't imagine the war being waged within. Her heart bled for his pain. He would make a magnificent father. She believed Anthony had so much love to give . . . if he'd let himself. She'd hoped his marrying Melissa might have burst the damn, but he'd managed to push her away, too.

She gazed at her husband. Her wonderful husband. She

would not fail today. She owed Anthony everything for he'd introduced her to Freddie.

She rose. "I have some correspondence to answer. I shall leave you three boys alone."

She gave Freddie a knowing look before closing the door quietly behind her.

Freddie stood looking down at him. In a soft voice he whispered, "What are you so afraid of?"

Anthony closed his eyes, his voice raw with emotion. "Don't do this to me, Freddie."

Freddie crouched down next to Anthony's chair and stroked a finger down his son's face. Lord Philip opened his eyes. Baby-blue eyes focused on Anthony, then Philip smiled.

Anthony's heart lurched, filling his chest to bursting point. Philip looked so much like Freddie.

Philip's little fists waved in the air, his little legs jerking against Anthony's arm.

His proud papa said, "Isn't he amazing? A true gift from God. To think Samantha and I created something so innocent, so helpless, so . . . perfect."

Without thinking, Anthony gave the baby his finger. Philip grabbed it with his tiny hand and made a gurgle of sound.

"He likes you."

Anthony couldn't tear his eyes away from the sight. Philip lay content, gripping his finger, kicking his legs and blowing bubbles of saliva out of his mouth.

Anthony's eyes lifted to Freddie. "You know me. You know what I am capable of. You know what I did when I was young."

Freddie looked at his son, then back at Anthony. "The boy, heavily under the influence of his father, is nothing like the man you have become. You should be proud. You survived." Freddie stood and moved back to lean against the mantelpiece. "Would you let anyone hurt him? Would you protect Philip?"

Anthony swore. "With my life."

Freddie nodded. "I need to know that if something should happen to me, my son would be raised by someone I trust. Someone who would not only protect him but teach him right from wrong, show him how to be a man, and most of all love him."

His eyes pierced Anthony. "You are that man. You know what is important to a child. You know how a child should be treated. If your father's cruelty taught you anything, he taught you how a child needs to be loved, should be loved."

His voice a ghost of a whisper, Anthony asked Freddie, "How do you know? How do you know I'm not like my father? Love is only a word to me. Am I even capable of love?"

"Look at you. You're holding my son as if he were the most precious thing in the world to you. I can see the emotion in your face. Fierce and proud."

Anthony raised his head, startled. Freddie was right.

"Now imagine what you'd feel if you were holding your own son."

The words sent a blinding image crashing through his head. A picture of a little girl laughing up at him. She had large hazel eyes, flowing black hair, and the face of an angel. Melissa's face.

A floodgate opened, and his heart filled with emotion until he thought it would explode from his chest. Tenderness and something deep, too deep for words, swam through his body, touching every part of him.

His child. Their child.

His throat clogged with emotion. Christ! He knew this infant was dangerous. He gathered Philip tightly against his chest. He loved this baby already. And he would love his own children, ensuring nothing hurt them. He would protect and cherish them.

Anthony rose and handed Philip back to Freddie, his eyes misty with unshed tears. "Thank you. Thank you for showing me."

"I have tried to show you for years, as has Rufus. You are not your father. "

Anthony gripped the mantel with both hands and hung his head. "Melissa. God, what have I done?"

"You love her." It wasn't a question. "I know because you pushed her away. If you had no feelings for her, you would have left her at Craven House. She'd have been no threat."

"It's frightening how well you know me." He turned to Freddie. "I think I've loved her from the moment I compromised her and she told me not to sacrifice myself for her. I simply refused to recognize the emotion. I didn't think I was capable of love."

"Love is scary. It's painful, frightening, and frustrating. But it's also the most noble of emotions. You'd do anything to hold on to it, to revel in its glow, and most importantly, to bestow it unconditionally on the people you love."

"I love her." His voice hitched. "I love Melissa."

"Of course you do. That's why you've been behaving like a man whose head is pounding from too much drink."

"I'm such a fool." He turned beseechingly to Freddie. "What should I do?"

Freddie smiled and held Philip up to his shoulder. "When everyone else looked down on Samantha and her background, when Society told me to throw her away, do you remember what you said to me? 'Selfless love is a gift so rare, a gift beyond measure, and a man should give up everything he owns just to have a glimpse of it.' You were right. To have what I have with Samantha I would have given up everything—including my pride."

The two men eyed each other.

"Go to her, Anthony, and even if you have to get down on your knees and beg for forgiveness until eternity, do it."

"What if that is not enough?"

"Then do whatever it takes until it is enough. You're the Lord of Wicked; surely you know how to woo a woman?"

"That's the problem. She was never terribly impressed with the Lord of Wicked."

Freddie simply smiled. "Then show her the man underneath. She won't be able to resist loving him."

Chapter 21

She'd managed to give her constant shadow the slip. Stubbs had been adamant that Mr. Dutton must accompany her whenever she left the immediate grounds of Bressington. Apparently there had been some thieves in the area attacking the wealthy. Stubbs felt responsible for her with her husband absent.

Nevertheless, today she needed to be alone. Alone to contemplate her next move. Was she brave enough to go to London and beg Anthony's forgiveness? What kind of reception would he give her?

The late afternoon sun warmed her skin as she steered her bay mare along the lush fields of Bressington. Melissa tried to ignore the churning despair grinding her stomach.

She was pregnant and Anthony had left her. She'd heard no word for almost six weeks. Where was he? Who was he with? Had he procured a mistress? Her eyes filled with tears. Of course he would have.

How ironic that the man she loved, the man she'd gifted her heart to, was unlikely to let her near enough to prove to him how rewarding their match could be.

If she chased after him, he'd push her away. He dealt with intimacy by seeking mindless pleasure and avoiding anything that truly made her feel. He protected himself by shielding his heart behind a stone fortress. She wasn't sure she had the strength or tenacity to chip away and free his heart, stone by stone.

For the child she carried she would try anything, do anything, to ensure their son or daughter knew its father's love.

After the way he'd made love to her, she had foolishly thought she'd penetrated his protective wall.

Then he'd calmly informed her he did not want children.

She'd realized her mistake too late. His wall had not been bridged, it was still impregnable. Making love, for him, was not about the joining of two souls. It was a pleasurable pastime. He'd tried to warn her of that once. He used pleasure to block out hurt and bitterness.

He could not grasp the fact that love was the only true protection. Nothing could hurt you, if you had love.

The pain his words had inflicted still knifed through her chest. He wanted a "white marriage" so that he would never father a child.

She placed a hand over her stomach. The thought of never having a child to love was like being told she had a cancer. She got down on her knees and thanked God that their very first union had produced this child, for if she could not win his favor, she did not think she'd ever be blessed with another.

Her senses skittered. If she had to choose between a loveless marriage and her child, there was no contest. She would face any exile as long as she could hold her child in her arms. She'd never let him take the baby from her—never. She'd flee to the ends of the earth.

She wanted the baby she carried. She wanted his child. This baby now meant more to her than life itself.

Guilt made her give a small sob. She would have to tell Anthony. He deserved to know he had a child. Perhaps—perhaps when he held his baby he'd change his mind. That's it. As soon as the child was born she would return to Anthony. Not before. The only way to break through to him would be to place their child in his arms. Make the child real to him.

She knew his battle with his inner demon. She knew Anthony was capable of love. He was just—scared . . .

Anthony was scared of love.

She would teach him. Teach him that there was nothing to fear. Their child would be their savior. Like everything in his life, he battled that which he was afraid of, that which he did not understand.

All she had to do was show him how to conquer his fear. Prove to him that letting love win was not losing—it would bring him more joy and happiness than anything he'd ever known.

He cared too much about people to let his own son become a stranger. Their child would be the solution. Their child would finally open his heart. Their child would win where she had failed.

Her stomach settled, and her breathing no longer caused pain in her chest. She had her answer, her plan.

A small voice inside her head issued a warning. Anthony might come to want his son, but that didn't mean he'd want her. She refused to dwell on that outcome.

Coming out of her daze, she took stock of her surroundings. She had ridden farther than she had anticipated. Looking around, she was surprised to see a figure sitting atop a black horse on the far side of the field. She did not recognize the rider. She turned in her saddle, confused. She was still on Bressington land. What did this stranger want?

He kicked his steed and slowly made his way across the field toward her. He began to take shape. He seemed somewhat familiar. Where had she met him before?

She became uneasy. Like snowflakes hitting her face, an icy chill seeped into her veins. It was the acquaintance of Anthony's from the slave auction. Every hair on her body prickled.

Swallowing her fear, she turned her horse and simultaneously clapped her heels to the mare's flanks. She heard the man curse and yell, "Don't let her get away."

Spooked by the man's bellow, and by her obvious fear and

urging, the mare shot off, streaking across the meadow, parallel to the copse.

The copse seemed to thunder into life as men and horses surged out of hiding.

Heart in her mouth, she swung the mare, cornering around the copse, forcing the men to wheel their horses before they could follow.

Melissa swallowed her fear. She rode with hands and knees, urging the little mare to fly.

The mare was nimble and had a good turn of speed. Melissa choked the reins. It had been years since she had ridden this fast, this recklessly. Fear and desperation pounded in her veins. She sensed the horses gaining on her; she didn't risk a glance back. If she was unseated, she not only risked them catching her, she might fall and hurt the baby.

She couldn't outrun them, not with a mare she'd ridden all afternoon. She would have to lose them before the mare lost her strength.

One paddock over was Blackwood Forest. Dense woodland with trees large enough to hide her, or at least give her mare a fighting chance.

She headed toward the woods, her closest cover. Her hands on the reins felt like ice.

She pressed her heels into her horse's heaving sides. The gallant mare responded as she veered north and tried to pick up the pace, racing as if chased by the devil.

Her hands shook. He was the devil. His men's curses carried on the breeze.

Facing forward, her lungs tight, she continued to urge the mare on. They were gaining on her, the ground shaking from their thunderous strides.

Sooner than she expected, a line of trees rose before her. She headed for them and swung along the line, searching for a bridle path. For safety.

Her eyes locked on a break in the tree line—an entrance. She was fifty yards from it when she took another look over her shoulder. With a grim grin she knew she'd make it.

Just as she swung her gaze back to the trees she saw the branch, but it was too late. She didn't have time to duck, and within a blink, pain struck her head and everything went black.

She didn't know where she was or how she'd got here. She felt weak, and it was an effort to breathe. A blacksmith was hammering in her head. She tried to sit up and groaned. The room swayed and the floor rushed up to greet her.

She lay back against the pillows. She looked down. Her riding jacket and boots gone, stripped off her while she'd been unconscious. Her uneasiness grew at the thought of strangers undressing her.

Where was she? She was not at Bressington. The room was unfamiliar and looked—different. *Think Melissa. What happened?*

Her mind began to clear, but she still felt as if she were—rocking. She heard men calling out, gulls screeching, and the smell of salt and sea overwhelmed her.

She was on a boat. Whose boat?

She remembered racing across the fields. A pain swamped her tired body, and she gave a low groan. She moved her hand and placed it tenderly over her stomach. A more paralyzing fear gripped her, making her chest contract so hard she could not breathe. What if she had lost the child? She felt between her thighs. There was no blood.

She heard footsteps steadily nearing her door. Her lips trembled, and she willed the choking panic to disappear. Sitting up, she swung her legs over the edge of the bunk and ignored the dizziness and light swaying. She had to remain calm. She ran her hands over her hair, which was still held in place by her combs. Apart from her clothing, she seemed to be all in one piece. She folded her hands demurely in her lap. All she wanted to know was whether she was still with child.

The door opened. It was the man from the slave auction, the man who'd stared at her on her horse. "Good, you're awake."

Her pulse raced even though the man did not appear to be too frightening. He was of average height, not much taller than she, and lean of build. His brown hair was cut short and hugged a noble head. His lips were full and his nose straight, adding to his aristocratic bearing. He was obviously a member of her class. A man of Society. She wondered why that frightened her more.

His face was quite alluring, classically chiseled, and his high cheekbones drew an onlooker upward to eyes of pale blue, the color of frozen ice. They were hypnotizing, framed by thick chocolate lashes, giving his face an air of femininity. Most women would find him very attractive, until they looked deep into those eyes.

Melissa's breath caught in her throat; they were eyes filled with pure evil. There was not one drop of humanity radiating from within their steely depths.

He advanced into the cabin and closed the door.

She went on the defensive. Her mouth was so dry she could barely form words. "How long have I been here?"

"How interesting. Not where am I, but how long have I been captive? It never ceases to amaze me how ladies of the *ton* hold their reputations in greater stead than their safety."

"Without our reputations what do we have?"

His laugh, as brittle as broken glass, filled the small space. "I do admire a woman who is direct. You have been in my keeping for a few days. The fall was not as bad as I'd expected. You landed on a thicket of small bushes. They miraculously broke your fall. You have a small bump on your head, that is all."

She gripped the bedcovers, willing her hand not to move to her stomach. Her child was safe—for now.

He smiled. Menace poured into the cabin with that smile, so much so that Melissa jerked backward on the bunk.

"Do you know who I am?"

Melissa still could not get a word out. She simply shook her head.

"But you recognized me. That is why you ran." His smile

widened and became somewhat grotesque. "I am Philip Drake, Baron Rothsay. I'm surprised your husband did not tell you about me. We were friends, once inseparable, sharing everything—and I mean everything. Ah, happy memories of the many times I have shared a bed with Anthony and one or two of his strumpets."

Melissa's face remained blank. She would not let his crudity shock her. She tried to remember, but she was certain she'd never heard the name. She'd only glimpsed him briefly at the slave auction.

"However, I am quite sure he would not want to share you—his wife."

Melissa's head jerked up, and a sliver of fear began to smother her.

Lord Rothsay laughed, the sound harsh and ugly. "When I said friend, I meant business rivals. Although we were friends once, a long time ago. I could tell you things about your husband that would make you wish you'd never met him."

Perhaps if she let the Baron know she and Anthony did not get on, he'd not be able to use her to whatever end he envisaged. "I already wish I'd never met him."

He laughed. "This is not about who loves whom. It's about possession. About ownership. These are what a man like Wickham understands."

Melissa glared at the man who was enjoying toying with her. "What do you want with me?"

He moved with calculated grace until he stood directly in front of her, staring down, his eyelids never blinking. He reached out his hand and trailed a finger down her left cheek. She had to tighten every muscle in her body to stop herself from flinching at his touch.

His head bent toward her face and unable to help herself, she turned her head away. He moved so close she could feel his breath against her ear, and he softly uttered, "I want revenge."

He said the words as if they were a caress. A promise of what was to come. Melissa's bones filled with dread. She stammered, "I—I do not understand. Revenge for what? I don't even know you."

"Ah, my sweet, not revenge against you, revenge against your husband." He reached up and withdrew the combs holding her hair, and using both hands, he loosened her tresses until they flowed down her back. "Unfortunately, you are simply a means to an end. A very beautiful means." He kissed the top of her head. "If you do not fight me, you may even enjoy our time together. I have many things I wish to teach you. When I return you to your husband, I want you to show him what an adept teacher I have been."

Her racing heart suddenly stilled. He was going to have his revenge on Anthony by hurting her. The irony of that was not lost on her. Little did the Baron know, her husband did not value her. If Lord Rothsay destroyed her reputation, Anthony would have the ammunition to divorce her. Anthony would likely thank him.

This time he held her chin in a vicelike grip and took her mouth in a bruising kiss. She tried to break his hold, her hands tugging at his, but he tightened his grasp until she thought her jaw would break. Her lips parted to let out a shriek of pain, and he took immediate advantage, sweeping his tongue so far inside her mouth she gagged.

Instinct took over, and she kicked out at him, catching him hard on his shin. He tore his lips from hers. "Oh, kick me harder, I love pain." Shrugging his shoulders he added, "You shouldn't fight me though, I like my women willing. Perhaps it's best to teach you immediately what happens when you displease me."

He turned from her and began removing his jacket. Icy fear gripped her innards.

"You can beat me all you like, but I will not submit to you."

He moved and opening the cabin door yelled, "Johnson, bring the child up from the pen."

Melissa's hand immediately went to her stomach.

Lord Rothsay turned back to face her. "There is nothing to

gain from beating you into submission, Lady Wickham. When I pleasure my women"—he raised his eyebrow at her look of disbelief—"you will feel pleasure, I assure you, my sweet. I prefer them to be beautiful, not a mass of cuts and bruises."

With a show of defiance she said scornfully, "I will never submit willingly to your touch, and I certainly won't feel pleasure." She stood up from the bed. "You are stronger than I and can no doubt take my body, but I will never give you what's inside. I shall lock my feelings away. It will be like taking a dead body."

He laughed. "Such an innocent. No one can resist my brewed aphrodisiac." His eyes narrowed and hardened. "I have many things to teach you, Melissa, and your first lesson is—you must learn never to say never." He moved quickly and pulled her tight into his embrace, pinning her arms to her side, locking his thighs about her legs so that she was unable to move. For such a slight man he was very strong.

"I have seen and done things that would make your skin crawl, my sweet. Most of them with your husband in our younger days. I've learned that anyone will do what you ask of them if the right pressure is applied." And he bent and took her mouth in another kiss, a kiss that was meant to brand her and scare her into submission.

Melissa simply froze and refused to respond.

He lifted away from her as the door behind them swung open, and a man entered dragging a little Negro girl of about ten.

The child was wide eyed and extremely scared.

"This is where things get interesting, Melissa. I shall give you a choice. You will agree to lay with me, to act as my lover, to perform as my mistress without damage to my person, or I shall take this girl instead . . . while you watch."

Melissa's mouth dropped open in horror. The smirk on the face of the man called Johnson told her Lord Rothsay was deadly serious. Melissa put her hands up in front of her. "But she is only a child."

Lord Rothsay's expression did not alter. "Yes, I enjoy them this young. They scream in pain, which I also enjoy, but being so small they are easy to overpower. After a while the screams of agony are a bit off-putting, but I simply clamp a hand over their mouths when it gets too much." He did not blink. "But for you, my dear, I shall not silence her. You may find her screams intolerable."

Melissa died inside. She'd never felt so powerless. Numbness engulfed her. She knew he would do what he so casually described, knew he would enjoy it, and knew she could not bear it.

She was so deep in shock, she could not answer. She never fathomed such evil existed in the world.

"By the way, there are ten more girls where she came from. I am sure by the third girl you will come around to my way of thinking."

Still she said nothing.

Sighing, Lord Rothsay signaled to Johnson as he began to unbutton the placket of his trousers. Johnson grabbed the young girl, and with two hands, he ripped the thin dress she was wearing off her body.

The girl began to whimper and tried to hide her nakedness. Her body was still prepubescent, and Melissa felt like she was going to be sick.

"Stop." Melissa fell to her knees sobbing. "Please don't touch her."

Lord Rothsay stilled his hands and moved to stand over her. "Do you agree to my terms, Lady Wickham? You will come to my bed willingly?"

"Yes," she whispered.

Lord Rothsay bent lower. "What did you say? I cannot hear you."

Melissa turned her face upward and glared at him. "Yes," she yelled into his cruel face.

Lord Rothsay smiled. A smile that was almost humanlike. "Too easy. Just like Anthony, your heart is too soft."

Melissa frowned. Anthony's heart was anything but soft. It was a stone fortress, impenetrable.

Rothsay laughed. "Anthony hasn't told you. He hasn't begged your forgiveness. I thought he would seek his redemption through you." He bent and whispered in her ear. "He raped a young Negro girl not much older than the child who's just left this room."

"No," Melissa cried out. She shook her head. "He'd never do—he'd never hurt—no. He just wouldn't. I'll not listen to your lies."

"Ask him. When you next see him, ask him why he's so consumed with guilt. Why he thinks he's so evil."

Melissa brushed her tears off her cheeks. *When she sees him*. The Baron was not going to kill her then. She cradled her stomach. She could bare anything as long as her baby survived.

"Now don't sulk. Over the coming days I will teach you how to enjoy making love in many different ways. A few new tricks in your repertoire to impress your husband."

Melissa's elation suddenly came to an end when he uttered that one word—days. In a trembling voice she asked, "How long do you intend to keep me here?"

He turned at the door. "Rest now. You'll need your strength. We have a long night ahead of us."

"You did not answer my question."

His smile chilled her to the bone. "Until I can send you back pregnant with my child. I know your husband does not share your bed, and I know why." He hesitated, and for a minute she feared he wasn't leaving. "I will send someone along to see to your bath and provide you with food. You need to eat. You'll need plenty of stamina for what I have planned this evening."

Melissa dropped her eyes from his knowing gaze. She instinctively knew she had to keep her face blank. What would he do if he found out she was already with child?

Once he left the room, she leaned over the bunk and was violently sick in the chamber pot.

Weak and scared, she lay on the rocking bunk and looked at the mirrors above her on the ceiling. She did not recognize the woman staring back. She looked empty, like there was nobody living inside her.

Her hand moved to cradle her stomach. She had to escape and soon. Rothsay was a monster, only God knew what he'd do if he found out she was already with child.

Anthony's child.

Chapter 22

A nthony returned to Craven House early in the afternoon. He sent a runner with a note for Rufus, asking him to attend him immediately. He wanted to explain his absence for the next few weeks and hand over the latest intelligence on the search for Rothsay's boat, *The Master*, before setting out for Bressington.

Rufus's men had lost track of Rothsay. They believed he was no longer in Norfolk. The fact their enemy continued to elude them was frustrating to say the least. Anthony was restless, impatient, and he wanted Rothsay's white slavery ring destroyed, along with the man running it.

He'd only just settled behind his desk to tidy up the last pieces of correspondence when the study door burst open and panic—in the shape of Richard and Rufus—rushed in.

"Melissa!" Richard's chest heaved. "She's been taken."

Anthony bolted to his feet. "Taken! What do you mean taken? Who? How . . . ?" But he knew. His body chilled as his eyes locked on Rufus and saw his confirmation.

Richard rushed, "I was passing Bressington and stopped in to visit with her. The house was in an uproar. I came to find you as quickly as I could. I met Rufus, just now, on your front steps. He seems to know who would want to take her."

Anthony swore, clenched his fists at his side, and stormed around the desk heading for the door.

"Who? Who would take her?" Richard asked.

"Rothsay." He saw his brother's face drain of color.

Rufus put his arm out, halting his departure. "This is not the time for rash actions. We need to think this through. Where would he take her?"

Anthony ignored his friend and opened the door, calling for Stevens. He appeared immediately. "Saddle Dark Knight—now!"

Richard put his hand on his brother's shoulder. "It's not certain Rothsay's the one who kidnapped Melissa. Even if he has, you don't know where he will have taken her."

Anthony closed his eyes, and for once in his life, prayed. "He'll have taken her to his ship, *The Master*. He'll want to sell her. I should have known. A perfect way to get revenge on me—taking my wife and leaving me to live with the knowledge she is in some Arabian brothel . . ." He punched the door frame. "If only we knew where the ship was docked."

Anthony had not noticed Stevens' entry, but the butler's gasp drew his gaze. "My lord, *The Master* is docked at Tower Hill." Three sets of eyes drilled into Stevens. "Lady Sudbury has just returned from a visit to the schooner."

Anthony stilled. "Rothsay's in London—with Lady Sudbury?" If Cassandra had any part to play in this, he'd wring her pretty neck.

"Yes, my lord."

Before he could ask another question, Rufus uttered in amazement, "How do you know this?"

Stevens' face reddened. "I'm not one for gossip, sir, but some of the staff do talk."

"Go on," Anthony encouraged.

"The cook's cousin, Tom—he's downstairs eating some of Cook's famous pork pie—is Lady Sudbury's driver. Has been for years." Stevens appeared to get more nervous.

"Come on, out with it, man," Rufus urged.

"Lady Sudbury and Lord Rothsay have an unusual relationship. They have a common—interest." Stevens closed his eyes and in a rush uttered, "They are both members of Spare the Rod."

The stunned silence was shattered with Anthony's curse. "Christ." He turned to Richard. "Did you know?"

"Absolutely not. I know of the establishment, but it's never been my cup of tea."

Rufus uttered, "I've been there." Richard let out a low whistle. "In the line of duty. It is not a place I'd wish to return to—ever."

Anthony dragged in a deep breath, held it for a second while he thought. "Rufus, go and get Cassandra and bring her here. We'll talk with Tom. Stevens, send him up in ten minutes. Richard, I want to know every detail of Melissa's abduction."

Rufus curtly nodded and left the study with Stevens close behind. Anthony, too wound up to sit, stalked back and forth before the windows. Richard took a chair and began.

"I was in Kent visiting Miss Thornton—"

"Do get on. I don't want a catalog of your social life."

"Do you want to know about Melissa or not?" Richard huffed, his face turning slightly pink. "I thought I'd drop in and have dinner with Melissa. She's been miserable since you banished her to Bressington." Richard's voice was filled with condemnation. "Well, anyway, I arrived to find Theresa in tears and Mr. Dutton and the grooms running around saddling horses, swearing and cursing at each other. Each blaming themselves that they hadn't accompanied her on her ride.

"One of your tenant farmers had seen her being chased on horseback by a group of men. He tried to follow, but when he caught up with them at Blackwood Forest, he saw them bundle a limp and lifeless Melissa across the back of one of the horses and gallop off."

Anthony swallowed down his fear. "She is not dead. He wants her alive." The anguish swamping him at the thought of losing Melissa filled him with such searing pain. It hurt to simply breathe. *This was why you didn't love.* He closed his eyes and prayed he'd get her back. Scarcely when he realized he didn't want to live his life without Melissa, he might lose her.

"We'll get her back, Anthony. I promise."

Richard's words sounded hollow. Anthony ran his hand through his hair and cursed, fighting back tears of frustration. "God, I hope we do. It's all my fault she's been taken. If I hadn't forced her to marry me. If I hadn't left her alone at Bressington. If I,"—he swallowed—"had not been such a coward and faced my feelings for her . . ."

He slammed his fist against the wall. "I couldn't bear to think of Melissa being sold off—ending up—a slave . . . I'd never stop searching for her. Never!"

Richard came to stand next to him and rested a hand on his shoulder. "You love her?" Anthony nodded. "We will get her back."

Anthony turned and strode back to his desk. "Not without a plan we won't. Where's Tom?"

Cassandra knew she should worry.

When Viscount Strathmore called for her, she'd been flattered. He was almost as handsome as Anthony and just as rich. Aside from an alternative husband, his presence could not be dismissed.

Rufus suggested a turn in the park with a quick stop at Craven House to drop a note off to Lord Wickham. Since getting in his carriage, however, Rufus's demeanor had cooled slightly. When they pulled up outside Craven House, she should have trusted her instincts, but when he invited her to accompany him inside, she had agreed.

He'd been a trifle rough escorting her into Anthony's study. She sensed she was in trouble.

She rubbed her elbow and studied Anthony's face as he stared at her in a manner that had the hairs on her arms lifting. He made no attempt to stand when she entered the small study.

The first thing she noticed, other than the anger evident in Anthony's taut jaw, were the maps strewn over the desk. "Going somewhere?" she asked, trying to smother the fear rapidly assailing her body.

"Once we have the destination from you, Lady Sudbury." Anthony rose and leaned forward, both hands planted flat on the desk, his eyes glinting like hard steel. "Where has Rothsay taken Melissa?"

Her throat constricted. She moved calmly into the room and took a seat. "I do not think I have had the pleasure of making Lord Rothsay's acquaintance, although I have heard the name."

Anthony's hand thumped the table, and his voice so low she almost couldn't hear him, said, "Don't play games with me, Cassandra, or I'll . . ."

"What? Hit me?" She couldn't withhold a smile. She thought she'd very much like being hit by Lord Wickham.

Anthony stood and fisted his hands at his side. "Does the club, Spare the Rod, jog your memory? Or perhaps being an accessory to kidnapping, likely rape, and murder? How about hanging by the neck until dead?"

Cassandra clutched her hands together. "What on earth are you talking about?" There was no way she was admitting any part in Rothsay's plan. If they caught him, hopefully they'd kill the bastard and no one would know the small part she'd played, plus she'd be debt-free. Her markers would die with Rothsay.

"Rothsay has taken Melissa."

She feigned horror, her hand rising to cover her mouth. "I had no idea."

"Then why lie to us?"

She didn't have to pretend her anger. "I am embarrassed. Society does not look favorably on my exotic tastes. I saw no reason to publish them." She leaned forward in her chair. "But if he has taken Melissa against her will—"

"Of course it's against her will."

She didn't deign to answer.

Rufus loomed over her. "Anthony and Richard, if you'd like to leave the room, I'm sure I can make Lady Sudbury provide us with the details we require."

She watched with amusement as Rufus's lips firmed. "Not very persuasive, Lord Strathmore. You've just learned I enjoy pain."

He bent low and stroked a finger down her face. "Such a beautiful face, it seems such a pity to mark it."

Her bravado dimmed. Not her face, not her meal ticket. She gathered her thoughts. There was no point in being difficult. It would make her look as if she'd had something to do with Rothsay's diabolic plot.

"I can see you are not playing a game. If my cousin really is in trouble, I want to help." She spread her hands wide. "What information do you need?"

She saw the relief in Anthony's stance.

"We need to know exactly where his schooner is or where else he might possibly take Melissa. How many men does he have? Was he planning on setting sail anytime soon?"

"His boat's docked at Tower Hill, berth nine. I have no idea what his plans are other than I was invited to a party on Wednesday night at his country house in Richmond." She smiled at Anthony. "Not a party you'd likely enjoy, a bit rough for you." She frowned and chewed her bottom lip, acting for all she was worth. "Now you mention it, Rothsay did say he had a new member for our little group. One of his new toys, as he likes to call them. Do you think he meant Melissa?"

Anthony growled.

"Oh, dear. I thought he simply meant one of his slaves. You remember the slaves, don't you, Anthony? Rothsay manages to find such exquisite female creatures—"

Rufus slapped a hand over her mouth. "Shall I gag her?" His voice betrayed his anger. She saw Anthony shake his head. "Get up. You're coming with us."

As the men marched her to Strathmore's curricle, she spied Tom sitting up top. "Why do you need me if you have Tom?"

Anthony pushed her into the carriage, his grip hard and painful. She liked it. "You'll guarantee our entry onto the boat. Besides, if anything has happened to Melissa, I'll need something to take my anger out on."

He slammed the door behind her, calling for his horse. But she was not alone. Rufus sat in the shadows across from her.

"I wouldn't want to be in your shoes should anything happen to Melissa. Anthony is not a forgiving man."

Every time Anthony thought of Melissa at the mercy of Rothsay, his heart lurched, his body chilled, and his mind filled with images of what Rothsay could be doing to her— with her. *Hold on, my darling, I'm coming.* Shutting off such thoughts, he concentrated on getting to *The Master* as fast as Dark Knight could gallop, heedless of the others following.

He would not let the ship set sail.

He couldn't lose her. Not now. Not when he'd finally found the one woman he loved.

Chapter 23

Melissa felt ravaged to the heart as she numbly sat in front of the gilt-edged mirror brushing her hair. She gave her hair one more stroke with the brush. With a spark of her old self, she threw the brush across the elegant cabin, sending it clattering to the floor. Why did she care how she looked? Rothsay wouldn't care—all he cared about was raping her.

And it would be rape. She didn't care how many drugs he gave her; he would be taking her against her free will.

She molded her hand tenderly over her stomach. He would never get her pregnant, because her true love already had. Anthony.

Where are you? Why have you not come for me?

She knew why. Anthony did not care about her. She was simply a way for him to continue living his life the way he wanted. A rake with no ties, no commitment, and no desire to beget an heir.

She moved to stare out of the tiny porthole, but she faced out into the river and could see nothing of what was happening on shore. She had no idea where she was or when Rothsay would send her home.

Home. She had no home. Not anymore. Who would want her after this? Once Anthony learned what Rothsay did to her, he'd have the perfect excuse to lock her away. She would be tarnished, thought of as a whore. Would he believe the child she carried was his?

She felt bruised, hollow inside.

God, if only this were a terrible nightmare and when dawn came tomorrow morning she'd wake up in her bed.

She didn't want to submit to Rothsay. She wanted to fight him until her last breath died on her lips, but she had a babe to think about. Plus the young girls he kept as slaves.

Tears slipped down her cheeks as memories of Anthony crowded her mind. His smile, his touch, his strength. She angrily swiped the tears away. She needed his strength. She would persevere. She would not let Rothsay win. She would protect the one thing she had left in this world—her child. Anthony did not need her. Did he know she'd been taken? Was he even trying to find her? Perhaps he would think his life would be easier if he simply left her lost.

The ashes of her grief filled her throat and choked her.

She lay down on the bunk and watched the afternoon shadows lengthen. Soon Rothsay would join her and force her to—she couldn't even think about what was to come. He would own her body. He would make the woman in the mirror do unspeakable things. She rubbed her eyes, pressing her palms so hard into her eye sockets she wondered if she'd ever see again.

Then she heard the footsteps in the hall. Melissa froze, ice forming in her veins. Rothsay.

She did not bother to move. She lay in the middle of the bunk waiting, waiting for the devil to come and claim her.

At Rothsay's entry, she turned her head and stared at him. He closed the door behind him. Melissa forced herself to sit up.

He walked to the edge of the bunk and stood looking down at her. He gave a soft laugh as he stroked down her cheek with his finger.

He pulled out a pair of black leather boots from behind his back and a translucent gown of fine white silk. "Put these on."

Heart pounding in her throat, she glanced up at her captor.

"Why?" Her voice dripped with sarcasm. "Am I going riding? I'll need more than boots and a thin negligee."

His hand slid around her neck, and she could feel her throat tighten as he squeezed. "Not to ride me, you won't." The pressure around her neck eased. He gestured to the clothes. "Put them on, or I shall have Johnson come dress you and whatever else he wishes to do. I don't care about a few bruises. All I care about is sending you back to your husband filled with my seed."

"You're pure evil."

He pulled her head up and bent to take her lips. He broke the hard kiss. "My child will become the next Earl of Wickham. I couldn't think of a sweeter revenge."

Rothsay's smile chilled her very blood. She felt her spine stiffen. She bluffed for all she was worth. "Perhaps I shall fight Johnson with everything I have. It would be fitting to die before you can take me."

The sharp twist of his mouth sent a fresh chill through her. "Then I will simply have to see to it myself. One more word of defiance and I'll have little Mary brought up here for our enjoyment. I'll force drugs down your slender throat and make you join in as I rape her—all because you are too stubborn to put on a pair of boots." He removed his jacket and dropped it to the floor.

She felt the fight leave her. She could not defeat an evil such as him. She was simply no match for the devil. His smile widened. She could see he recognized her surrender in the droop of her shoulders.

Through clenched teeth he said, "Now put them on. We have a long night ahead of us."

She climbed off the bed, so weary she had to grip the bedpost to keep from slipping to the floor. He stood watching her, his eyes leering at her. Hot with excitement. Hot with victory. He pulled the silk garment backward and forward between his hands, savoring the feel.

She turned her back to begin undressing.

"No, face me. Let me see you. I want to soak in your

beauty." She had no choice but to obey, but she tried to block him from her mind as she began to disrobe. Finally naked she reached for the degrading garment he held.

Rothsay did not hand it to her. "Boots first." He shot her a cool glance. "You are a beautiful woman, and I will enjoy having you in my bed." His face twisted in his lust. Her stomach heaved. She knew the look well. "Boots first. Then the negligee."

She couldn't halt the shake in her fingers. She took her time, trying to delay what was to come. Once she'd finished, he undid his cravat and pulled his shirt over his head.

He made her stand in the middle of the cabin and he strolled around her, staring at her like she was some painting on his wall. She could not even summon up a shred of embarrassment.

He came up behind her and pulled her back against him. She could feel his erection through his breeches prodding her buttocks. His hands cupped each breast, and he kneaded them, moving his lips softly against her neck.

"You're beautiful. Wickham is going to be in hell when he learns I have you, knowing what I am doing to you, and knowing he can do nothing about it."

A tear slid down Melissa's cheek. How wrong this man was. Her husband most likely wouldn't care. Anthony did not love her.

"Turn around." She saw he'd begun to unbutton the placket of his trousers.

She felt the bile rising in her throat. "I thought you were going to drug me."

"Later." He pulled his erection free. "I want you alert and angry for this."

Melissa inwardly raged. *Don't upset him. Just get through this. Think of the baby.*

"Get down on your knees." His tone was composed, but she heard desire in the notes.

When she was not quick enough, he forced her down. She let out a cry of pain as her knees hit the hard wooden floor.

His hands tangled viciously in her hair. "It will bring me great pleasure to have Anthony's wife down on her knees servicing me with her mouth like a whore."

Suddenly she was filled with such rage, such anger—she wanted this man dead. He was a monster. He deserved to die.

Through a mist of tears, she saw his discarded jacket and a small pistol that had fallen out of one of the pockets.

Could she reach it without him noticing?

The hand holding her head tight against him relaxed. She concentrated on the pistol, her other hand stretching for the jacket.

Her fingers strained along the floor, inching forward, stretching until she thought her knuckles would pop. Finally, she gripped the edge of the material.

She slowly drew it toward her, sliding the pistol across the floor, all the while keeping his attention focused on how good her mouth and hand felt on him. He groaned, and his head dropped back, his eyes closing.

She lifted the gun into her hand. She raised her eyes to look up at the monster above her. He cried out, his knees buckling under the power of his climax. He landed on all fours at eye level with her.

Melissa wiped her hand over her mouth and fought the urge to vomit.

A taunting evil smile of satisfaction and victory lit his face. "That was perfect. The bite at the end, inspirational; perhaps I won't have to teach you much after all. The sight of a woman on her knees, my dick in her mouth, is delicious." His smile disappeared. "Now get up on the bed."

"No."

"Do I need to remind you of little Mary?"

She raised the gun and pointed it directly at his chest. "Little Mary would be safer if you were dead."

He eyed the gun warily. "A gun that size won't kill me."

She aimed for his groin. "Perhaps not. But it will relegate your favorite pastime to the impossible."

On shaky legs, she stood and then froze as she heard several footsteps racing toward the cabin. Not now, not when she was this close to escape. She bit her lip. Now what could she do? There was no way Johnson and his men would ever let her leave here alive.

The footsteps seemed to get faster the closer they got to her door. Before she could think of her next move, the door crashed open and at first Melissa thought she was dreaming.

Anthony.

Anthony and Richard stood in the doorway.

"Ah . . . Anthony. What bad timing. You've just missed your wife and I having a very pleasant interlude."

"Richard, keep your gun on him." Anthony crossed to Melissa, trying to ignore Rothsay's state of undress, the placket of his breeches hanging open, and . . . Taking a blanket off the bed, he draped it around her shoulders and scooped her gently into his arms. "You're alive. Thank God."

She touched his face. "You came for me?"

"Shh . . . I've got you."

Before he could say more, Rufus appeared at the door.

His face gentled into a look of relief at the sight of Melissa in Anthony's arms.

Richard urged, "We have to go—now. Rothsay may have more men working on the docks."

Melissa cupped Anthony's face. "The girls. You have to save the young girls. I don't know where he has them locked up."

Anthony gently kissed the top of her head and nodded to Richard. "We will find them. We won't leave without them."

The relief at seeing Melissa safe quickly became an all-consuming fury directed at the man on his knees before him. If not for Melissa in his arms, he'd have beaten Rothsay to death.

He looked at the scum before him and turned to the door. Over his shoulder he growled, "Richard, bring him."

Much to Rothsay's dismay, the rescue party made it back to Anthony's house with the freed slaves and the children.

Most of his men had either fled, been captured, or were killed in the rescue.

Rufus undid the shackles around Rothsay's wrists and pushed him into the Craven House cellar.

Rothsay spun and in the darkness was just about to offer Rufus a taunt when the world exploded into fireworks as a shattering blow hit him in the side of the head. He crashed to the floor, too stunned to protect himself from an enraged Anthony Craven who was standing over him, fists raised.

"Don't damage him too much. I want to see him stand trial. We have the evidence. The hold contained five white women he'd abducted off the streets," Rufus said before closing the cellar door.

The room flooded with shadow, only a small window at the top of one wall letting in a fraction of light. Rothsay's dizzied gaze saw the murderous silver eyes pinning him in a stare full of red-hot hatred.

"Get up, you miserable excuse for a human being," Wickham said, his lips curving into a bitter smile. "Believe me when I say I don't care if you ever stand trial. This is between you and me."

He staggered to his feet, but before he could even raise his arms, Wickham punched him across the face. "This is for Melissa."

Rothsay cursed at the thunderous blow, which was followed by a kick in the groin. He dropped to the floor, the pain taking his very breath. Usually he enjoyed pain, but delivered by a man—especially this man—it was not pleasant.

He balled up on the floor, sprawled against the door. He goaded his former friend and bitter enemy. "What? No foreplay? No wonder Melissa was grateful for my ministrations."

"Get up," Wickham spat out.

Rothsay realized the restraint his nemesis was using. He climbed cautiously to his feet. Wickham swung at him again, a big punch connecting under his jaw, making his head snap back.

"Defend yourself or is it that there is no one here to do your dirty work for you," Wickham cursed.

Rothsay felt a tooth loosen. He bent, placing his hands on his knees and let the blood drip down. "I don't think so. You're just looking for an excuse to beat me to death."

"Why shouldn't I after what you have done to Melissa."

"Did she tell you what I did to her and how much she enjoyed it?"

Rothsay watched Wickham's eyes darken with anger, the cords in his neck jumping. He spat at Rothsay's feet. "Enjoy! That's why she had a gun trained on you."

"Well, I enjoyed it anyway. Your wife's mouth has a better use than simply talking." The look on Anthony's face was worth the broken nose he got from the next punch.

He looked up through the blood filling his eyes and mouth. "You don't want this to come to trial, Anthony." For the first time in several hours, he gave a genuine smile. "Melissa's reputation will be ruined. Her word against mine."

"You bastard. You kidnapped her—"

"No, I didn't. She came willingly. Having been left by her husband and ignored for over a month, she did not need any encouragement to come play with me." He stood up straight. "At least that's the story the jury will hear." He spread his hands wide. "Given the scandal already surrounding your marriage—how she tricked you into the wrong bed—I doubt the jury will believe a word your wife says."

Rothsay didn't even see the punch coming, and he crumpled to his knees once more. It would only take a few more hits and he'd be unconscious.

"Then you'll stand trial for white slavery."

He laughed in Anthony's face. "I don't think so. I'd have to tell the whole story—the whole story of how a jealous husband planted women on my boat, so enraged with jealousy over his wife's affair."

Anthony stood there fuming, his chest heaving. He refused to accept the truth of Rothsay's words. Before he could think of a thing to say, the cellar door flew open.

A woman was silhouetted in the doorway, the light hiding her features.

"Stand back," Anthony warned through gritted teeth. He looked closely, his eyes adjusting to the flood of light. "Is that you, Cassandra?"

Rothsay laughed. "She's my favorite plaything. Have you missed me, Cassandra?"

She didn't make a move to enter. She simply raised her arm and pointed a pistol directly at Rothsay's heart. "Viscount Strathmore tells me you're going to stand trial for running a white slavery ring. You'll likely get transported to Australia. That's not good enough." Her words were barely audible in the quiet of the cellar.

Suddenly Rufus was behind her. "Don't be rash, Lady Sudbury. He is not worth killing."

Cassandra's voiced wobbled. "It is worth it to repay him for all the terrible things he made me do." She spat. "You pig."

Rothsay took a step toward her. "You enjoyed every minute of it. You love being down on your knees." Rothsay laughed in Anthony's face. "She wants me dead because I hold the marker to all her debts. Very well played, my dear."

Before either Anthony or Rufus could react, she'd moved closer. "This time, you get down on your knees. Now!"

As Rothsay made to comply, he warned, "Don't do this, Cassandra. One word from me, and these gentlemen wouldn't care if I snapped your pretty neck."

Cassandra cocked the pistol.

"She was the one that suggested I get rid of Melissa. She wanted you for herself. She's broke." Rothsay turned his head and sneered at Anthony. "However, Cassandra wanted her dead. But I was going to return her to you. Just used a bit. Wouldn't it be ironic if my son became the next Earl of Wickham?"

Anthony lashed out. Another punch sent Rothsay forward toward Cassandra. "Cassandra, watch out!" Anthony roared, but he was too late.

Rothsay shot out his hand and grabbed her by the hair, yanking her toward him. She shrieked as she stumbled against him, and he whipped the pistol out of her hand before any of them could stop him and put the gun to her head.

Cassandra screamed.

"Stay back or she dies," the Baron warned with a wolfish grin.

"Shoot him," Cassandra screamed. "Kill him."

"Shut up, slut," he growled at her.

"Rothsay, let her go. This is between you and me," Anthony said in deadly quiet.

Rothsay tried to drag Cassandra to the door, but she refused to cooperate. She sunk down to the floor. "I'm not going anywhere with you. You'll have to kill me."

Rufus stood blocking the cellar door. He had not moved an inch. His gun was primed and fixed on Rothsay. "I'd let her go, Rothsay. If what you say is true, and she was responsible for you kidnapping Melissa, I don't care if you shoot her. I'll simply shoot you as soon as she's dead."

Anthony hoped Rothsay didn't know Rufus was bluffing. Rufus would never let Rothsay kill the woman.

Suddenly Cassandra screamed and twisted in Rothsay's hold, grabbing at the pistol. They scuffled and fought. There was a loud shot and a puff of smoke as the gun discharged. Cassandra and Rothsay stood looking at each other, eyes wide. Then as if time had slowed, Rothsay slid to the floor. Dead.

Rufus checked his gun. "Go to your wife. I'll clean up here."

As Anthony made for the door, Cassandra grabbed at his arm. "It's not true you know. I'd never have asked him to hurt Melissa."

But she couldn't look him in the eye. He shook off her hold. "Get out of my sight. If I see you near me or Melissa ever again, I'll kill you." He left without a backward glance.

He wanted Melissa.

He wanted his wife.

Chapter 24

Anthony paced the hall, waiting for the doctor to finish his examination. He couldn't forget the sight that greeted him when he'd burst into the schooner's cabin. He knew as he'd raced to her rescue what Rothsay would likely be doing to her. His fists clenched at his side. It was not her fault. She did not willingly go to his bed. Still, Anthony couldn't get the sight of her standing before Rothsay clad in only thigh-high leather boots and a sheer negligee out of his mind. Had Rothsay raped her or had he saved her in time?

Guilt ate at him. He should never have left her alone at Bressington. He should have foreseen Rothsay's plan.

His fists clenched and unclenched at his sides. He was glad Rothsay was dead. He would have liked to have killed him with his bare hands.

The door to Melissa's bedchamber opened, but it was only Theresa.

"Is she—all right?"

Theresa patted his hand. "The doctor will be out soon. I'm off to organize the hot water for a bath. She wants to wash the feel of Rothsay off her skin."

Visions of what Theresa's words inferred had Anthony stumbling for the hallway chair. Theresa had already hurried off down the stairs before he could clarify. Anthony licked his lips. If she had been raped, he'd deal with it. It didn't change how he felt about her. If Rothsay had got her with child . . . he swallowed, he would accept that, too.

But would it change how she felt about him? He'd not saved her? He'd left her alone to become a weapon of revenge. He brought her into his world, his world of evil.

He dropped his head in his hands. If Rothsay had forced himself on her, then Rothsay's vision might come true. He hadn't slept with Melissa for over six weeks. If he made love to his wife now and she delivered a child in nine months, he would never know whose it was. Pain knifed through him. This was a fitting punishment for the way he'd treated her.

Anthony was so deep in his misery he didn't hear the doctor leave her room until he put his hand on Anthony's shoulder. Anthony stood up with a start. "How is she, doctor?"

Doctor Kilmer was a kindly gent. Anthony saw the pity shining in his eyes and expected the worse. "She's bearing up remarkably well. She needs a bath, some food, and a good night's sleep."

Anthony gulped. "Did he—is she hurt?"

Kilmer took pity on him. "Rothsay did not rape her if that is what you are trying to ask."

Anthony sagged against the wall. "I got to her in time."

"Yes. For a woman in her condition, she has come through her ordeal a picture of health."

Anthony grabbed the doctor's arm. "Condition?"

"Congratulations, my lord. You are to be a father in around seven months' time."

His eyes opened wide in amazement. It was almost two months to the day that he'd mistakenly taken her virginity. Warmth blossomed in his chest. He wanted to tell the whole world. He was going to be a father. He felt no fear, no terror, merely mind-numbing happiness.

"Can I see her?"

Doctor Kilmer chuckled. "She wants to bathe and dress first. While you wait, why don't we go to your study and celebrate with a glass of that fine brandy you keep?"

* * *

Melissa sank into the hot water and sighed. Her shoulders were still knotted with tension even though she knew she was safe. She wished she could stay here for hours. The thought of getting dressed and facing Anthony sickened her. He would want to know what happened. She didn't know whether she should tell him what Rothsay had forced her to do.

Anthony had suffered enough disappointment and pain in his life. She wanted to shield him from any more.

She felt ill remembering the feel of Rothsay in her mouth. She'd already washed her mouth out with brandy many times. She still couldn't get rid of the taste of him.

"Theresa, are you there? Can you bring me another glass of brandy please?"

She lay her head back on the edge of the tub and closed her eyes. Warmth infused her skin, and it wasn't from the hot water. She remembered the look on Anthony's face when he'd stormed into the room and saw she was safe. It was a definite look of profound relief.

At first she thought it was from guilt. But he'd cradled her tightly against his chest on the trip back to Craven House, whispering endearments in her ear and placing gentle kisses against the top of her head.

He'd come for her.

"This is the third glass you've had. It is not like you to drink hard spirits." Theresa eyed her suspiciously as she handed her the glass. "What did you not tell the doctor? Did you lie? Did Rothsay force himself on you?" Theresa pulled up a stool next to the tub.

Theresa's face lost its smile when she saw the tears well in her eyes, and Melissa would not answer her. Instead Theresa said, "Would you like me to wash your hair?"

Melissa nodded and, after taking a large gulp, handed the glass to Theresa.

She sat upright in the tub, screwed her eyes shut, and

tipped her head back. Theresa poured the hot water through her hair and then gathered the soap and began to massage it through her scalp. Her hands were gentle and soothing.

In a small voice Melissa said, "Rothsay didn't exactly rape me." She couldn't see the look on Theresa's face since her eyes were still closed, but she felt Theresa's hands stop for a moment on her scalp.

"What did he do, Mel?"

She shuddered. Tears began to leak out from under her eyelids. She screwed her eyes up tighter, trying to keep the tears from flowing. She was safe; the baby was safe, which was all that mattered.

"He forced me to pleasure him with my mouth." She couldn't help the sob that escaped with her words. Her body began to shake.

Heedless of the water, Theresa pulled her into her arms, rocking her gently and cooing, "That's it, let it all out. You cry all you want. I've got you."

Melissa cried and cried until she had no more tears to cry. Then she pushed out of Theresa's arms and wiped away her tears with her hand. "Anthony is going to ask me what happened. What should I tell him? Should I tell him the truth?"

Theresa hesitated. "Is there any need for him to know? Men may seem tough on the outside, but they often hide a soft inner center. They crumble and are consumed with guilt over not being there to protect those they love. Telling his lordship would only bring him pain over something he cannot change. Unless you cannot bear to carry the burden of your secret on your own?"

Melissa shook her head. "If I can bear being forced to do it, I can bear keeping it secret. I do not wish to hurt Anthony."

"Good girl. You're strong. You won't let a man like Lord Rothsay destroy you."

Melissa smiled and ran her hand lovingly over her belly. "Not when I have so much to live for. I've never wanted to hurt anyone before, but when I pointed the pistol at Roth-say's chest, I so wanted to shoot him."

"I for one am glad you didn't. Apparently his lordship and Viscount Strathmore had been staking Rothsay out for the last few months. Viscount Strathmore was going to ensure he stood trial for running a white slavery ring."

"Was?" A cold chill raced through her. "They haven't let him go?"

"Bless me, no. Lady Sudbury shot him with her gun."

"What's Cassandra doing here?"

Theresa held up the towel for her to step into. "She was with the men when they rescued you."

As if a strong wind rose up and blew out a candle, the hope and happiness she had in her chest petered out. He hadn't come to rescue her; he'd been on a government mission. She'd simply been lucky enough to be taken by the one man they were watching. Would Anthony have bothered to come for her otherwise?

She knew the answer. Probably not. Anthony had brought Cassandra with him. Had he broken his promise? Was Cassandra now his mistress? Is this who he'd been spending the past six weeks with? Did Cassandra share his bed?

All her fears and doubts flooded back. She made it to her bed before she collapsed. Once again, she'd simply been his obligation. He had to save his wife. Society would expect nothing less. It was really closing down a white slavery ring that was important.

Not her. Never her.

Knowing Anthony's lover was under the same roof, she couldn't face him.

"Pass my nightgown, Theresa. I don't want any dinner. I'm exhausted. I want to go to bed and sleep."

Theresa helped her into her gown and tucked her into bed. "Shall I tell his lordship to pop up to say good night?"

"No." She bit her lip. "That is tell him I need a good night's sleep and I shall see him in the morning."

*   *   *

"She doesn't wish to see me?" Anthony asked incredulously. With sinking heart, he knew why. Melissa hated him. He'd banished her to Bressington and left her to be kidnapped by a heinous monster. He did not blame her for never wanting to see him ever again.

His punishment was to be forever despised by the only woman he loved. To live as her husband and never be able to touch her, love her. His innards gripped with pain.

Doctor Kilmer picked up his hat and gloves. "If you'll excuse me, my lord, I shall take my leave. I'll call tomorrow morning to see how the Countess is faring." He closed the study door softly behind him.

Theresa curtsied and made to follow.

"Is she all right, Theresa? Please tell me he didn't hurt her. I couldn't bear it if he's hurt her." Anthony sunk back into his chair and rested his head on his hands.

Theresa hesitated at the door. She turned to face him. "Your wife is strong. She wouldn't let an animal like Rothsay cause her one moment of concern. Your problems are not caused by Rothsay."

Shame made him unable to meet Theresa's knowing gaze. "God, I've made such a mess of things."

"Anything can be fixed if you want it bad enough." Theresa stepped forward. "Do you? Do you want her?"

Anthony raised his head. "I love her. I need her more than she'll ever need me."

Theresa smiled. "There is your answer. You know what you have to do." Theresa turned to leave.

Anthony rose from his chair, panic gripping his voice. "What answer? Theresa, what am I supposed to do? Tell me. I'll do anything."

"Just love her." She closed the door softly behind her.

Chapter 25

The next afternoon, Anthony infused himself with courage. He lowered his head, then walked with measured paces to the door of the morning room, opened it, and entered, shutting the door behind him. Melissa had refused to see him last night, citing exhaustion. He was sure it had been an excuse. As the day progressed, it was obvious she was trying to avoid him. He'd not seen her all morning.

Enough was enough. His guilt, and fear of what she would tell him, had stopped him from acting sooner. Melissa could not continue to ignore him, ignore their marriage. What hurt him more than anything was the thought that she might blame herself for anything Rothsay might have done to her. She had done nothing wrong. Everything was his fault. He hadn't protected her.

The doctor said Rothsay had not raped her, but Rothsay's taunts about his wife echoed constantly in his head. He couldn't bear to think Melissa had been tainted by any of Rothsay's perversions. It would be one more sin he could never atone for.

The door clicked shut. He heard her start and move in her chair.

He turned from the door to face her and met her gaze with cool determination. She looked away. He closed his eyes and willed himself to continue. They had to face the aftermath of his desertion and her abduction. They couldn't, or he wouldn't, continue as they were.

His tongue seemed to swell in his mouth. He didn't know what to say to her. "Good afternoon, Melissa. I hope you are fully recovered from your ordeal. I missed you at breakfast this morning." God, he was lame.

She refused to look him in the eye. "I did not feel like food this morning."

Earlier, Anthony had heard her through the open door of the bedchamber adjoining his, retching. Theresa told him Melissa was violently ill most mornings, but by midday the nausea and dizziness passed.

"If you are hungry, I could organize a servant to fetch you something. A cup of tea perhaps?"

His inquiry seemed to startle her. She flashed him a quick look from under her beautiful, long, black eyelashes. "There is no need to pretend to play the part of the concerned husband."

He tried to keep the impatience out of his voice. "But *I am* your concerned husband."

"Really! That's why I haven't seen or heard from you in over six weeks," she said bluntly.

He walked to stand by her chair, at a loss for words. She was right; he had ignored her, but she'd never been out of his thoughts, out of his dreams. He could see her anger in the way she held her body straight and taut in the chair. Getting her to forgive him was not going to be easy. "I think you need to stay and rest. You have been through quite an ordeal."

He got down on his knees before her. Her eyes widened in surprise. He took one of her tiny hands in his, stroking her palm with his thumb. "Did he . . . did he hurt you?" Her eyes welled with tears, and she hung her head. His breath caught in his throat. "Did he . . ." he couldn't get the words out. "Did he rape you, Melissa?"

Her anguished cry of "No," filled the room. She tore her hand from his and leaped from her chair, moving to stare out the window. He could hear his heart pounding in relief above the silence.

He moved to stand behind her, pulling her back against him. So softly, he almost didn't hear her, she whispered, "I'm so sorry to disappoint, but if you want to get rid of me, you'll not be able to use rape as an excuse," she bit out bitterly.

Anger flashing through him, he swung her around to face him. "You must think me a monster to want my wife to be used by another man. Christ, Melissa." He struggled for control. "I would never wish that experience on any woman. Especially my wife."

She heard the pain in his voice. She instinctively raised her hand and stroked his face. His handsome face. How she had missed it. But it didn't change anything. It didn't change the fact he hadn't wanted her. He'd saved her out of obligation and duty. She meant nothing to him.

"I have already ordered Theresa to pack my things. I assume you wish me to return to Bressington as soon as possible." Her voice was unnervingly quiet.

He couldn't tell whether the prospect of leaving him saddened her or not. "Do you want to return to Bressington?"

At his question she raised her lovely hazel eyes and looked directly at him. "I don't want to be in your way." He noted her movement. She tenderly rested her hand on her stomach.

He'd asked the doctor and Theresa not to inform Melissa that he knew about the pregnancy. He wanted her to tell him herself. "Is there something you wish to tell me?" he asked softly.

"Only that I shall be inviting Lady Albany to stay with me at Bressington for a while. I hope that doesn't break the conditions of my banishment."

"Do you hate me that much?"

Her voice rose as her anger grew. "How can you think that? I've done everything in my power to make you want me. But you've made it very plain you have no feelings for me.

You never really wanted me, and now I'm sure you deeply regret ever marrying me."

Anthony paused and looked at her, really looked at her. He clearly saw what she had tried to hide from view all her life. She wanted to matter, desperately wanted to be loved. His heart swelled to overflowing. He so very much wanted to be the man whom she'd allow to love her.

"I've never regretted anything less in my life." He paused. "I have so many regrets; I don't know where to begin. But marrying you was not one of them. It's the smartest thing I've ever done."

Her brain attempted to understand the words she was hearing. His hair was tousled, and his silky fringe was shielding his eyes. She longed to brush it aside. His eyes could not shield his true thoughts from her. She tried very hard not to let his beauty distract her. He was trying to tell her something important, she was sure. "But you don't love me. You've never loved me. You pushed me away," she said in an undertone of hurt.

Anthony reached up to touch her cheek. "I have been such a fool. I have made many mistakes in my life." Her breath caught as his thumb brushed the corner of her mouth. "Some I will never be forgiven for. Please tell me I'm not too late, that pushing you away has not lost me a second chance?"

In a daze, she sat back down on the large upholstered chair by the fire. He still had not told her he loved her. Anthony moved forward slowly until he stood in front of her, his gray eyes darkly mournful. He grabbed a footstool and sat down at her feet.

Melissa licked her lips, almost too scared to say the words, not wanting to hear the answer. "You would not be so cruel as to expect me to stay here with your mistress living under the same roof."

"My mistress? What the hell are you talking about? I don't have a mistress."

Her eyes narrowed. "Cassandra. I know Cassandra is here. Don't deny it."

"Rufus has escorted Cassandra home and will see to it that she leaves England on the next boat and does not return for quite some time. If I ever see Cassandra again, I shall throttle the last breath out of her."

"Mistresses appear to be easier to shed than wives," she retorted.

"I have never broken my promise to you. Cassandra has never shared my bed. She was here solely to help me find you. She is Rothsay's plaything." He watched the emotions play across her sweet face. She'd never looked more beautiful or more fragile. He moved closer, wanting to haul her into his arms. "I have not bedded another woman since I married you. Thoughts of you have been driving me mad during the day and haunting me at night. I do not wish to be rid of you, Melissa. I want you to be my wife in every sense of the word."

Melissa's hand went to her abdomen. "What about your reluctance to have children? I can't simply be a vessel for your lust. That would destroy me. I'm not sure anything has really changed. You are simply relieved I am unhurt."

Hope faded, and his heart grew heavy in his chest. To earn her forgiveness he was going to have to confess all. He knew what he was about to tell her would either help them heal or drive her away completely. His skin crawled with the thought he might lose her, but if he didn't share his past with her, he'd lose her anyway.

"There is something important I wish to tell you." He swallowed hard. His heart was pounding recklessly. He took a deep breath. "I need to tell you about my past. I'm not looking for pity, merely understanding. I'm hoping when you hear my tale, you might be able to forgive me."

She sat above him like a marble statue, so beautiful his breath hitched in his throat. He felt physically ill at the prospect of her rejection, but he knew he was going to lose her if he didn't say what needed to be said.

Her palm cradled his cheek. "You don't need to do this."

"I do. I want a new start. If you bless me with one, I won't allow there to be any secrets." He took her hand in his and got down on his knees before her. He had to prove to her that he'd share his life with her. All of it. The good and the ugly.

"You once asked me how I got this scar." He traced the deep groove on his left cheek. "I raped a woman, a girl really"— he stammered—"she was a black slave girl about the same age as I was at the time, fourteen." His voice was so quiet she barely heard the words. All she concentrated on was the pain radiating from within the sounds.

"My father decided to introduce me to manhood, and she was my birthday present. I knew it was wrong. I could clearly see she was terrified. I refused his gift." He all but spat the word. "But my father had other plans. It was to be another one of his lessons—the lesson of power. The strong conquering the weak. I was forced to do what my father wanted or he would have given her to his men and made me watch." He drew an unsteady breath while Melissa observed every nuance of tormented emotion that flitted across his face.

"I knew what they would do to her. Even at that young age, I had heard enough women's screams to last me a lifetime. I thought if it was me, and only me, she would not suffer as much. I would be gentle, and it would be over quickly." His head dropped to his chest. "But it was worse than I could ever imagine. Her pitiful cries, the tears streaking her face, she struggled. . . And to my shame I reached my pleasure from the act." He clenched his fists at his sides, shuddering. "You see you were correct in your assessment of me. I'm weak. I didn't stand up to my father and help the girl."

She thought of Rothsay and the choice he had given her. Inwardly she balked; there had been no choice. The emotional blackmail he applied by using Mary, the young girl, was far stronger than anything he physically could have inflicted upon her. Her heart went out to the young Anthony and the choice he was forced to make.

"Shhhh. You were fourteen years old. What could you have done against your father and his men? You did what you thought would hurt her least."

With a snarl of anguish he said, "It was all for nothing. My father gave her to his men afterward anyway. I tried to stop them, but my father struck me across my face with the butt of his pistol."

His voice dropped to a deadly low. "Something inside of me died that day. I swore from that moment on, I'd never care for anyone again. To care for another . . . the pain of hearing her screams, knowing I hadn't saved her, still eats at my soul. What if I loved someone and I couldn't save them? What if I became like my father, cold and cruel?"

She bent over him, holding him in tender strength. He kept his head down, burying his face in her hair as it spilled over him.

"Rothsay and his father were there that day. His father gifted him a present, too, and he reveled in the screams. That was the day our friendship ended. He has despised me for my weakness ever since, while I hated him for his cruelty."

"That is why closing down his white slavery ring was so important to you. You know how evil he is."

Anthony nodded. "Again, I have been less than noble. I have tried to atone for my past. When I learned that Rothsay had taken you, I was terrified," he whispered. "I thought it was God punishing me for my sins. Just as I'd come to love, he handed the person I love most in the world, you, to the devil himself. I'd do anything, and I mean anything, to get you back. I thought I would never see you again. The thought of him hurting you . . ."

She touched his face in wordless empathy. He pressed his cheek into her hand, but she could not bring herself to meet his gaze. He might see more than he could bear. She would never tell him. Never hurt him with the truth. He might not be able to forgive himself.

Anthony sighed. "All my life I have believed it was better not to feel. I learned to bury my feelings deep inside. I thought I could protect myself, stop myself from being hurt, stop myself from becoming the monster that was my father."

More words tumbled out of him with such heated passion, her chest ached. "When I met you, the very first time you looked into my eyes and told me you would not make me marry you, I was shaken down to my very soul." He stroked her face with his finger. "Most women I knew would have rushed me to the altar that night, simply for the money and power I could give them, but not you. I knew you were different. I knew you were special. I pushed for the wedding, knowing that if I did not grab your goodness, my soul would be lost forever."

They were both silent for a long moment.

"I couldn't tell you about not wanting children. You wouldn't have married me. I would have had to explain my past. I didn't want you to know the type of man I was," he said, barely audible. "I thought I was my father's son and should not pass on my seed."

"You are your father's son. You can't escape the fact of your birth."

Her words tore at his heart. She did despise him.

"You don't understand how hard I have worked to atone for my past. But if I lose you, if you don't love me, I won't survive—" He cut his words off and lowered his head, hating himself. He felt himself crumbling, finally, the view down into his black soul beckoned.

She stroked his head. "Let me finish. You are nothing like your father, except in looks. You have a heart big enough to withstand more cruelty than any person should have to bear, yet it still has room for love. It has room for me."

His eyes welled with tears. "I'm sorry. I'm so sorry. I tried so hard to push you away. I'm sorry I wasn't strong enough to love you as you deserve. But most of all I'm sorry for introducing you to the evil that was Rothsay." Anthony stared pleadingly at her. "If he laid a hand on you . . ."

* * *

"No, he didn't hurt me." It wasn't a lie. A man like Rothsay could never hurt her. Not when she had Anthony's love.

At her simple denial, a shudder racked him and slowly he lowered his head all the way to her lap. He clung to her, unworthy as he was, and prayed she would forgive him. "I fought against loving you," he murmured. "I tried to convince myself that what I felt was merely lust. But deep down, I recognized the truth. That's why I was determined to push you away."

She held him in her embrace for a long moment, nuzzling his cheek with her soft lips as she bent over his back and stroked him lovingly.

She still hadn't said she forgave him. His voice was muffled from her embrace "I can perfectly understand if you hate me. I hate myself."

"I don't hate you." Her voice was barely audible.

Anthony pulled out of her embrace and threw his hands up in the air. "Despise me then—God knows I despise myself."

She gave a whispered reply. "I don't despise you, either."

Emotion flickered in her eyes, brief, but there for an instant, the one he wanted so desperately to see.

Anthony closed his eyes and drew in a deep breath. His body shook from the effort of keeping his voice low and even. "Do you forgive me?"

"Anthony." She curled her fingers around his trembling hands, gazing at him intensely. "You don't need *my* forgiveness—"

Despair wrenched at his gut. "I do . . ."

She shook her head. "No. You need to forgive yourself. You'll always have my forgiveness. I love you."

He lifted his shattered gaze and stared at her, lost.

"I love you, you fool. I've always loved you. But the only person who can heal you is you. Let go of the past. Open your heart to love and heal." She leaned forward and kissed his lips. "I love you," she murmured again and again.

He groaned. "I love you, too. I only want you. Say you won't leave me. I am not as strong as you. I would not survive without you."

"You are the strongest man I know."

Without any hesitation Anthony declared, "Not without you. Not without you by my side." He paused. "Not without you and our child."

"Our child," she repeated softly with a hint of warmth. "You know?" she said, and her voice filled with wonder.

He nodded. "I'm no longer afraid. I know how to love a child. I'll love our child. A child who deserves both his parents. A child who deserves a warm, loving family. We can give him that—together."

She looked into her husband's silver-gray eyes, so filled with love she thought her heart would fracture. She didn't deserve a man with such courage. To have overcome his upbringing and to survive with a heart still whole was truly inspiring.

She caught his face, framed it in both hands, held it so she could see every nuance. "You really love me? And you want our child?"

"I need you. I want you. I love you. Always."

His words burned in her brain. "I never thought I'd be so lucky."

He rose and swept her up into his arms. "I'm the one who has been blessed with luck. More, much more. I've been blessed with your love." He stalked across the room, bid her open the door, and then in front of gawking servants, climbed the stairs to his bedchamber. Not stopping until he'd laid her gently on his bed.

He stood staring down at her, soaking in her beauty. "I'm so thankful Richard gave me the wrong directions and I found you, because you've captured my soul. I love you so much that when you are not with me I am only half a man."

She gave a shaky laugh. "I've loved you almost since the first time I saw you. I think I recognized a kindred soul. We both have known little of love."

He came down on the bed beside her and stroked his hand over her stomach. "We will learn together. I'll work hard to be a husband you can be proud of. I'll love, honor, and cherish you for all the world to see. I want to be a family."

She felt the passion behind his declaration. "That is all I've ever wanted. A family to love and to love me."

Her radiant smile, the one he'd kept in his head over the long lonely weeks, made it seem as if the sun had suddenly begun to shine within his bedchamber. Tenderly, he pulled her into his arms, holding her close.

"You truly don't regret being forced to marry me?" It seemed his lovely wife needed more assurance.

"Hush, you idiot. I love you, Melissa, and I'm not letting you go—ever." His voice softened. "You've saved me from a life of living hell."

"You saved yourself."

"I tried desperately not to love you, but you were so very hard to resist, especially when you blatantly set out to seduce me. God, I thought I was going to go mad with desire."

"I wasn't very good at it. You still left me."

He slowly began the delicate task of unfastening the hooks and tapes of her clothing, turning her disrobing into an exercise in sensual pleasure. "If you'd not been so good at it, I would not have had to run away from you." Finally he bared her completely. He was getting drunk on her beauty.

She lay before him in her natural splendor. "I was good at it? I made you want me?"

He shuddered, his hungry gaze lingering on the pale flesh he'd exposed. "So good, if I hadn't taken your virginity I would be asking you some very pertinent questions."

He reached out to stroke her. His palm barely brushed her nipple, and she arched her back in ecstasy.

"It was Cassandra's book," she sighed.

"I really should read more." His lips curved in a smile as he bent his head and took her nipple between his lips.

Melissa's breathing changed, going more shallow as his hand roamed lower to the soft curls between her thighs. "Madame du Barry's book, the French courtesan, taught me a lot, but some of her teachings I just could not . . ."

He lifted his head from her breast and looked into her eyes. "Couldn't what?"

Her faced flamed with color. "I couldn't understand how they would work."

He smiled tenderly at his wife. "You don't need any book to learn about making love. I'll teach you everything you need to know. In fact, I probably won't ever let you leave this bed."

"You won't tire of me?"

His heart melted at the probing, insecure note in her voice. "I have not had a mistress, or any other woman, since the night I mistakenly came to your bed."

"I suppose you have been busy chasing Rothsay and his white slavery ring."

"I don't have a mistress because I don't want one. I haven't thought about another woman or wanted one since I met you."

"You haven't?"

Anthony rolled her beneath him. He held her gaze and nudged her thighs apart, settling between them. "I couldn't get a black-haired regal temptress out of my head. I don't want anyone but you."

"Truly? The Lord of Wicked is no more?"

Something twisted in his chest, making it difficult to take a breath. "Of all the women in the world, there is none I want to devote my life to, none I want to love more, none I need more, than you." His voice became teasing. "I still want to be wicked, but only with you. Will you let me show you?"

She could see it in the silver heat of his eyes, see the fire and the feeling behind his heartfelt statement. He bent his head and kissed her—long and deep.

It was minutes later before he caught his breath enough to murmur, "You forgive me?"

She reached up and placed a gentle kiss on his lips. "You have not been listening, my darling man—there is nothing to forgive. You love me. That is all that matters."

In that moment he knew, not only that he loved her, loved her and their child more than his own life, but that no matter what, he always would.

She smiled in fervent ardor. Reaching up, she drew his head down, kissed him—delicately, tantalizingly, holding at bay the fire that was beginning to rage between them. "I love you. I want to be a proper wife to you." She whispered the words against his lips. "Take me. Show me how much you want me. Brand me with your love so that I never forget you are mine, as I am yours—always."

"You don't know how hard I prayed to hear those words." He took control of the kiss, plundering her mouth, then tilted her hips and entered her. He drank her gasp as he inexorably pressed into her tight sheath. All the way in. He loved her, wanted her, and needed her.

Melissa gave herself up to it, up to him—surrendered completely. She trusted him to protect her, to love her, and to cherish her. She opened her body to him, opened her heart, and offered him her soul.

It felt right, it felt comfortable, and it felt amazing. She belonged here—in Anthony's bed. Finally, she was his wife in more than name.

Their breaths mingled through the shattered sobs and low groans, as their heated bodies moved together. As the pace increased and the depth of his passion and need broke over her—buffeted her, pleasured her—a deeper understanding dawned.

He was showing her that he loved her, that she was all that mattered. She would never love him more than she did at that precise moment.

He sensed her release, and she felt his control slip. His desire broke free, took hold, and drove him relentlessly, while she sobbed and held him to her as he came apart in her arms.

His last coherent thought was of their child, the product of a mistaken night. A mistake he would be eternally grateful for having made. As the wave broke and took him, left him gasping and thoroughly sated, he felt the ghosts of his past lift from his shoulders.

As they drifted, buoyed on the fading glory, she felt a peace in her heart. She'd found her prince, her friend, her lover. . . . Together they could face anything. They belonged together—him for her, her for him.

Two halves of the same coin, bonded by a power nothing could break. Together, their life would be filled only with joy.

She was sure of it.

For she had tamed, captured, and claimed the heart of the Lord of Wicked. She gave a little giggle and inwardly admitted she hoped he'd not be too tame. She thought of her favorite book, *The Secrets of a French Courtesan*. Lessons she hoped to put to use very soon. Her quiet laughter filled the bedchamber. There was no time like the present.

Anthony stretched beside her. "I am out of practice. You shouldn't have the energy to laugh after I have ravished you." His fingers toyed with her, fondling her breasts, caressing them with both hands. "I shall have to try harder."

A breathless moan was her response. "Oh, I do hope so, my lord." Impatiently, she pushed Anthony onto his back and rose up over him, trailing kisses across his chest. "I'm sure I could provide you with a few instructions. You'll find I am a match for the Lord of Wicked."

He pulled her down, hard against him, letting her feel his burgeoning erection, and reverently whispered against her lips, "I know you are, my love. My perfect match."

Epilogue

London, four months later. . .

With enraptured eyes, Anthony watched the raven-haired beauty cradle the baby in her arms and state her vow, before God, to love him. Lord Philip Dorrington, who only a minute ago had been squealing in Anthony's arms, as he'd made his own vows of God parenting, lay cooing quietly in his wife's gentle hold.

He took pride in the woman standing beside him, all eyes watching as she quietly and earnestly agreed to look after Philip. Anthony's love for her was heightened by the joyful knowledge that soon he would be holding their own child in his arms. Melissa, though round in her pregnancy, looked radiant, glowing with health and happiness. Her fair skin luminous in the candlelit, shadow-filled church.

As she handed the baby back to his mother, Melissa lifted her face and smiled her heart-stopping smile. The smile that every day made him feel incredibly blessed and thoroughly loved. Her gaze cloaked him in love. Her love. He would never get enough of it.

The christening service ended, and they made their way back out into the late January sunshine. Anthony stopped on the steps of the church, immune to the cold, watching his wife laugh and chat with the other guests as they drifted toward the group of carriages on the street below. How barren his life would have been had his brother not played him false and tricked him into her bed, compelling him to wed her.

Richard had no idea how much Anthony owed him. He'd never be able to repay his twin if he lived to be a hundred.

He felt his body stirring as he watched her. The carriage ride back to Freddie's house would take at least half an hour. A devilish smile formed on his lips. Melissa turned and caught his look. The smile Melissa sent him in response was so arousing, so womanly, so inviting—that need slammed into his chest and he descended the church steps and hurried toward his carriage.

In the past few months, Melissa had made them experiment with every position in her courtesan's book. Even the Lord of Wicked was sometimes surprised, or maybe the pleasure was more enhanced because of the deep abiding love he felt for her. They spent magical hours learning about each other's bodies, becoming true lovers, delighting in each other's passion, always ending by making hot passionate love wherever and whenever they could. They fell deeper in love every day.

He pictured Melissa naked in their bed . . . perhaps they wouldn't be missed at the christening party.

Anthony lifted Melissa into the carriage and felt the tremble running through her hands. His body throbbed contemplating her response once the doors closed.

Once seated inside, Melissa scolded, "You can wipe that look off your face. I am not missing Philip's christening party. We are his godparents, after all."

He pulled her onto his lap, his hands finding the silken skin of her thighs beneath her skirts. "I wouldn't dream of missing the event." His lips brushed hers gently. "It's a half hour journey; I can think of several ways to ensure we stay warm for the duration."

The smoldering look in her eyes made his breath catch.

"I'm as big as a horse. The Lord of Wicked can't possibly find me attractive in this condition."

"The Lord of Wicked, no," he said softly. "But the man who loves you with all his heart and soul does, and always will."

He bent his head to kiss her, to show her his love. Anthony felt himself tremble with desire. Desire for this woman, his woman. He'd never felt more contented.

Melissa was the chief reason he felt such peace. Even when he'd given her no reason to love him, she had wrapped him in her healing embrace, giving him solace with her unreserved love. Until his dying day he would return the favor and love her unconditionally. Nothing would make him happier or give him more joy.

"All my life, I've felt as if my soul were missing. You've helped me find myself. You've helped me to forgive myself."

His kiss deepened and his desire soared as he felt her small hands fumble with the placket of his trousers. His fingers moved to stroke between her thighs. As usual her passion matched his own. She was wet and eager to receive him. He lifted her astride him and gently lowered her onto his pulsing member, relishing the feel of her rounded belly pushing against him.

He raised his hands to her full breasts and eased them out of her bodice. Leaning forward he tenderly suckled one nipple, glorifying in the way she ground down onto him.

He lifted his head from her breast and met the brilliant sparkle of her hazel eyes and felt lust and love surge through him. "I think we should move more vigorously if we are to keep warm. Are you up for the ride?"

"My darling man, I'm relieved to see that though you may have given up the title, you are still a little bit wicked."

He surged farther into her hot sheath, his hardness filling her to the hilt. "I hope I'm more than a little, madam."

Melissa giggled, but his next few thrusts filled the carriage with her passionate cries. She could feel him pulse and throb within her. His thick shaft felt huge and hot, and she sunk lower onto him, fully absorbing its swollen length.

"I love feeling you so deep inside me," she whispered on a breathless sigh. "I love you, Anthony . . ."

Their gazes locked. "And I love you, Melissa. Don't you ever doubt it. I'll always need you, want you, love you, and protect you."

"We'll love each other, always." Her hands gripped his shoulders, and she rose and sank down hard, impaling herself on him.

He shuddered and felt his gentleness fraying. He surged inside her. Melissa's fingers dug into his shoulders as she met him stroke for stroke. His hands gripped the soft globes of her bottom and raised her higher, moving her faster. In only a moment their joining turned frenzied, the rhythm building until her cries of release mingled with his harsh groans. Anthony poured himself into her welcoming body, shaking with the force of their joint convulsive pleasure, while Melissa collapsed sated against his chest.

They sat intimately joined, the gentle rocking of the carriage sending jolts of delicious, lingering pleasure through them both. Melissa nuzzled her cheek in the curve of his shoulder, her fingers twining in his hair.

"Warm enough?" he asked, stroking the white skin above her breasts, marveling at the changes her pregnancy was having on her body.

"Yes." His simple smile, so filled with love for her, warmed her every day.

His hand gently caressed her bump, where their child lay quietly growing inside her. Sometimes, she woke in the night, scared that this was all a dream, that her darling man was a figment of her imagination. But then he'd pull her tight against his body, holding her in his arms, whispering words of love in her ear and making slow passionate love to her.

Hearing the carriage begin to slow, Melissa hurriedly moved off his lap and tried to right her clothes. "Here let me help," he offered. His hands found her breasts but seemed to fondle her more than help her. He couldn't seem to get enough of his wife.

"You are scandalous," she accused. "A fine example to young Philip we will be, if I arrive in a state of undress."

Anthony's mother, and most of the other guests, did not miss the flushed and bedraggled picture young Lord Dorrington's godparents made as they entered the house. Melissa looked as if she'd just been thoroughly ravished, and her son's eyes blazed with happiness.

She never thought she'd live to see this day—her eldest son happy, and with the next Wickham heir on the way. Anthony came forward to press a kiss to her cheek.

She couldn't resist saying, "I knew the right woman would be the making of you. I'm only sorry I could not help your father the way Melissa has helped you."

He squeezed her hand. "Unlike Father, I wanted to be saved. Don't blame yourself for his shortcomings."

Tears welled in her eyes, and she cupped his cheek in her palm. "Thank you."

Anthony placed a kiss on her hand and strolled across the room to join the proud father.

Richard watched his brother. He would never have believed Anthony was the same man who, only a little over six months ago, railed against the world. He'd been quite certain Anthony would never find happiness, that he'd never forgive himself for their father's past sins. Despondent, full of self-pity, and suffering for deeds not of his making, Anthony was lost to the world.

But Anthony hadn't just survived, he'd flourished. Flourished because of a woman. A woman he'd tricked his brother into compromising on the advice of his mother. He swallowed. It could have all gone so horribly wrong. But Melissa had opened Anthony's heart and led him down the path of redemption.

Their family owed Melissa everything.

Anthony, on the other hand, owed him a thank-you. He thought it time his brother ate humble pie.

Chuckling, Richard sauntered over to where Rufus, Freddie, and Anthony sat, glasses of whiskey in hand, toasting the proud father.

He sat across from his twin and raised his glass. "As we appear to be toasting, I'd like to raise a toast to me."

Rufus coughed, while Freddie laughed.

Anthony said, "Other than causing another scandal, being caught in Lady Kettering's bedchamber by her husband last week, what have you got to celebrate?"

Richard couldn't help his smug smile. "I have single-handedly, oh, all right, with help from Mother, brought down the Lord of Wicked. He is now resoundly caught in the parson's noose."

"And loving every minute of it," Anthony declared.

"So, Anthony. I'm still waiting for that thank-you. I told you on the very night you met Melissa, you'd thank me one day. Well, brother, that day is here."

"I'm glad he's not my brother. He's going to be impossible to live with, Anthony. You'll be thanking him for the rest of your life," Freddie said, and gulped down the rest of his whiskey.

"And so I should." Anthony stood and bowed to Richard. "I thank you, my wife thanks you, and the Lord of Wicked thanks you. Actually, the Lord of Wicked has retired." Anthony's lips curved in relief. "And I haven't even missed him."

Richard smiled. "Not the most profuse thanks in the world." He shifted forward in his seat. "As my reward, may I take up your mantle? The Lord of Wicked always got all the women. I'd make an excellent substitute." He hesitated. "Unless one of you fellows wants the title?"

Freddie raised an eyebrow. "If you want it, take it. I'm sure you can live up to your brother's reputation. I don't want it. I'm happily married. The only wicked thing I can get away with is to have one too many drinks after dinner."

"Damn it, Freddie, Richard doesn't need any encouragement to be wicked." Anthony eyed his good friend, Rufus. "I pass the mantle of Lord of Wicked onto you. You never know, it might change your life, too."

Richard cocked his head to one side, shaking it in a negative response. "No, the title doesn't suit Rufus. He is far too honorable to wear the title."

Rufus appeared to look at the twins in amusement. "Christ, I hope that is not your way of telling me I'm boring, Richard. Working for the Foreign Secretary, in times of war, is anything but."

Richard slapped his knee. "That's it. Perfect." He grinned at the other three men.

"Well, don't keep us in suspense," they all urged at the same time.

"It appears it is to be the day of christenings. I christen Rufus Knight, Viscount Strathmore, Lord of Danger."

Anthony tipped his head back and roared with laughter.

Melissa looked across the room, a room filled with family and friends, at her husband. A man who not long ago rarely smiled and never laughed.

Her heart, so full of love, did a little flip in her chest. She thought his raucous chortle was the most beautiful sound she'd ever heard.

Play a sexy game of TRUTH OR DEMON
with Kathy Love's latest,
available now . . .

What the hell?

Killian blinked up at the unfamiliar ceiling—a dingy white ceiling. Not the crisp, new white of his ceiling at home. Nor was he in his own bed. This one was decidedly feminine, covered in a ruffled bedspread plastered with pink and red cabbage roses. Nothing like his black silk sheets.

He glanced to the right to see an antique nightstand. On it, in its full flowered and beaded glory, sat a lamp that looked as if it came from a yard sale circa 1959. An Agatha Christie was opened, facedown on the doily-covered surface. Several medication bottles were lined up beside that.

Great, not only was he in a strange bed, but it appeared to be that of an elderly woman.

He glanced to his left, hoping he'd see something that would make sense to him. He definitely needed an explanation for this predicament—and why he didn't seem to recall how he got here. But instead of some clue, he found someone staring back at him.

It was the ugliest, mangiest cat he'd ever seen. It stared at him with its one good eye. An eerie yellow eye, while the other was stuck together into a crusted black line. Its long, white fur—or at least he thought it was white—had a matted, gray tinge as if it had rolled in ashes. Damp ashes.

Maybe Killian was still in Hell. But he suspected that even demons would throw this thing back.

Keeping his movements slow and subtle, Killian levered himself up onto his elbows, concerned that even the slightest move would set the beast into attack mode.

The cat hissed, its back arching and its tail, once broken or maybe just as naturally ugly as the rest of it, shot up like a tattered flag at half-mast. It hissed again, louder, its lips curling back to reveal a splintered fang and some serious tartar buildup.

Killian braced himself for what appeared to be an inevitable fur-flying assault, but instead the feline monster darted over the chair and disappeared under the bed, surprisingly fast for such a massive creature.

"Great," he said, peering over the edge. Now he felt like he was stuck in some horror movie where the monster under the bed would lunge out and grab him as soon as he set a foot on the floor.

He fell back against the mattress. The scent of musty pillow, masked only slightly by some kind of stale, powdery perfume, billowed up around him.

Where the hell was he?

He lay there, searching his brain, but nothing came back to him. His last memory was getting off work and going home. But he was clearly no longer in Hell. This place was very definitely the dwelling of a human. Humans had a completely different energy from demons.

Had he gone home with some human woman for a little nocturnal fun? Not his usual behavior, but not unheard of either.

He glanced around the room with its flowered walls and damask curtains. A pink housecoat was draped over a rocking chair in the corner.

He cringed at the sight. Not unless he'd suddenly developed a taste for the geriatric set.

"At least let it have been the hot granddaughter," he said aloud. The monster under the bed hissed in response. Probably not a good sign.

He remained there for a moment longer, then decided he

couldn't stay trapped in this sea of frills and flowers indefinitely. He had to figure out where he was—and more importantly, why.

He sat up, steeling himself for his next move. Then in one swift action, he swung his feet over the edge of the bed and gave himself a hard push against the mattress, vaulting a good three feet across the floor.

The dust ruffle quivered, then a paw with claws unsheathed shot out and smacked around, hoping to connect and maim. Finding nothing, it snapped back under the bed's depths. The bed skirt fluttered, then fell still.

"Ha," he called out to the animal, feeling smug. Then he just felt silly. He was a demon who'd managed to outsmart a cat. Yeah, that was something to get cocky over. Especially since he was a demon who had somehow managed to forget where the hell he was.

He stepped out of the bedroom into a small hallway. Directly in front of him was a bathroom that revealed more flowers on the shower curtain and on the matching towels hanging on a brass rack. Even the toilet seat cover had a big rose on it.

To his right was another bedroom. A dresser, a nightstand and a brass bed—and, of course, more flowers.

He frowned. Would he really hook up with a human who was this obsessed with floral prints—very *bold* floral prints? He didn't think so, but anything seemed possible at this point.

He wandered to a living room with swag draperies and ancient-looking velvet furniture. Ben-Gay, hand lotion, Aleve, a crystal bowl filled with mints and a box of tissues were arranged on another doily-covered table beside a tatty-looking recliner. A crocheted afghan was draped over the back.

"Let there be a granddaughter . . . let there be a granddaughter," he muttered, even though he'd seen not a single sign of youth so far.

He crossed the room to a fireplace, looking at the framed

photos crowded along the mantel. Only one woman kept reappearing in the pictures and she didn't look to be a day younger than eighty. But he didn't recognize her. In fact, none of the people in the pictures jogged his memory.

"Maybe I don't want to remember," he said, grimacing down at a picture of a group of elderly women on what appeared to be adult-sized tricycles beside some beach.

Then his own shirt sleeve caught his attention—or more accurately his cuff link, deep red garnets set in a charm of a ferry boat: the symbol of his position and job in Hell.

He set down the picture and inspected himself. He was still dressed in his standard work uniform, a white shirt with a tab collar, a black vest and black trousers. He'd taken off his greatcoat sometime during the evening, but he was relieved to see that the rest of his clothing was intact.

A good sign nothing untoward had happened, but it still didn't give him any hint as to where he was or how he got here.

"Just get out of here," he told himself. He could just as easily contemplate this bizarre situation in the luxury of his own place.

He closed his eyes, picturing his ultra-modern dwelling with its clean lines and stark colors. Not a single flower to be found anywhere. He visualized the living room with its black leather furniture. The bedroom with its king-size bed and dark red walls. He especially visualized his black granite bar and the bottle of Glenfiddich Scotch Whisky sitting on it.

A nice glass or two of fifty-year-old scotch and a little xBox 360 on his big screen television seemed exactly like what he needed after all this strangeness. There was nothing like expensive liquor and "Modern Warfare 2" to get him calmed down. Then maybe he'd recall his lost evening.

Let there be a hot granddaughter, he added again.

Then with his creature comforts affixed in his mind, he willed himself away from this odd apartment and back to his own world. . . .

Except nothing happened.

No whirring sound, no sense of whisking through space and time. No—nothing.

He opened his eyes to find himself still surrounded by flowers and the scent of old age.

Pulling in a deep breath, he closed his eyes again, and really focused. But this time he noticed something he hadn't the first time. It was a sort of weighted feeling as if leg irons were around his ankles, keeping him in this dimension.

He released the breath he didn't even realize he was holding pent up in his lungs. What was going on? Why shouldn't he be able to dematerialize out of the human realm?

But then he realized *shouldn't* wasn't the right word. He felt like he *couldn't*. No, that wasn't exactly the right word either.

For the first time since waking up in this place, a sensation akin to panic constricted his chest. He forced himself to ignore the feeling, chanting over and over in his head that there was a reasonable explanation for all of this.

"Just go to a bar here," he muttered to himself. "Have a stiff drink—and relax."

Things were bound to make sense if he just calmed down. How could he expect to think clearly surrounded by floral chaos?

Just then the cat from the bedroom leapt up onto the recliner, the springs creaking under its massive bulk. It peered at him from its one good eye, then hissed.

"Yeah. I'm outta here."

He left the living room, striding toward a door at the end of another small hallway. It had to be the exit. But when he reached the door, he stopped. Everything within him told him to just grab the doorknob, turn it and leave, but again something stopped him. Told him he had to stay right here.

"Just go," he growled.

But he couldn't bring himself to move. That was until he heard the rattle of the doorknob, jiggling as if someone was inserting a key from the other side.

Killian glanced around trying to decide what to do. He

noticed the kitchen to his right and side-stepped into the narrow little room, leaning against an avocado-colored refrigerator as he listened. He heard the whoosh and creak of the door opening.

"Where is he?" a female voice said. A young female voice. The granddaughter?

"He's got to still be here," another female voice said.

Hmm, he hadn't considered there might have been more than one granddaughter. That certainly made things more interesting—and worth remembering.

Killian decided there was no point in hiding. After all, they were expecting him to be here. At least, he thought they were talking about him, and they were the ones who could likely offer him the information he wanted.

He stepped out of the kitchen to see three young girls. And *girls* was definitely the operative word.

Dear Lucifer, was there *any* middle ground here?

As soon as they saw him, in almost comical unison, the girls screamed. And with the familiarity of that piercing sound, all his lost memories rushed back. The screaming girls, the flying snack foods, the thwack to the head.

Killian raised a hand, frowning down at his, for all practical purposes, abductors. Surprisingly, his gesture silenced them.

"Why did you bring me here?"

If his memories of the night before were any indication, he needed to get an answer as quickly as possible, before another candlestick-wielding woman appeared.

He shot a quick look over his shoulder, just for good measure.

The girl with a smattering of freckles across her nose and dark brown eyes moved out of the doorway, waving to the other two to join her. The other dark-haired girl joined her inside the apartment. Only the cherubic blonde hesitated behind them. But finally, and clearly against her better judgment, she followed, although Killian noticed she didn't release the doorknob.

Ready for a speedy escape. Smart girl. He was not in a good mood. And he was a demon. Never a great combination.

"Who are you? And why did you bring me here?" he demanded.

The girls all shifted, nervous.

Then to his surprise, the freckle-faced one straightened to her full height—maybe a whopping 5'2"—and met his gaze directly.

"I'm Daisy."

Killian tried not to make a face. Of course, *more* flowers.

"This is Madison," Daisy said, gesturing to first one girl, then the other. "And Emma."

Madison surprised him by meeting his eyes too. She sported that ennui that all kids seemed to master as soon as their age hit double digits. Killian was tempted to point out to her she hadn't looked quite so bored just moments earlier when she was squealing, but he remained silent. Emma still clutched the doorknob, managing none of her friends' cool boredom. Quite the opposite. As soon as his gaze moved to her, she tensed as if she was ready to dart—or pass out. Her blue eyes widened and seemed to eat up half her face.

A twinge of sympathy pulled at him. He ignored it.

"I was the one who conjured you," Daisy said, her expression neither blasé nor frightened. This girl was simply direct and calm.

A girl with a mission.

"We all conjured you," Madison corrected her, giving Daisy a pointed look.

"Yes." Daisy acknowledged her friend, but remained undaunted. "We all did. But we conjured you to fulfill my wish."

"Which we should have negotiated," Madison muttered, collapsing against the wall in a perfected slouch of disgust.

Daisy didn't even glance at her friend this time. She stayed focused on him. "We called you to—"

"Do something impossible," Madison interjected.

This time Daisy did shoot a censorious look at her friend.

Then she said, "No. It might be a little tricky but not impossible."

Madison rolled her eyes. Emma swayed. Apparently passing out was still an option for the silent friend.

"What is this tricky—possibly impossible task?" Killian asked, growing tired of the teenage bickering.

This wasn't his usual thing. Hell, he'd never been conjured before, and he had very little experience with teenagers. But even with his admittedly limited experience, he wasn't prepared for what the earnest girl in front of him said next.

"I want you to find my sister a boyfriend."

If you liked this book,
try Rebecca Zanetti's FATED,
in stores now . . .

"Mama! Mama, wake up." Tiny hands clutched at Cara's worn nightshirt, shaking with all their might. Cara's eyes flew open, and her heart hitched in her chest. Terrified blue eyes speared her through the dusk of the morning. The little girl must have had another nightmare. "Janie, sweetheart, what?"

"They're coming. They're coming now, the bad men. We have to run." Janie's breath came in sharp gasps before she let out a high-pitched sob.

Cara shook her head, reaching out to enfold her daughter in a hug. She slowed her own breathing, the need to comfort her child overwhelming her. Poor Janie. Not another nightmare. She reached for her reading glasses on the table only to realize she'd fallen asleep with them on. Again. The newest edition of *Botanical Magazine* hadn't been the barn-burner she'd expected.

She smoothed Janie's hair down while silence echoed around them. Now more than ever, she wished Simon had lived, maybe he could have soothed their daughter's fears. She flipped on the antique pink Depression glass lamp. "It's okay, sweetheart. I'm sure it was just a bad drea—"

A loud crash came from the other room and Cara yelped. The sound of splintering wood propelled her to action. She leapt from the bed, yanked Janie into her arms, and sprinted for the master bath, barely missing the potted fern in the corner. Her heart slamming against her ribs, she locked the door and rushed toward the small window. She failed to unlock it before the thin door burst open behind her.

A broad hand stopped the door from clanging against the wall. At least six and a half feet of muscle-packed male filled the doorway.

With a cry, she dropped Janie to her feet and dodged in front of the four-year-old. The air caught in her throat and her ears started to ring as adrenaline spiked through her blood. This was not happening. She yanked her head to the side and forced herself to accept the situation. Accept that she needed to fight. She dragged oxygen into her tight lungs and searched the tiled counter for a weapon—her tweezers probably wouldn't harm anybody.

She pushed Janie back against the wall. Retreating a step, she held one hand out to ward off the threat. His size made her gulp. Brown eyes raked her from his hard cut face, and raven black hair reached his collar with a freedom that disavowed any ties to the military—although he wore the requisite flack boots and dark jeans under a bulletproof vest. She'd seen the gear on a Discovery Channel special about soldiers.

The energy emanating from him stole her breath.

"Get out," she said, shielding her child. Trying to shield herself from the feelings he threw at her. Anger, passion, and urgency all swirled together, mixing with her own panic and making her lightheaded. Her knees wobbled, and her head began to ache. She usually blocked better than this. Or maybe his emotions were just that strong.

"We need to go." His tone was water over sharp rocks, as if he was trying to gentle a naturally rough voice. Then his eyes dropped to her faded nightshirt to see the image of Einstein surrounded by shopping bags—"Quantum Shopping." His top lip quirked up and a dimple winked. Her heartbeat slowed in response. Then he stalked a step closer, his hands at his sides, and her gaze flew to the gun on his hip, to the several knives secured in his vest.

Her heart leapt back into action. "You have the wrong

house." She glared up at his implacable face—a face cut from granite with a jaw made to take a punch. She'd have to jump to even come close.

The scent of spiced pine and male infused the room.

He shook his head. A pit the size of a large rock settled in her stomach as adrenaline slammed the room into sharp focus. Her breath came in short pants, and her scientific mind sought an answer. A way to take his massive frame down. She stamped down on the rising panic when nothing came to mind, and again searched for a weapon, spotting the tiny Fittonia "White Anne" in the terra-cotta planter. She couldn't throw Annie at the man; the plant would never survive.

The intruder took another step to peer over her shoulder. "It will be okay. We have to go." His large hand encircled Cara's bicep before dragging her into the bedroom. Fear seized her vocal cords for a moment, and her mind scattered. Should she tell Janie to run? Could she slow him down long enough?

Then, with a muffled curse, he dropped her arm. A low growl emanated from him as he peered at his hand. He wiped it on his pant leg and grabbed her again. What had been on her shirt?

The phone near the bed caught her eye, and she lunged for it. He jerked her back, his hand warm and firm on her arm. Cara dug her feet into the carpet but their forward momentum didn't slow, so she tried to yank away as he pulled her toward a basket of clothes at the foot of the bed.

"Janie, follow us," he tossed over his shoulder.

Cara coughed out air. He knew Janie's name. This wasn't random. Fear choked her again. "How do you know her name?"

He pivoted until she smacked flush against him. Heat filled her, surrounded her. His hands settled on her arms, and his determination and intent beat at her. Damn it. She couldn't block him—she sucked as an empath. Then he lowered his head.

"I know both of your names, Cara. Listen. My name is Talen Kayrs, and I won't hurt you. I'm here to help." Determined eyes captured hers while he gave her a moment. "Take a deep breath. I can feel your power. You can find the truth here. You know I won't hurt you." His voice rumbled low. Soothing.

Her body softened from his tone even as her mind rebelled. Her breathing evened out. Danger radiated out of the man, but she could sense no intention to harm her. Or Janie.

Janie tugged on her waist. "It's okay, Mama. We have to go. They're coming."

Cara stepped to the side and nodded. "Fine. We'll leave. We can follow you." If she could just get Janie to the car—

He grinned, flashing even white teeth. "You can't lie worth spit. You have one minute to throw on clothes." The sound of his rough voice shot nerve endings alive through her skin. But not from fear. He turned toward the door.

"No." She again tried to wrench away while her body tingled where it met his.

"Then you go in your pajamas." He grabbed the basket of clothes in his other arm while he towed her into the hallway. "Keep up, Janie." The little girl stumbled behind, keeping her hands glued to Cara's waist.

"Wait, no, Mama," Janie cried out, pulling on her mother. "I need Mr. Mullet." Her voice rose to a shrill sob.

Talen whirled around and squinted over Cara's shoulder. "Mr. Mullet?" He eyed the living room entrance and then focused on the little girl.

Cara pressed a hand against his chest, settling her stance to protect her child. "Mr. Mullet is her stuffed bear—she doesn't go anywhere without him." If Janie could leave the room, Cara could really fight.

Talen raised an eyebrow, his gaze thoughtful. "Hurry, Janie. Get the bear—we have to go."

Quick as a flash, Janie darted from the room. Dark eyes met Cara's and she wavered, then shot her knee upward to his groin, simultaneously punching her fist toward his face with a fierce grunt.

He shifted, allowing her knee to connect to the muscle of his upper thigh while his arm shot out to stop her punch. His broad hand enclosed her fist inches away from his chin, and the slap of skin on skin echoed around the room. The basket of clothes remained safe in his free arm.

Pain lanced through her leg, and fear cascaded down her spine. Panting out breath, she waited for retaliation. If he hit her, he'd knock her out. What about Janie?

Talen tilted his head to the side, his hand warm around hers. "Is your leg all right?"

He asked about her leg? Seriously? She'd just tried to turn him into a eunuch. "Fine," she hissed through her teeth.

"Hmmm," he said, twisting his hand to grasp her wrist and yank her into the living room. "You might want to work on not broadcasting your intent with those pretty blue eyes next time." Mere politeness colored his tone, not an ounce of anger to be found.

Cara stumbled, truly off balance for the first time that evening.

"I got him, Mama," Janie chirped, running into the room with the stuffed bear and her worn blankie. "We can go now."

The front door hung drunkenly split in two. At the sight, Cara began to struggle again. With an exasperated sigh, Talen dropped the basket of clothes, shifted her to the side, and lifted Janie into his arms.

"No!" Cara cried out, reaching for her daughter before pounding on his broad back. Pure instinct moved her to protect Janie, and rage choked her as she beat on his dark vest.

"Get the clothes and move it," he growled over his shoulder. He crossed the front porch, heading toward a black Hummer idling at the curb.

Cara threw herself against the man holding her child, knocking over the basket. Clothes scattered across the wooden planks.

"Let her go, you bastard!"

He may not intend harm, but he had no right to kidnap them. She clutched one arm around his massive neck as her knees dug into his spine. She jerked hard against his windpipe. A rush of anger slammed through her body, pushing out the fear.

Even with her struggling on his back, his long strides continued toward the vehicle unhampered. He yanked open the rear door, placed Janie in a booster seat, and buckled her in with quick motions. Cara moved to jump off him, only to have him close the door, grab her arm, and pull her around. Two strong hands held her aloft. Hard steel met her backside when he stepped into her, his face lowering to hers. "Stop fighting me."

His strength was unbelievable. Her own vulnerability beat into her as she realized her nightshirt had risen to reveal pale pink panties. The cool night air rushed across her bare legs. Dark denim scratched the tender skin of her inner thighs, and she opened her mouth to scream.

One swift movement and his mouth covered hers. Hot, firm, and somehow restrained. The effort of his restraint belted into her. He fought to control himself. Heat slammed through her. A roaring filled her ears and her breath hitched. Her heart slowed, and time stopped. For a brief moment, *his* heartbeat echoed throughout her body to a spot below her stomach.

He growled low and his mouth moved over hers, no longer silencing her, but tasting. Exploring. One thick arm swept around her waist and pulled her into him; the other lifted to tangle a hand in her hair. He tugged, angled her head more to the side. He went deeper.

She moaned as his tongue met hers. He explored her mouth like he owned it. For a moment, he did. She forgot everything. There were only his lips on hers, demanding. Promising. His heat warmed her as she returned his kiss, pushing closer into his hard body, forgetting reality.

Pure strength surrounded her. Hot. Dangerous. Tempting.

Don't miss A SENSE OF SIN,
the second novel from Elizabeth Essex,
in stores next month!

Del had not known who she was when he first laid eyes upon her, but he instinctively didn't like her. He distrusted beauty. Because beauty walked hand in hand with privilege. Unearned privilege. And she was certainly beautiful. Tall, elegant, with porcelain white skin, a riot of sable dark curls and deep dark eyes—a symphony of black and white. She surveyed the ballroom like a queen: haughty, serene, remote and exquisitely pretty. And beauty had a way of diverting unpleasantness and masking grievous flaws of character. No, beauty was not to be trusted.

Her name was confirmed by others attending the select ball at the Marquess and Marchioness of Widcombe's. It wafted to him on champagne-fueled murmurs from the hot, crowded room: "Dear Celia," and "Our Miss Burke." And the title that everyone seemed to call her, "The Ravishing Miss Burke," as if it were her rank and she the only one to wear that crown.

The ravishing Miss Celia Burke. A well-known, and even more well-liked local beauty. And here she was, making her serene, graceful way down the short set of stairs into the ballroom as effortlessly as clear water flowed over rocks in a hillside stream. She nodded and smiled in a benign but uninvolved way at all who approached her, but she never stopped to converse. She processed on, following her mother through the parting sea of mere mortals, those lesser human beings who were nothing and nobody to her but playthings.

Aloof, perfect Celia Burke. *Fuck you.*

Yes, by God, he would take his revenge and Emily would have justice. Maybe then he could sleep at night.

Maybe then he could learn to live with himself.

But he couldn't exact the kind of revenge one takes on another man: straightforward, violent and bloody. He couldn't call Miss Burke out on the middle of the dance floor and put a bullet between her eyes or a sword blade between her ribs at dawn. No.

His justice would have to be more subtle, but no less thorough. And no less ruthless.

"You were the one who insisted we attend this august gathering. So what's it to be? Delacorte?" Commander Hugh McAlden, friend, naval officer and resident cynic, prompted again.

McAlden was one of the few people who never addressed Del by his courtesy title, Viscount Darling, as they'd known each other long before he'd come into the bloody title and far too long for Del to give himself airs in front of such an old friend. And with such familiarity came ease. With McAlden, Del could afford the luxury of being blunt.

"Dancing or thrashing? The latter, I think."

McAlden's usually grim mouth crooked up in half a smile. "A thrashing, right here in the Marchioness's ballroom? I'd pay good money to see that."

"Would you? Shall we have a private bet, then?"

"Del, I always like it when you've got that look in your eye. I'd like nothing more than a good wager."

"A bet, Colonel Delacorte? What's the wager? I've money to burn these days, thanks to you two." Another naval officer, Lieutenant Ian James, known from their time together when Del had been an officer of His Majesty's Marine Forces aboard the frigate *Resolute*, broke into the conversation from behind.

"A private wager only, James." He would need to be more circumspect. James was a bit of a puppy, happy and eager, but untried in the more manipulative ways of society. There was no telling what he might let slip. Del had no intention of getting caught in the net he was about to cast. "Save your fortune in prize money for another time."

"A gentleman's bet then, Colonel?"

A *gentleman's* bet. Del felt his mouth curve up in a scornful smile. What he was about to do violated every code of gentlemanly behavior. "No. More of a challenge."

"He's Viscount Darling now, Mr. James." McAlden was giving Del a mocking smile. "We have to address him with all the deference he's due."

Unholy glee lit the young man's face. "I had no idea. Congratulations, Colonel. What a bloody fine name. I can hear the ladies now: *my dearest, darling Darling.* How will they resist you?"

Del merely smiled and took another drink. But it was true. None of them resisted: high-born ladies, low-living trollops, barmaids, island girls or *senoritas.* They never had, bless their lascivious hearts.

And neither would *she*, despite her remote facade. Celia Burke was nothing but a hothouse flower just waiting to be plucked.

"Go on, then. What's your challenge?" McAlden's face housed a dubious smirk as several more Navy men, Lieutenants Thomas Gardener and Robert Scott joined them.

"I propose I can openly court, seduce and ruin an untried, virtuous woman." He paused to give them a moment to remark upon the condition he was about to attach. "Without ever once touching her."

McAlden gave a huff of bluff laughter. "Too easy, in one sense, too hard, in another," he stated flatly.

"But how can you possibly ruin someone without touching them?" Ian James protested.

Del felt his mouth twist. He had forgotten what it was like

to be that young. While he was only six and twenty, he'd grown older since Emily's death. Vengeance was singularly aging.

"Find us a drink would you, gentlemen? A real drink and none of that lukewarm swill they're passing out on trays." Del pushed the youths off in the direction of a footman.

"Too easy to ruin a reputation with only a rumor," McAlden repeated in his unhurried, determined way. "You'll have to do better than that."

Trust McAlden to get right to the heart of the matter. Like Del, McAlden had never been young. And he was older in years as well.

"With your reputation," McAlden continued as they turned to follow the others, "well deserved, I might add, you'll not get within a sea mile of a virtuous woman."

"That, old man, shows how little you know of women."

"That, my darling Viscount, shows how little you know of their Mamas."

"And I'd like to keep it that way. Hence the prohibition against touching. I plan on keeping a very safe distance." While he was about this business of revenging himself on Celia Burke, he needed to keep himself safe—safe from being forced into doing the right thing should his godforsaken plan be discovered or go awry. And he didn't *want* to touch her. He didn't want to be tainted by so much as the merest brush of her hand.

"Can't seduce, really *seduce*, from a distance. Not even you. Twenty guineas says it can't be done."

"Twenty? An extravagant wager for a flinty, tight-pursed Scotsman like you. Done." Del accepted the challenge with a firm handshake. It sweetened the pot, so to speak.

McAlden perused the crowd. "Shall we pick now? I warn you, Del, this isn't London. There's plenty of virtue to be had in Dartmouth."

"Why not?" Del felt his mouth curve into a lazy smile. The town may have been full of virtue, but he was full of vice. And he cared about only one particular woman's virtue.

"You'll want to be careful. Singularly difficult things, women," McAlden offered philosophically. "Can turn a man inside out. Just look at Marlowe."

Del shrugged. "Captain Marlowe married. I do not have anything approaching marriage in mind."

"So you're going to seduce and ruin an innocent without being named, or caught? That *is* bloody minded."

"I didn't say innocent. I said untried. In this case, there is a particular difference." He looked across the room at Celia Burke again. At the virtuous, innocent face she presented to the world. He would strip away that mask, until everyone could see the ugly truth behind her immaculately polished, social veneer.

McAlden followed the line of his gaze. "You can't mean— That's Celia Burke!" All trace of joviality disappeared from McAlden's voice. "Jesus, Del, have you completely lost your mind? As well as all moral scruple?"

"Gone squeamish?" Del tossed back the last of his drink. "That's not like you."

"I *know* her. Everyone in Dartmouth knows her. She is Marlowe's wife's most particular friend. You can't go about ruining—*ruining* for God's sake—innocent young women, like her. Even *I* know that."

"I said she's *not* innocent."

"Then you must've misjudged her. She's not fair game, Del. Pick someone else. Someone I don't know." McAlden's voice was growing thick.

"No." Darling kept his own voice flat.

McAlden's astonished countenance turned back to look at Miss Burke, half a room away, now smiling sweetly in conversation with another young woman. He swore colorfully under his breath. "That's not just bloody minded, that's sui- cidal. She's got parents, Del. Attentive parents. Take a good hard look at her mama, Lady Caroline Burke. She's nothing less than the daughter of a Duke, and is to all accounts a complete gorgon in her own right. They say she eats fortune hunters, not to mention an assortment of libertines like you, for breakfast. And what's more, Miss Burke is a relation of the Marquess of Widcombe, in whose ballroom you are currently *not dancing*. This isn't London, you are a guest here. My guest, and therefore Marlowe's guest. One misstep like that and they'll have your head. Or, more likely, your bollocks. And quite rightly. Pick someone else for your challenge."

"No."

"Delacorte."

"Bugger off, Hugh."

McAlden knew him well enough to hear the implacable finality in his tone. He shook his head slowly. "God's balls, Del. I didn't think I'd regret having you to stay so quickly." He ran his hand through his short, cropped hair and looked at Del with a dawning of realization. "Christ. You'd already made up your mind before you came here, hadn't you? You came for her."

Under such scrutiny, Del could only admit the truth. "I did."

"Damn your eyes, Delacorte. This can only end badly."

Del shrugged with supreme indifference. "That will suit me well enough."

They called it blackmail, though the letter secreted in Celia Burke's pocket was not in actuality black. It had looked innocuous enough: the same ivory-colored paper as all the other mail, brought to her on a little silver tray borne by the butler, Loring. It would have been much better if the letter had actually been black, because then Celia would have known not to open it. She would have flung it into the fire before it could poison her life irrevocably. The clenching grip of anxiety deep in her belly was proof enough the poison had already begun its insidious work.

"Celia, darling? Are you all right? Smile, my dear. Smile." Lady Caroline Burke whispered her instructions for her daughter's ears only, as she smiled and nodded to her many acquaintances in the ballroom as though she hadn't a care in the world.

Celia shoved her unsteady hand into her pocket to reassure—no, not reassure—*convince* herself—the letter was still there. And still real. She had not dreamt up this particular walking nightmare.

She released the offensive missive and clasped her hands together tightly to stop them from trembling. She had no more than a moment or two to compose herself before the opening set was to begin.

Blackmail. The letter, dated only one day ago, was clear and precise, straight to the point.